15TH
ANNIVERSARY

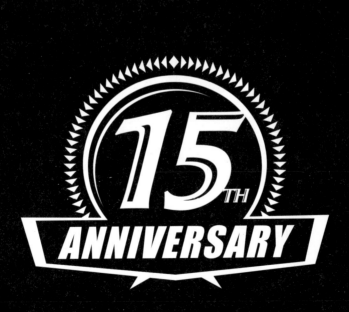

the Ri

BURNING

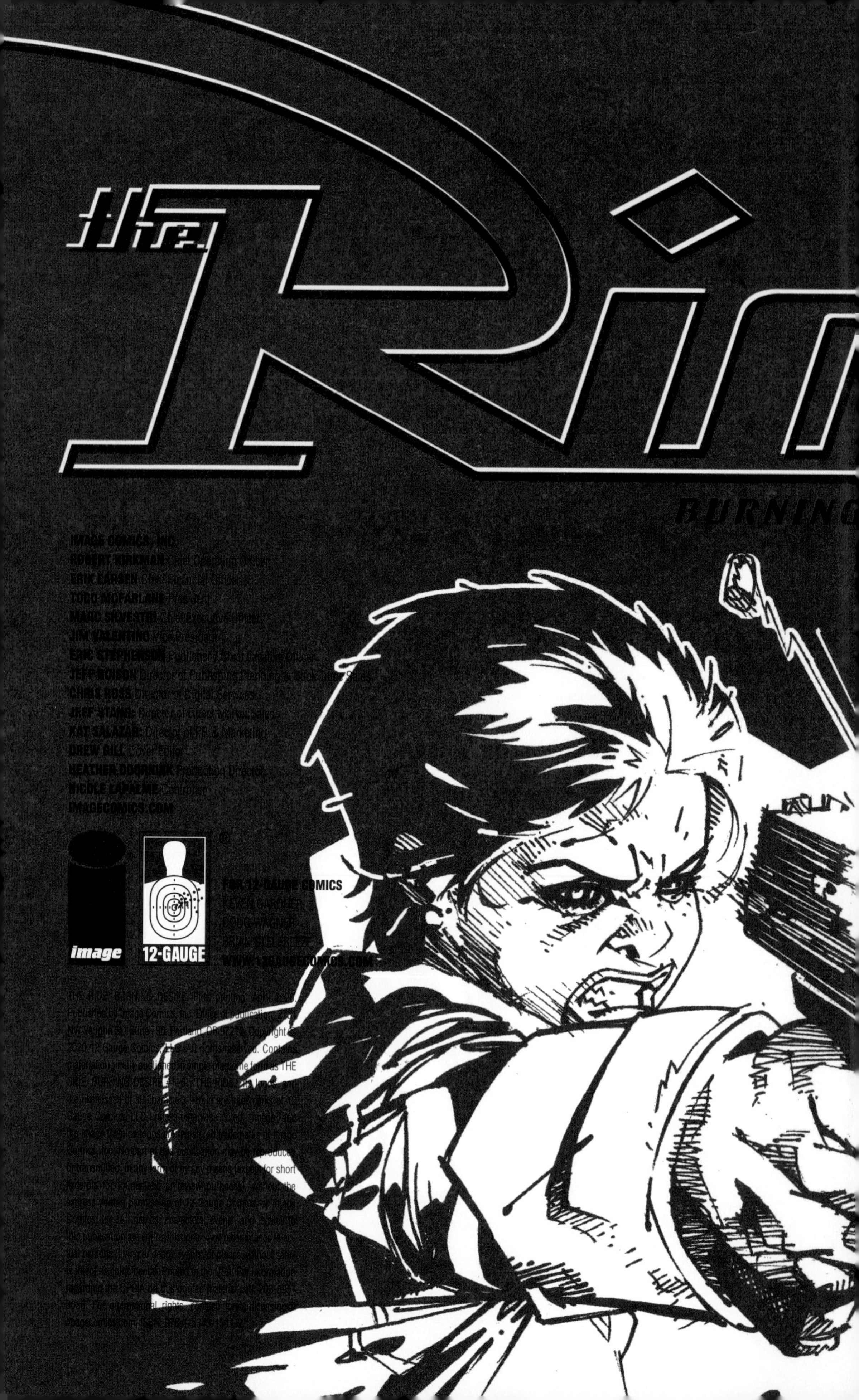

FOR 12-GAUGE COMICS
KEVIN GARDNER
DOUG WAGNER
BRIAN STELFREEZE
WWW.12GAUGECOMICS.COM

WRITTEN BY **DOUG WAGNER**

LETTERS BY **ED DUKESHIRE**

"BURNING DESIRE"

ART BY **DANIEL HILLYARD**

COLOR BY **LAURA MARTIN** (CHAPTERS 1 – 3)

& **CHARLIE KIRCHOFF** (CHAPTERS 3 – 5)

LAURA MARTIN: CHAPTER 3, PAGES 1 – 6 & 10 – 13
CHARLIE KIRCHOFF: CHAPTER 3: PAGES 7 – 9 & 14 – 16

"SPARKLES"

ART & COLOR BY **ADAM HUGHES**

"ASH"

ART BY **CHRIS BRUNNER**

COLOR BY **RICO RENZI**

"FOO"

ART BY **CULLY HAMNER**

COLOR BY **NAYOUNG KIM**

"NUN"

ART BY **TOMM COKER**

"ARNIE & ALBERT"

ART & COLOR BY **DOUG DABBS**

BOOK DESIGN BY **SASHA E HEAD**

PRODUCED & EDITED BY **KEVEN GARDNER**

BURNING DESIRE
CHAPTER ONE

DOUG WAGNER

STORY

DANIEL HILLYARD

ART

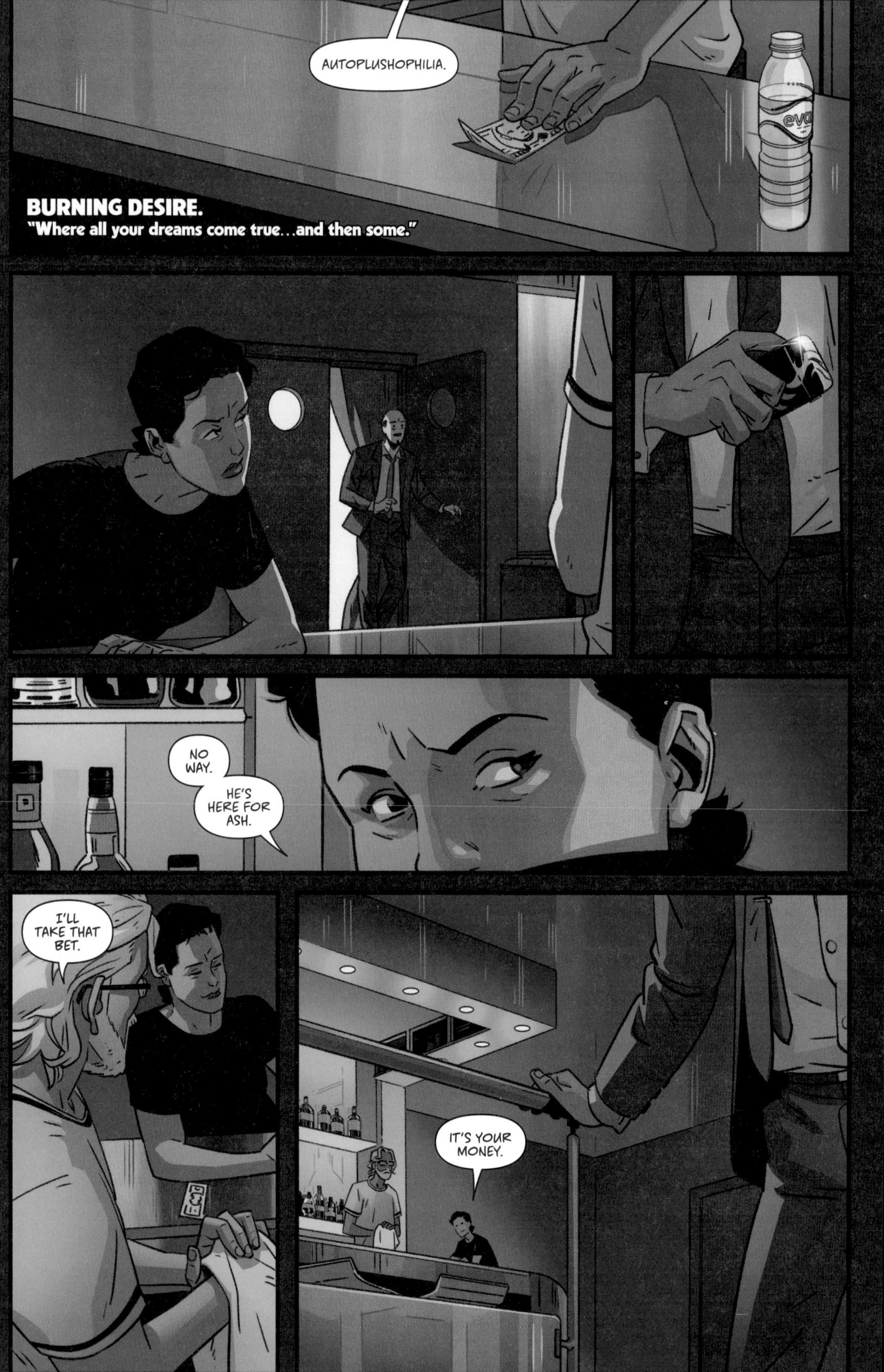
AUTOPLUSHOPHILIA.
BURNING DESIRE.
"Where all your dreams come true...and then some."
NO WAY.
HE'S HERE FOR ASH.
I'LL TAKE THAT BET.
IT'S YOUR MONEY.

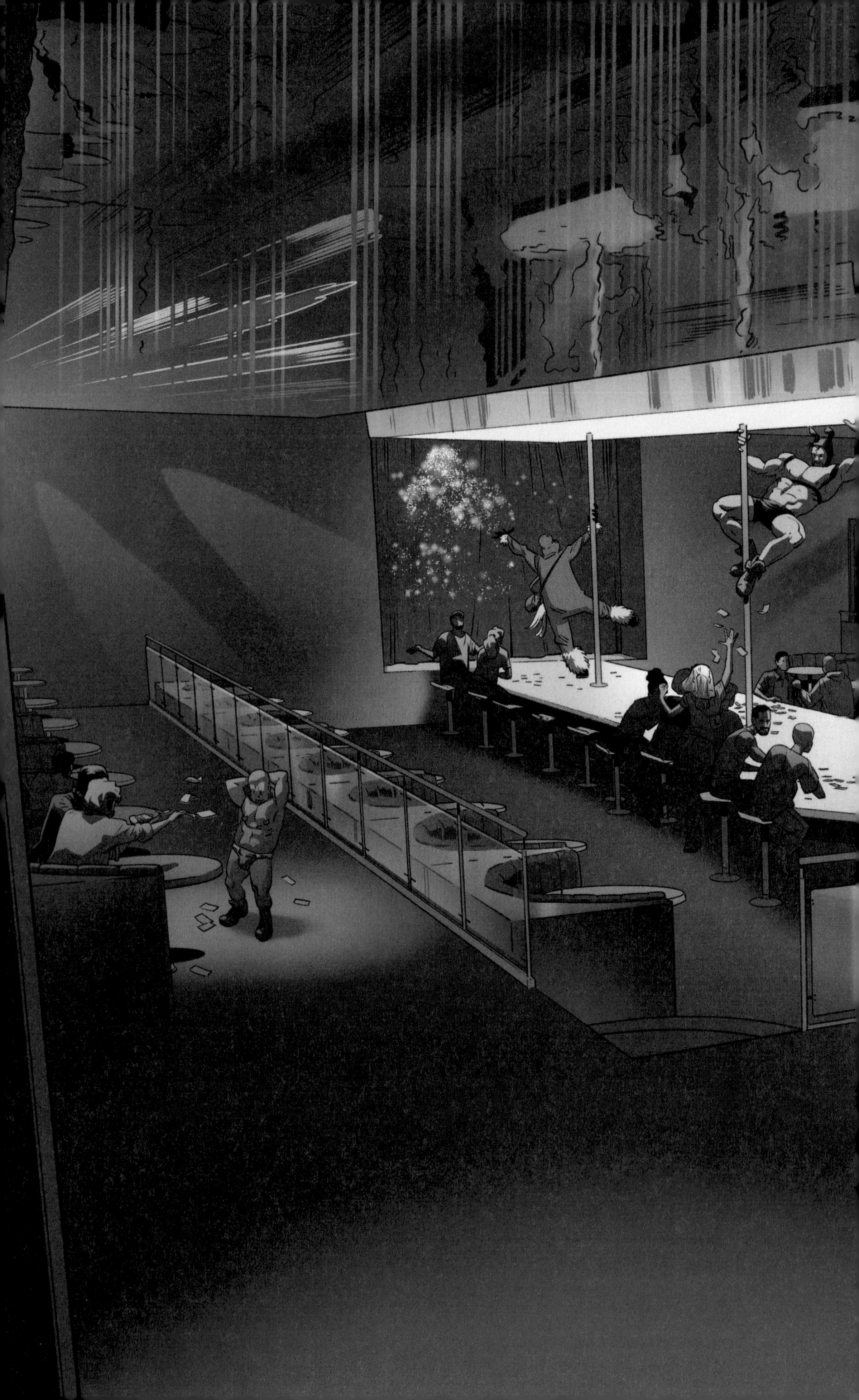

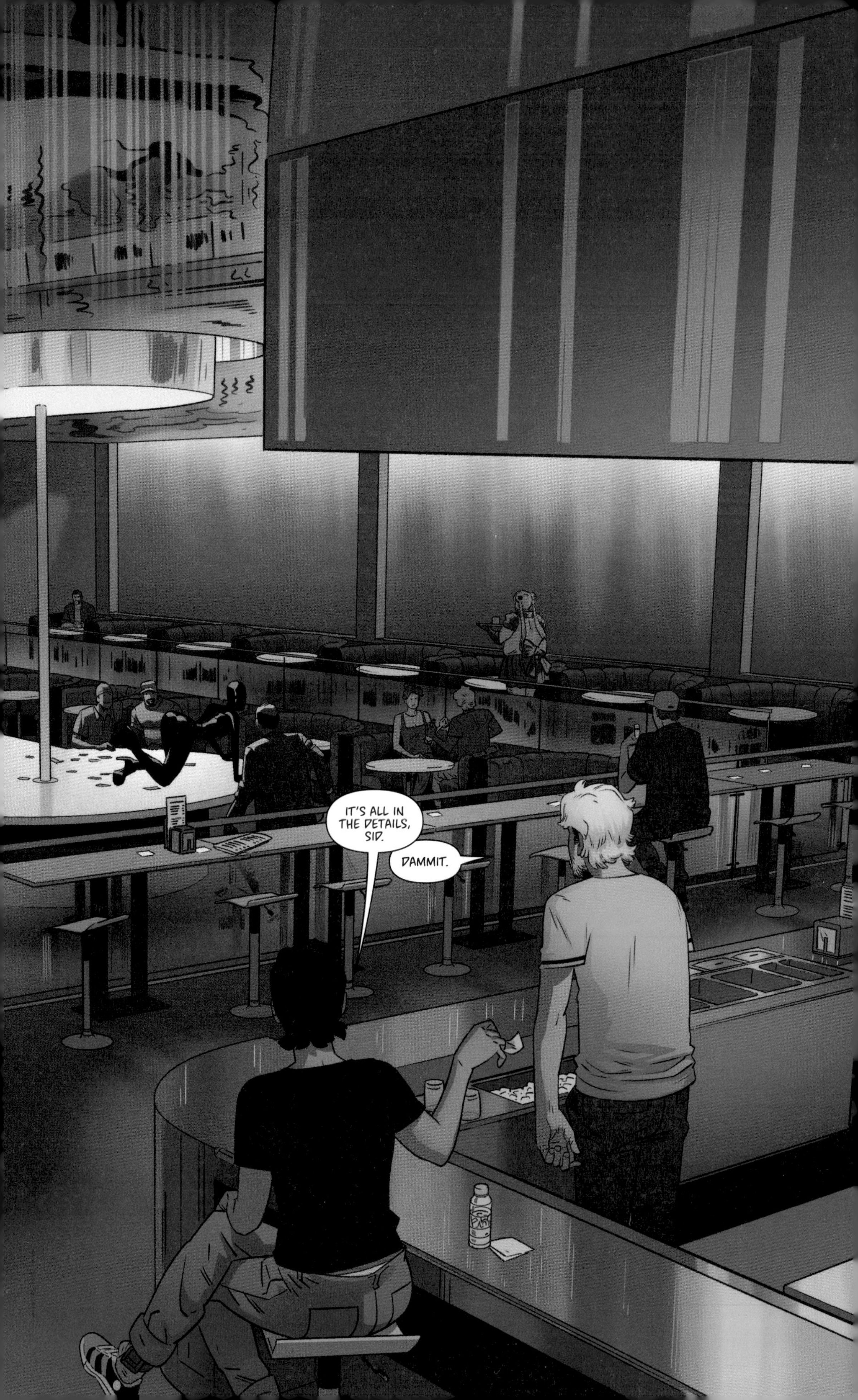
IT'S ALL IN THE DETAILS, SID.
DAMMIT.

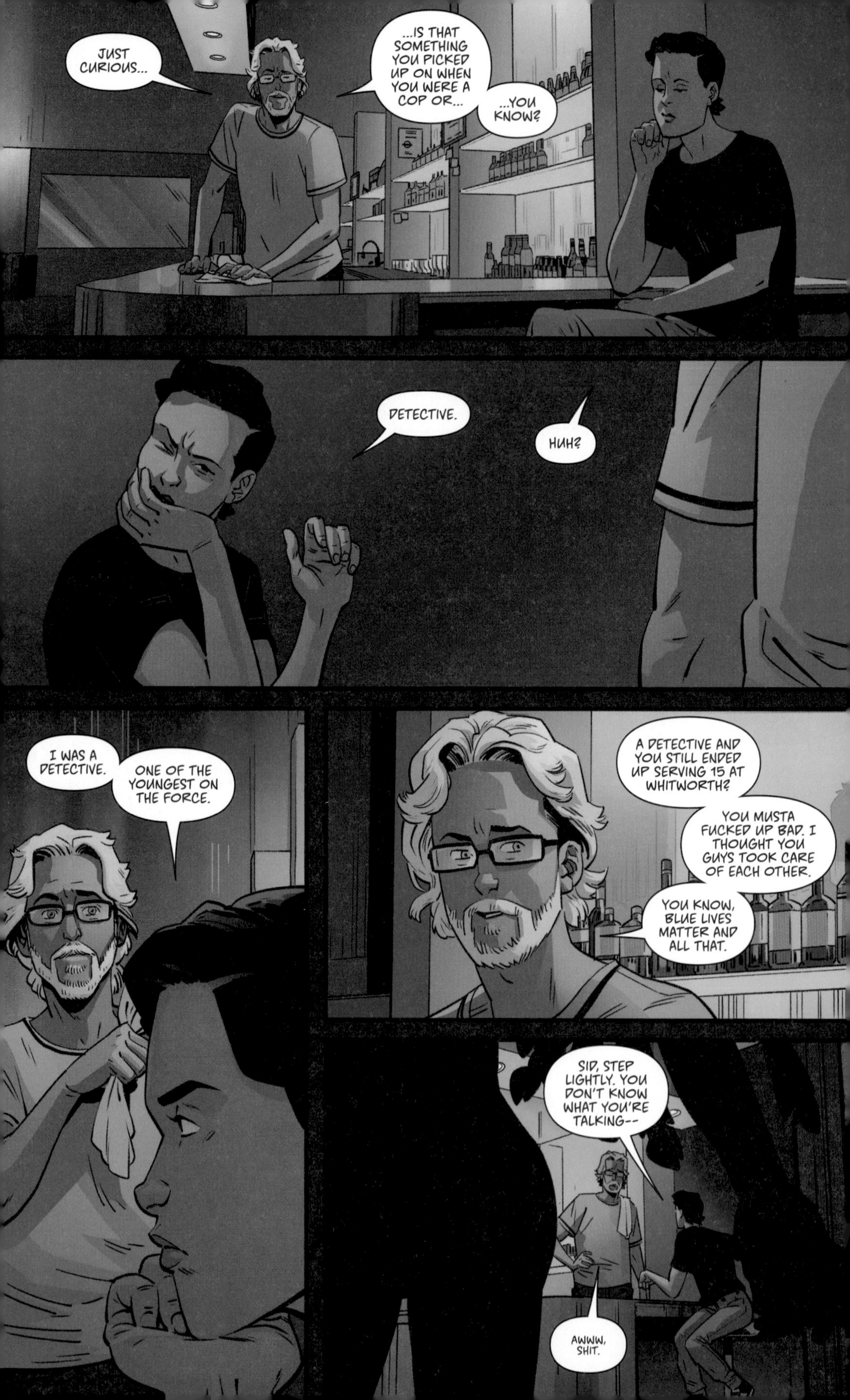
JUST CURIOUS...
...IS THAT SOMETHING YOU PICKED UP ON WHEN YOU WERE A COP OR...
...YOU KNOW?
DETECTIVE.
HUH?
I WAS A DETECTIVE.
ONE OF THE YOUNGEST ON THE FORCE.
A DETECTIVE AND YOU STILL ENDED UP SERVING 15 AT WHITWORTH?
YOU MUSTA FUCKED UP BAD. I THOUGHT YOU GUYS TOOK CARE OF EACH OTHER.
YOU KNOW, BLUE LIVES MATTER AND ALL THAT.
SID, STEP LIGHTLY. YOU DON'T KNOW WHAT YOU'RE TALKING--
AWWW, SHIT.

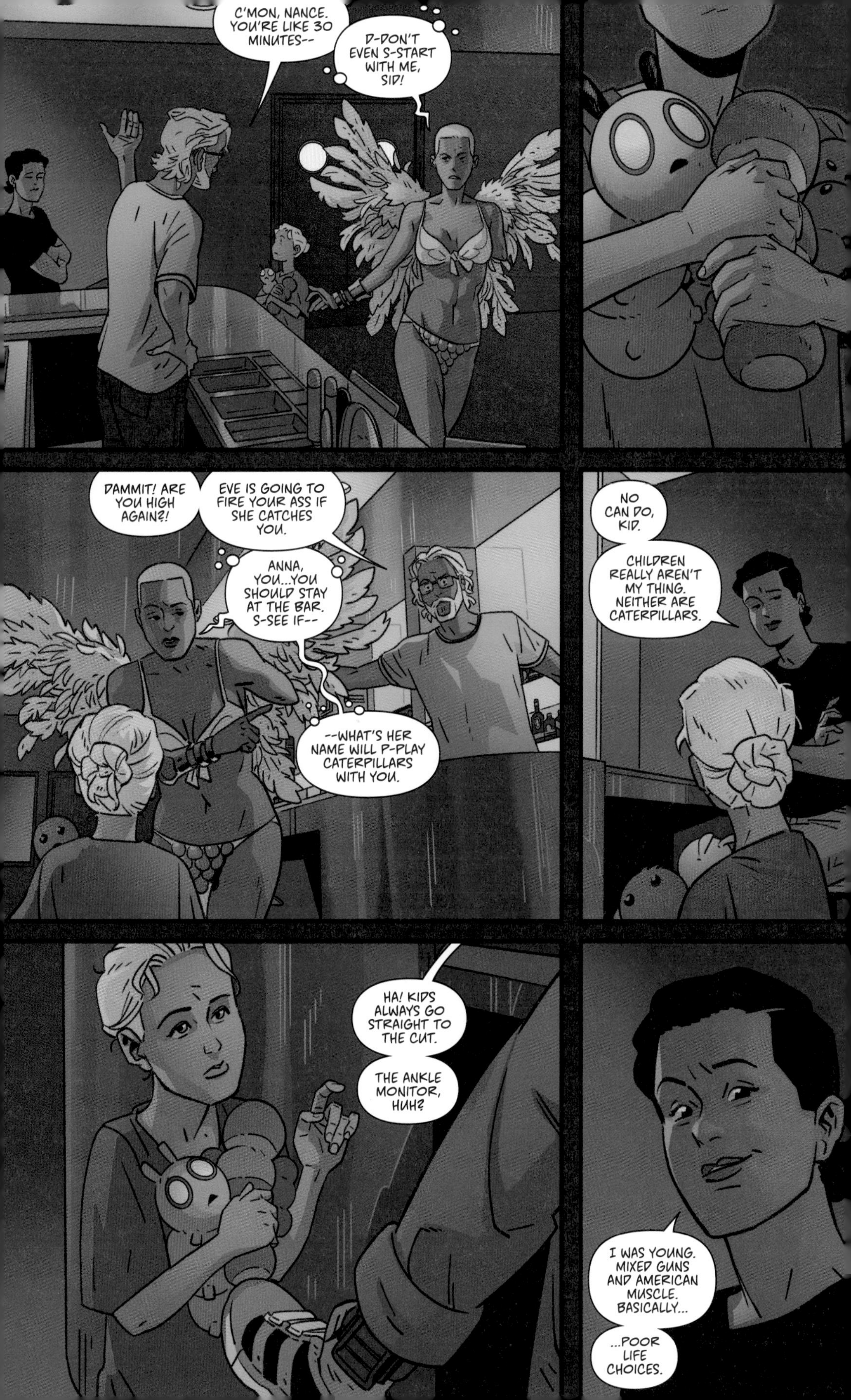
C'MON, NANCE. YOU'RE LIKE 30 MINUTES--
D-DON'T EVEN S-START WITH ME, SID!
DAMMIT! ARE YOU HIGH AGAIN?!
EVE IS GOING TO FIRE YOUR ASS IF SHE CATCHES YOU.
ANNA, YOU...YOU SHOULD STAY AT THE BAR. S-SEE IF--
--WHAT'S HER NAME WILL P-PLAY CATERPILLARS WITH YOU.
NO CAN DO, KID.
CHILDREN REALLY AREN'T MY THING. NEITHER ARE CATERPILLARS.
HA! KIDS ALWAYS GO STRAIGHT TO THE CUT.
THE ANKLE MONITOR, HUH?
I WAS YOUNG. MIXED GUNS AND AMERICAN MUSCLE. BASICALLY...
...POOR LIFE CHOICES.

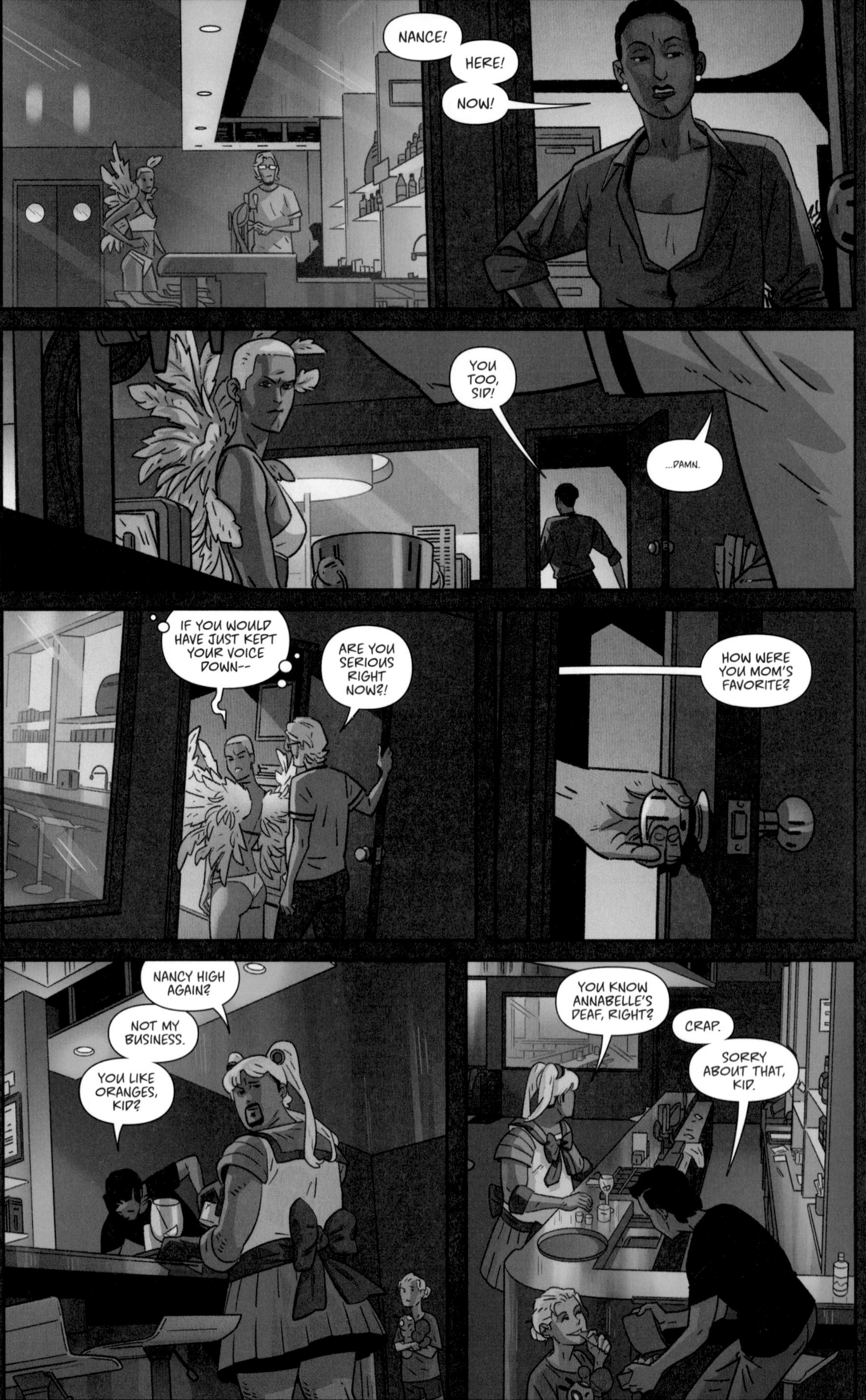
NANCE!
HERE!
NOW!
YOU TOO, SID!
...DAMN.
IF YOU WOULD HAVE JUST KEPT YOUR VOICE DOWN--
ARE YOU SERIOUS RIGHT NOW?!
HOW WERE YOU MOM'S FAVORITE?
NANCY HIGH AGAIN?
NOT MY BUSINESS.
YOU LIKE ORANGES, KID?
YOU KNOW ANNABELLE'S DEAF, RIGHT?
CRAP.
SORRY ABOUT THAT, KID.

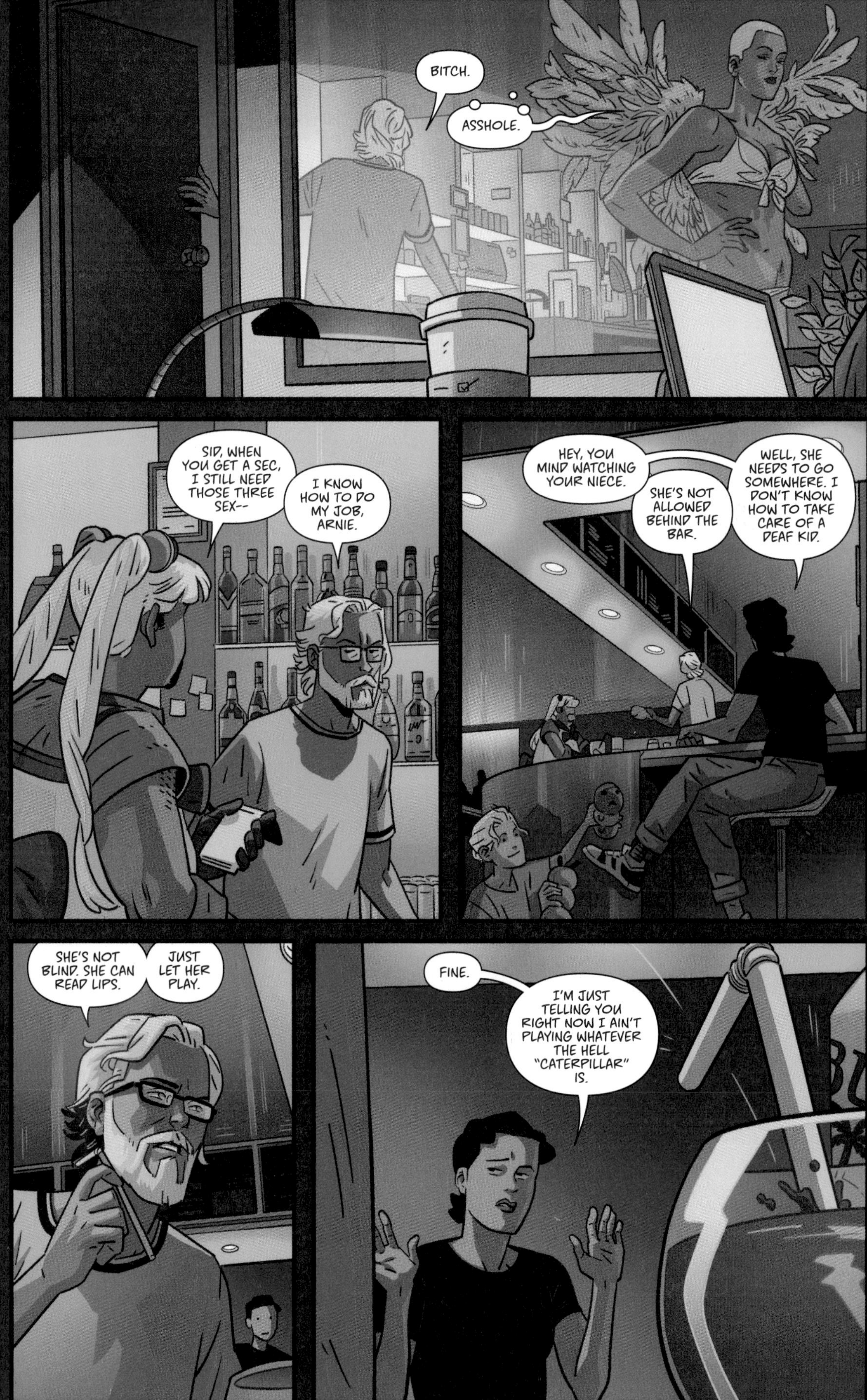
BITCH.
ASSHOLE.
SID, WHEN YOU GET A SEC, I STILL NEED THOSE THREE SEX--
I KNOW HOW TO DO MY JOB, ARNIE.
HEY, YOU MIND WATCHING YOUR NIECE.
SHE'S NOT ALLOWED BEHIND THE BAR.
WELL, SHE NEEDS TO GO SOMEWHERE. I DON'T KNOW HOW TO TAKE CARE OF A DEAF KID.
SHE'S NOT BLIND. SHE CAN READ LIPS.
JUST LET HER PLAY.
FINE.
I'M JUST TELLING YOU RIGHT NOW I AIN'T PLAYING WHATEVER THE HELL "CATERPILLAR" IS.

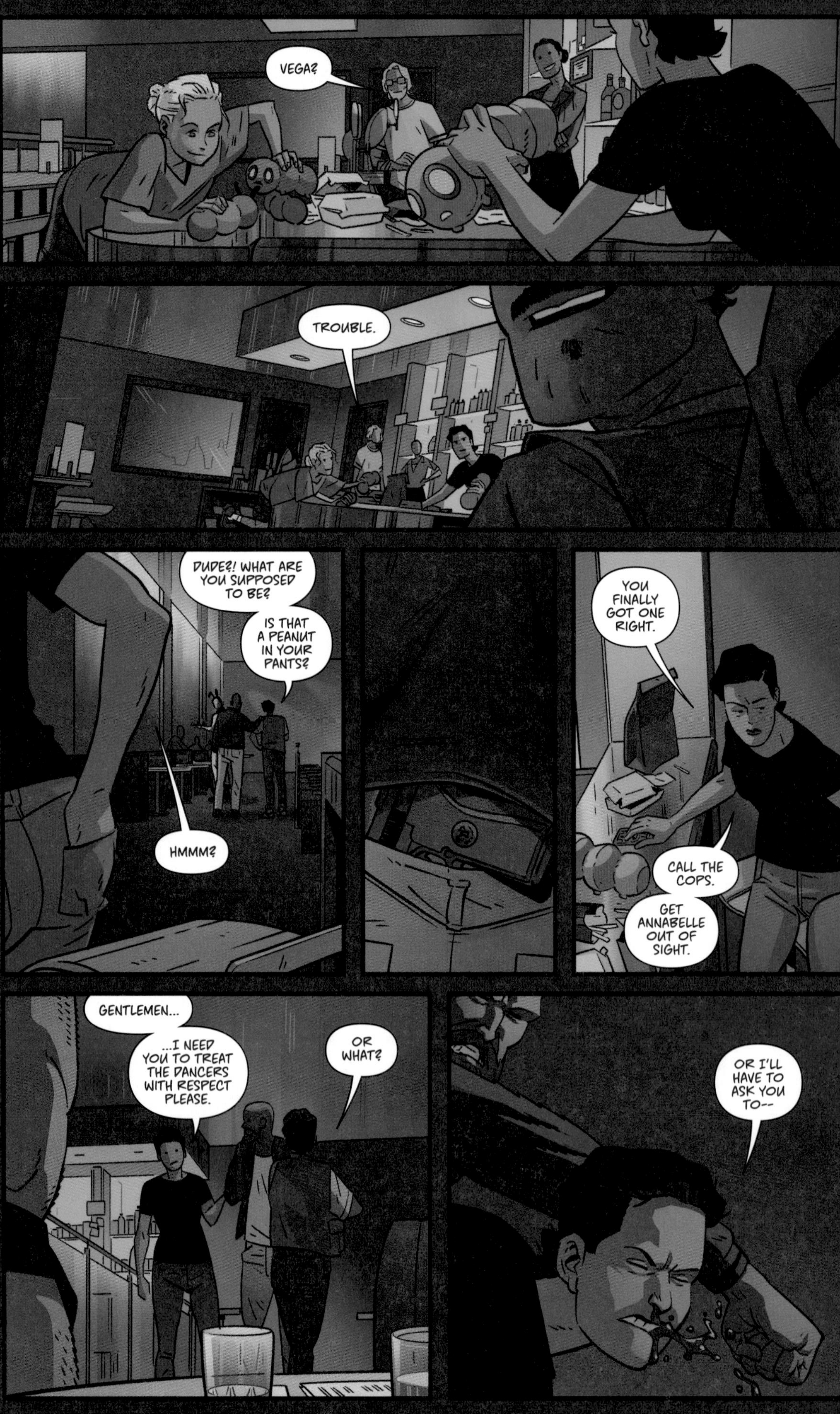
VEGA?
TROUBLE.
DUDE?! WHAT ARE YOU SUPPOSED TO BE?
IS THAT A PEANUT IN YOUR PANTS?
HMMM?
YOU FINALLY GOT ONE RIGHT.
CALL THE COPS.
GET ANNABELLE OUT OF SIGHT.
GENTLEMEN...
...I NEED YOU TO TREAT THE DANCERS WITH RESPECT PLEASE.
OR WHAT?
OR I'LL HAVE TO ASK YOU TO--

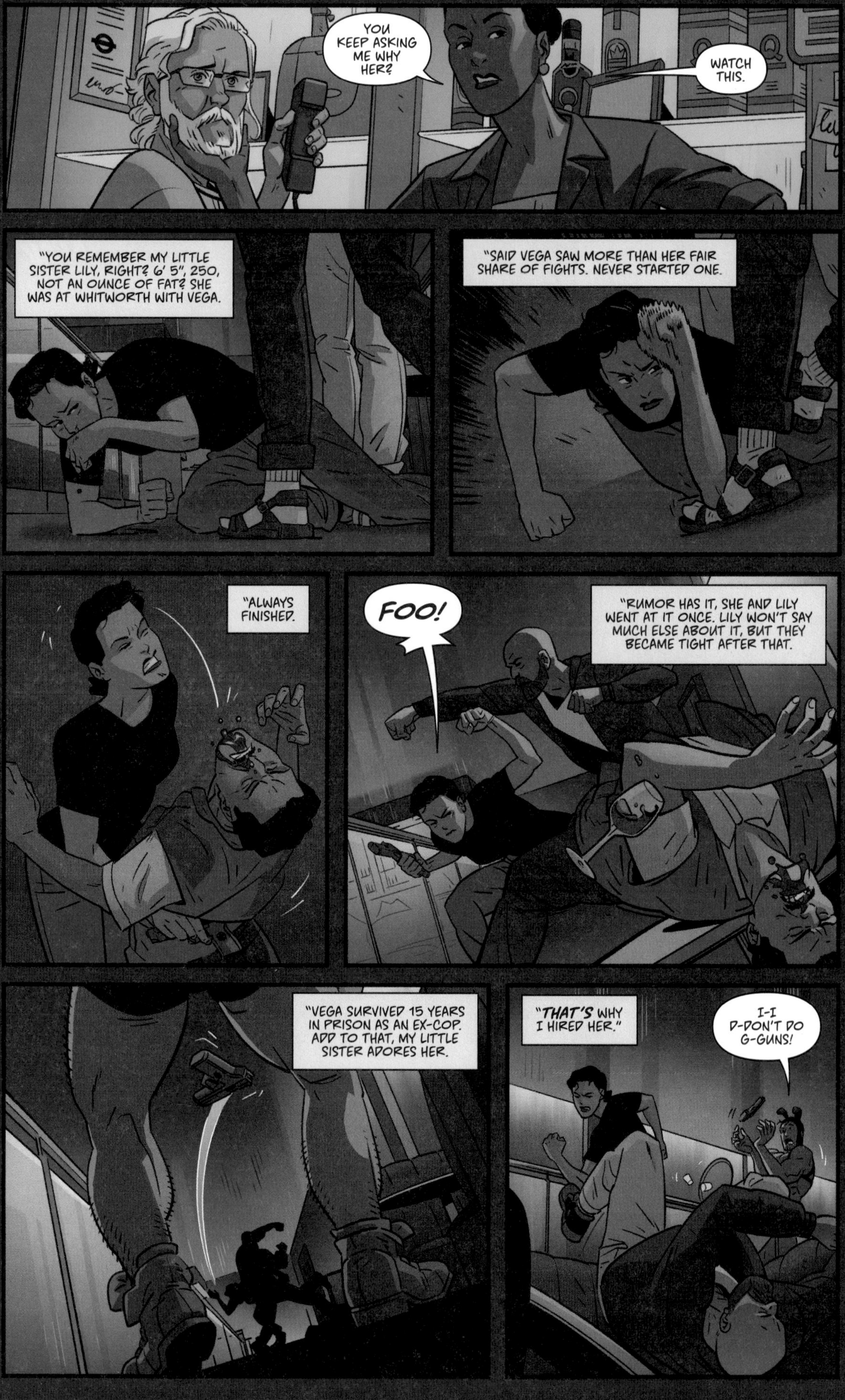
YOU KEEP ASKING ME WHY HER?
WATCH THIS.
"YOU REMEMBER MY LITTLE SISTER LILY, RIGHT? 6' 5", 250, NOT AN OUNCE OF FAT? SHE WAS AT WHITWORTH WITH VEGA.
"SAID VEGA SAW MORE THAN HER FAIR SHARE OF FIGHTS. NEVER STARTED ONE.
"ALWAYS FINISHED.
FOO!
"RUMOR HAS IT, SHE AND LILY WENT AT IT ONCE. LILY WON'T SAY MUCH ELSE ABOUT IT, BUT THEY BECAME TIGHT AFTER THAT.
"VEGA SURVIVED 15 YEARS IN PRISON AS AN EX-COP. ADD TO THAT, MY LITTLE SISTER ADORES HER.
"*THAT'S* WHY I HIRED HER."
I-I D-DON'T DO G-GUNS!

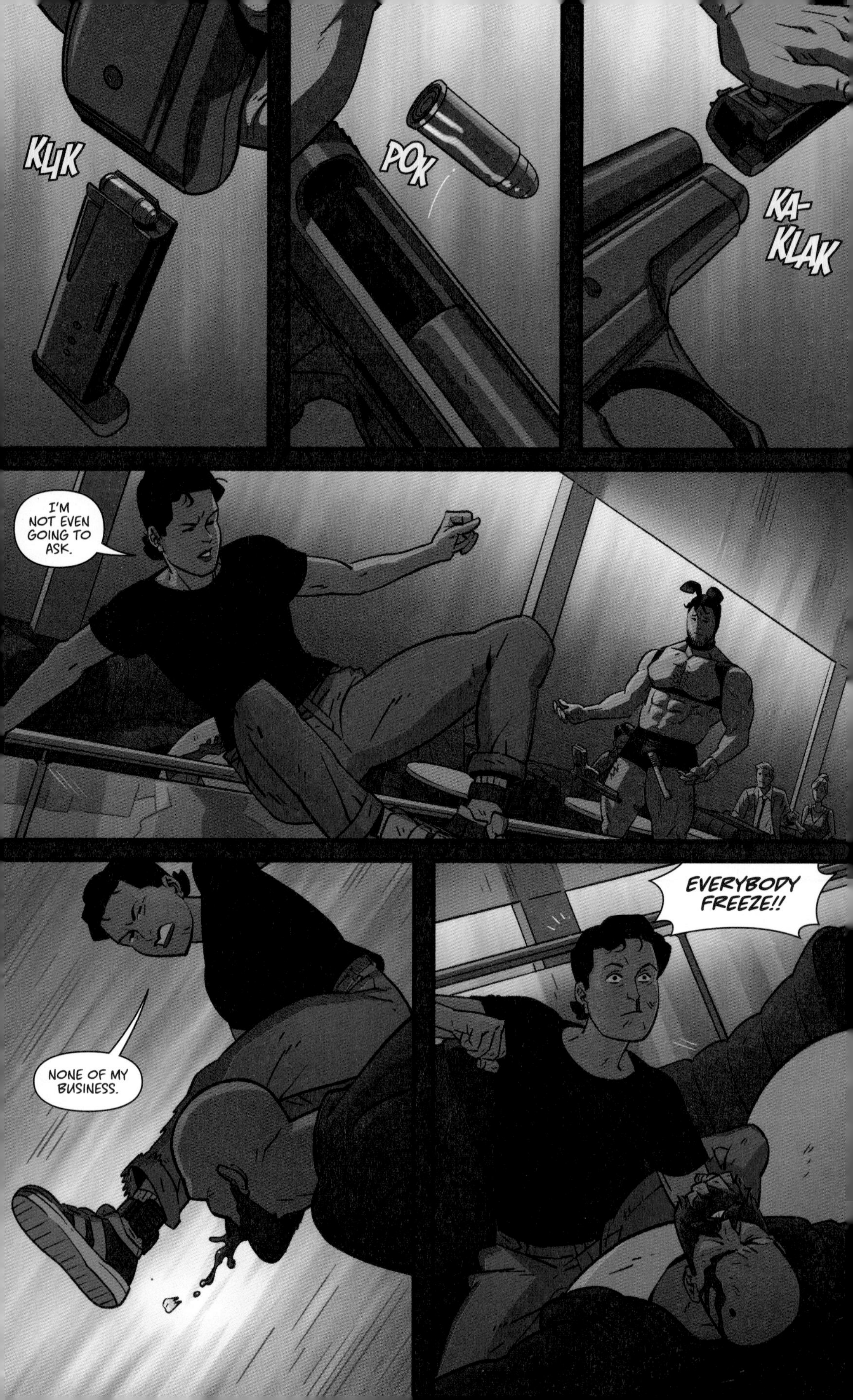
KLIK
POK
KA-KLAK
I'M NOT EVEN GOING TO ASK.
NONE OF MY BUSINESS.
EVERYBODY FREEZE!!

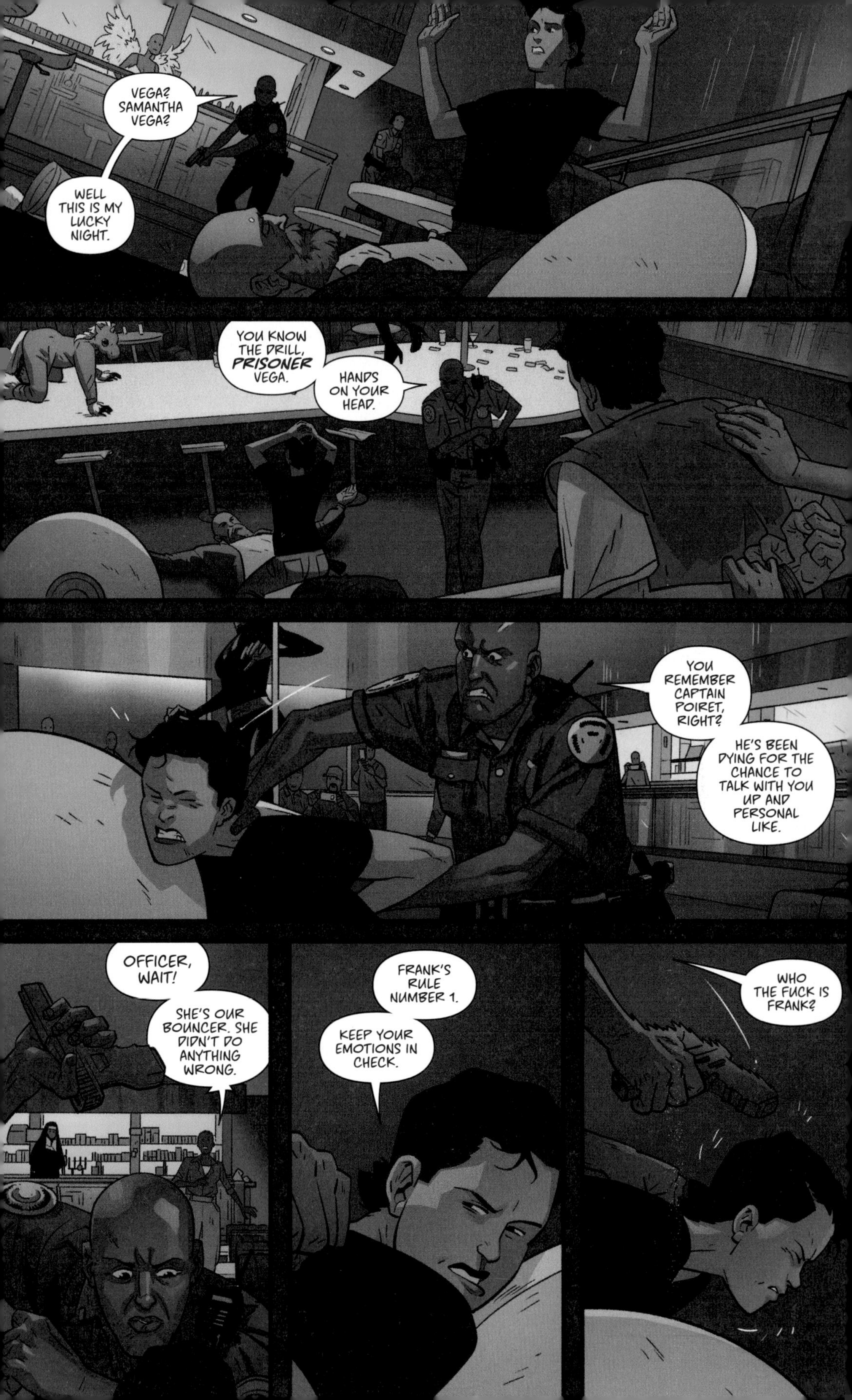
VEGA? SAMANTHA VEGA?
WELL THIS IS MY LUCKY NIGHT.
YOU KNOW THE DRILL, PRISONER VEGA.
HANDS ON YOUR HEAD.
YOU REMEMBER CAPTAIN POIRET, RIGHT?
HE'S BEEN DYING FOR THE CHANCE TO TALK WITH YOU UP AND PERSONAL LIKE.
OFFICER, WAIT!
SHE'S OUR BOUNCER. SHE DIDN'T DO ANYTHING WRONG.
FRANK'S RULE NUMBER 1.
KEEP YOUR EMOTIONS IN CHECK.
WHO THE FUCK IS FRANK?

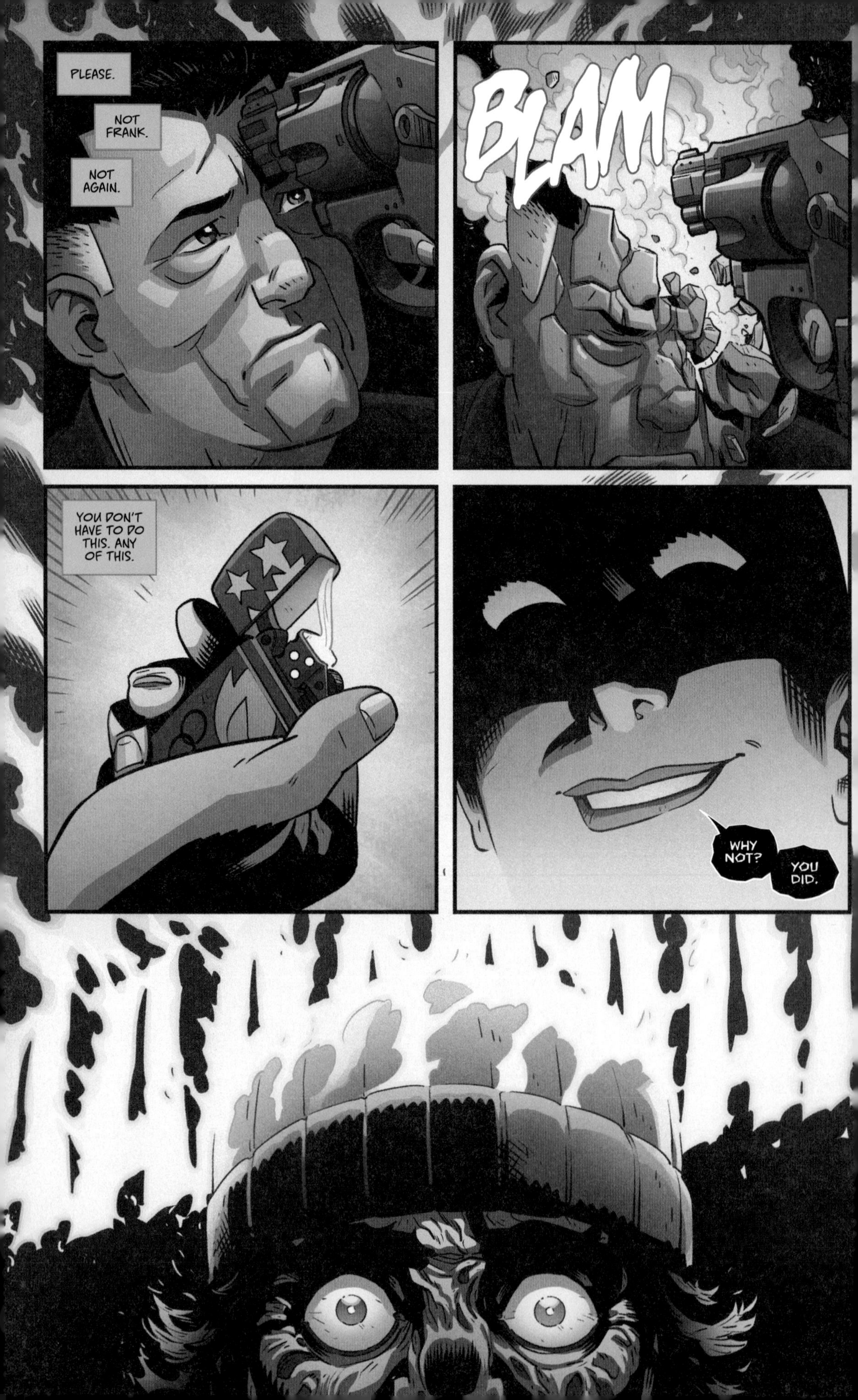

PLEASE.
NOT FRANK.
NOT AGAIN.
BLAM
YOU DON'T HAVE TO DO THIS. ANY OF THIS.
WHY NOT?
YOU DID.

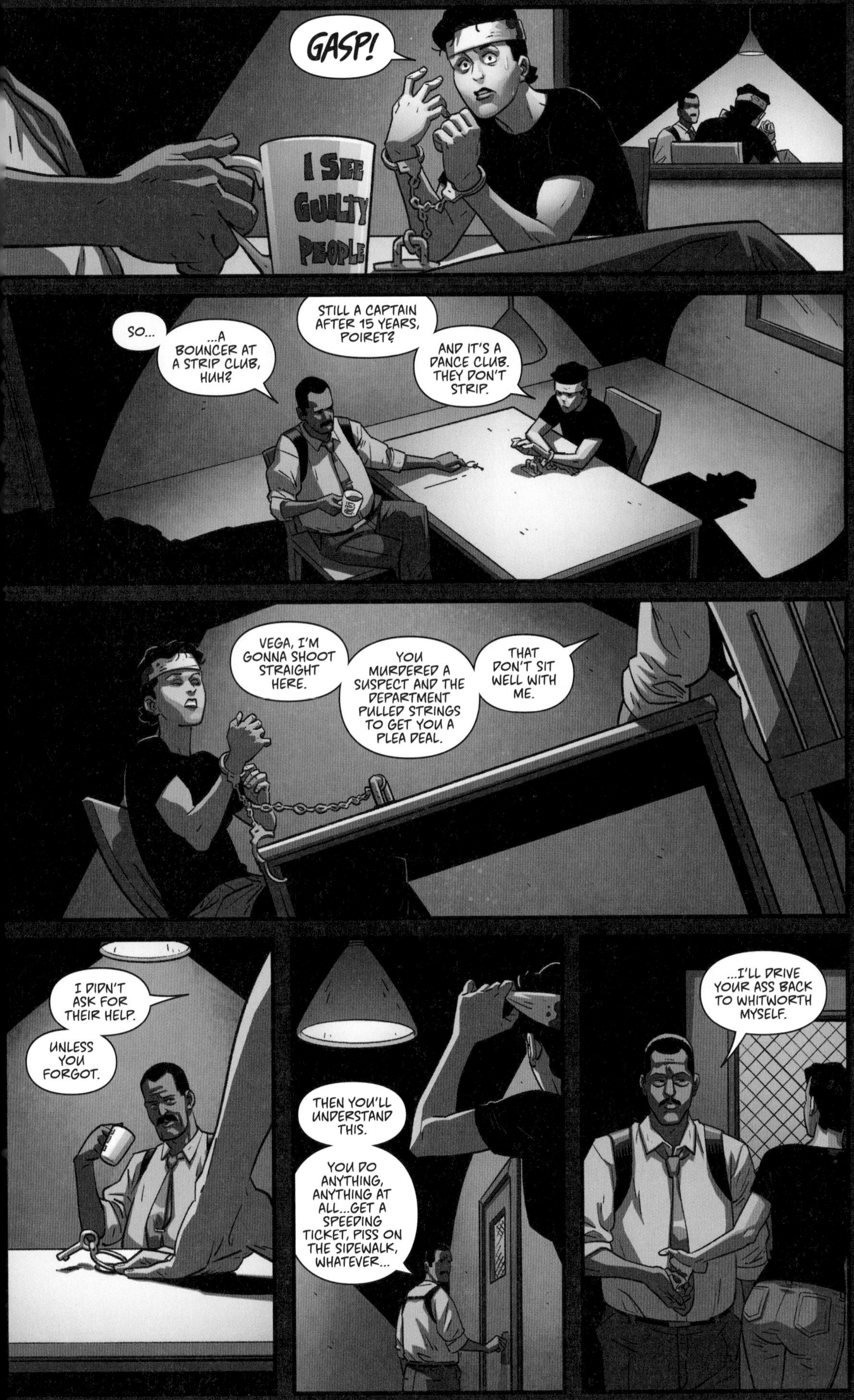
GASP!
I SEE GUILTY PEOPLE
SO...
...A BOUNCER AT A STRIP CLUB, HUH?
STILL A CAPTAIN AFTER 15 YEARS, POIRET?
AND IT'S A DANCE CLUB. THEY DON'T STRIP.
VEGA, I'M GONNA SHOOT STRAIGHT HERE.
YOU MURDERED A SUSPECT AND THE DEPARTMENT PULLED STRINGS TO GET YOU A PLEA DEAL.
THAT DON'T SIT WELL WITH ME.
I DIDN'T ASK FOR THEIR HELP.
UNLESS YOU FORGOT.
THEN YOU'LL UNDERSTAND THIS.
YOU DO ANYTHING, ANYTHING AT ALL...GET A SPEEDING TICKET, PISS ON THE SIDEWALK, WHATEVER...
...I'LL DRIVE YOUR ASS BACK TO WHITWORTH MYSELF.

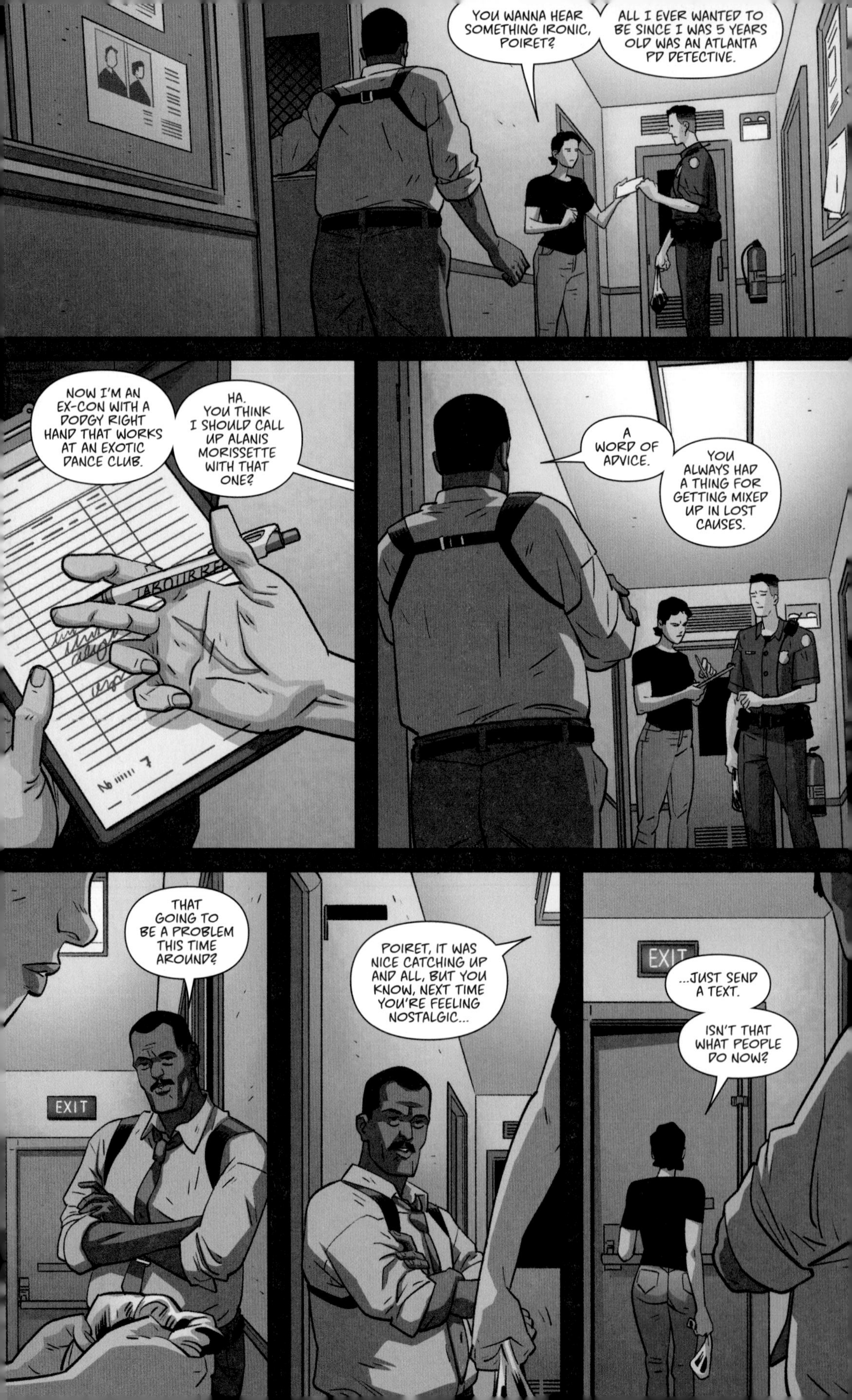
YOU WANNA HEAR SOMETHING IRONIC, POIRET?
ALL I EVER WANTED TO BE SINCE I WAS 5 YEARS OLD WAS AN ATLANTA PD DETECTIVE.
NOW I'M AN EX-CON WITH A DODGY RIGHT HAND THAT WORKS AT AN EXOTIC DANCE CLUB.
HA. YOU THINK I SHOULD CALL UP ALANIS MORISSETTE WITH THAT ONE?
A WORD OF ADVICE.
YOU ALWAYS HAD A THING FOR GETTING MIXED UP IN LOST CAUSES.
THAT GOING TO BE A PROBLEM THIS TIME AROUND?
EXIT
POIRET, IT WAS NICE CATCHING UP AND ALL, BUT YOU KNOW, NEXT TIME YOU'RE FEELING NOSTALGIC...
EXIT
...JUST SEND A TEXT.
ISN'T THAT WHAT PEOPLE DO NOW?

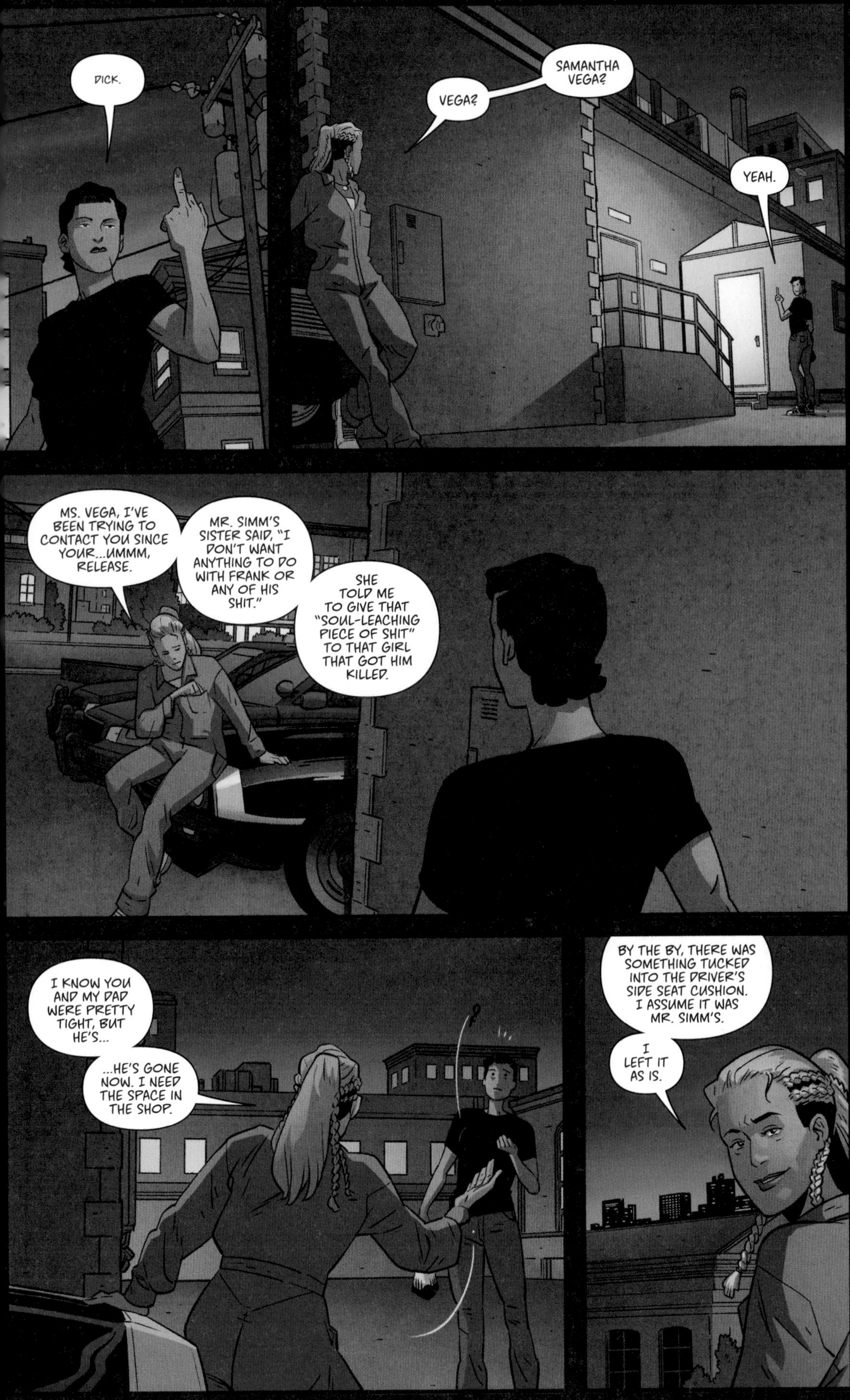
DICK.
VEGA?
SAMANTHA VEGA?
YEAH.
MS. VEGA, I'VE BEEN TRYING TO CONTACT YOU SINCE YOUR...UMMM, RELEASE.
MR. SIMM'S SISTER SAID, "I DON'T WANT ANYTHING TO DO WITH FRANK OR ANY OF HIS SHIT."
SHE TOLD ME TO GIVE THAT "SOUL-LEACHING PIECE OF SHIT" TO THAT GIRL THAT GOT HIM KILLED.
I KNOW YOU AND MY DAD WERE PRETTY TIGHT, BUT HE'S...
...HE'S GONE NOW. I NEED THE SPACE IN THE SHOP.
BY THE BY, THERE WAS SOMETHING TUCKED INTO THE DRIVER'S SIDE SEAT CUSHION. I ASSUME IT WAS MR. SIMM'S.
I LEFT IT AS IS.

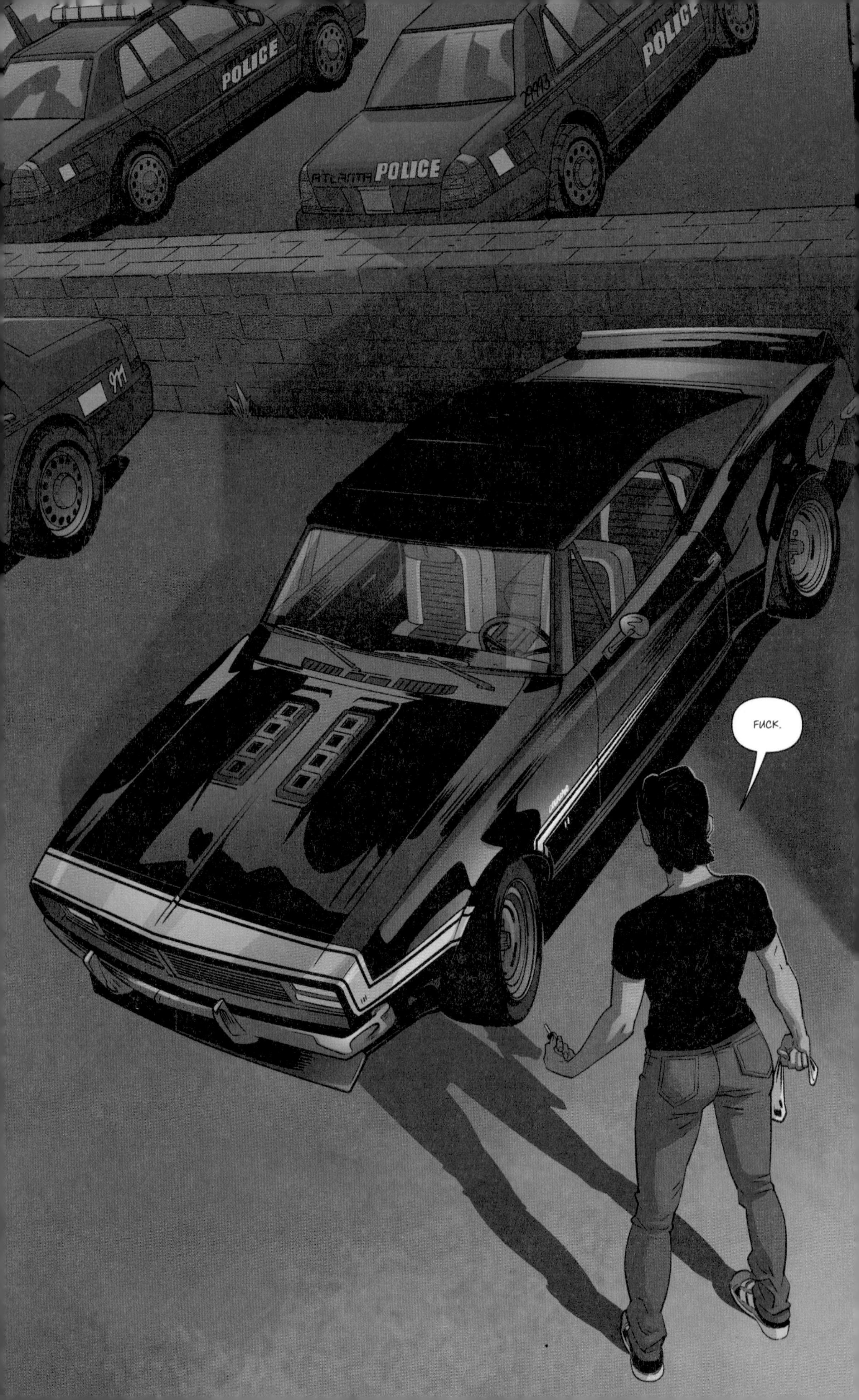
POLICE
ATLANTA POLICE
POLICE
FUCK.

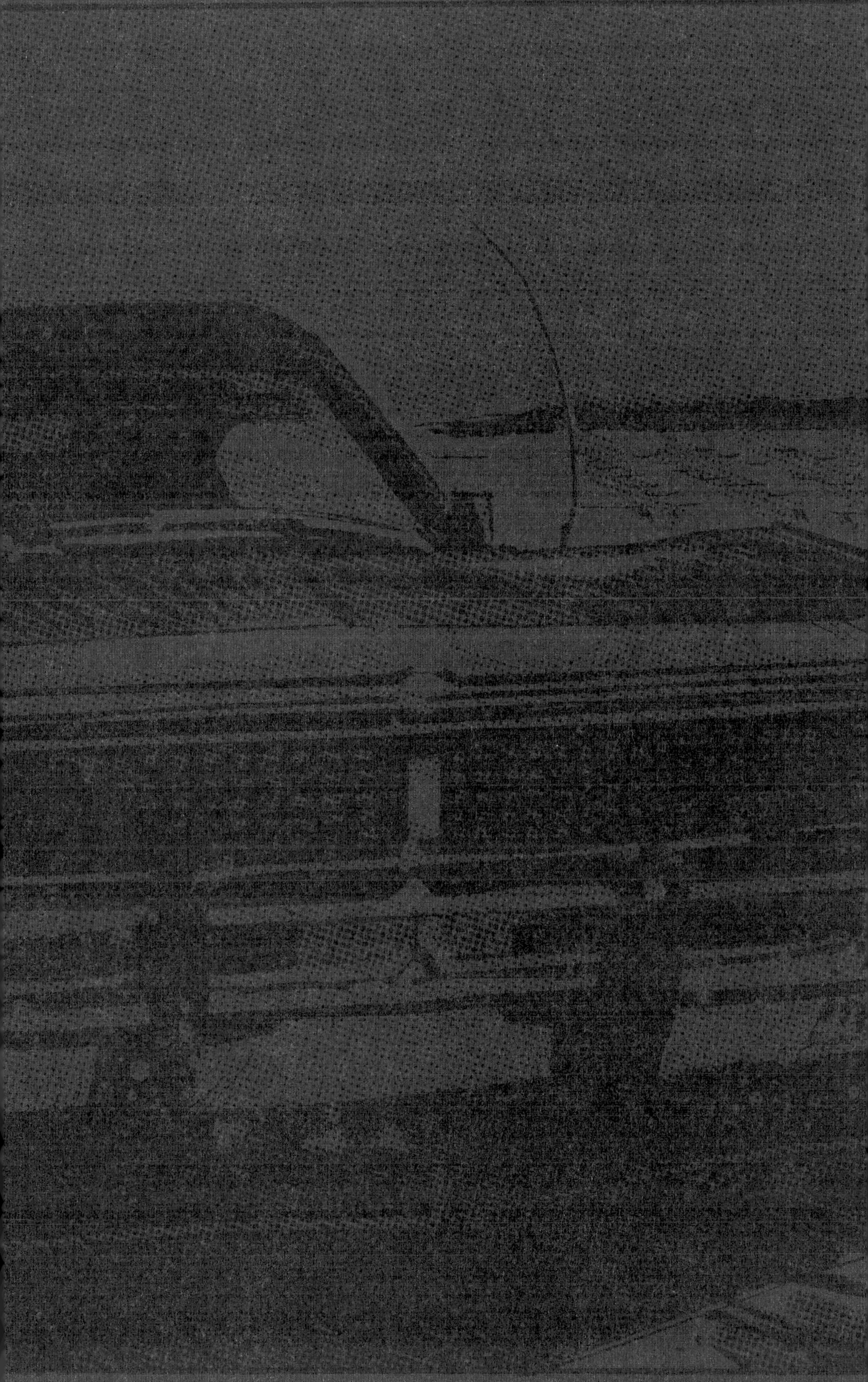

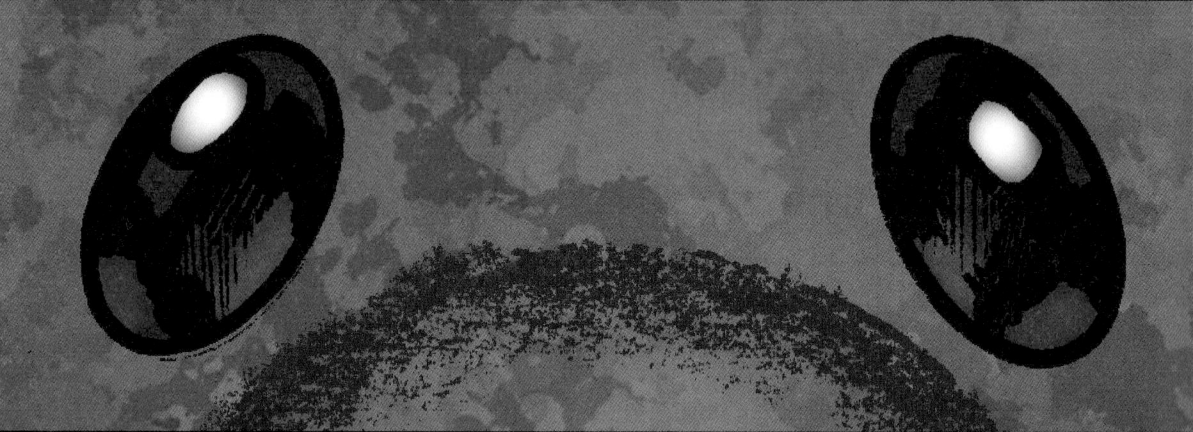

DOUG WAGNER

STORY

ADAM HUGHES

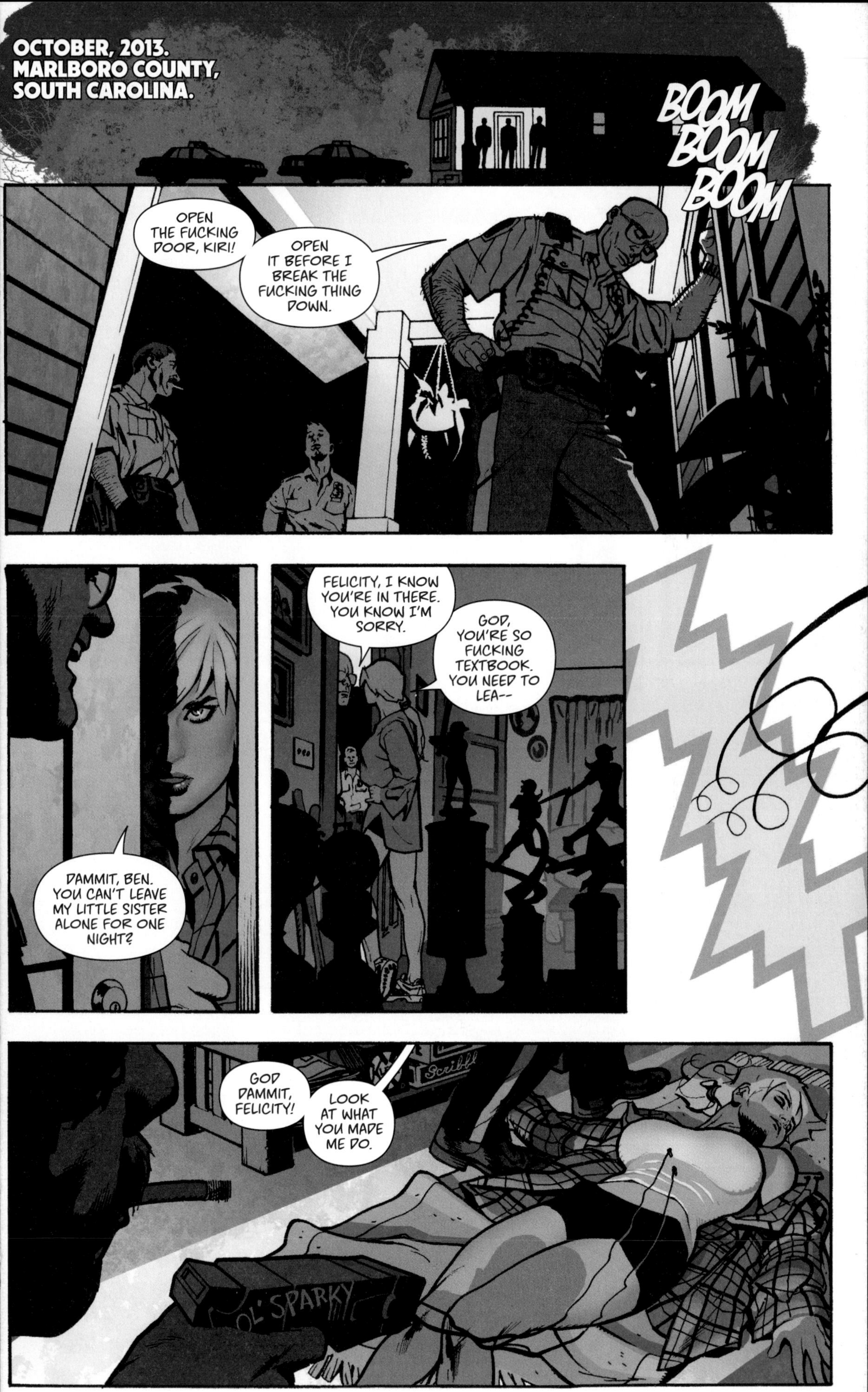
OCTOBER, 2013. MARLBORO COUNTY, SOUTH CAROLINA.
BOOM BOOM BOOM
OPEN THE FUCKING DOOR, KIRI!
OPEN IT BEFORE I BREAK THE FUCKING THING DOWN.
DAMMIT, BEN. YOU CAN'T LEAVE MY LITTLE SISTER ALONE FOR ONE NIGHT?
FELICITY, I KNOW YOU'RE IN THERE. YOU KNOW I'M SORRY.
GOD, YOU'RE SO FUCKING TEXTBOOK. YOU NEED TO LEA--
GOD DAMMIT, FELICITY!
LOOK AT WHAT YOU MADE ME DO.
OL' SPARKY

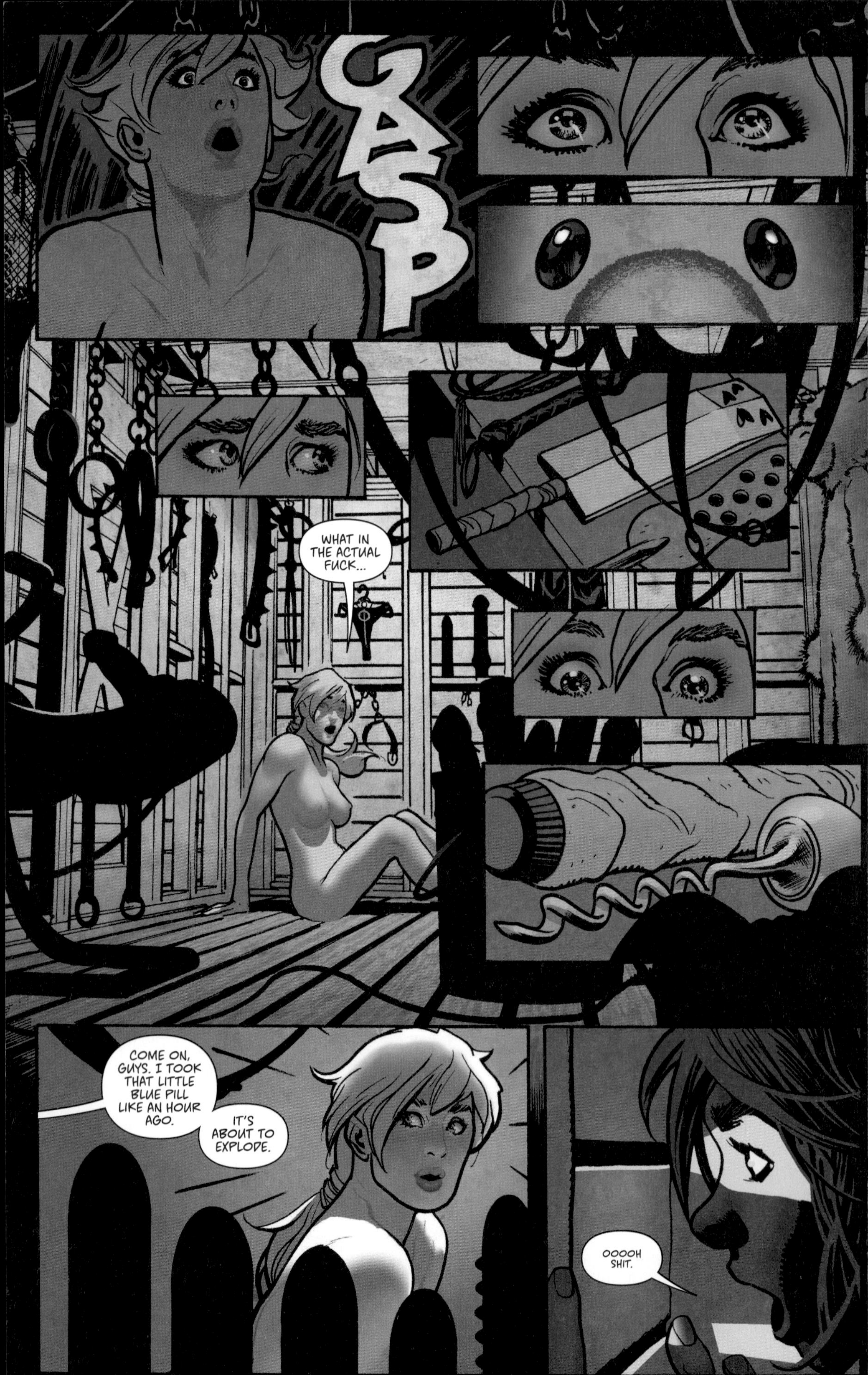
GASP
WHAT IN THE ACTUAL FUCK...
COME ON, GUYS. I TOOK THAT LITTLE BLUE PILL LIKE AN HOUR AGO.
IT'S ABOUT TO EXPLODE.
OOOOH SHIT.

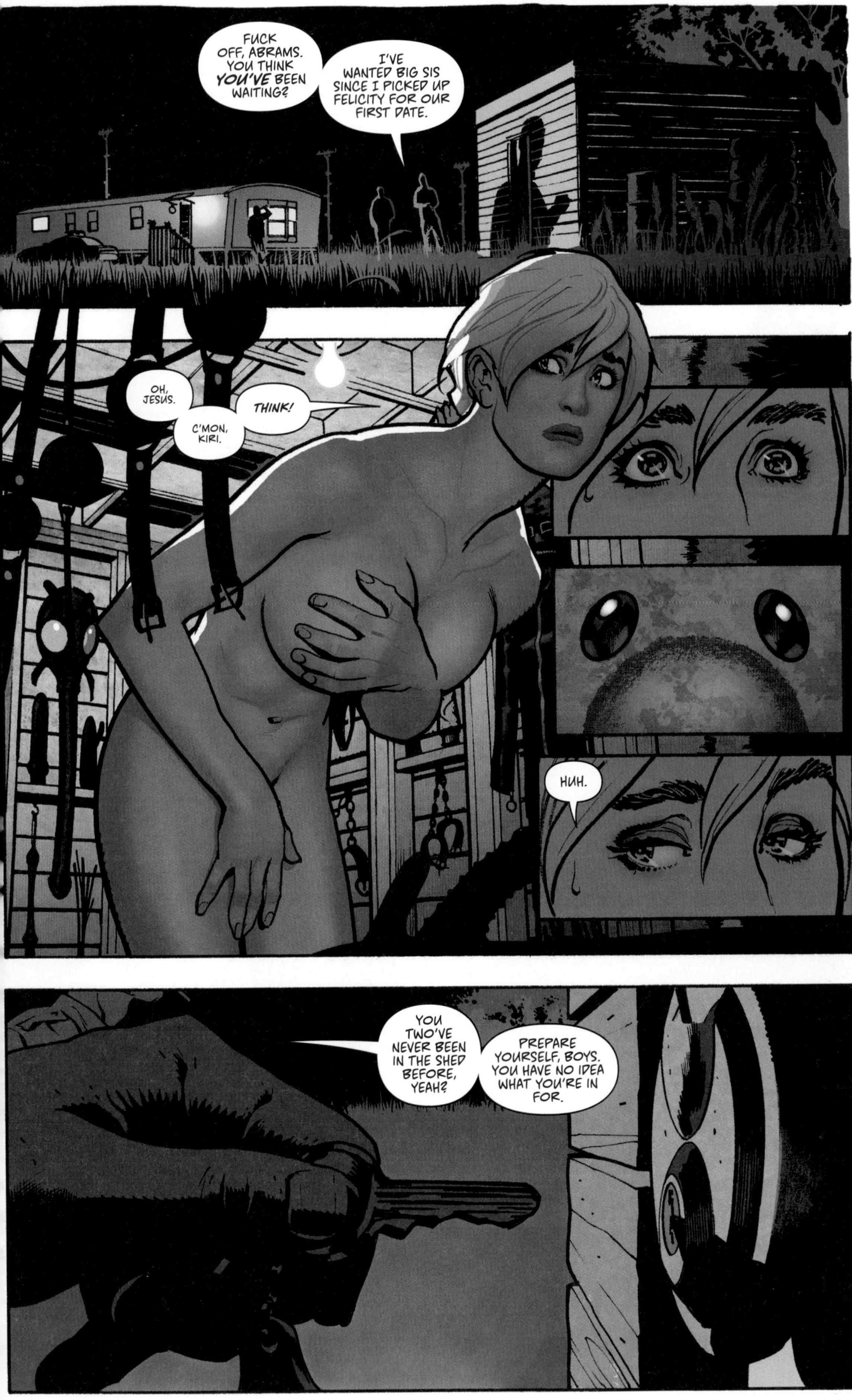
FUCK OFF, ABRAMS. YOU THINK YOU'VE BEEN WAITING?
I'VE WANTED BIG SIS SINCE I PICKED UP FELICITY FOR OUR FIRST DATE.
OH, JESUS.
C'MON, KIRI.
THINK!
HUH.
YOU TWO'VE NEVER BEEN IN THE SHED BEFORE, YEAH?
PREPARE YOURSELF, BOYS. YOU HAVE NO IDEA WHAT YOU'RE IN FOR.

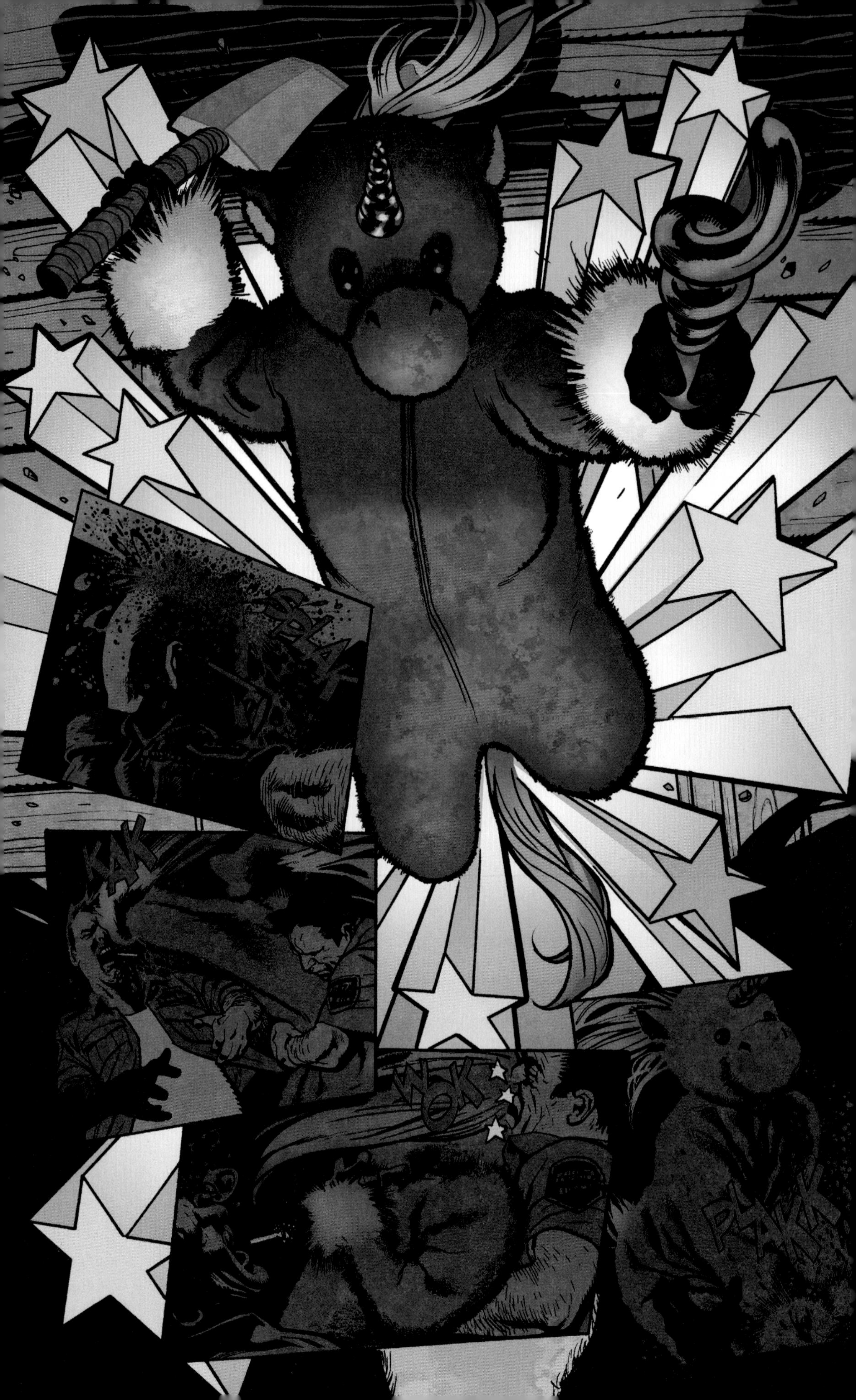
KAK
WOK

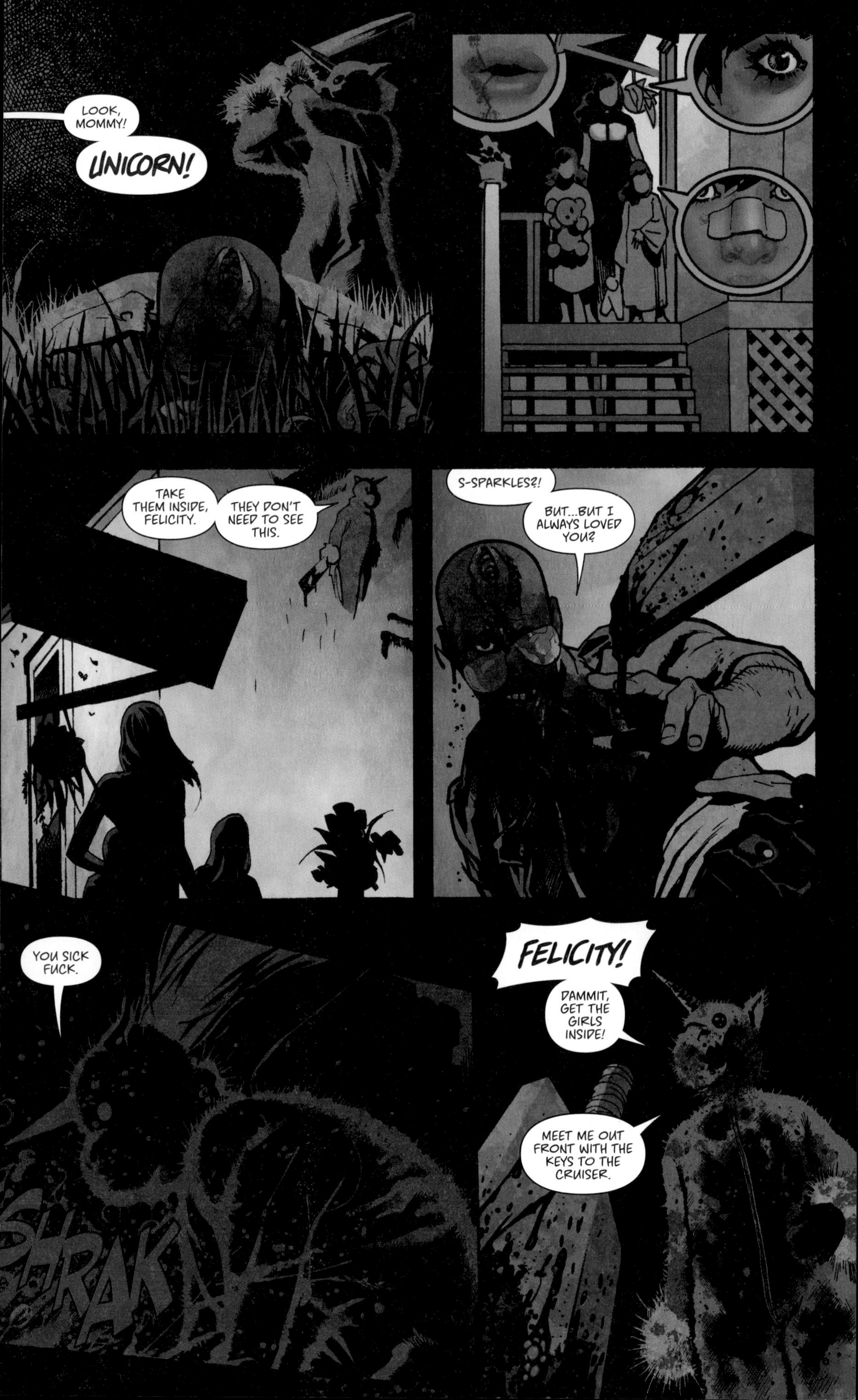
LOOK, MOMMY!
UNICORN!
TAKE THEM INSIDE, FELICITY.
THEY DON'T NEED TO SEE THIS.
S-SPARKLES?!
BUT...BUT I ALWAYS LOVED YOU?
YOU SICK FUCK.
SHRAK
FELICITY!
DAMMIT, GET THE GIRLS INSIDE!
MEET ME OUT FRONT WITH THE KEYS TO THE CRUISER.

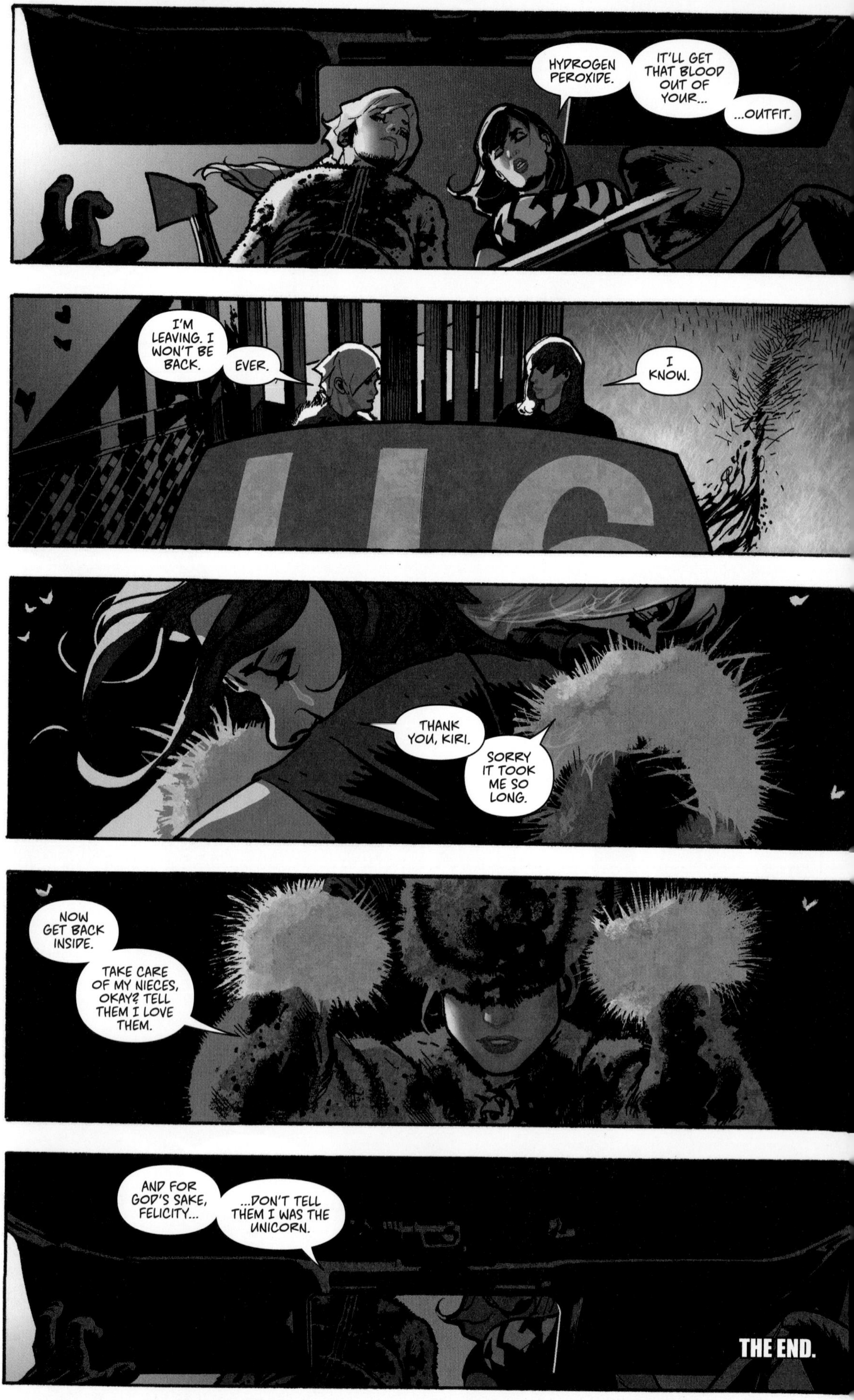
HYDROGEN PEROXIDE.
IT'LL GET THAT BLOOD OUT OF YOUR...
...OUTFIT.
I'M LEAVING. I WON'T BE BACK.
EVER.
I KNOW.
THANK YOU, KIRI.
SORRY IT TOOK ME SO LONG.
NOW GET BACK INSIDE.
TAKE CARE OF MY NIECES, OKAY? TELL THEM I LOVE THEM.
AND FOR GOD'S SAKE, FELICITY...
...DON'T TELL THEM I WAS THE UNICORN.
THE END.

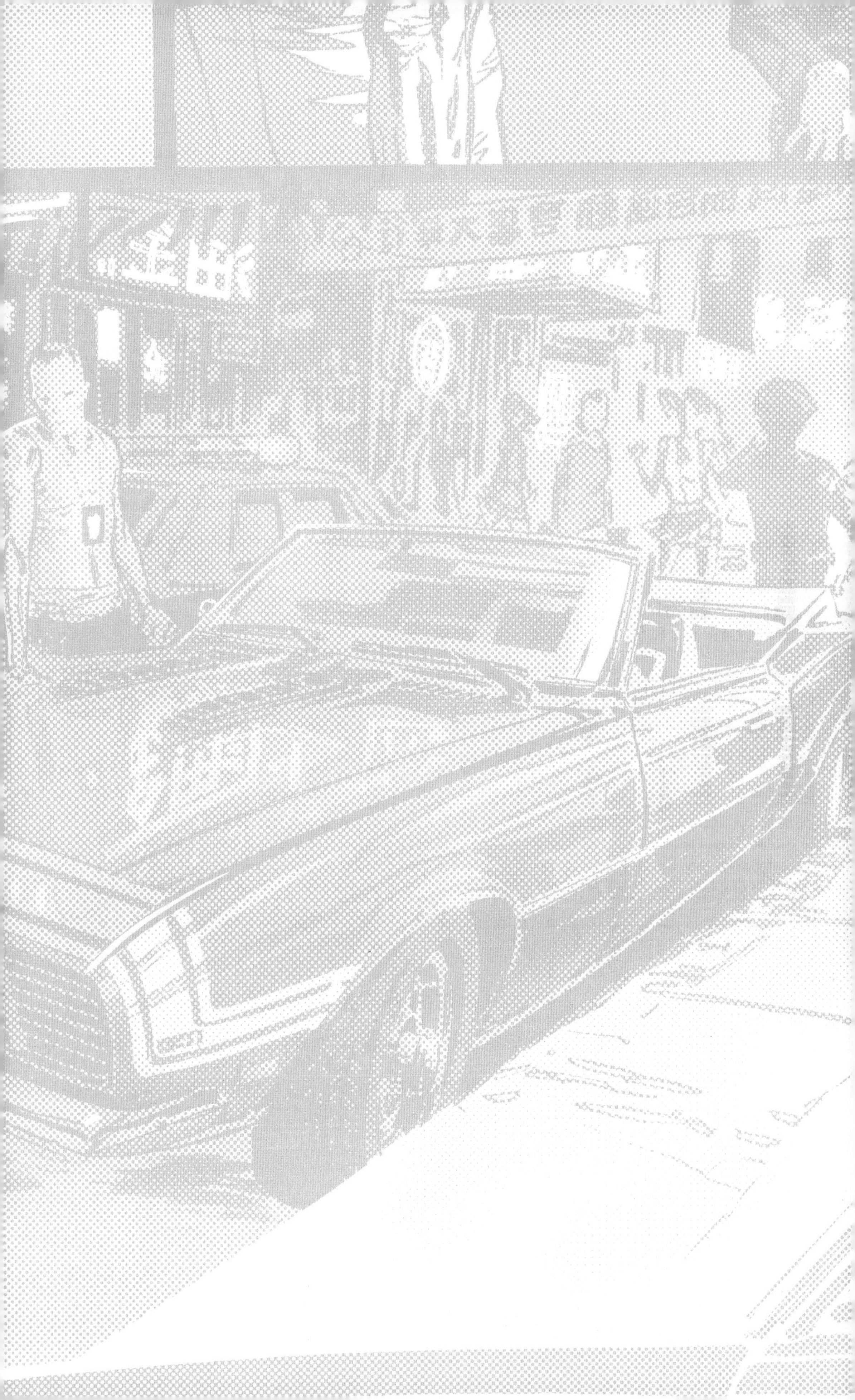

BURNING DESIRE
CHAPTER TWO

DOUG WAGNER
STORY

DANIEL HILLYARD
ART

LAURA MARTIN
COLORS

ED DUKESHIRE
LETTERS

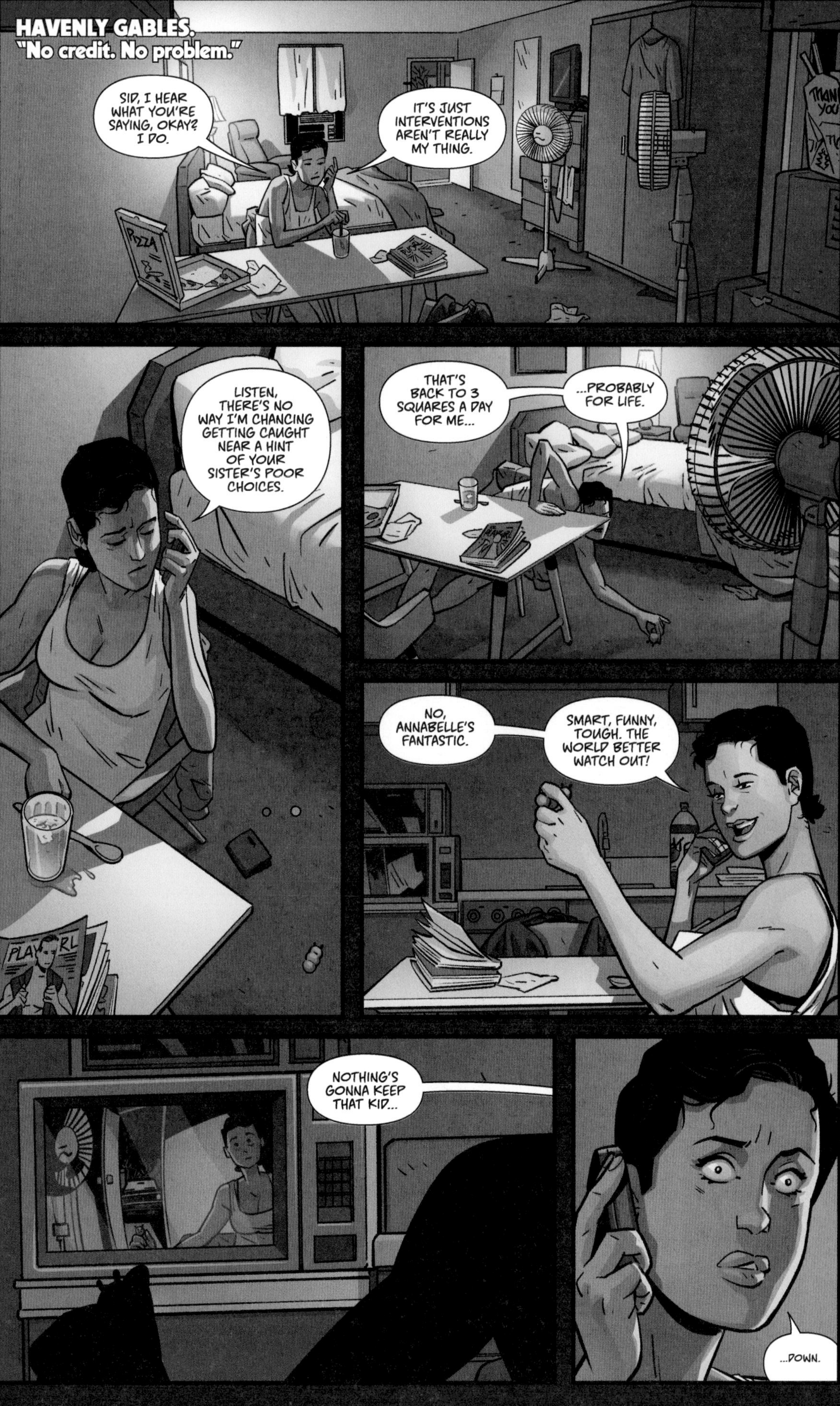
HAVENLY GABLES.
"No credit. No problem."
SID, I HEAR WHAT YOU'RE SAYING, OKAY? I DO.
IT'S JUST INTERVENTIONS AREN'T REALLY MY THING.
PIZZA
LISTEN, THERE'S NO WAY I'M CHANCING GETTING CAUGHT NEAR A HINT OF YOUR SISTER'S POOR CHOICES.
PLAYGIRL
THAT'S BACK TO 3 SQUARES A DAY FOR ME...
...PROBABLY FOR LIFE.
NO, ANNABELLE'S FANTASTIC.
SMART, FUNNY, TOUGH. THE WORLD BETTER WATCH OUT!
NOTHING'S GONNA KEEP THAT KID...
...DOWN.

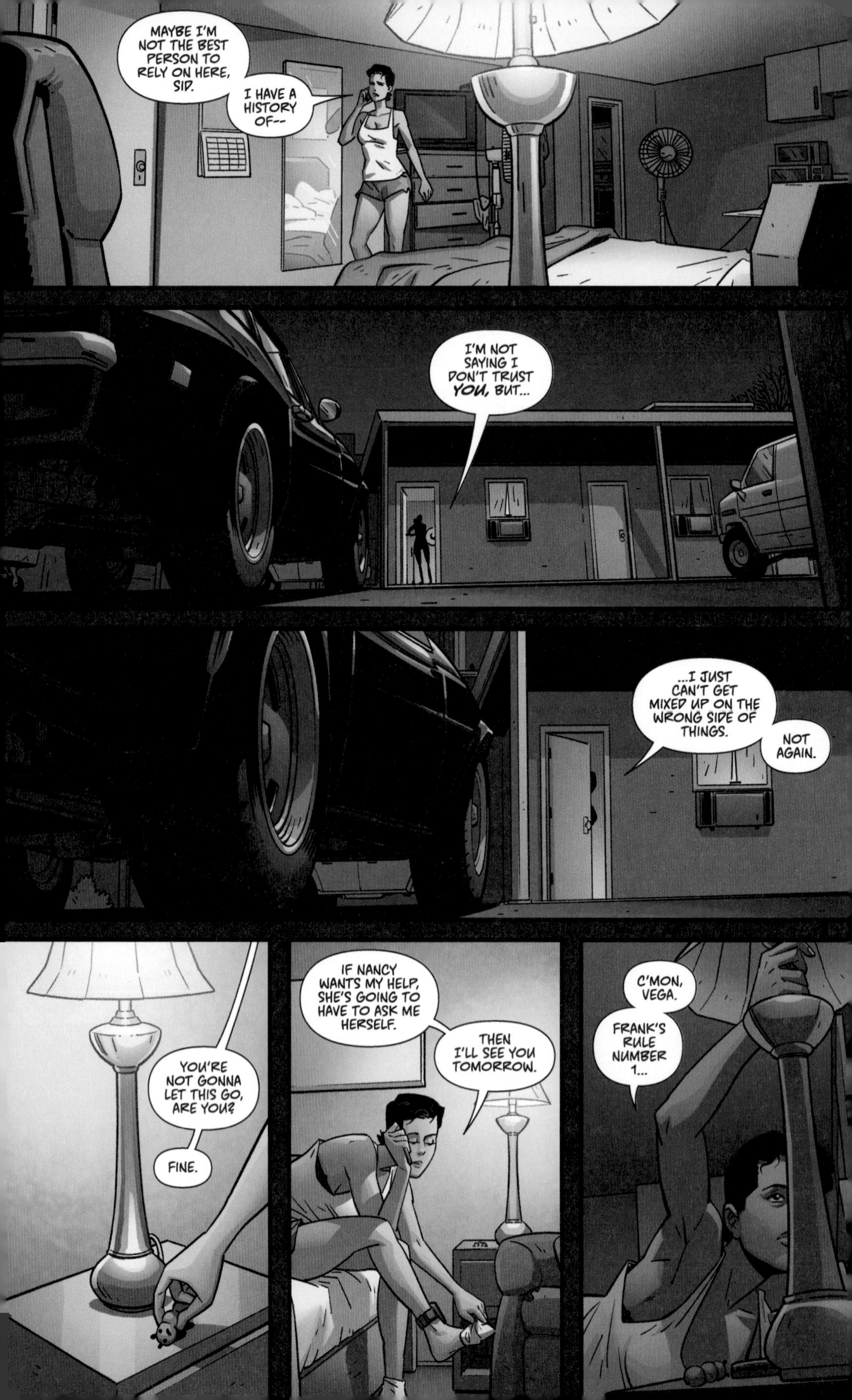
MAYBE I'M NOT THE BEST PERSON TO RELY ON HERE, SID.
I HAVE A HISTORY OF--
I'M NOT SAYING I DON'T TRUST *YOU*, BUT...
...I JUST CAN'T GET MIXED UP ON THE WRONG SIDE OF THINGS.
NOT AGAIN.
YOU'RE NOT GONNA LET THIS GO, ARE YOU?
FINE.
IF NANCY WANTS MY HELP, SHE'S GOING TO HAVE TO ASK ME HERSELF.
THEN I'LL SEE YOU TOMORROW.
C'MON, VEGA.
FRANK'S RULE NUMBER 1...

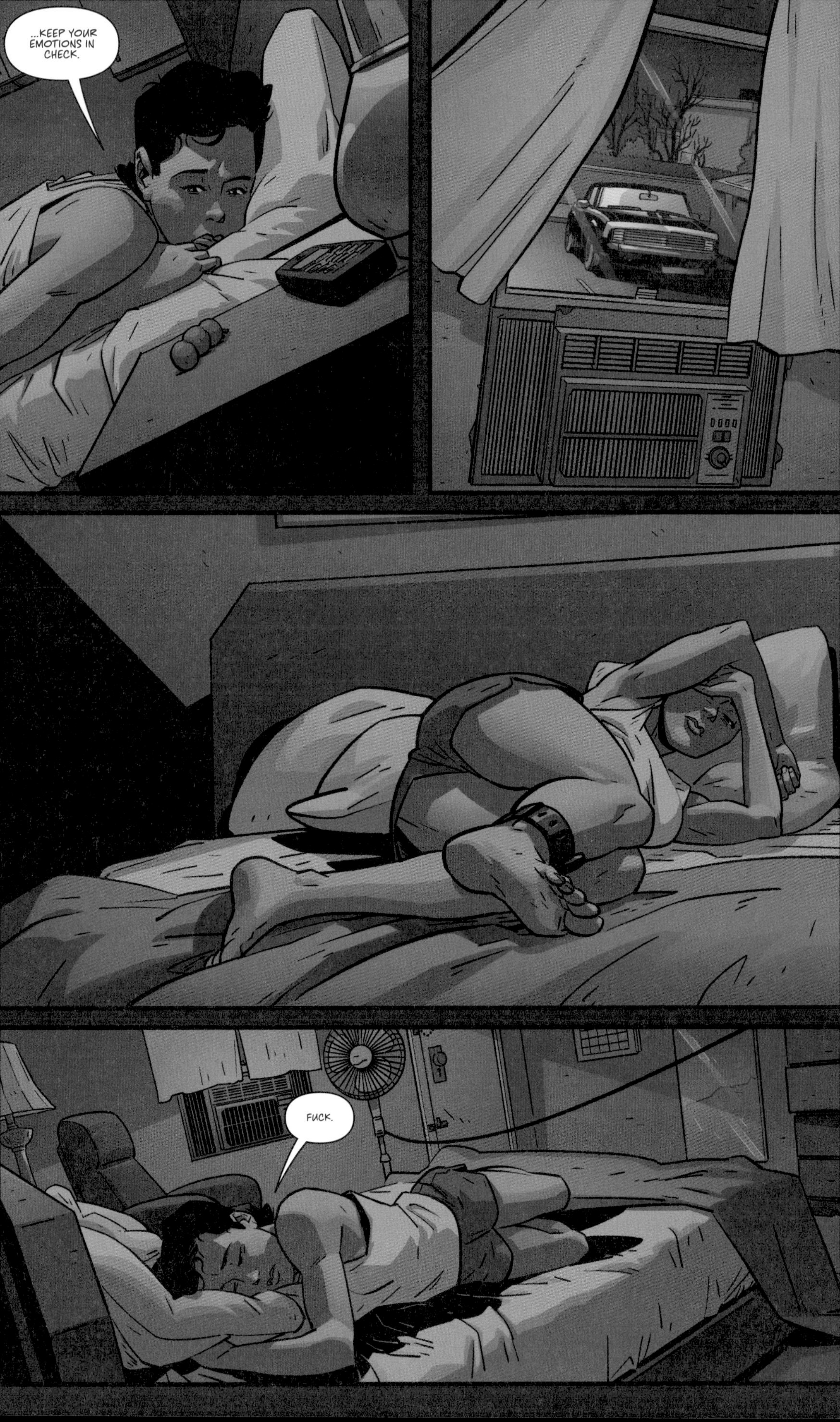
...KEEP YOUR EMOTIONS IN CHECK.
FUCK.

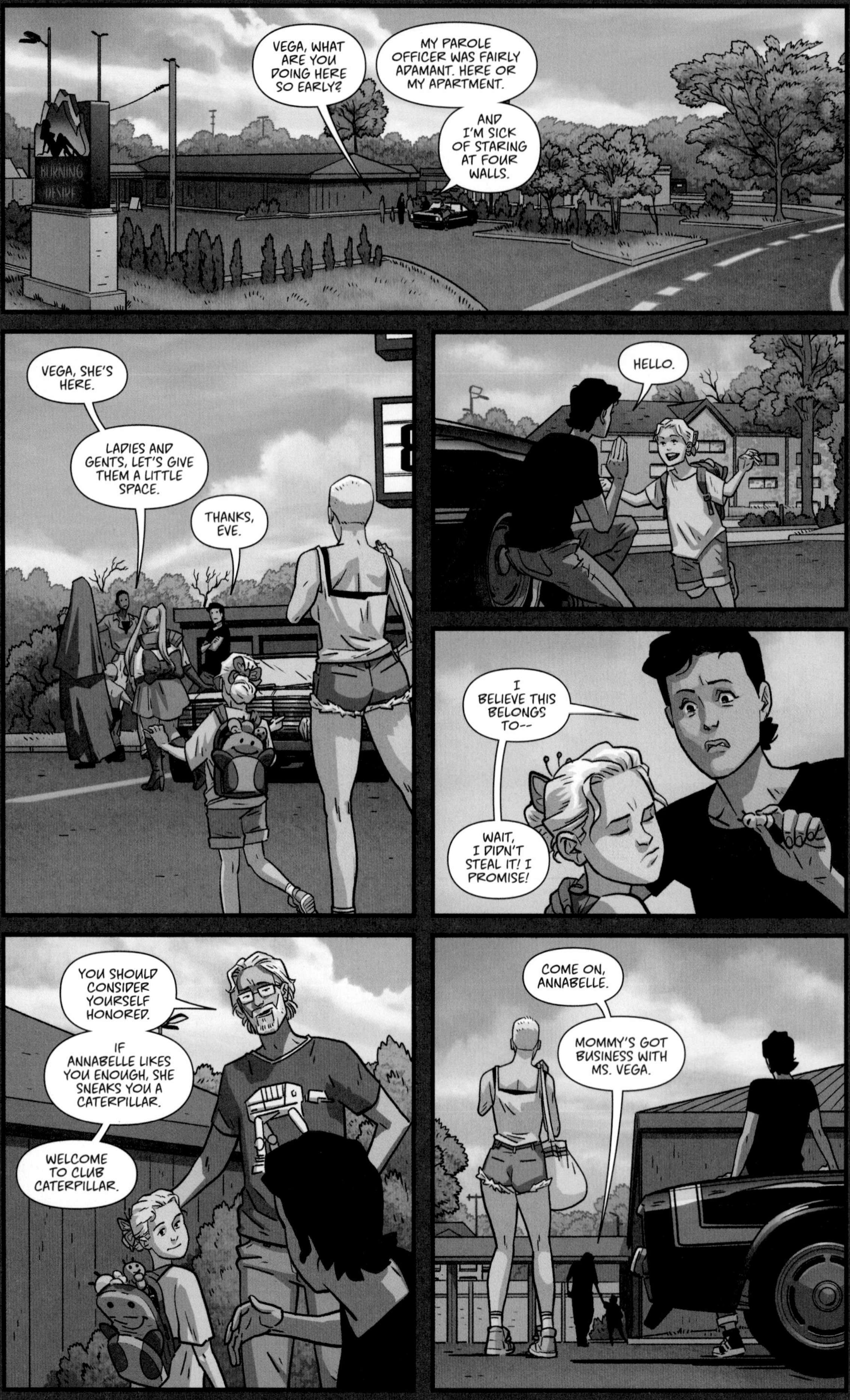
BURNING DESIRE
VEGA, WHAT ARE YOU DOING HERE SO EARLY?
MY PAROLE OFFICER WAS FAIRLY ADAMANT. HERE OR MY APARTMENT.
AND I'M SICK OF STARING AT FOUR WALLS.
VEGA, SHE'S HERE.
LADIES AND GENTS, LET'S GIVE THEM A LITTLE SPACE.
THANKS, EVE.
HELLO.
I BELIEVE THIS BELONGS TO--
WAIT, I DIDN'T STEAL IT! I PROMISE!
YOU SHOULD CONSIDER YOURSELF HONORED.
IF ANNABELLE LIKES YOU ENOUGH, SHE SNEAKS YOU A CATERPILLAR.
WELCOME TO CLUB CATERPILLAR.
COME ON, ANNABELLE.
MOMMY'S GOT BUSINESS WITH MS. VEGA.

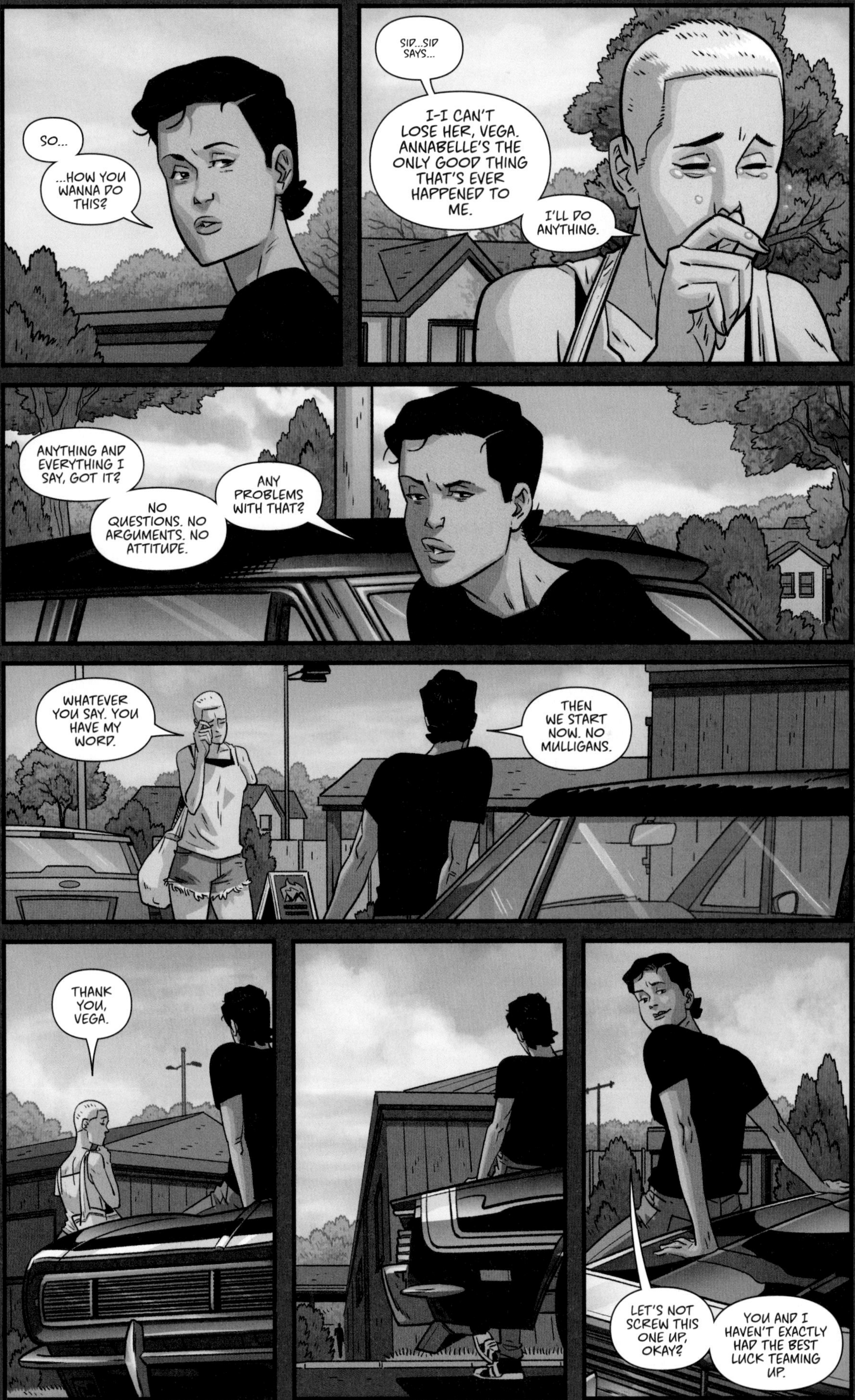
SO...
...HOW YOU WANNA DO THIS?
SID...SID SAYS...
I-I CAN'T LOSE HER, VEGA. ANNABELLE'S THE ONLY GOOD THING THAT'S EVER HAPPENED TO ME.
I'LL DO ANYTHING.
ANYTHING AND EVERYTHING I SAY, GOT IT?
NO QUESTIONS. NO ARGUMENTS. NO ATTITUDE.
ANY PROBLEMS WITH THAT?
WHATEVER YOU SAY. YOU HAVE MY WORD.
THEN WE START NOW. NO MULLIGANS.
THANK YOU, VEGA.
LET'S NOT SCREW THIS ONE UP, OKAY?
YOU AND I HAVEN'T EXACTLY HAD THE BEST LUCK TEAMING UP.

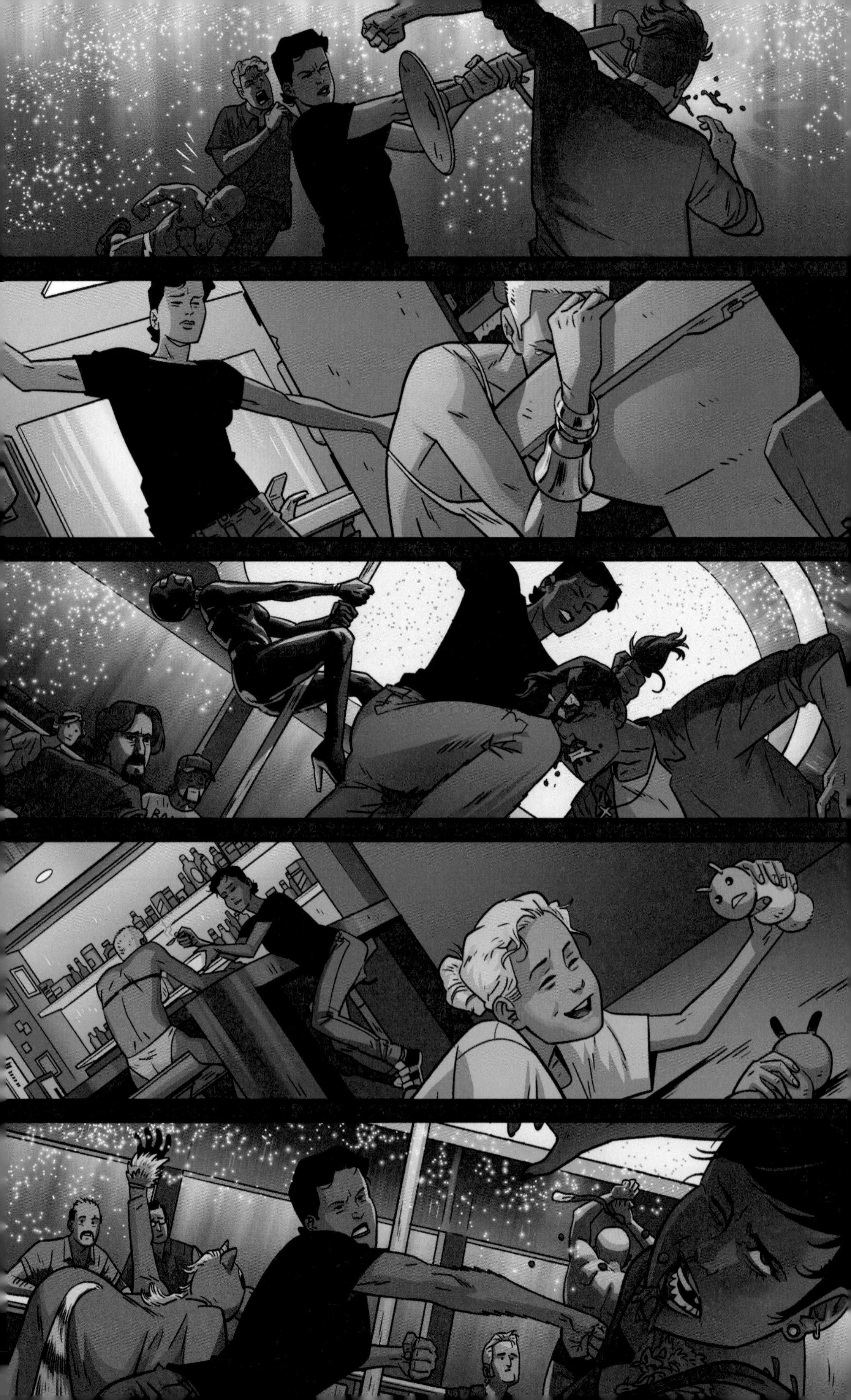

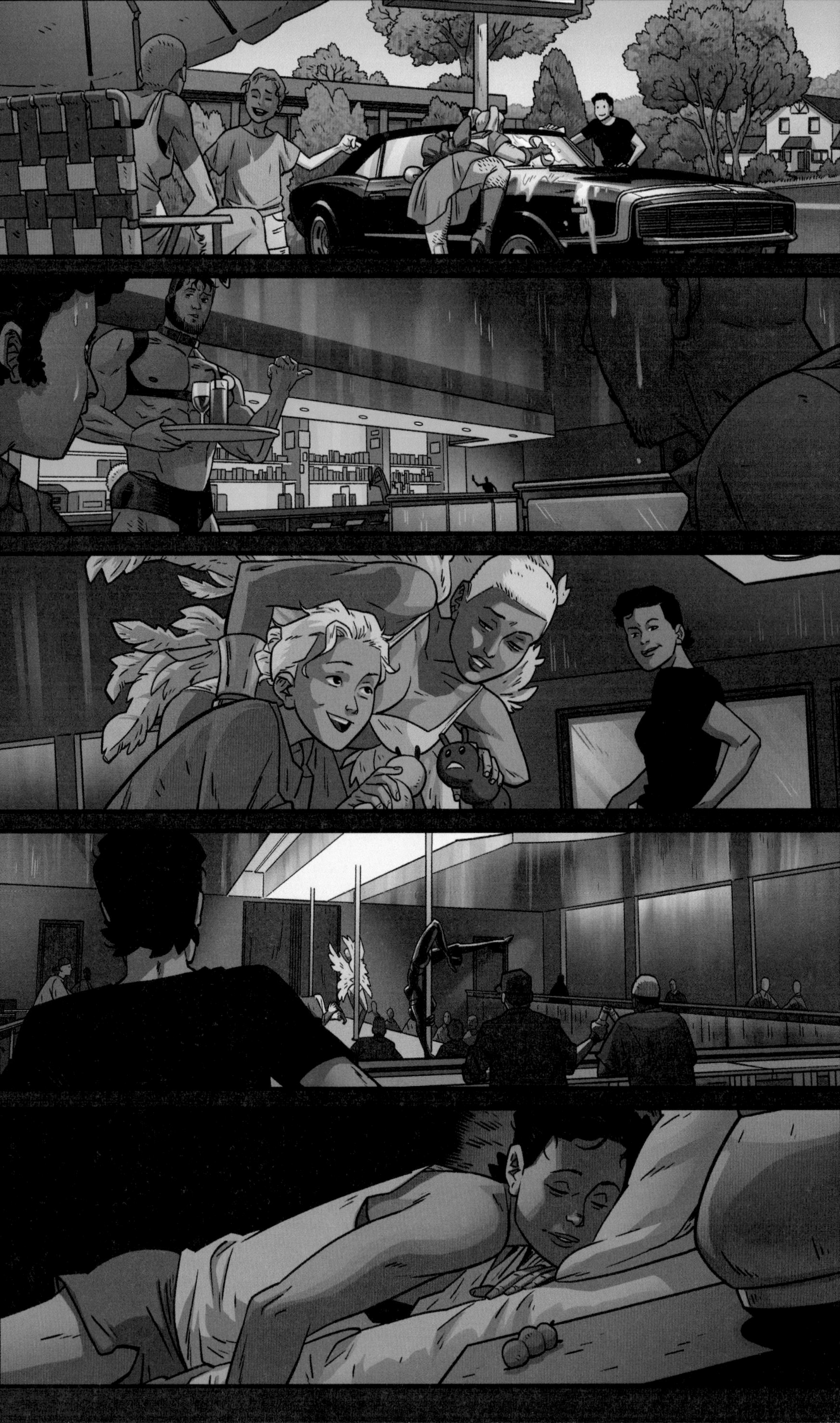

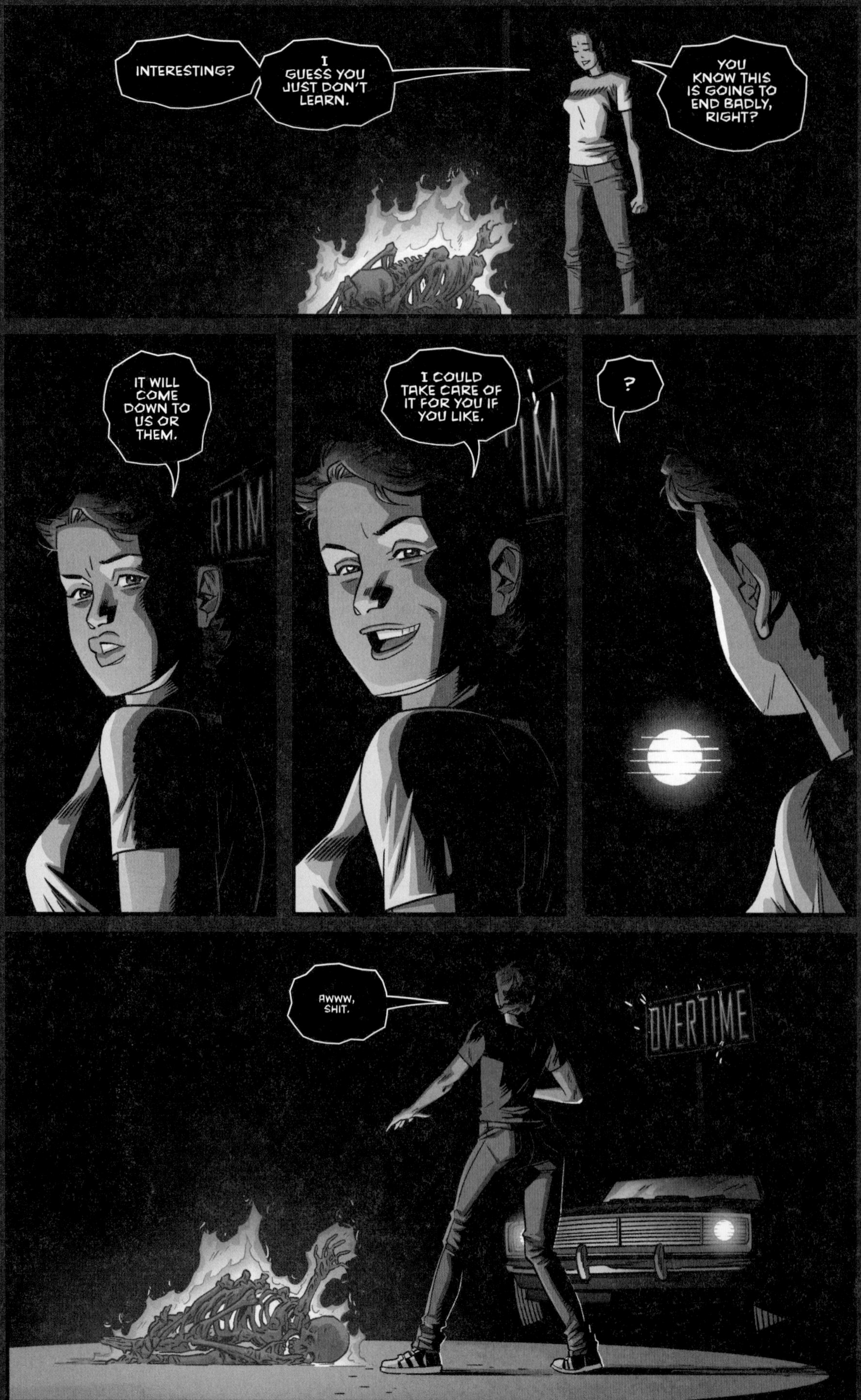
INTERESTING?
I GUESS YOU JUST DON'T LEARN.
YOU KNOW THIS IS GOING TO END BADLY, RIGHT?
IT WILL COME DOWN TO US OR THEM.
I COULD TAKE CARE OF IT FOR YOU IF YOU LIKE.
?
AWWW, SHIT.
OVERTIME

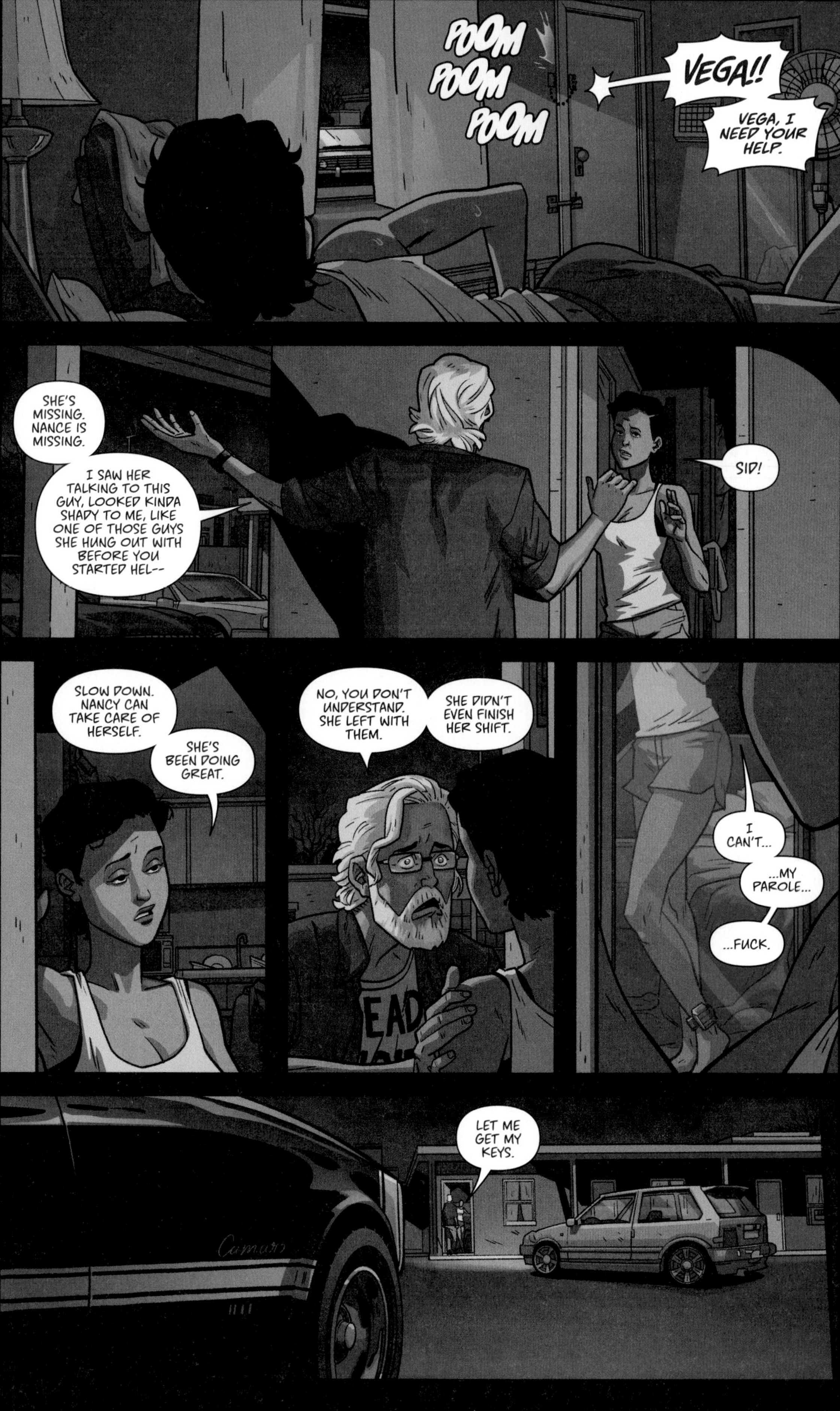
POOM POOM POOM
VEGA!!
VEGA, I NEED YOUR HELP.
SHE'S MISSING. NANCE IS MISSING.
I SAW HER TALKING TO THIS GUY, LOOKED KINDA SHADY TO ME, LIKE ONE OF THOSE GUYS SHE HUNG OUT WITH BEFORE YOU STARTED HEL--
SID!
SLOW DOWN. NANCY CAN TAKE CARE OF HERSELF.
SHE'S BEEN DOING GREAT.
NO, YOU DON'T UNDERSTAND. SHE LEFT WITH THEM.
SHE DIDN'T EVEN FINISH HER SHIFT.
I CAN'T...
...MY PAROLE...
...FUCK.
LET ME GET MY KEYS.

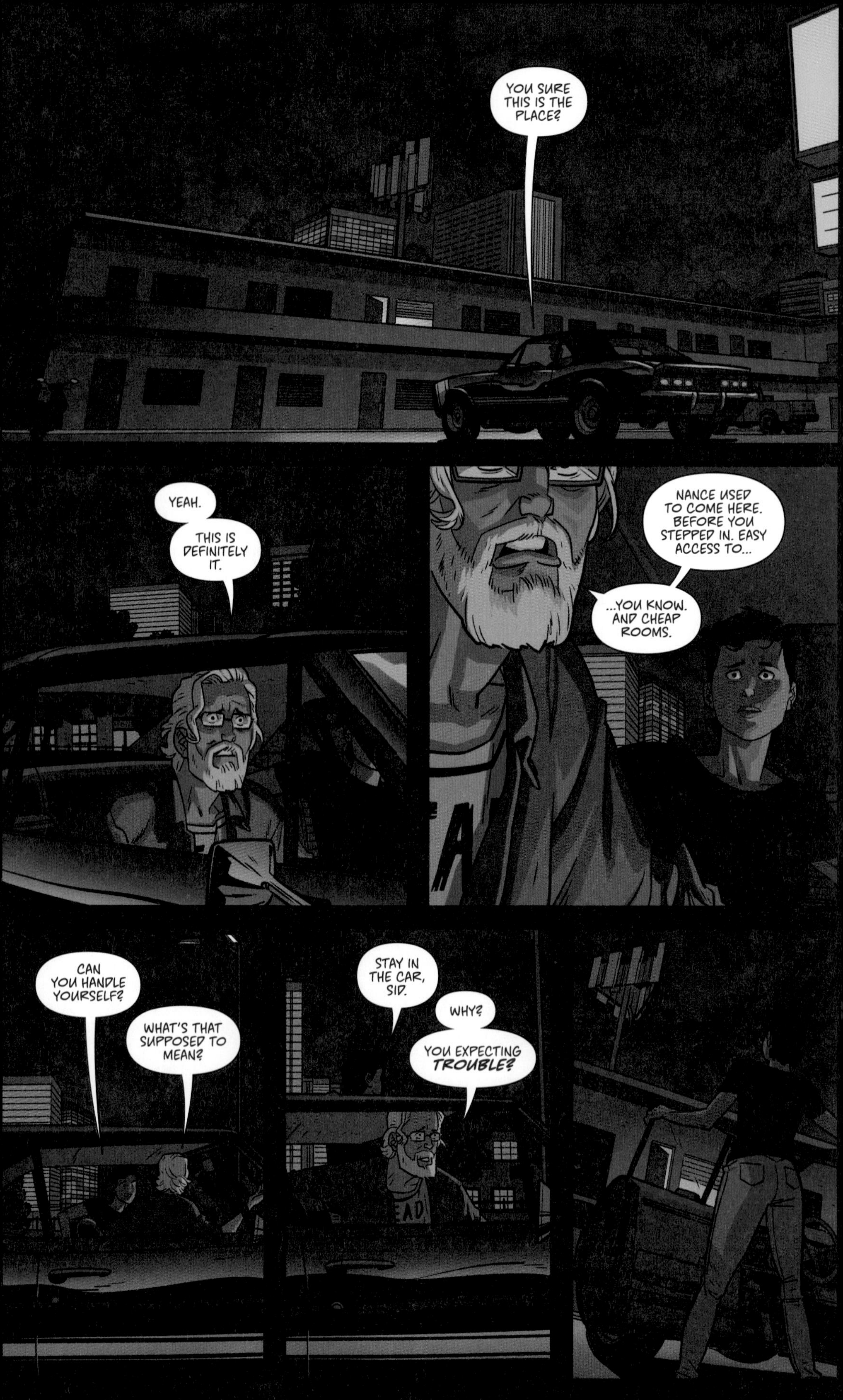
YOU SURE THIS IS THE PLACE?
YEAH.
THIS IS DEFINITELY IT.
NANCE USED TO COME HERE. BEFORE YOU STEPPED IN. EASY ACCESS TO...
...YOU KNOW. AND CHEAP ROOMS.
CAN YOU HANDLE YOURSELF?
WHAT'S THAT SUPPOSED TO MEAN?
STAY IN THE CAR, SID.
WHY?
YOU EXPECTING *TROUBLE?*

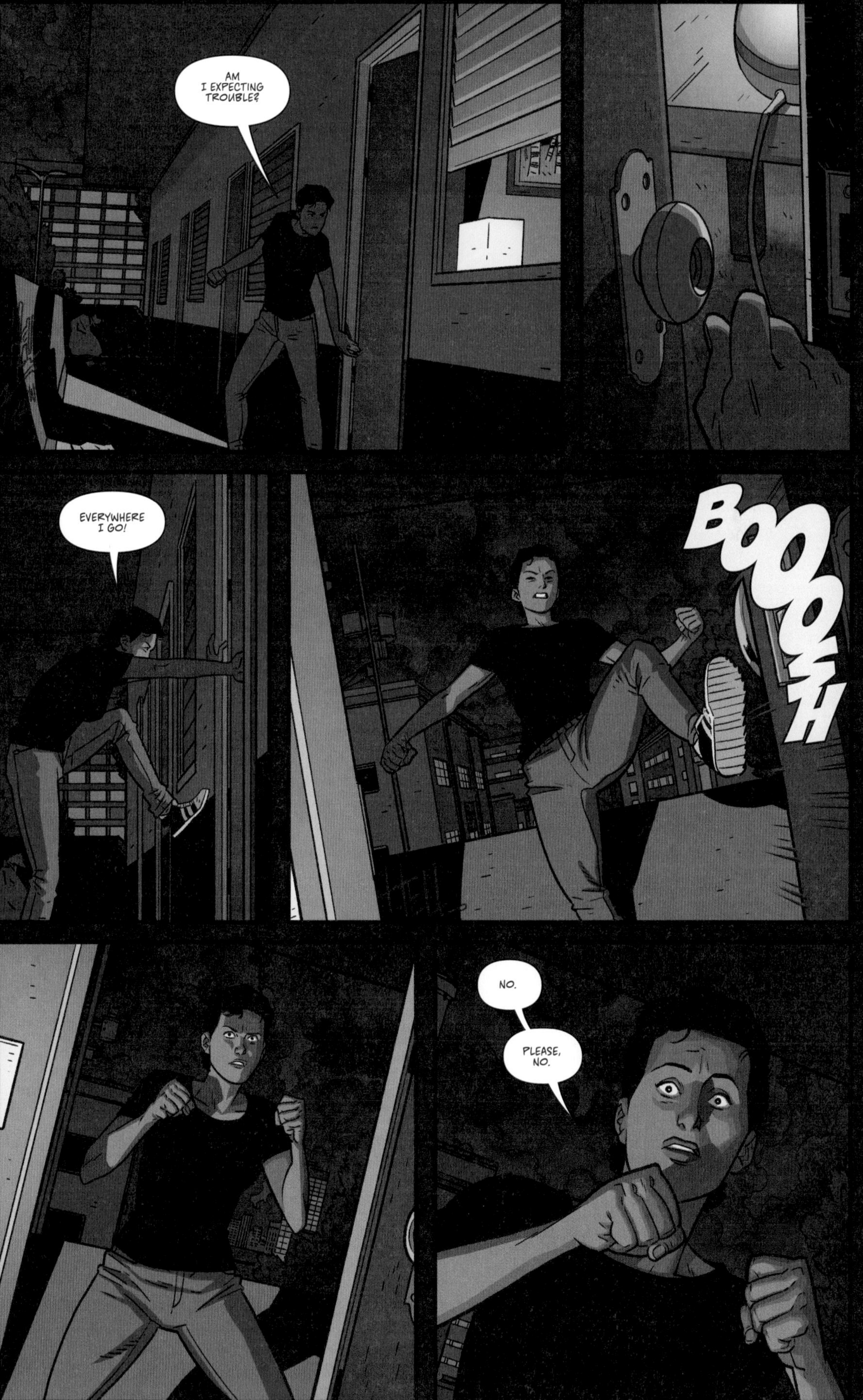
AM I EXPECTING TROUBLE?
EVERYWHERE I GO!
BOOOOWH
NO.
PLEASE, NO.

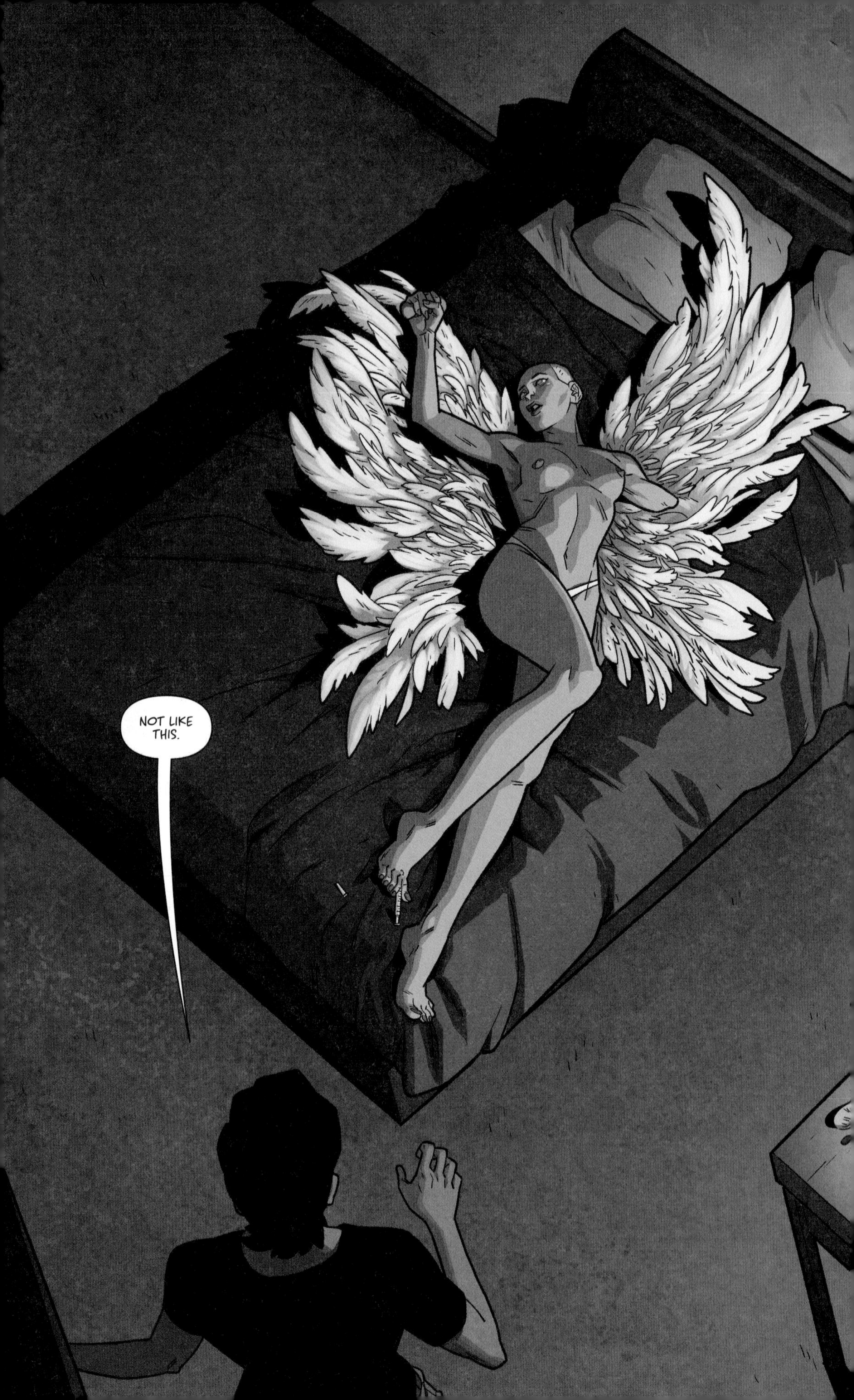
NOT LIKE THIS.

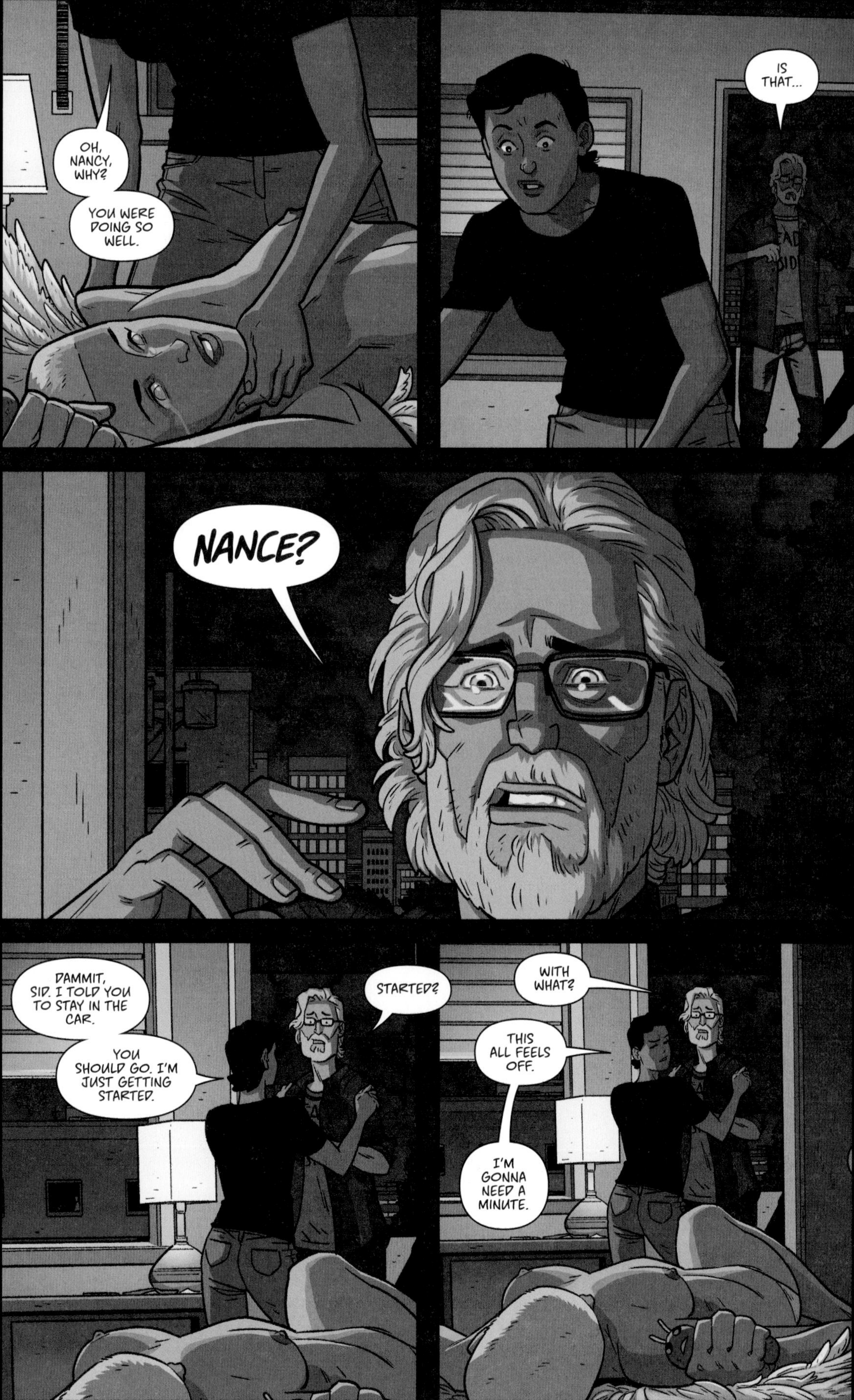
OH, NANCY, WHY?
YOU WERE DOING SO WELL.
IS THAT...
NANCE?
DAMMIT, SID. I TOLD YOU TO STAY IN THE CAR.
YOU SHOULD GO. I'M JUST GETTING STARTED.
STARTED?
WITH WHAT?
THIS ALL FEELS OFF.
I'M GONNA NEED A MINUTE.

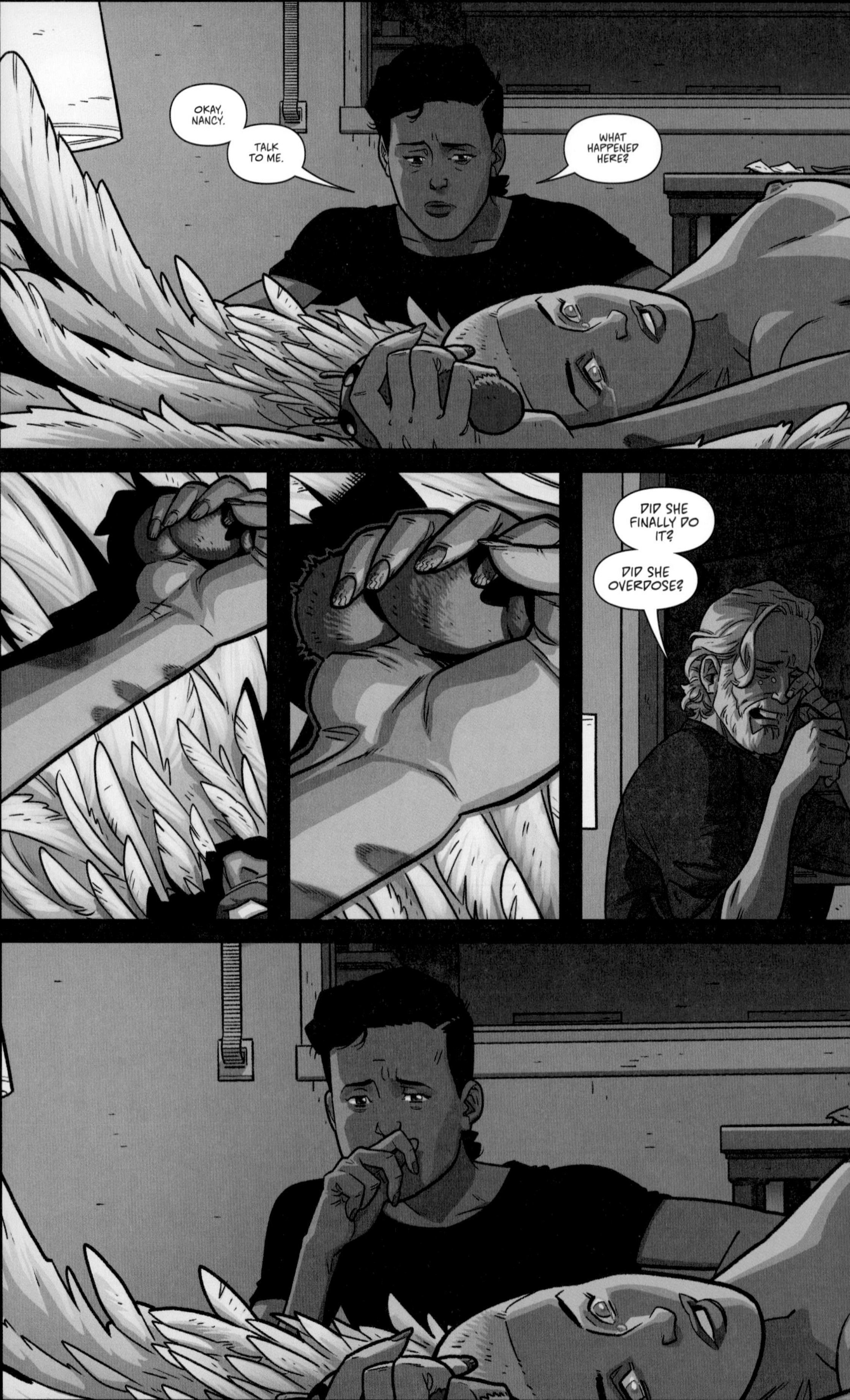
OKAY, NANCY.
TALK TO ME.
WHAT HAPPENED HERE?
DID SHE FINALLY DO IT?
DID SHE OVERDOSE?

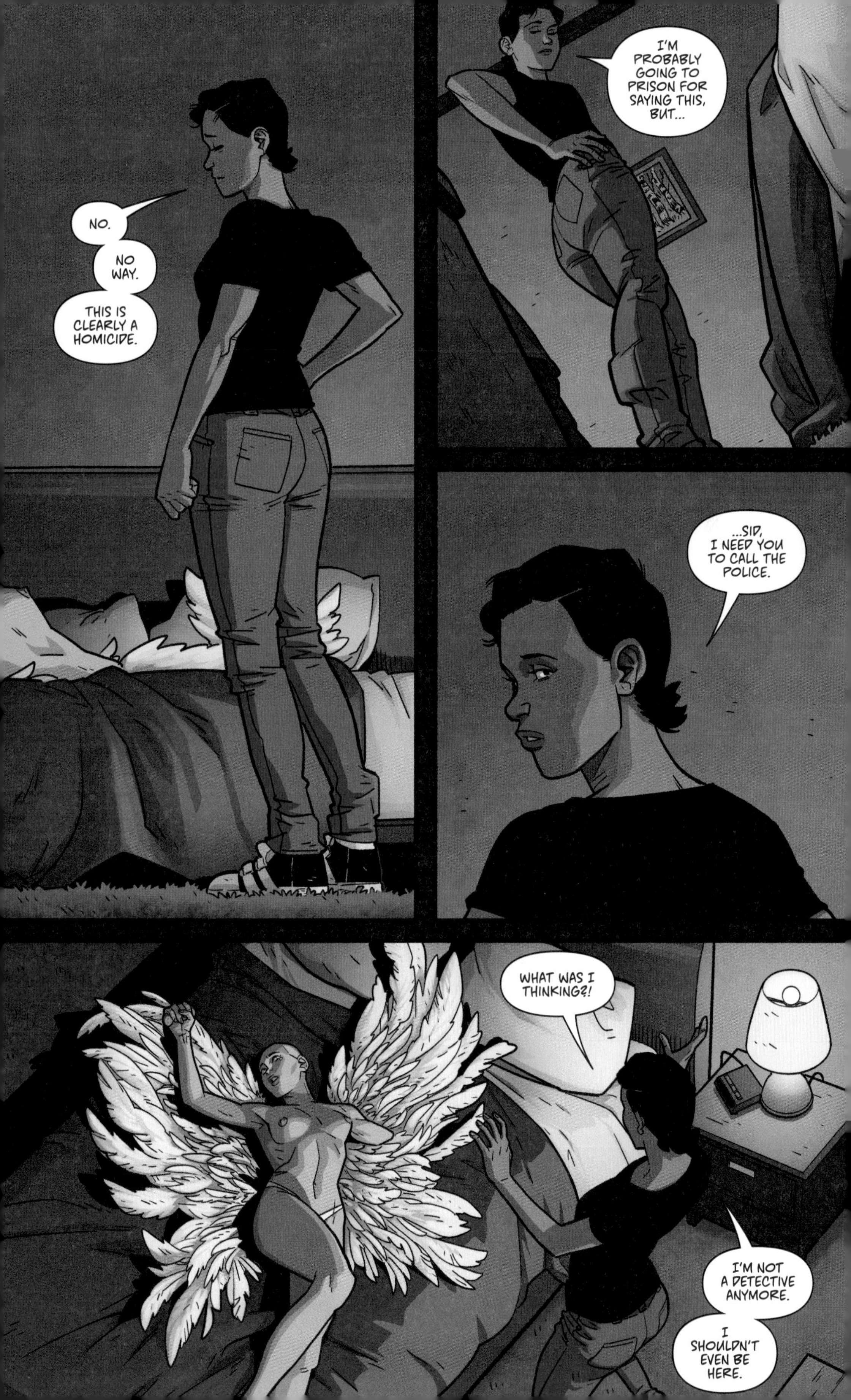
NO.
NO WAY.
THIS IS CLEARLY A HOMICIDE.
I'M PROBABLY GOING TO PRISON FOR SAYING THIS, BUT...
...SID, I NEED YOU TO CALL THE POLICE.
WHAT WAS I THINKING?!
I'M NOT A DETECTIVE ANYMORE.
I SHOULDN'T EVEN BE HERE.

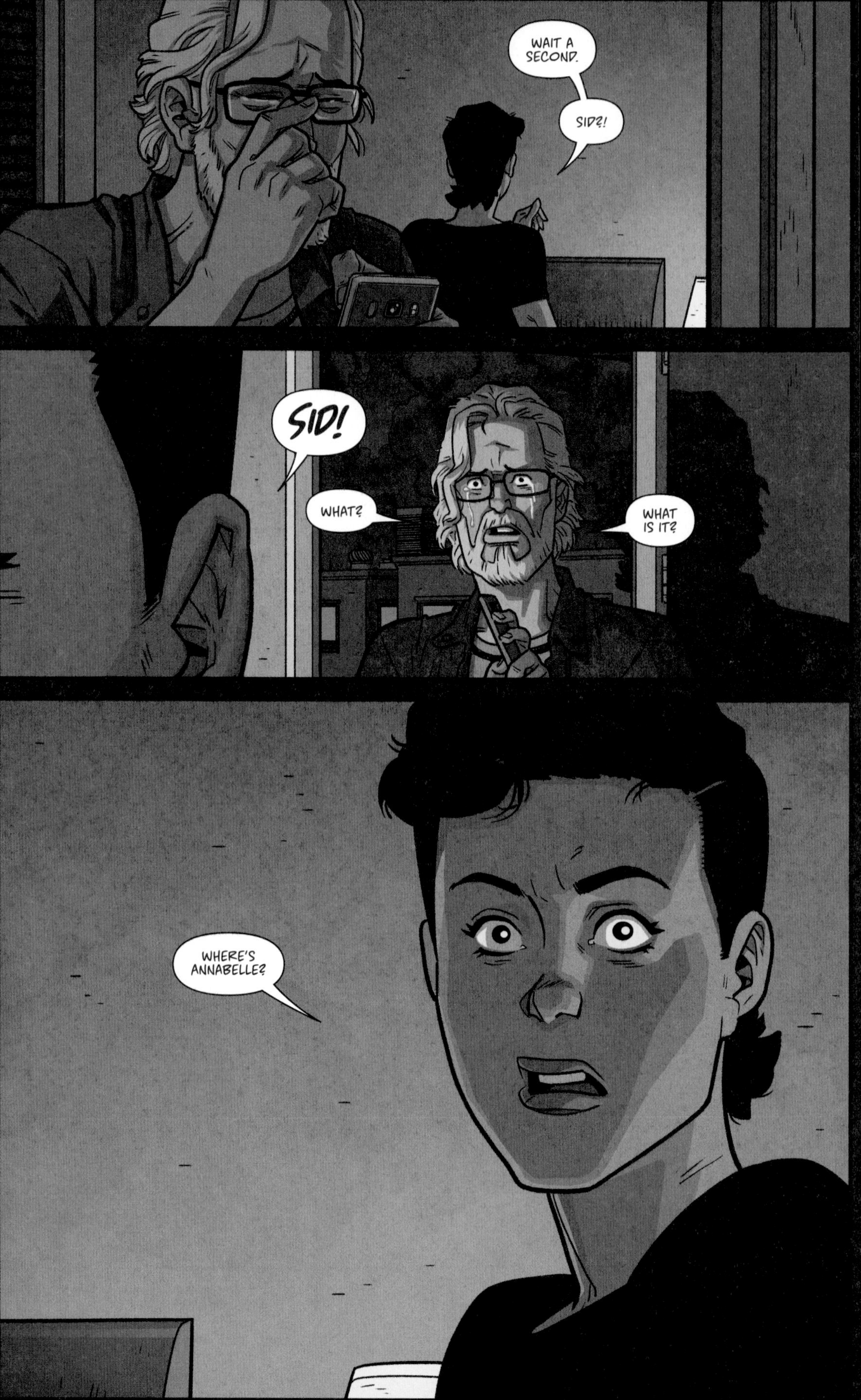
WAIT A SECOND.
SID?!
SID!
WHAT?
WHAT IS IT?
WHERE'S ANNABELLE?

"Ash"

DOUG WAGNER

STORY

CHRIS BRUNNER

ART

RICO RENZI

COLORS

ED DUKESHIRE

LETTERS

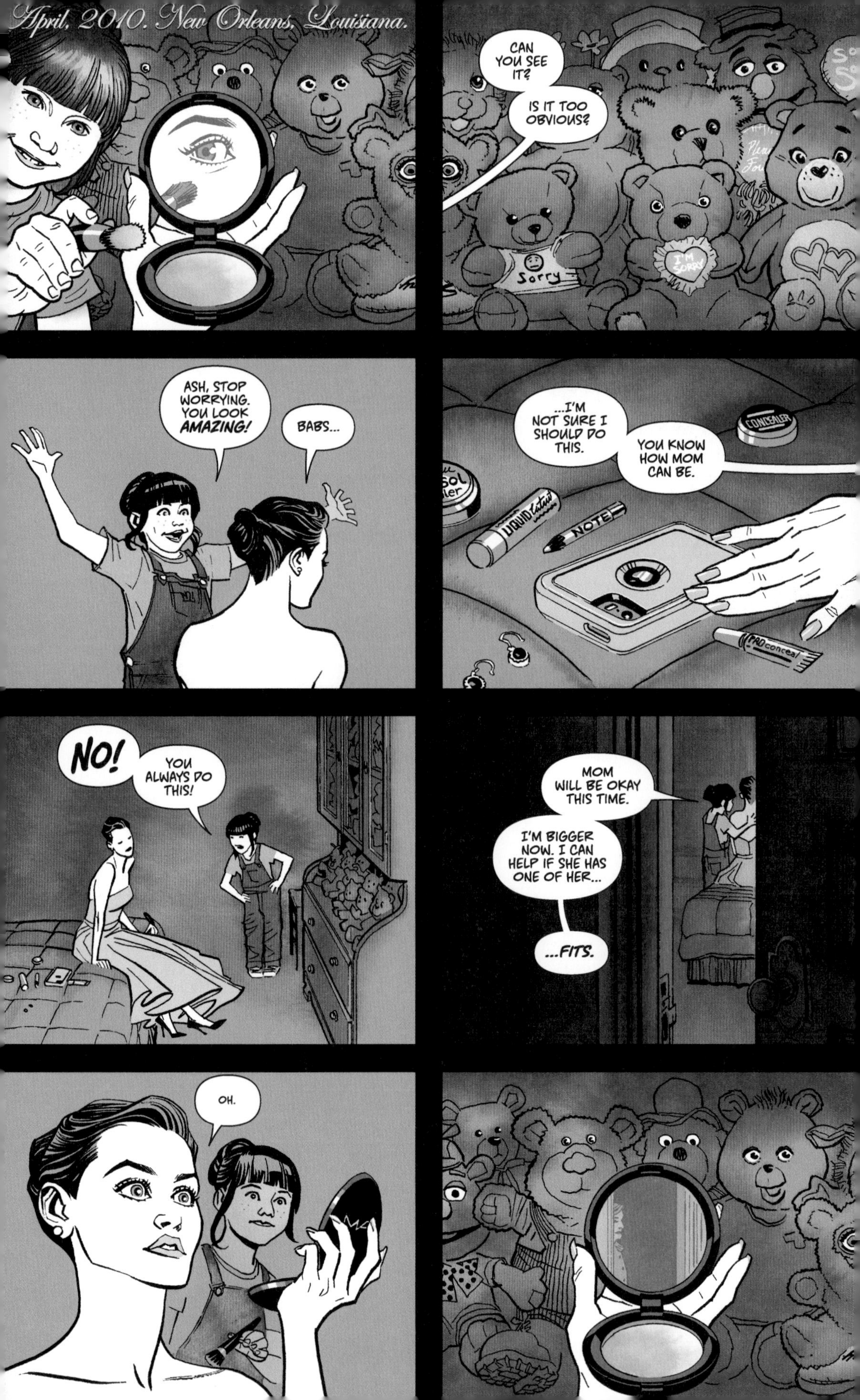
April, 2010. New Orleans, Louisiana.
CAN YOU SEE IT?
IS IT TOO OBVIOUS?
Sorry
I'M SORRY
ASH, STOP WORRYING. YOU LOOK AMAZING!
BABS...
...I'M NOT SURE I SHOULD DO THIS.
YOU KNOW HOW MOM CAN BE.
CONCEALER
LIQUID tatuú
NOTE
PRO conceal
NO!
YOU ALWAYS DO THIS!
MOM WILL BE OKAY THIS TIME.
I'M BIGGER NOW. I CAN HELP IF SHE HAS ONE OF HER...
...FITS.
OH.

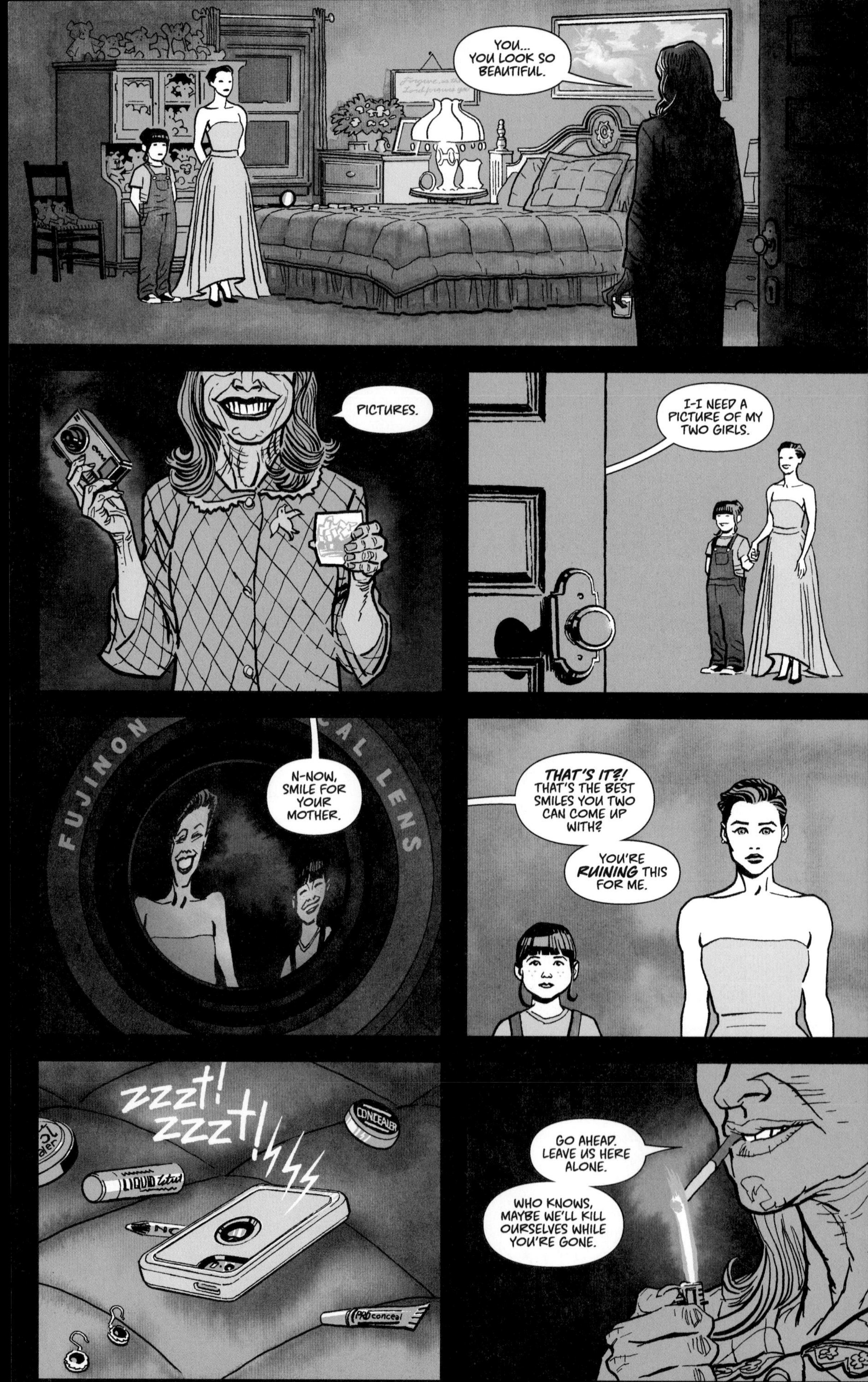
YOU... YOU LOOK SO BEAUTIFUL.
PICTURES.
I-I NEED A PICTURE OF MY TWO GIRLS.
FUJINON
N-NOW, SMILE FOR YOUR MOTHER.
THAT'S IT?! THAT'S THE BEST SMILES YOU TWO CAN COME UP WITH?
YOU'RE RUINING THIS FOR ME.
zzzt! zzzt!
CONCEALER
LIQUID
PRO conceal
GO AHEAD. LEAVE US HERE ALONE.
WHO KNOWS, MAYBE WE'LL KILL OURSELVES WHILE YOU'RE GONE.

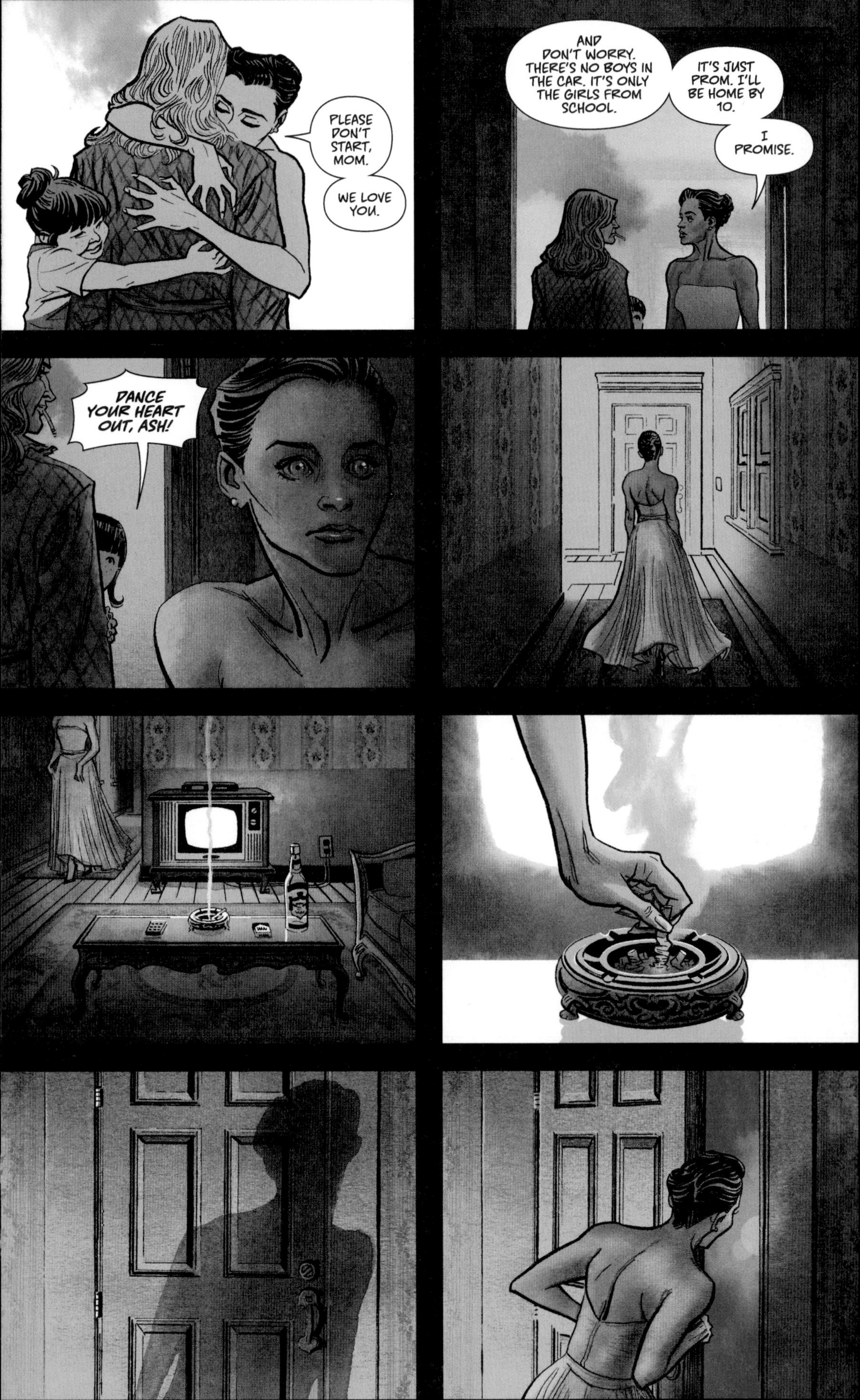
PLEASE DON'T START, MOM.
WE LOVE YOU.
AND DON'T WORRY. THERE'S NO BOYS IN THE CAR. IT'S ONLY THE GIRLS FROM SCHOOL.
IT'S JUST PROM. I'LL BE HOME BY 10.
I PROMISE.
DANCE YOUR HEART OUT, ASH!

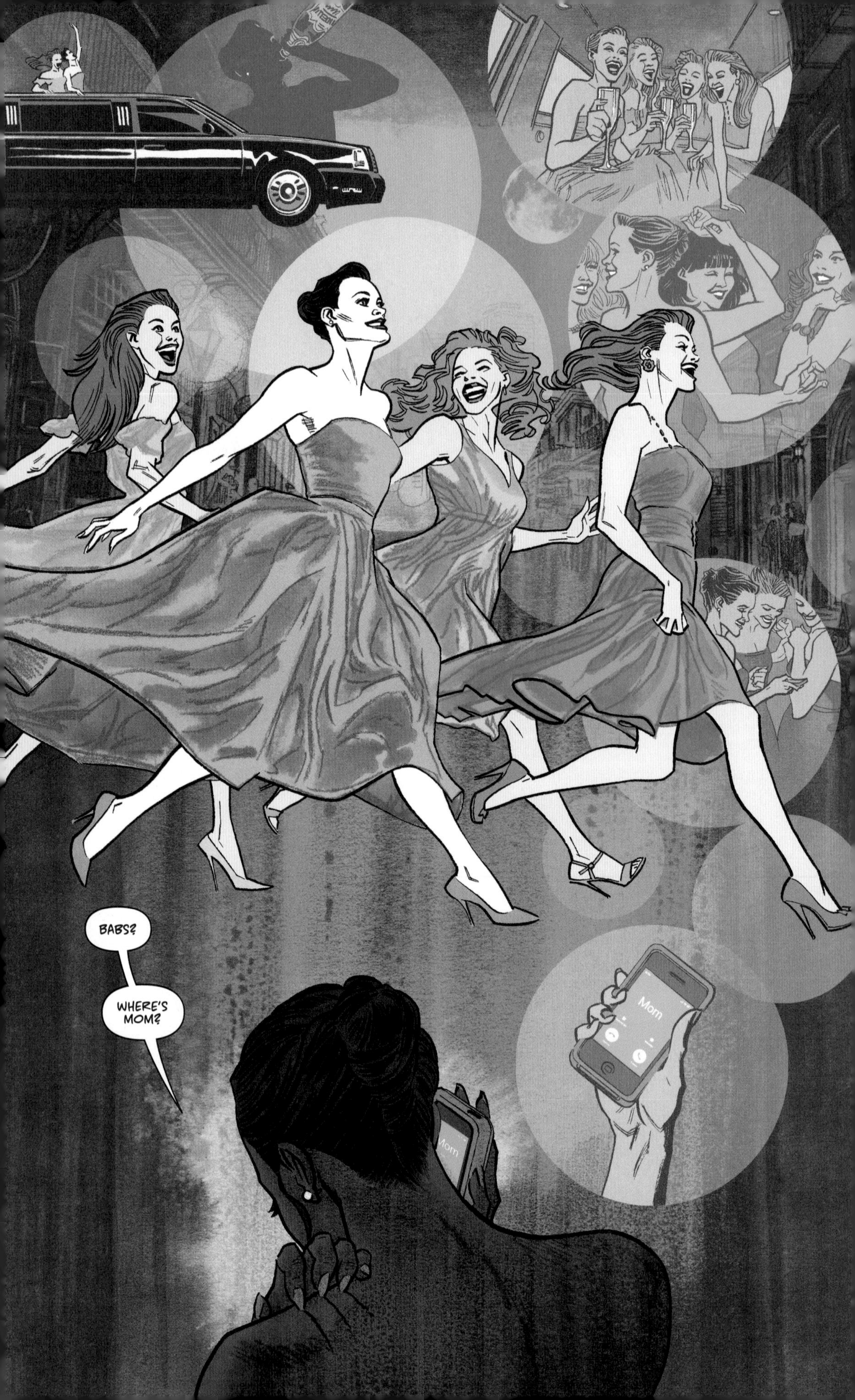
BABS?
WHERE'S MOM?
Mom
Mom

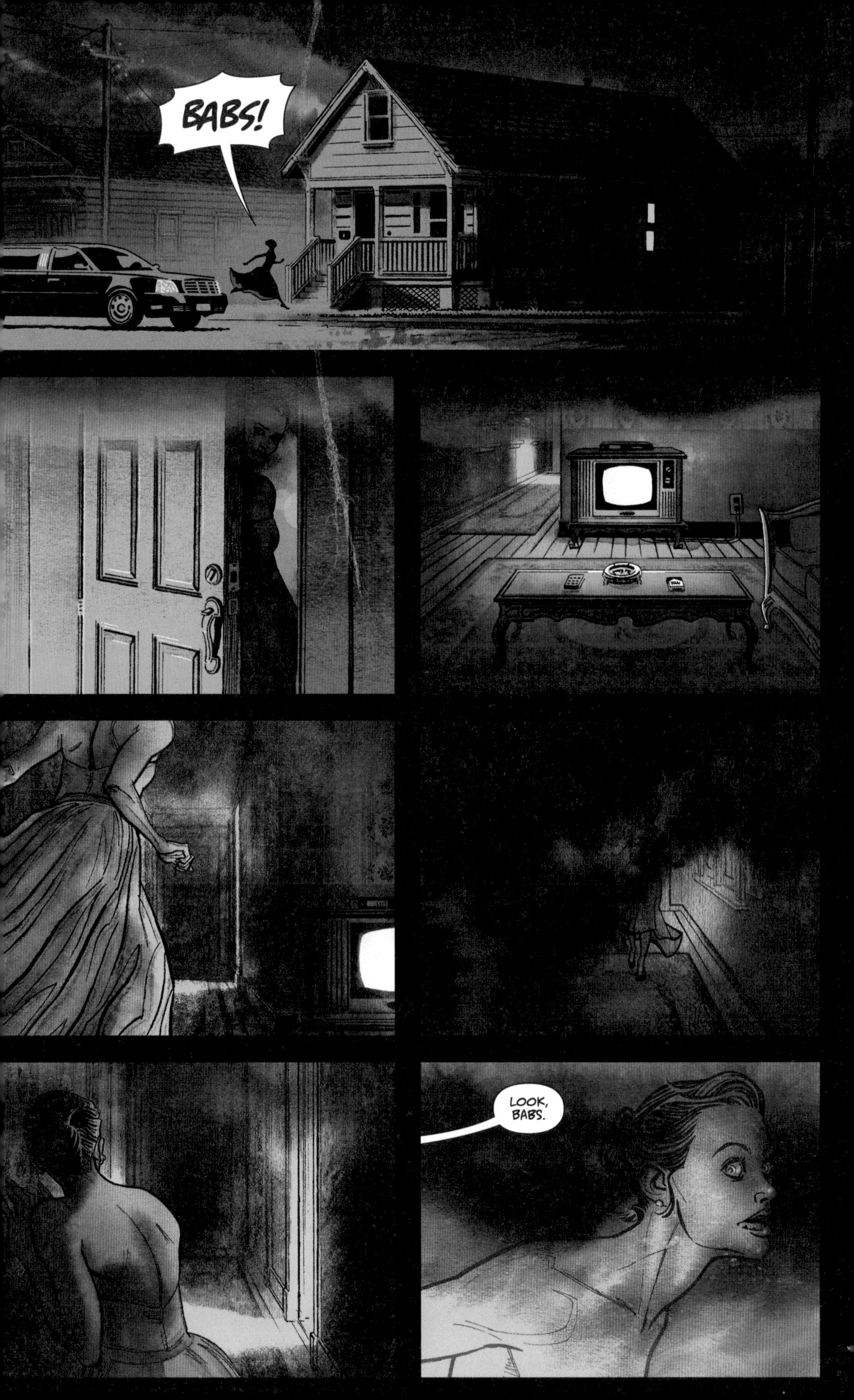
BABS!
LOOK, BABS.

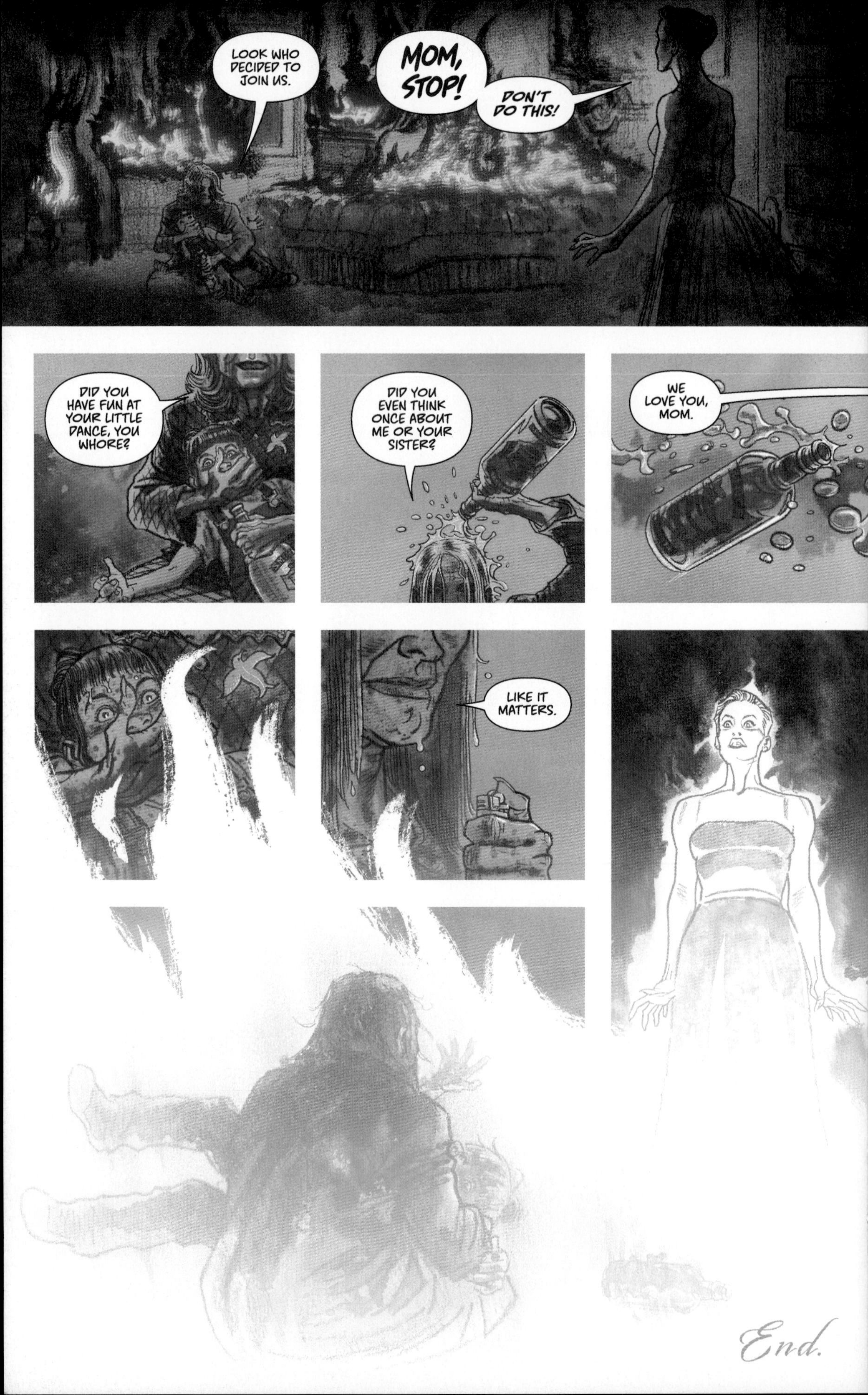
LOOK WHO DECIDED TO JOIN US.
MOM, STOP!
DON'T DO THIS!
DID YOU HAVE FUN AT YOUR LITTLE DANCE, YOU WHORE?
DID YOU EVEN THINK ONCE ABOUT ME OR YOUR SISTER?
WE LOVE YOU, MOM.
LIKE IT MATTERS.
End.

BURNING DESIRE
CHAPTER THREE

DOUG WAGNER
STORY

DANIEL HILLYARD
ART

LAURA MARTIN
CHARLIE KIRCHOFF
COLORS

ED DUKESHIRE
LETTERS

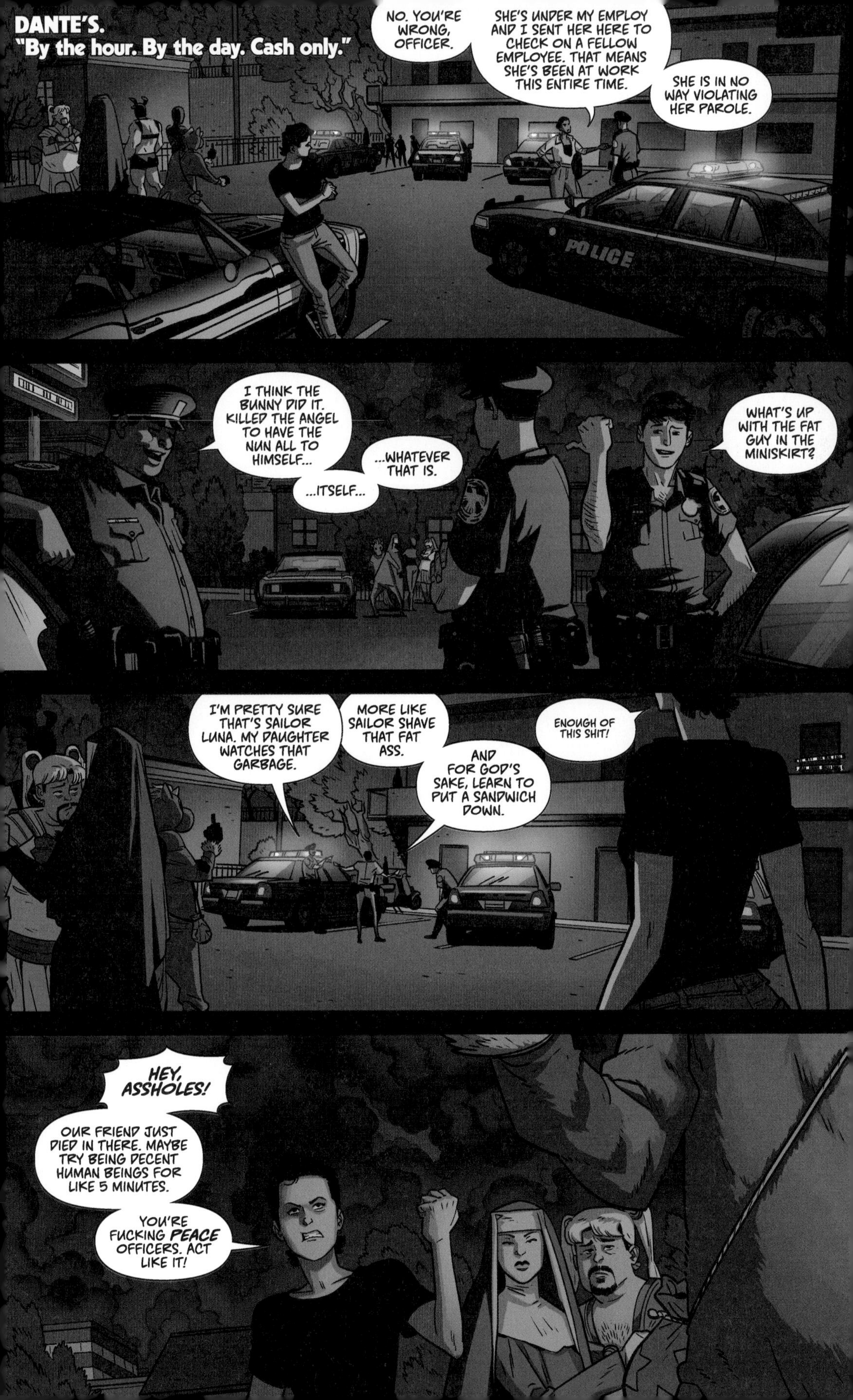
DANTE'S.
"By the hour. By the day. Cash only."
NO. YOU'RE WRONG, OFFICER.
SHE'S UNDER MY EMPLOY AND I SENT HER HERE TO CHECK ON A FELLOW EMPLOYEE. THAT MEANS SHE'S BEEN AT WORK THIS ENTIRE TIME.
SHE IS IN NO WAY VIOLATING HER PAROLE.
POLICE
I THINK THE BUNNY DID IT. KILLED THE ANGEL TO HAVE THE NUN ALL TO HIMSELF...
...ITSELF...
...WHATEVER THAT IS.
WHAT'S UP WITH THE FAT GUY IN THE MINISKIRT?
I'M PRETTY SURE THAT'S SAILOR LUNA. MY DAUGHTER WATCHES THAT GARBAGE.
MORE LIKE SAILOR SHAVE THAT FAT ASS.
AND FOR GOD'S SAKE, LEARN TO PUT A SANDWICH DOWN.
ENOUGH OF THIS SHIT!
HEY, ASSHOLES!
OUR FRIEND JUST DIED IN THERE. MAYBE TRY BEING DECENT HUMAN BEINGS FOR LIKE 5 MINUTES.
YOU'RE FUCKING *PEACE* OFFICERS. ACT LIKE IT!

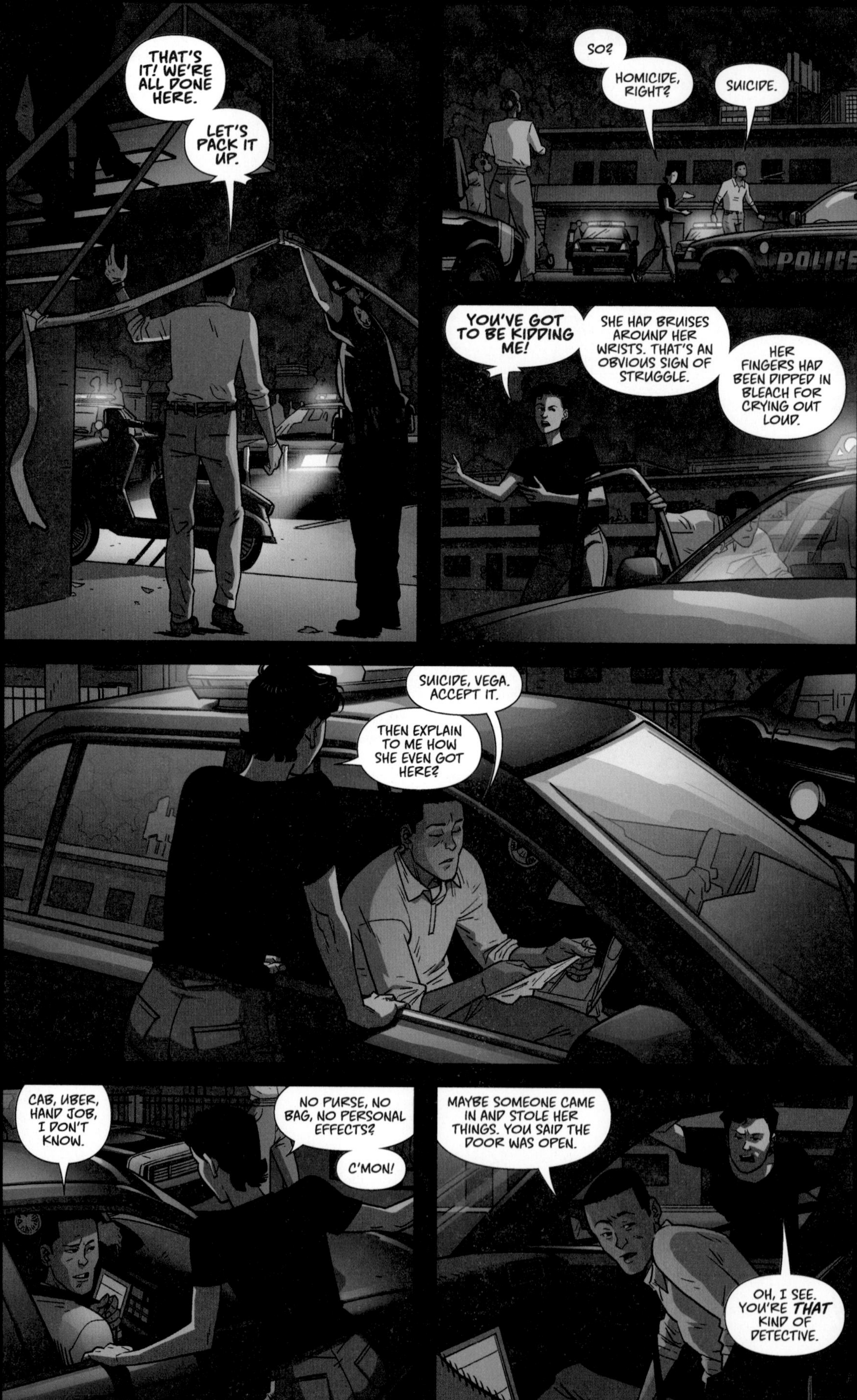
THAT'S IT! WE'RE ALL DONE HERE.
LET'S PACK IT UP.
SO?
HOMICIDE, RIGHT?
SUICIDE.
POLICE
YOU'VE GOT TO BE KIDDING ME!
SHE HAD BRUISES AROUND HER WRISTS. THAT'S AN OBVIOUS SIGN OF STRUGGLE.
HER FINGERS HAD BEEN DIPPED IN BLEACH FOR CRYING OUT LOUD.
SUICIDE, VEGA. ACCEPT IT.
THEN EXPLAIN TO ME HOW SHE EVEN GOT HERE?
CAB, UBER, HAND JOB, I DON'T KNOW.
NO PURSE, NO BAG, NO PERSONAL EFFECTS?
C'MON!
MAYBE SOMEONE CAME IN AND STOLE HER THINGS. YOU SAID THE DOOR WAS OPEN.
OH, I SEE. YOU'RE *THAT* KIND OF DETECTIVE.

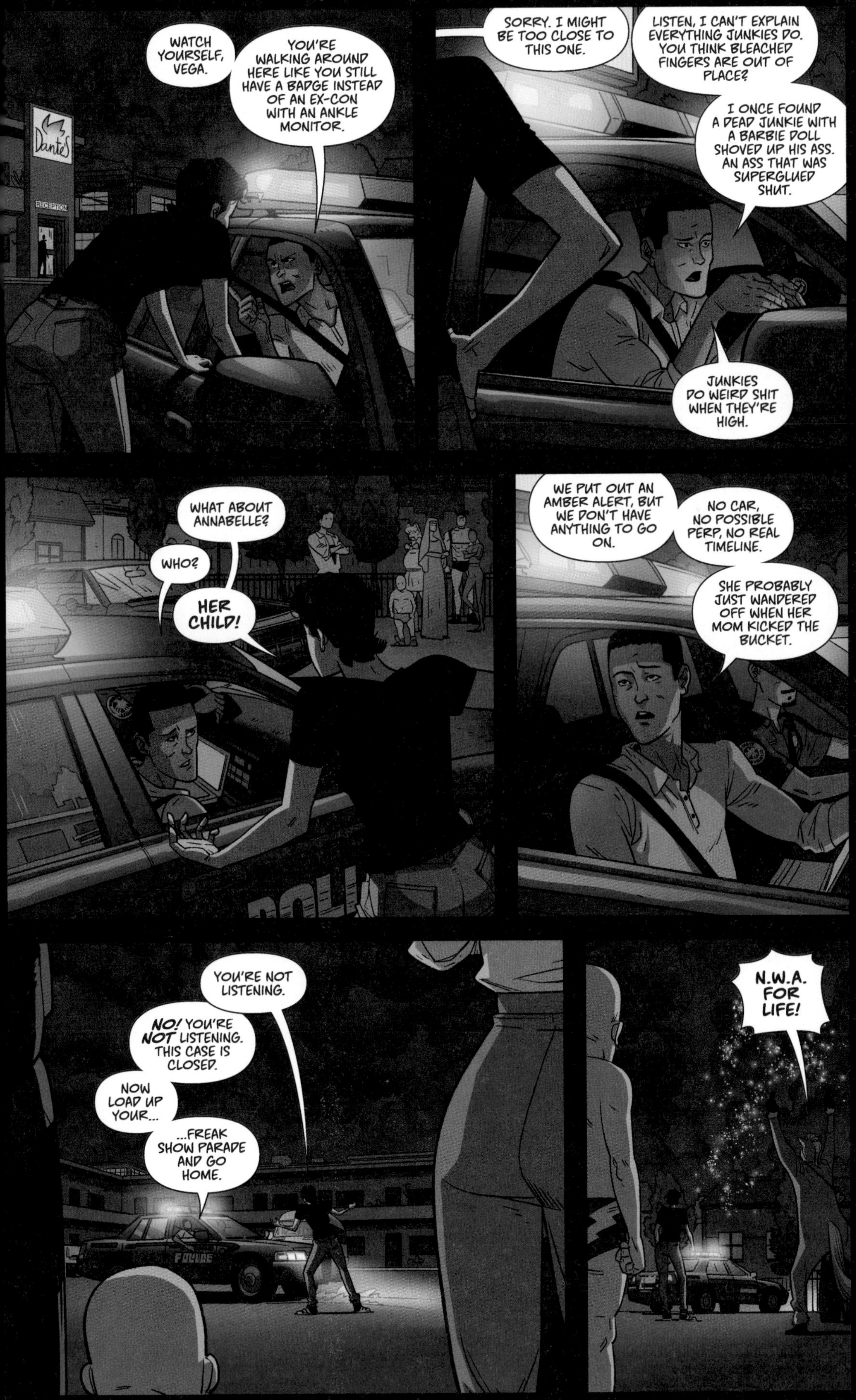
WATCH YOURSELF, VEGA.
YOU'RE WALKING AROUND HERE LIKE YOU STILL HAVE A BADGE INSTEAD OF AN EX-CON WITH AN ANKLE MONITOR.
SORRY. I MIGHT BE TOO CLOSE TO THIS ONE.
LISTEN, I CAN'T EXPLAIN EVERYTHING JUNKIES DO. YOU THINK BLEACHED FINGERS ARE OUT OF PLACE?
I ONCE FOUND A DEAD JUNKIE WITH A BARBIE DOLL SHOVED UP HIS ASS. AN ASS THAT WAS SUPERGLUED SHUT.
JUNKIES DO WEIRD SHIT WHEN THEY'RE HIGH.
WHAT ABOUT ANNABELLE?
WHO?
HER CHILD!
WE PUT OUT AN AMBER ALERT, BUT WE DON'T HAVE ANYTHING TO GO ON.
NO CAR, NO POSSIBLE PERP, NO REAL TIMELINE.
SHE PROBABLY JUST WANDERED OFF WHEN HER MOM KICKED THE BUCKET.
YOU'RE NOT LISTENING.
NO! YOU'RE NOT LISTENING. THIS CASE IS CLOSED.
NOW LOAD UP YOUR...
...FREAK SHOW PARADE AND GO HOME.
N.W.A. FOR LIFE!

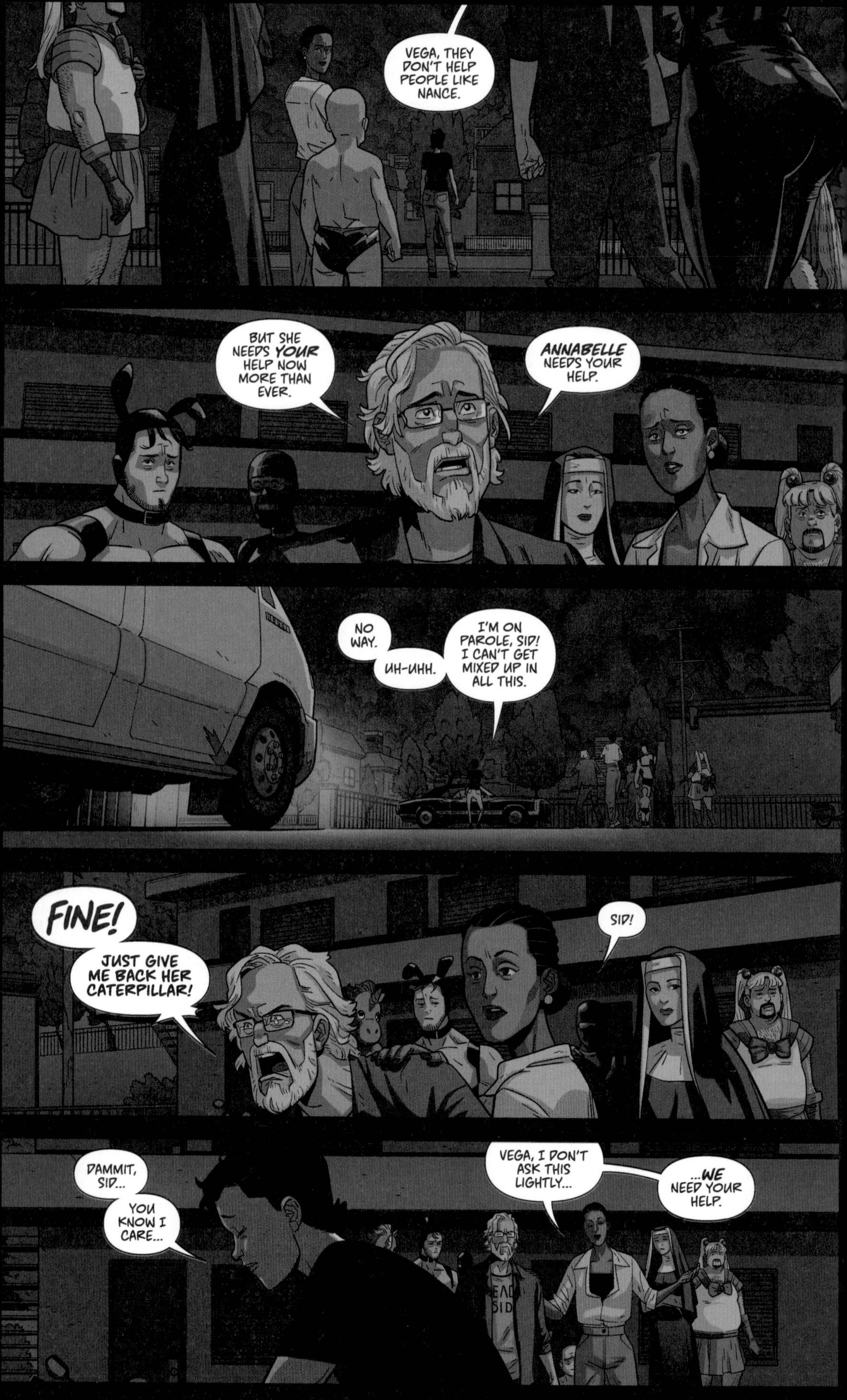
VEGA, THEY DON'T HELP PEOPLE LIKE NANCE.
BUT SHE NEEDS YOUR HELP NOW MORE THAN EVER.
ANNABELLE NEEDS YOUR HELP.
NO WAY.
UH-UHH.
I'M ON PAROLE, SID! I CAN'T GET MIXED UP IN ALL THIS.
FINE!
JUST GIVE ME BACK HER CATERPILLAR!
SID!
DAMMIT, SID...
YOU KNOW I CARE...
VEGA, I DON'T ASK THIS LIGHTLY...
...WE NEED YOUR HELP.

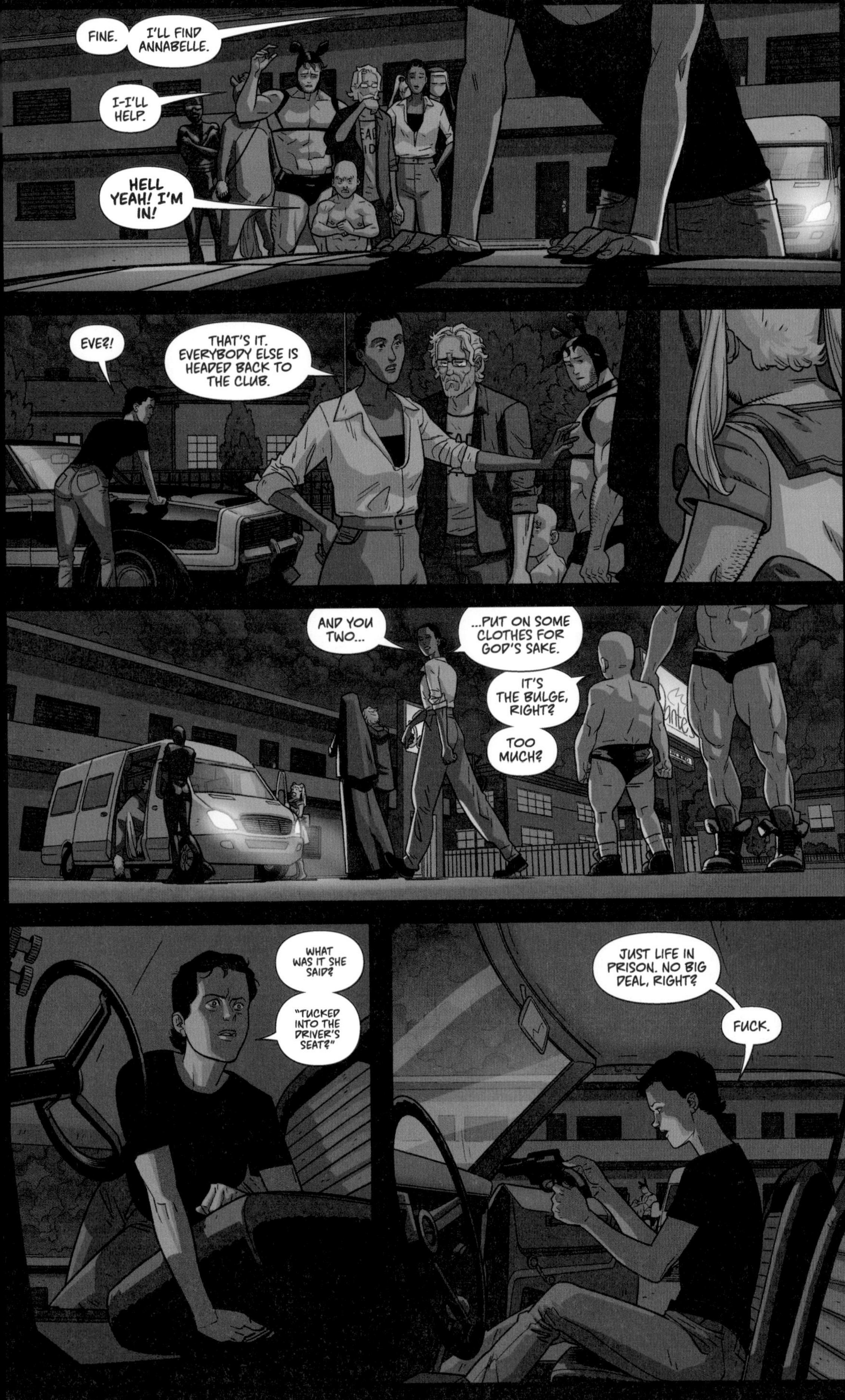
FINE.
I'LL FIND ANNABELLE.
I-I'LL HELP.
HELL YEAH! I'M IN!
EVE?!
THAT'S IT. EVERYBODY ELSE IS HEADED BACK TO THE CLUB.
AND YOU TWO...
...PUT ON SOME CLOTHES FOR GOD'S SAKE.
IT'S THE BULGE, RIGHT?
TOO MUCH?
WHAT WAS IT SHE SAID?
"TUCKED INTO THE DRIVER'S SEAT?"
JUST LIFE IN PRISON. NO BIG DEAL, RIGHT?
FUCK.

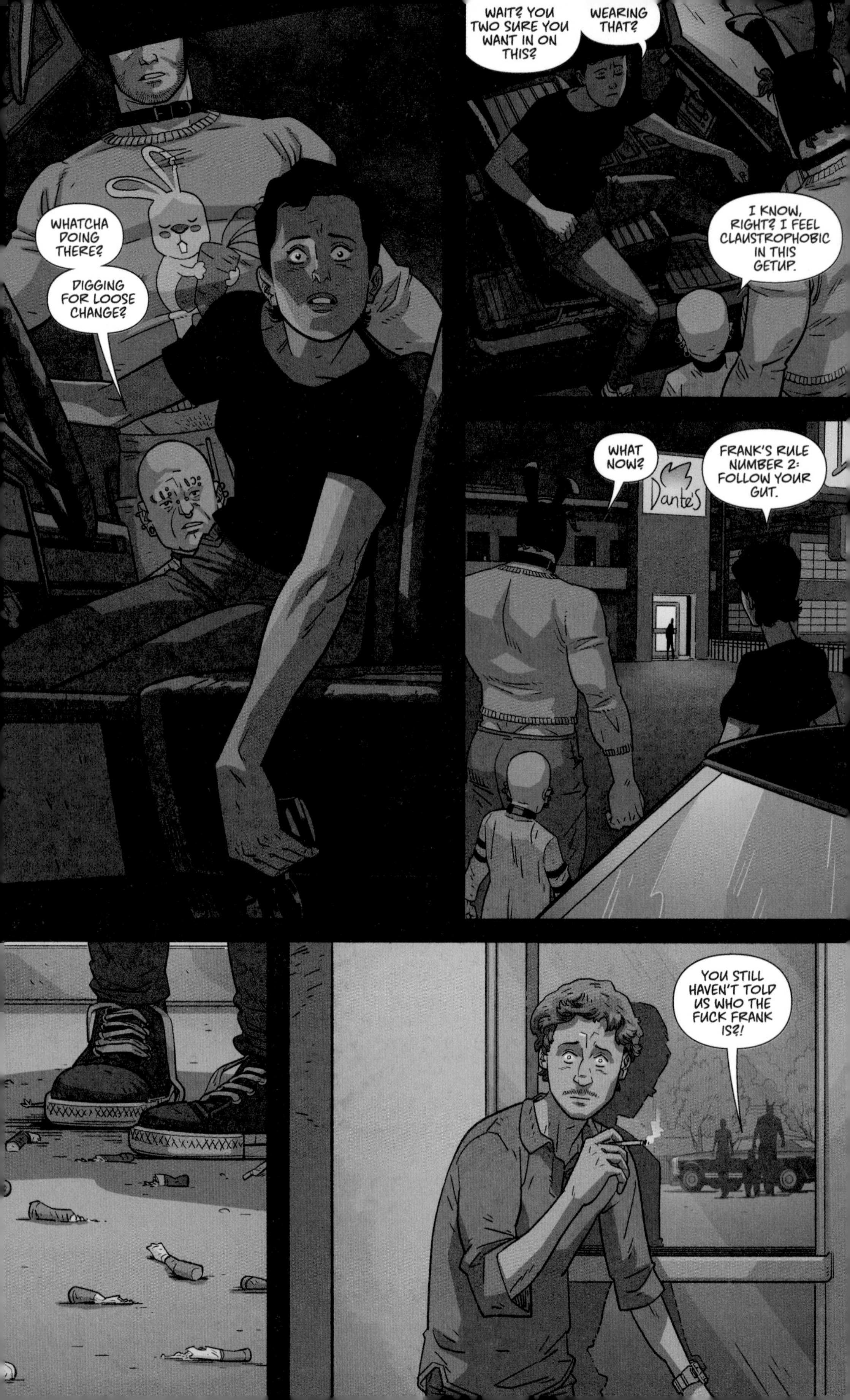
WHATCHA DOING THERE?
DIGGING FOR LOOSE CHANGE?
WAIT? YOU TWO SURE YOU WANT IN ON THIS?
WEARING THAT?
I KNOW, RIGHT? I FEEL CLAUSTROPHOBIC IN THIS GETUP.
Dante's
WHAT NOW?
FRANK'S RULE NUMBER 2: FOLLOW YOUR GUT.
YOU STILL HAVEN'T TOLD US WHO THE FUCK FRANK IS?!

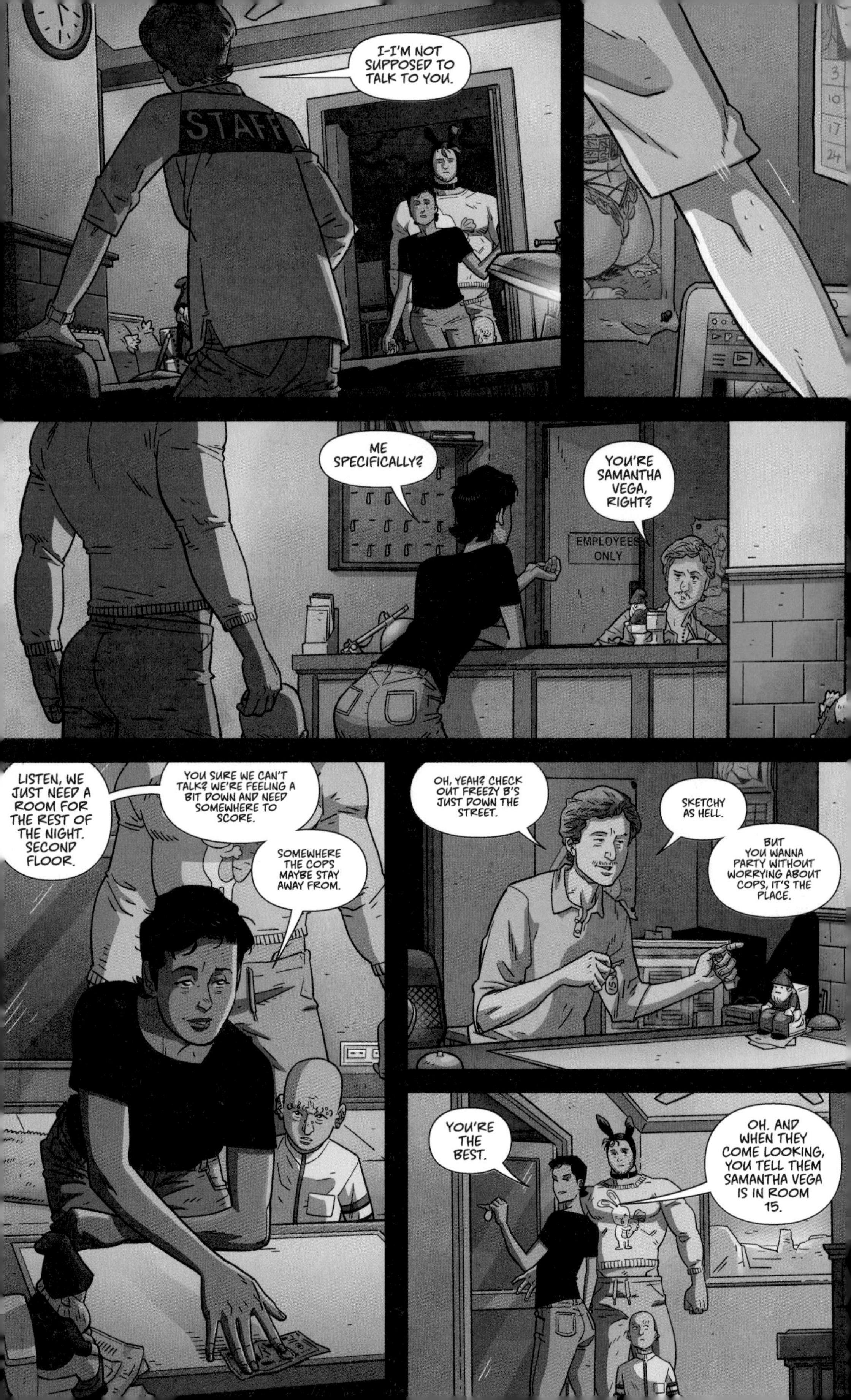
I-I'M NOT SUPPOSED TO TALK TO YOU.
3
10
17
24
ME SPECIFICALLY?
YOU'RE SAMANTHA VEGA, RIGHT?
EMPLOYEES ONLY
LISTEN, WE JUST NEED A ROOM FOR THE REST OF THE NIGHT. SECOND FLOOR.
YOU SURE WE CAN'T TALK? WE'RE FEELING A BIT DOWN AND NEED SOMEWHERE TO SCORE.
SOMEWHERE THE COPS MAYBE STAY AWAY FROM.
OH, YEAH? CHECK OUT FREEZY B'S JUST DOWN THE STREET.
SKETCHY AS HELL.
BUT YOU WANNA PARTY WITHOUT WORRYING ABOUT COPS, IT'S THE PLACE.
YOU'RE THE BEST.
OH. AND WHEN THEY COME LOOKING, YOU TELL THEM SAMANTHA VEGA IS IN ROOM 15.

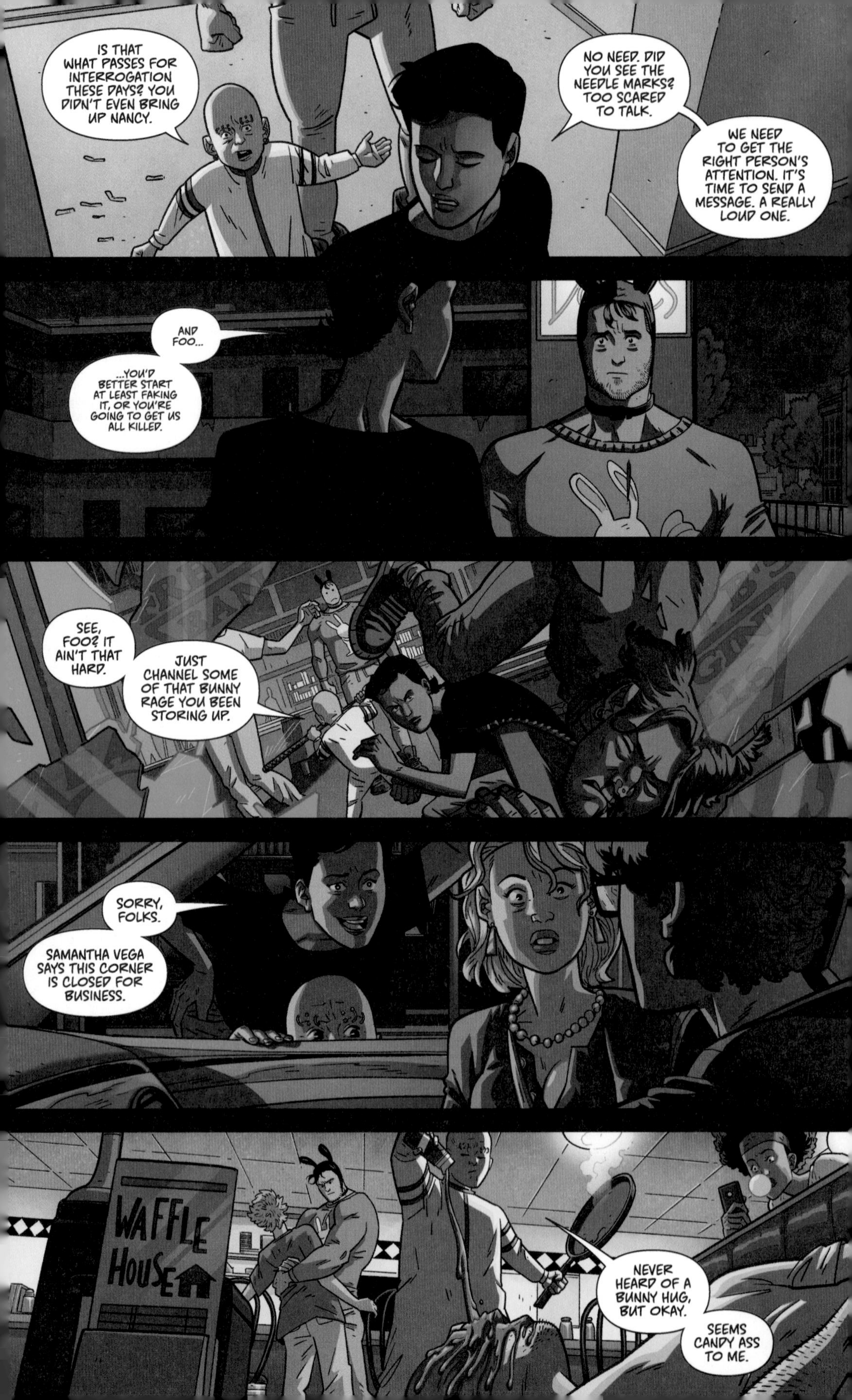

IS THAT WHAT PASSES FOR INTERROGATION THESE DAYS? YOU DIDN'T EVEN BRING UP NANCY.
NO NEED. DID YOU SEE THE NEEDLE MARKS? TOO SCARED TO TALK.
WE NEED TO GET THE RIGHT PERSON'S ATTENTION. IT'S TIME TO SEND A MESSAGE. A REALLY LOUD ONE.
AND FOO...
...YOU'D BETTER START AT LEAST FAKING IT, OR YOU'RE GOING TO GET US ALL KILLED.
SEE, FOO? IT AIN'T THAT HARD.
JUST CHANNEL SOME OF THAT BUNNY RAGE YOU BEEN STORING UP.
SORRY, FOLKS.
SAMANTHA VEGA SAYS THIS CORNER IS CLOSED FOR BUSINESS.
WAFFLE HOUSE
NEVER HEARD OF A BUNNY HUG, BUT OKAY.
SEEMS CANDY ASS TO ME.

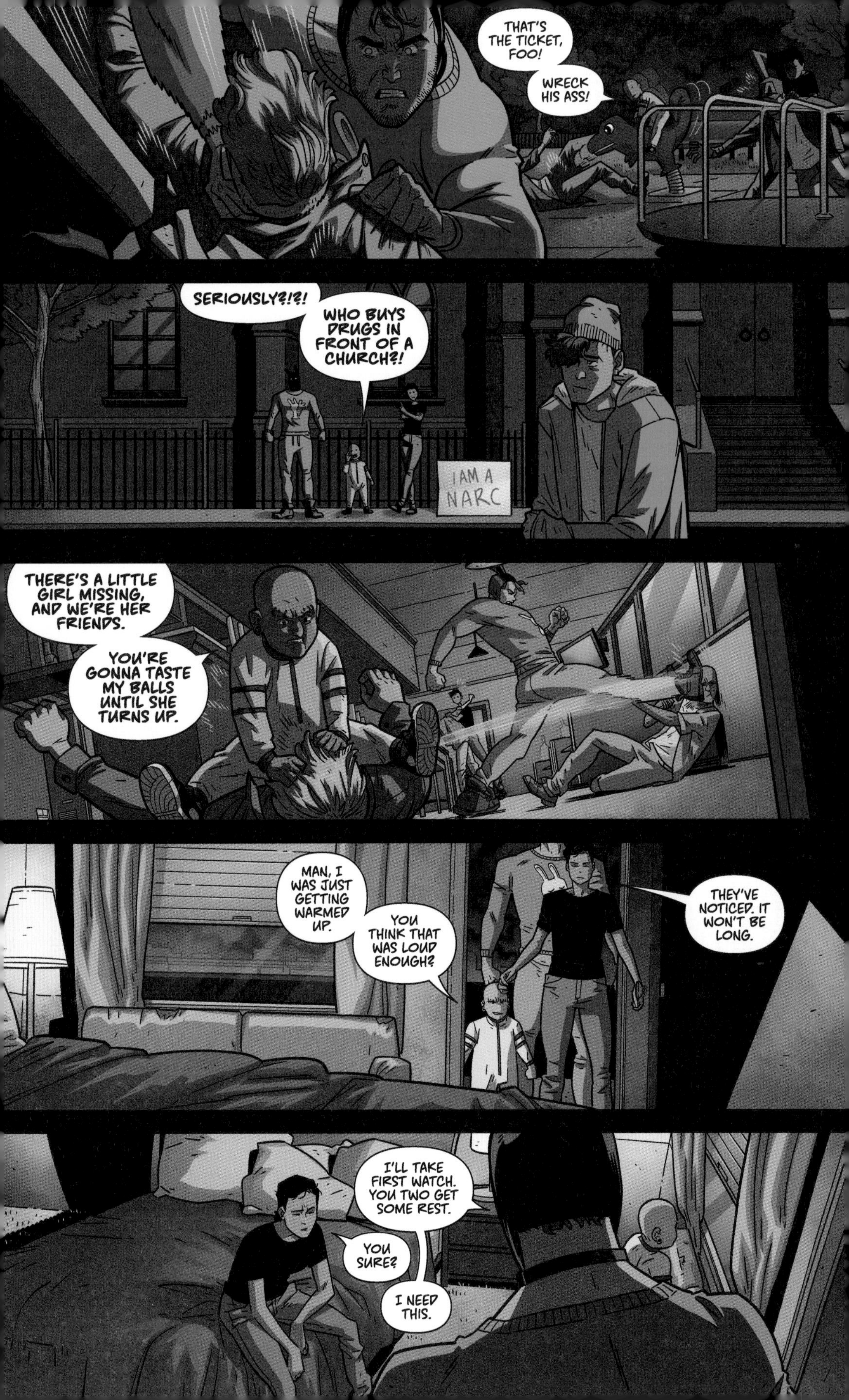
THAT'S THE TICKET, FOO!
WRECK HIS ASS!
SERIOUSLY?!?!
WHO BUYS DRUGS IN FRONT OF A CHURCH?!
I AM A NARC
THERE'S A LITTLE GIRL MISSING, AND WE'RE HER FRIENDS.
YOU'RE GONNA TASTE MY BALLS UNTIL SHE TURNS UP.
MAN, I WAS JUST GETTING WARMED UP.
YOU THINK THAT WAS LOUD ENOUGH?
THEY'VE NOTICED. IT WON'T BE LONG.
I'LL TAKE FIRST WATCH. YOU TWO GET SOME REST.
YOU SURE?
I NEED THIS.

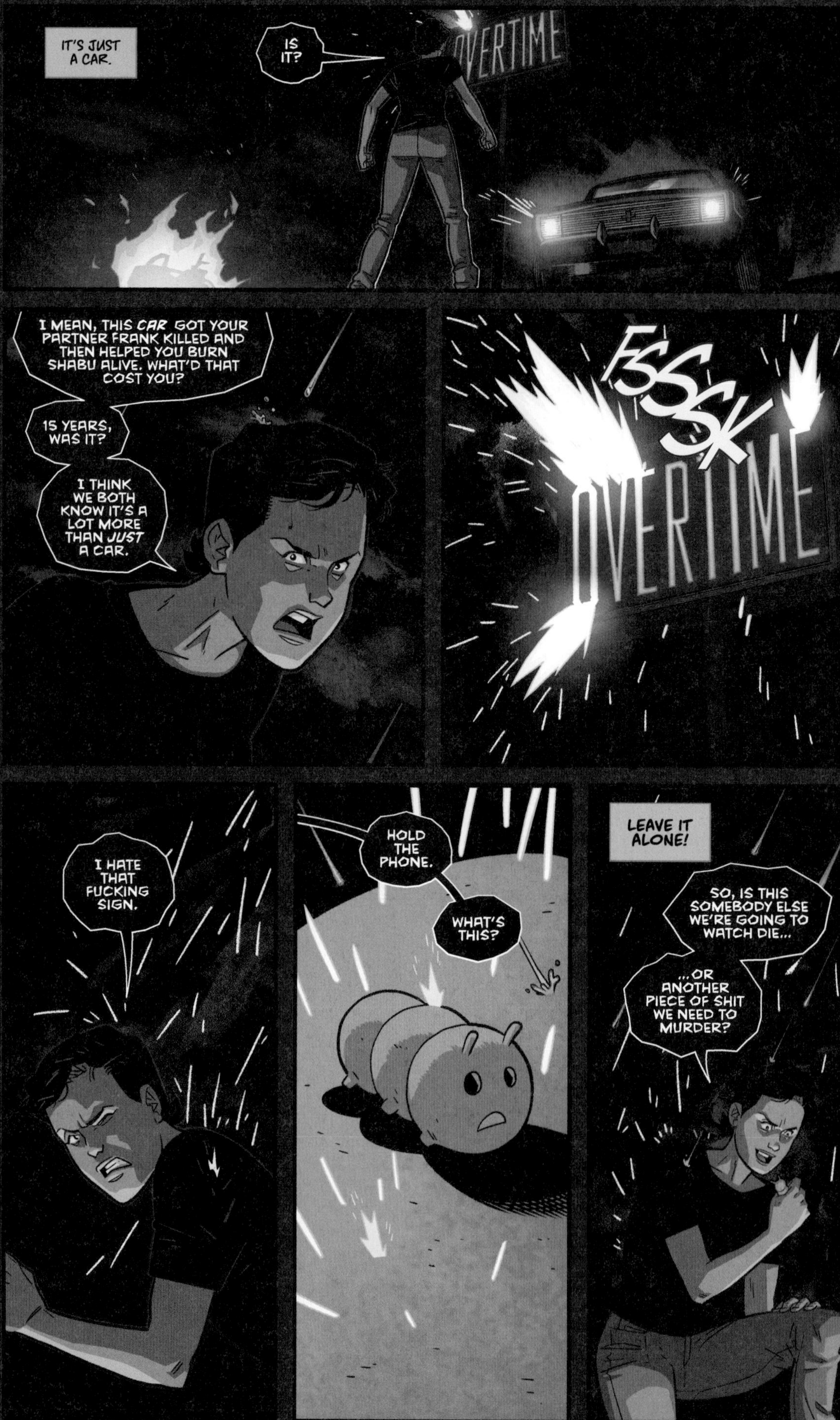
IT'S JUST A CAR.
IS IT?
OVERTIME
I MEAN, THIS CAR GOT YOUR PARTNER FRANK KILLED AND THEN HELPED YOU BURN SHABU ALIVE. WHAT'D THAT COST YOU?
15 YEARS, WAS IT?
I THINK WE BOTH KNOW IT'S A LOT MORE THAN JUST A CAR.
FSSSK
OVERTIME
I HATE THAT FUCKING SIGN.
HOLD THE PHONE.
WHAT'S THIS?
LEAVE IT ALONE!
SO, IS THIS SOMEBODY ELSE WE'RE GOING TO WATCH DIE...
...OR ANOTHER PIECE OF SHIT WE NEED TO MURDER?

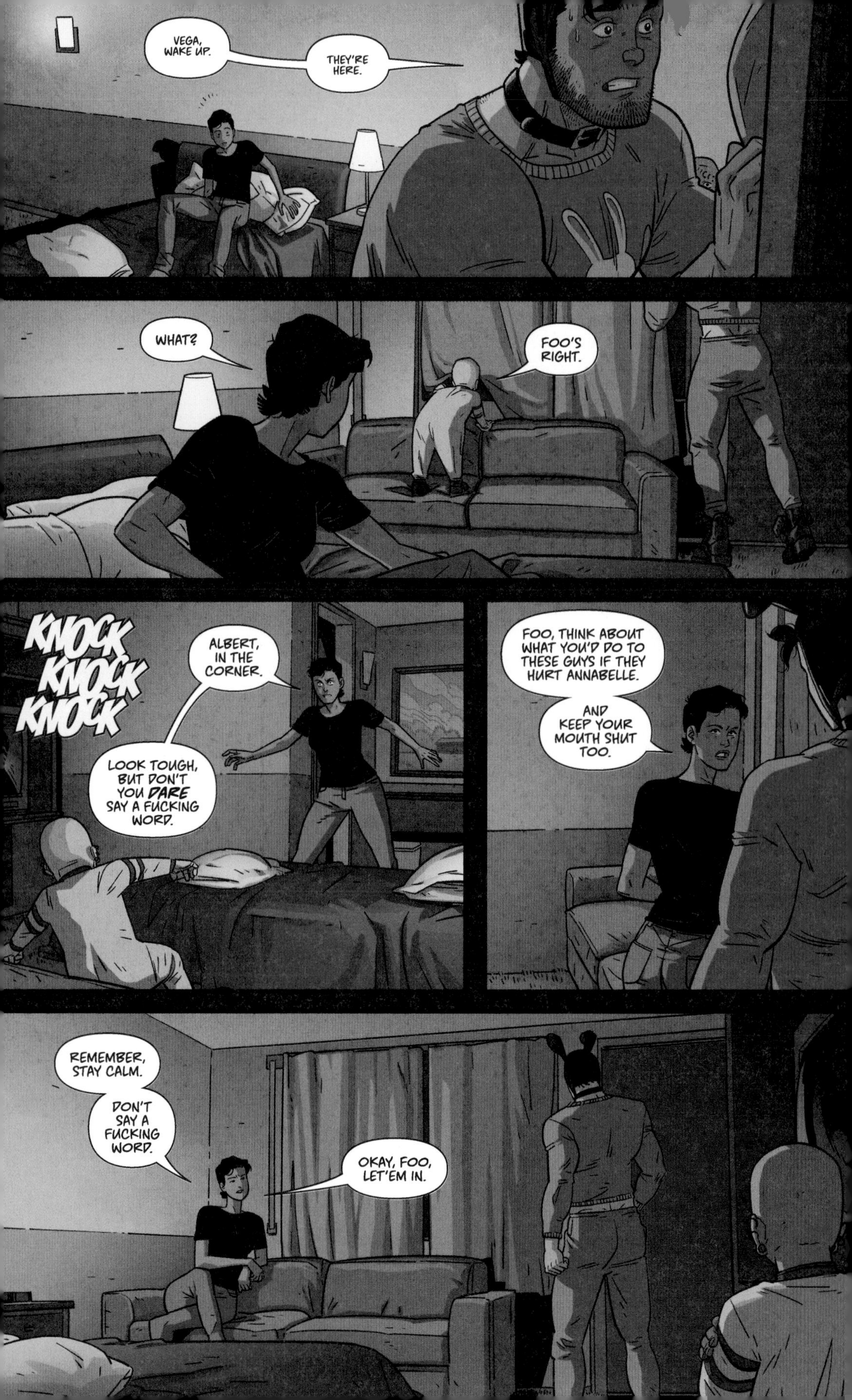
VEGA, WAKE UP.
THEY'RE HERE.
WHAT?
FOO'S RIGHT.
KNOCK KNOCK KNOCK
ALBERT, IN THE CORNER.
LOOK TOUGH, BUT DON'T YOU DARE SAY A FUCKING WORD.
FOO, THINK ABOUT WHAT YOU'D DO TO THESE GUYS IF THEY HURT ANNABELLE.
AND KEEP YOUR MOUTH SHUT TOO.
REMEMBER, STAY CALM.
DON'T SAY A FUCKING WORD.
OKAY, FOO, LET'EM IN.

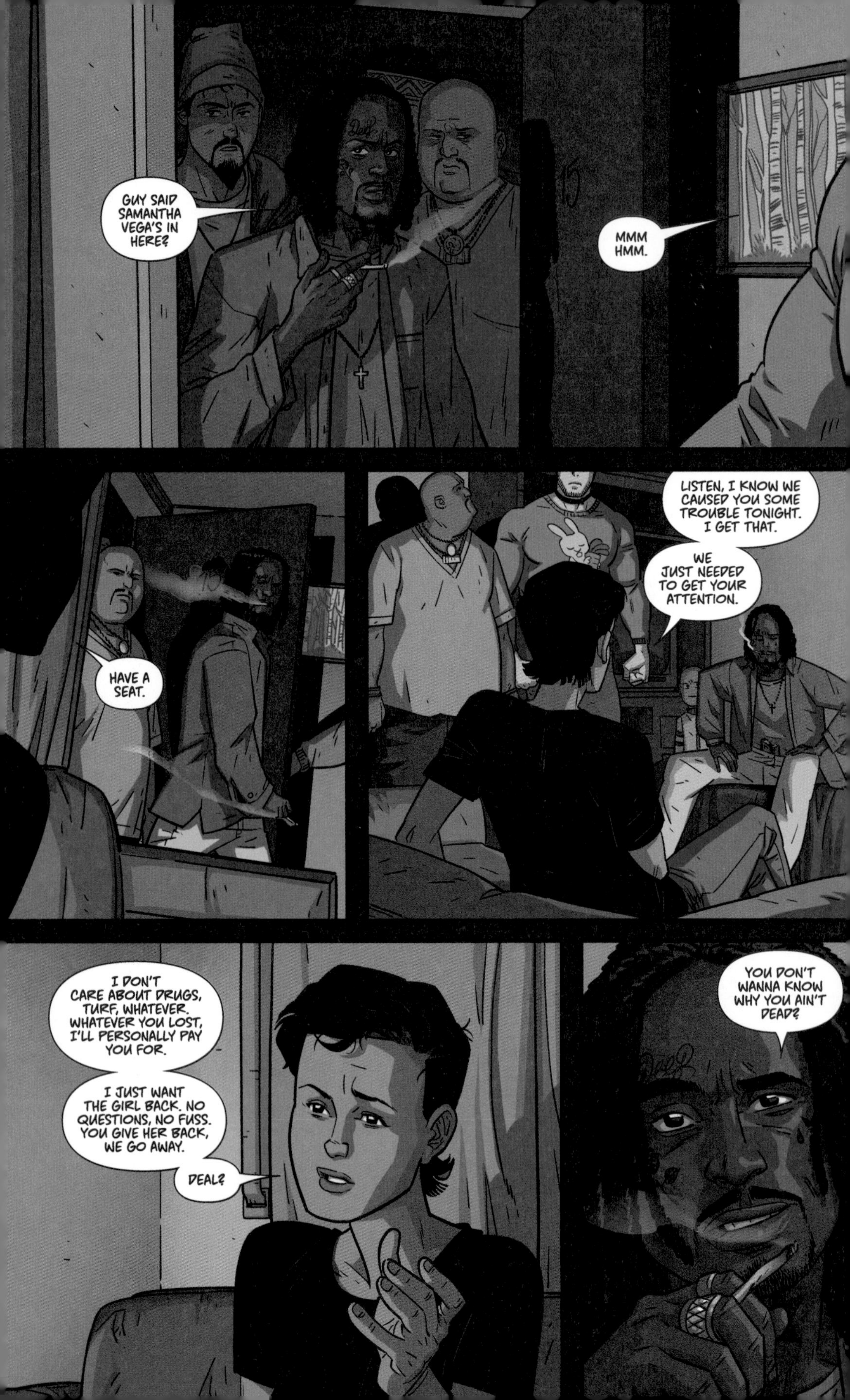
GUY SAID SAMANTHA VEGA'S IN HERE?
MMM HMM.
HAVE A SEAT.
LISTEN, I KNOW WE CAUSED YOU SOME TROUBLE TONIGHT. I GET THAT.
WE JUST NEEDED TO GET YOUR ATTENTION.
I DON'T CARE ABOUT DRUGS, TURF, WHATEVER. WHATEVER YOU LOST, I'LL PERSONALLY PAY YOU FOR.
I JUST WANT THE GIRL BACK. NO QUESTIONS, NO FUSS. YOU GIVE HER BACK, WE GO AWAY.
DEAL?
YOU DON'T WANNA KNOW WHY YOU AIN'T DEAD?

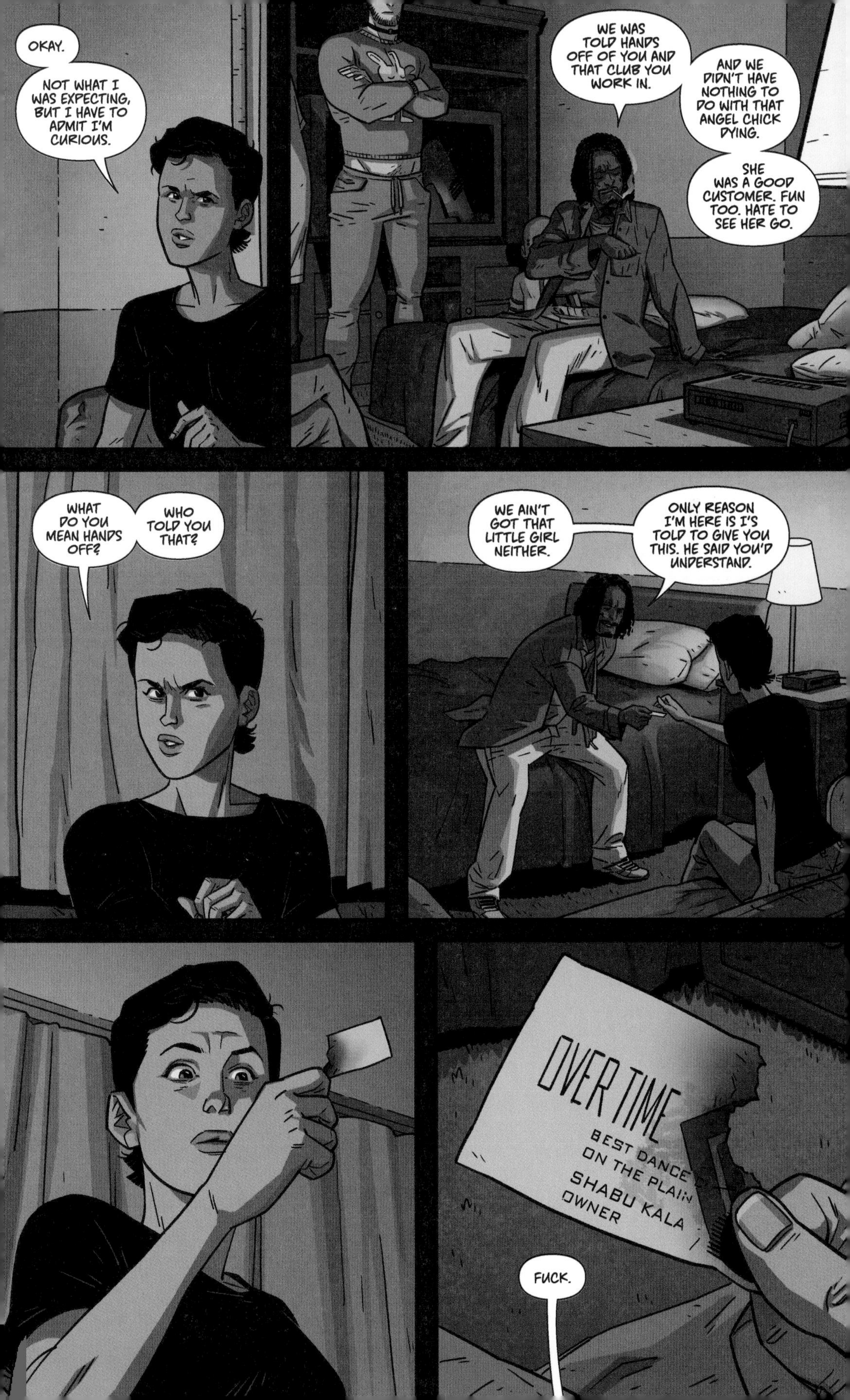

OKAY.
NOT WHAT I WAS EXPECTING, BUT I HAVE TO ADMIT I'M CURIOUS.
WE WAS TOLD HANDS OFF OF YOU AND THAT CLUB YOU WORK IN.
AND WE DIDN'T HAVE NOTHING TO DO WITH THAT ANGEL CHICK DYING.
SHE WAS A GOOD CUSTOMER. FUN TOO. HATE TO SEE HER GO.
WHAT DO YOU MEAN HANDS OFF?
WHO TOLD YOU THAT?
WE AIN'T GOT THAT LITTLE GIRL NEITHER.
ONLY REASON I'M HERE IS I'S TOLD TO GIVE YOU THIS. HE SAID YOU'D UNDERSTAND.
OVER TIME
BEST DANCE
ON THE PLAIN
SHABU KALA
OWNER
FUCK.

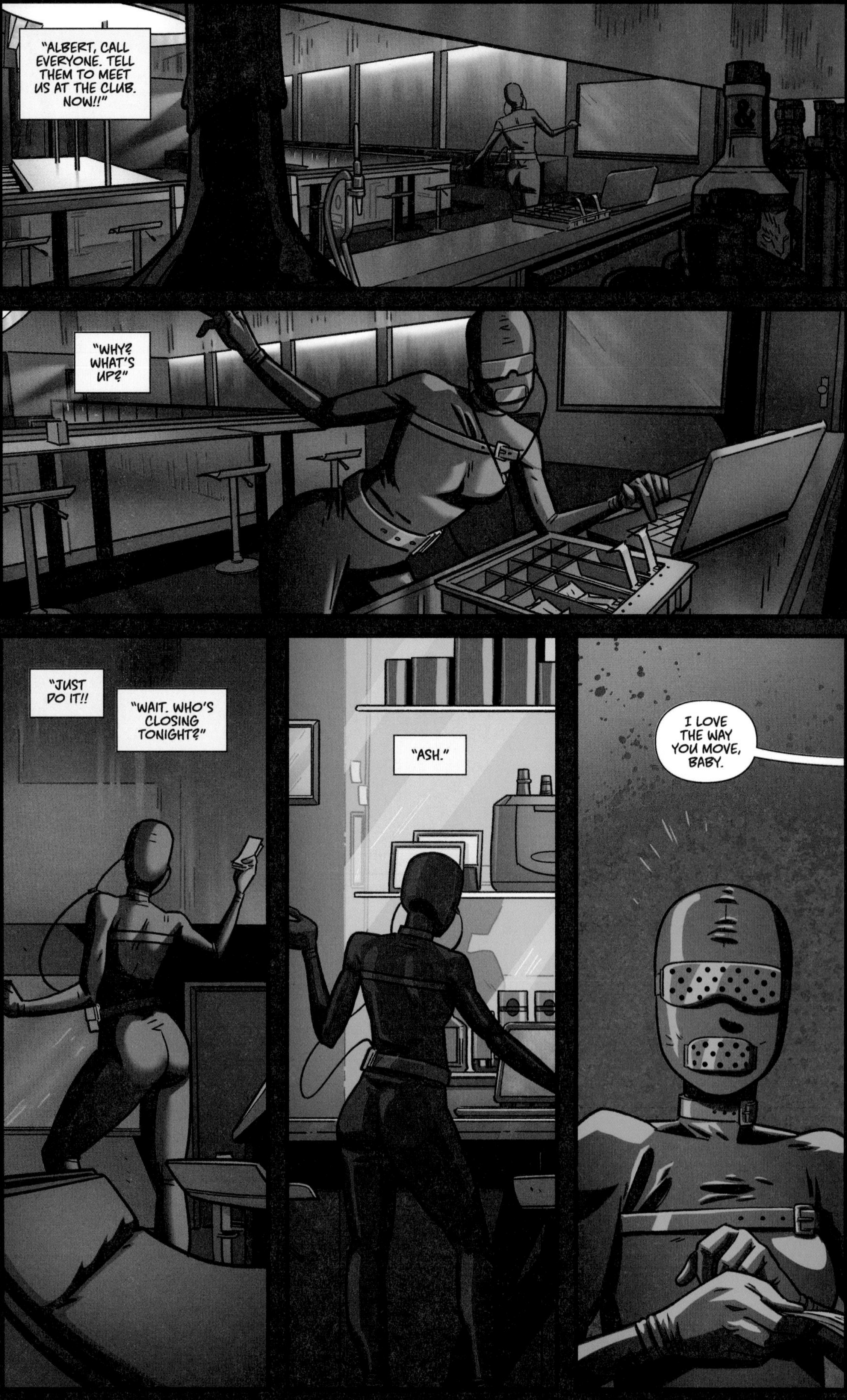
"ALBERT, CALL EVERYONE. TELL THEM TO MEET US AT THE CLUB. NOW!!"
"WHY? WHAT'S UP?"
"JUST DO IT!!
"WAIT. WHO'S CLOSING TONIGHT?"
"ASH."
I LOVE THE WAY YOU MOVE, BABY.

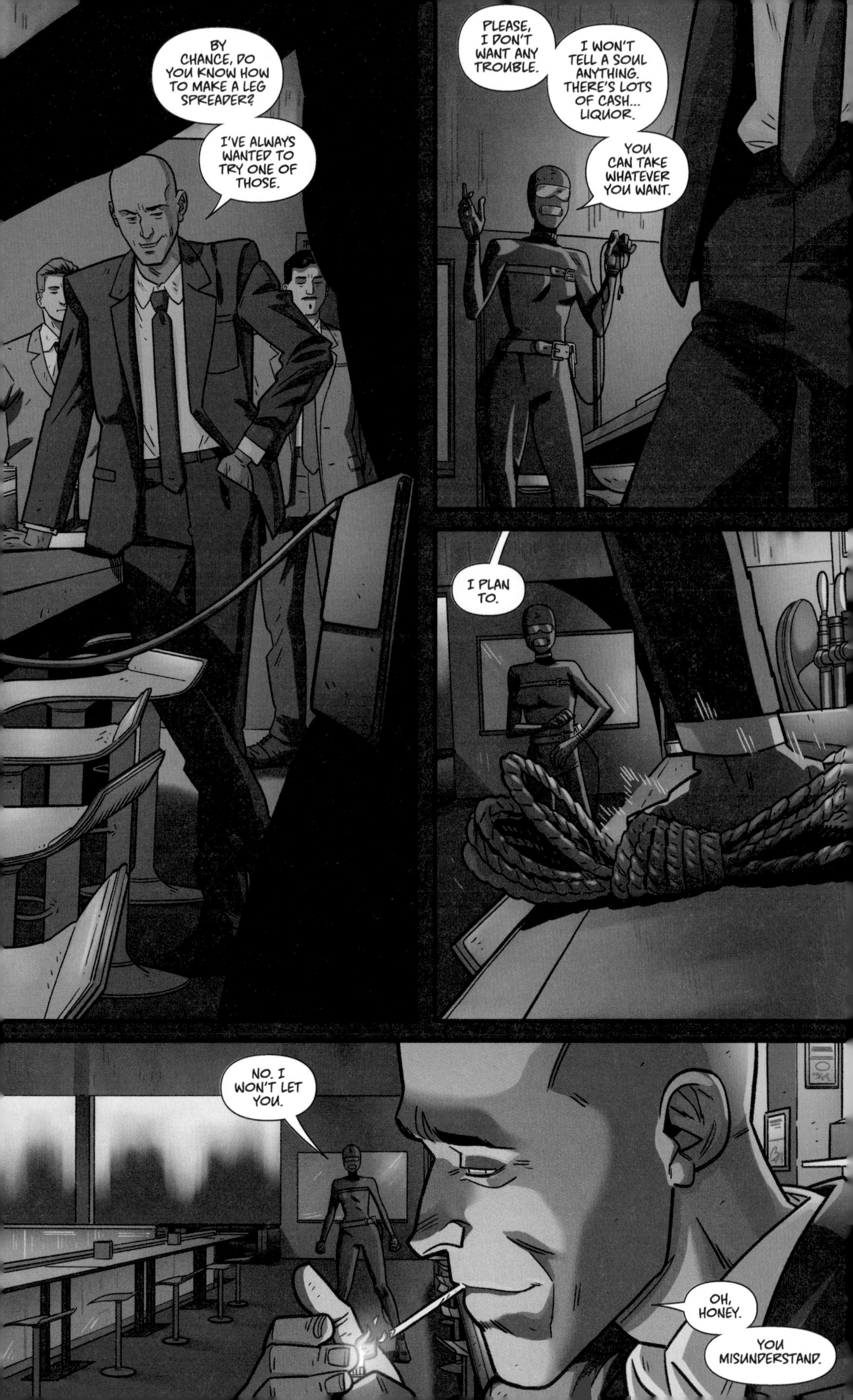
BY CHANCE, DO YOU KNOW HOW TO MAKE A LEG SPREADER?
I'VE ALWAYS WANTED TO TRY ONE OF THOSE.
PLEASE, I DON'T WANT ANY TROUBLE.
I WON'T TELL A SOUL ANYTHING. THERE'S LOTS OF CASH... LIQUOR.
YOU CAN TAKE WHATEVER YOU WANT.
I PLAN TO.
NO. I WON'T LET YOU.
OH, HONEY.
YOU MISUNDERSTAND.

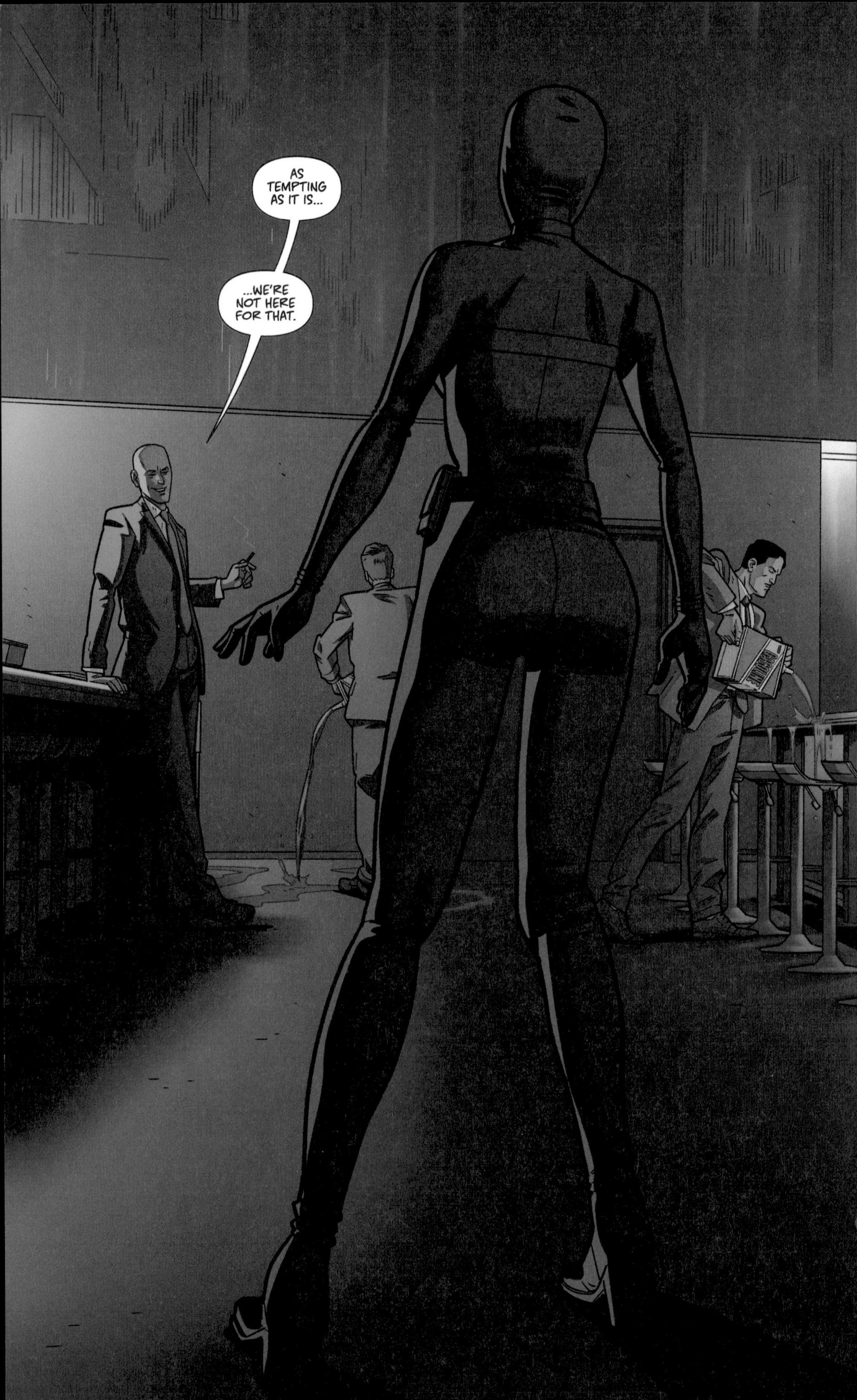
AS TEMPTING AS IT IS...
...WE'RE NOT HERE FOR THAT.

"Foo"

DOUG WAGNER

STORY

CULLY HAMNER

ART

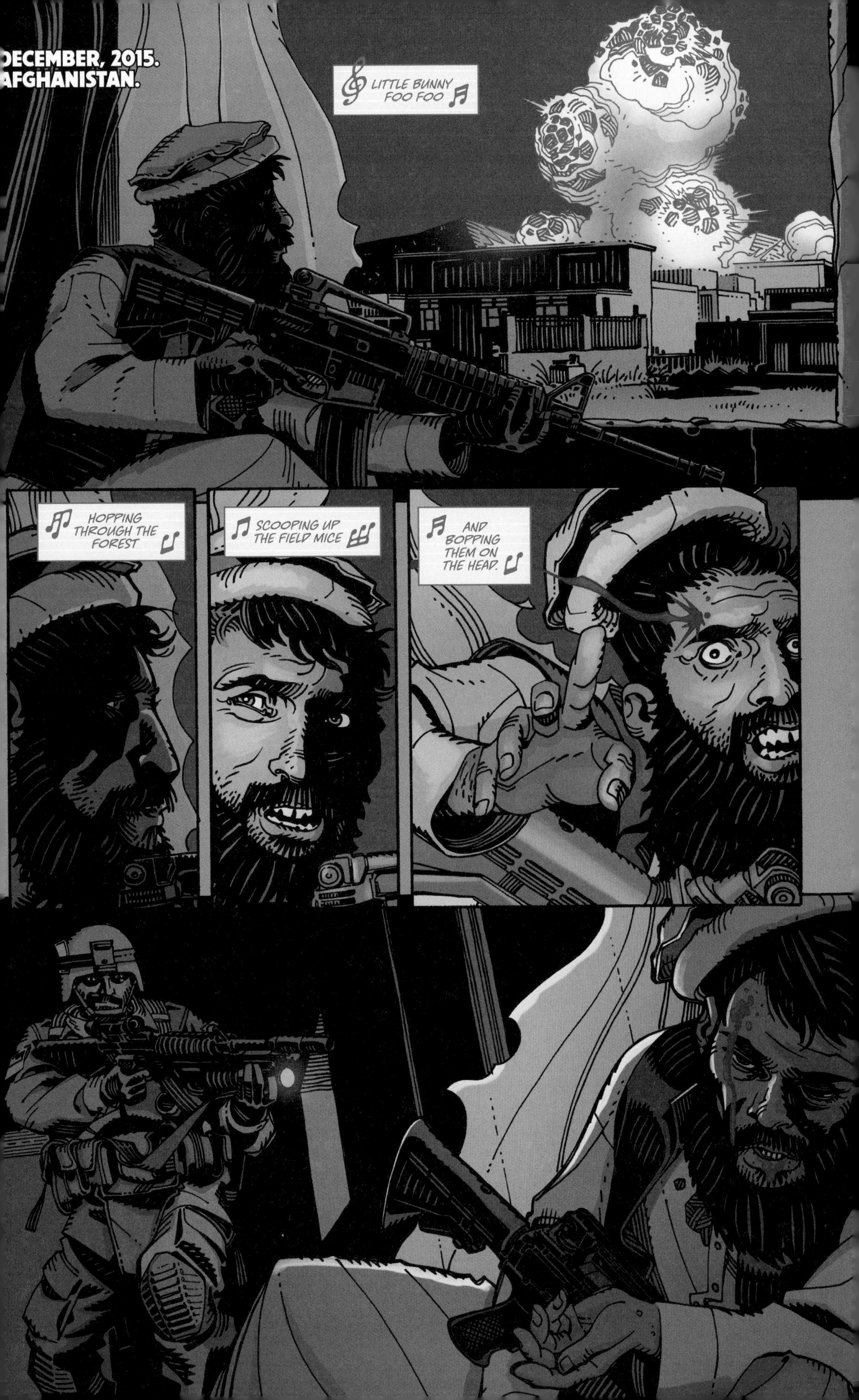
DECEMBER, 2015.
AFGHANISTAN.
LITTLE BUNNY FOO FOO
HOPPING THROUGH THE FOREST
SCOOPING UP THE FIELD MICE
AND BOPPING THEM ON THE HEAD.

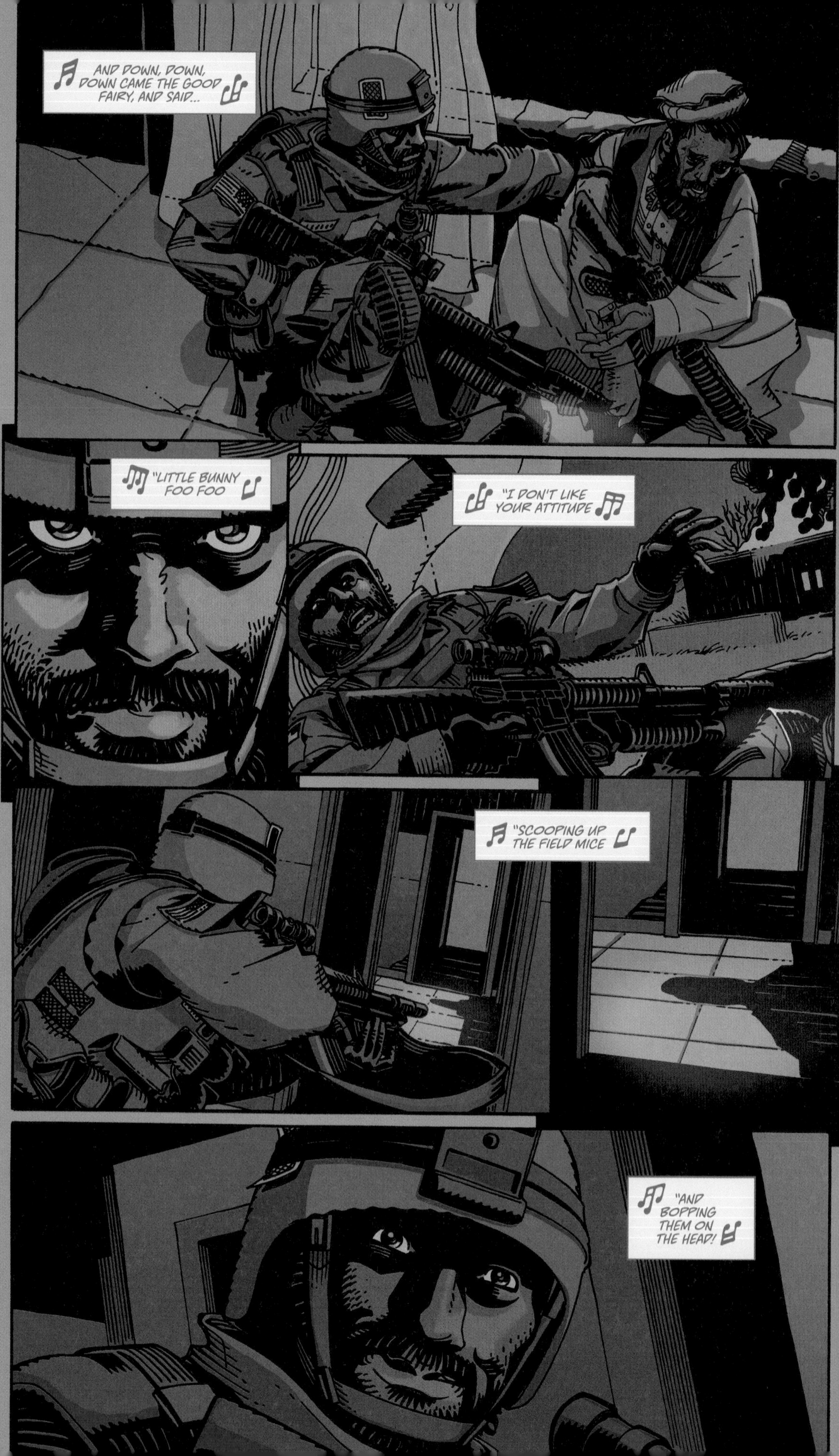
AND DOWN, DOWN, DOWN CAME THE GOOD FAIRY, AND SAID...
"LITTLE BUNNY FOO FOO
"I DON'T LIKE YOUR ATTITUDE
"SCOOPING UP THE FIELD MICE
"AND BOPPING THEM ON THE HEAD!

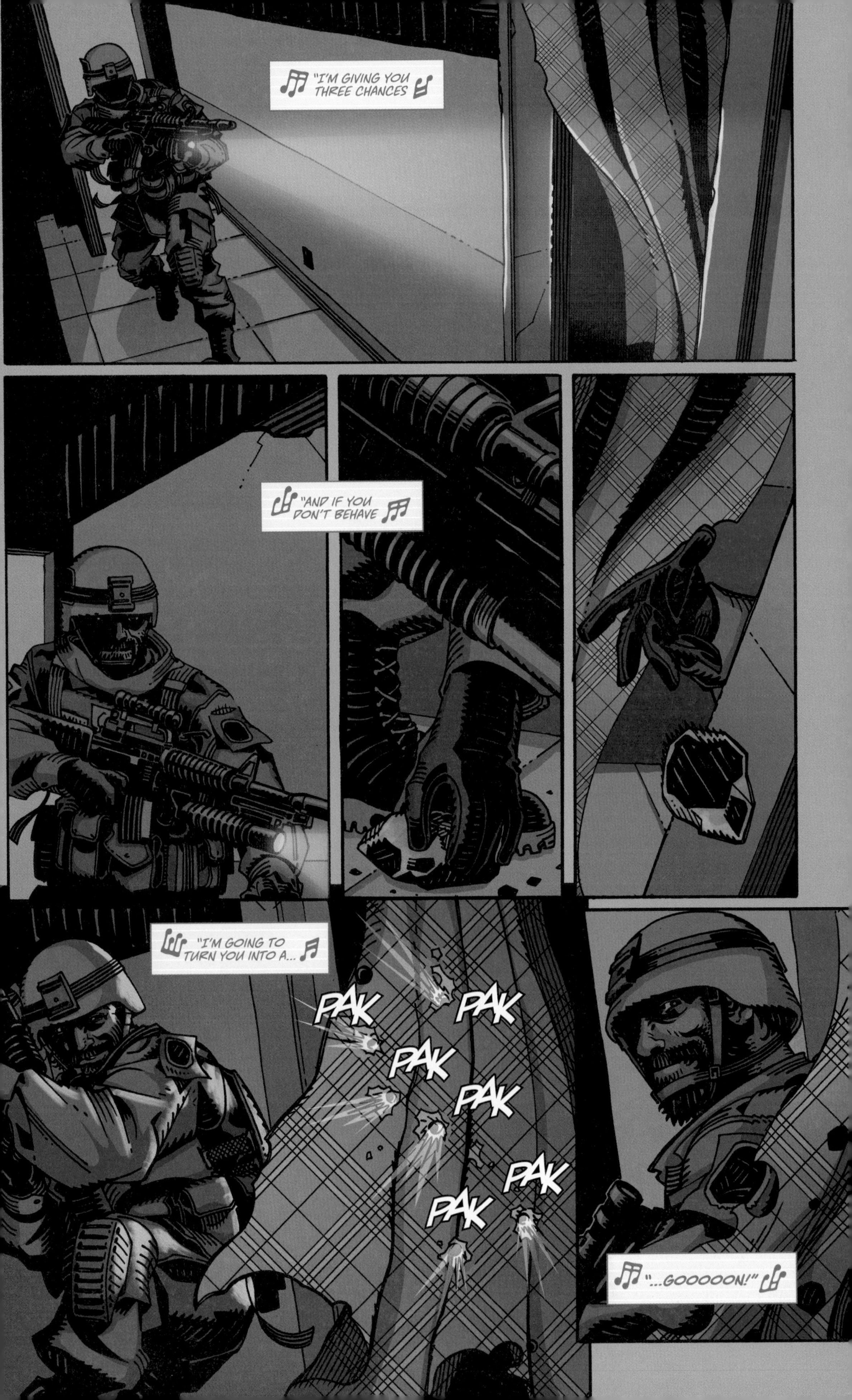
"I'M GIVING YOU THREE CHANCES
"AND IF YOU DON'T BEHAVE
"I'M GOING TO TURN YOU INTO A...
PAK
PAK
PAK
PAK
PAK
PAK
"...GOOOOON!"

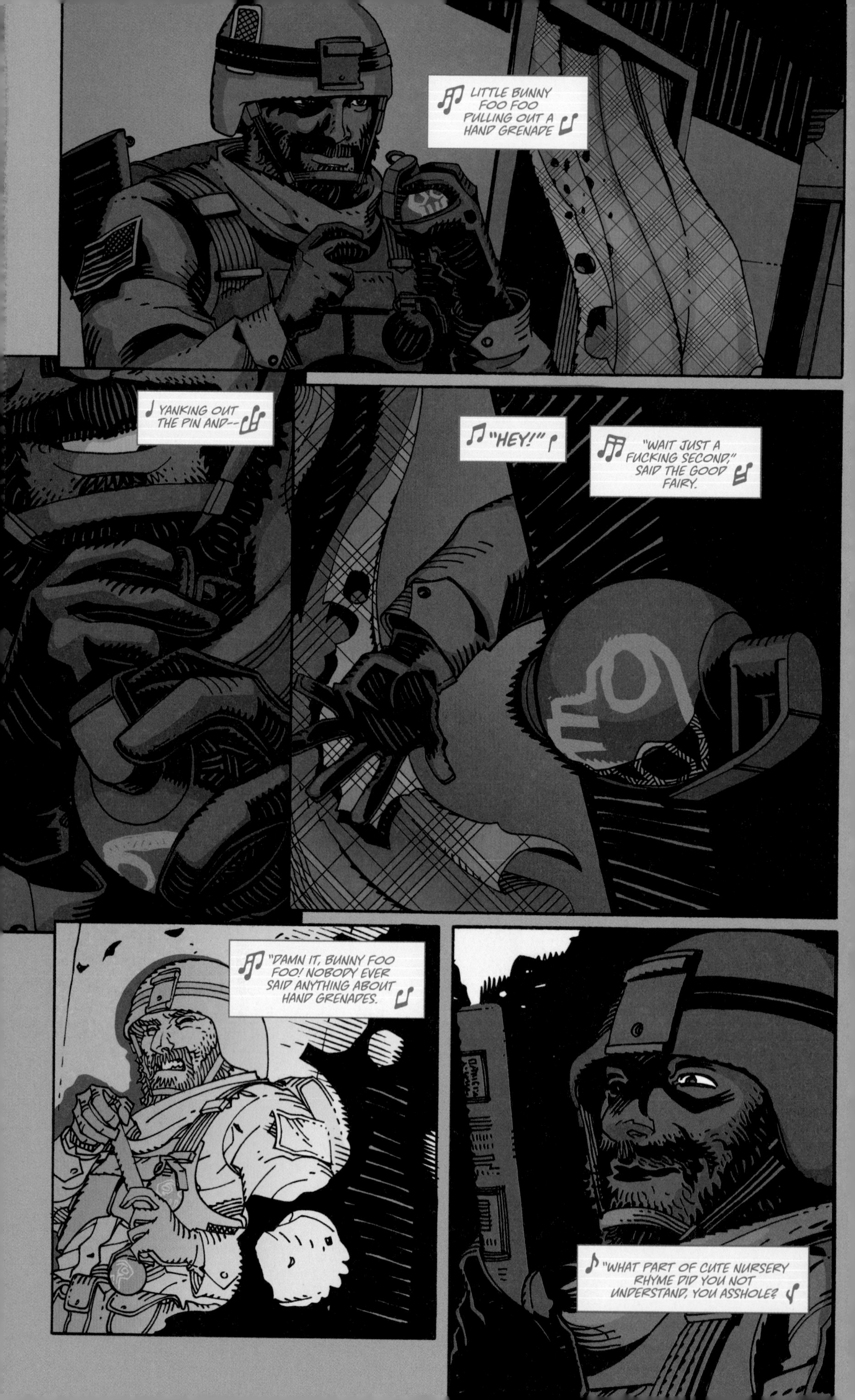
LITTLE BUNNY FOO FOO PULLING OUT A HAND GRENADE
YANKING OUT THE PIN AND--
"HEY!"
"WAIT JUST A FUCKING SECOND," SAID THE GOOD FAIRY.
"DAMN IT, BUNNY FOO FOO! NOBODY EVER SAID ANYTHING ABOUT HAND GRENADES.
"WHAT PART OF CUTE NURSERY RHYME DID YOU NOT UNDERSTAND, YOU ASSHOLE?

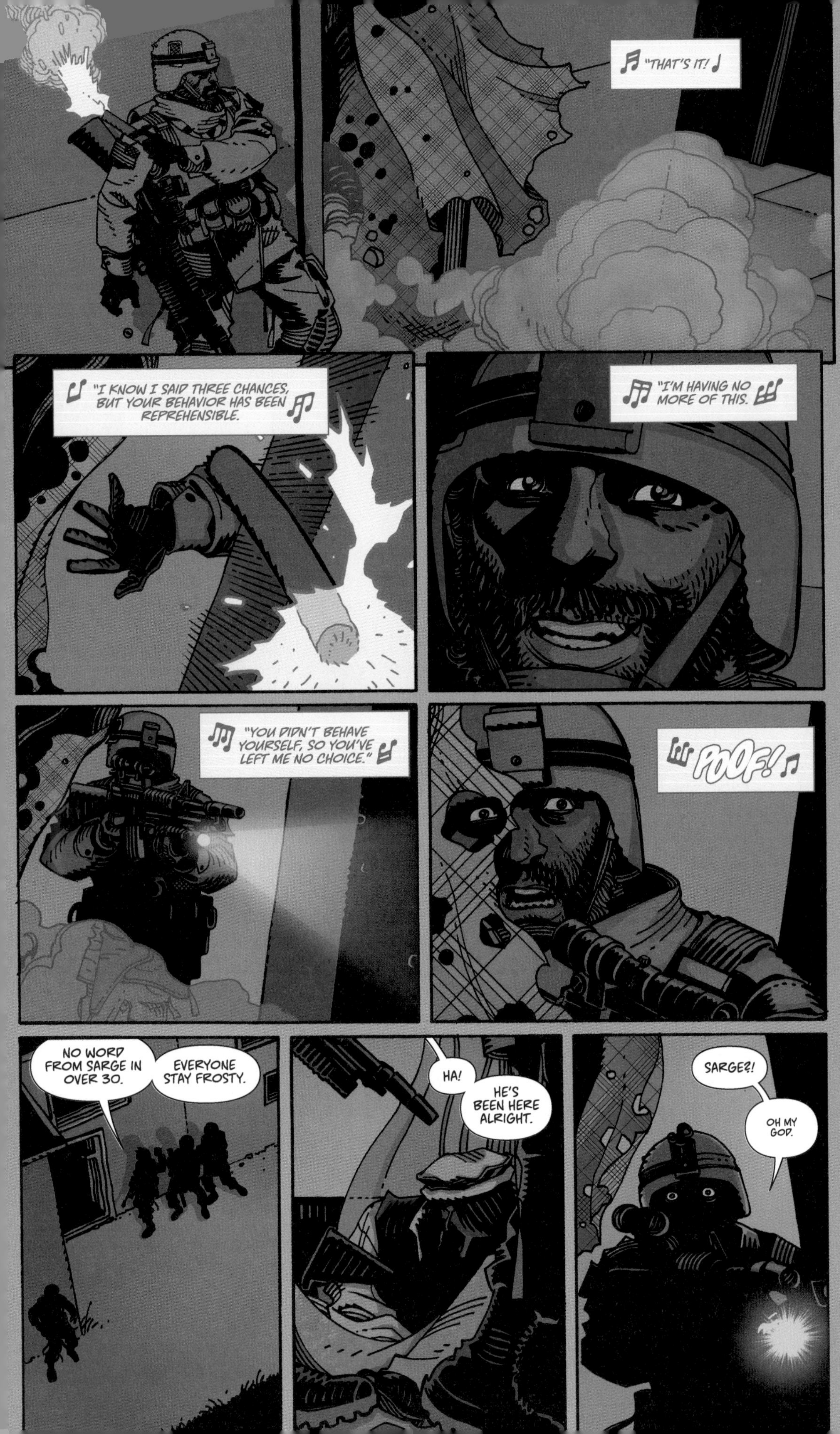
"THAT'S IT!
"I KNOW I SAID THREE CHANCES, BUT YOUR BEHAVIOR HAS BEEN REPREHENSIBLE.
"I'M HAVING NO MORE OF THIS.
"YOU DIDN'T BEHAVE YOURSELF, SO YOU'VE LEFT ME NO CHOICE."
POOF!
NO WORD FROM SARGE IN OVER 30.
EVERYONE STAY FROSTY.
HA!
HE'S BEEN HERE ALRIGHT.
SARGE?!
OH MY GOD.

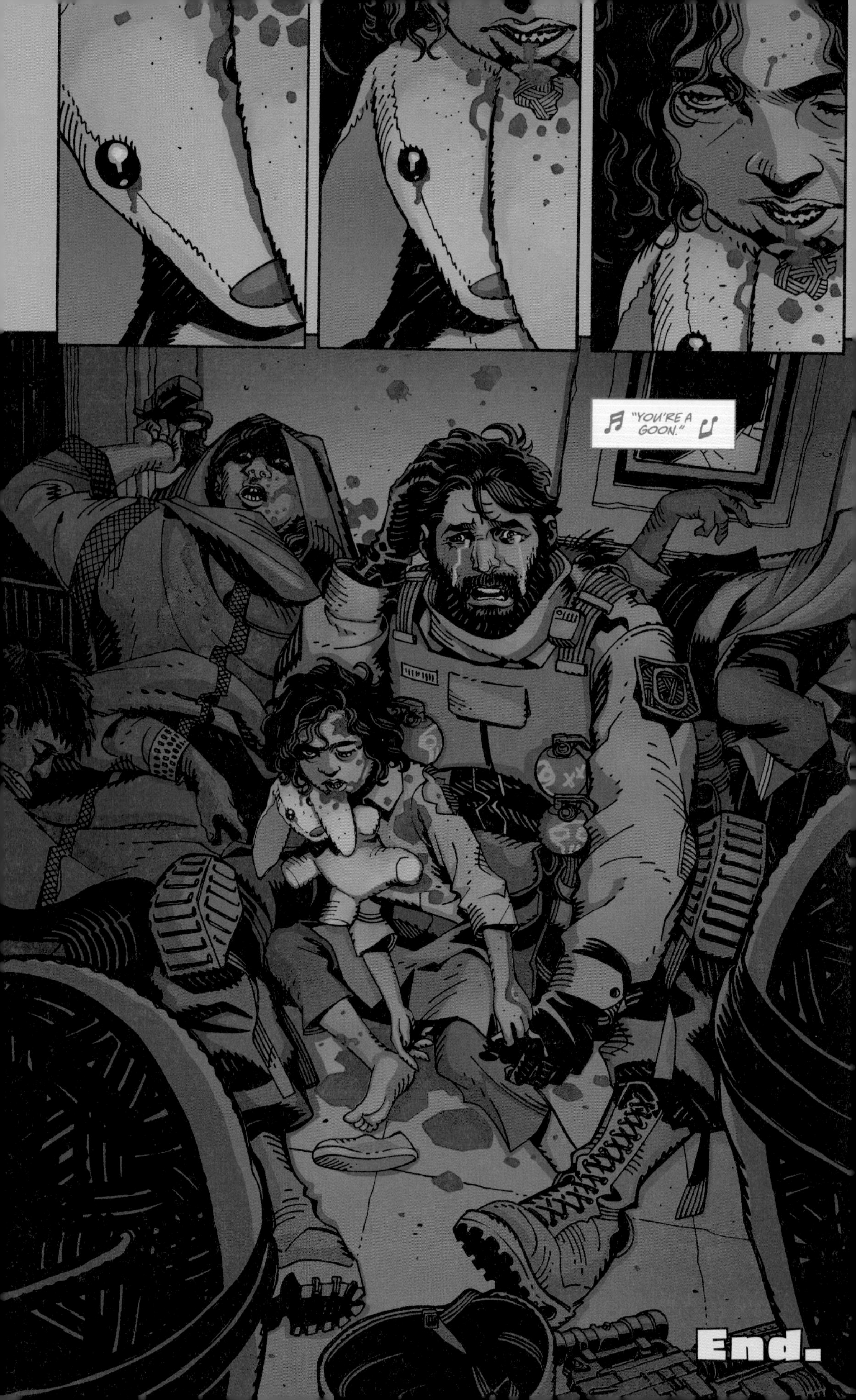
"YOU'RE A GOON."
End.

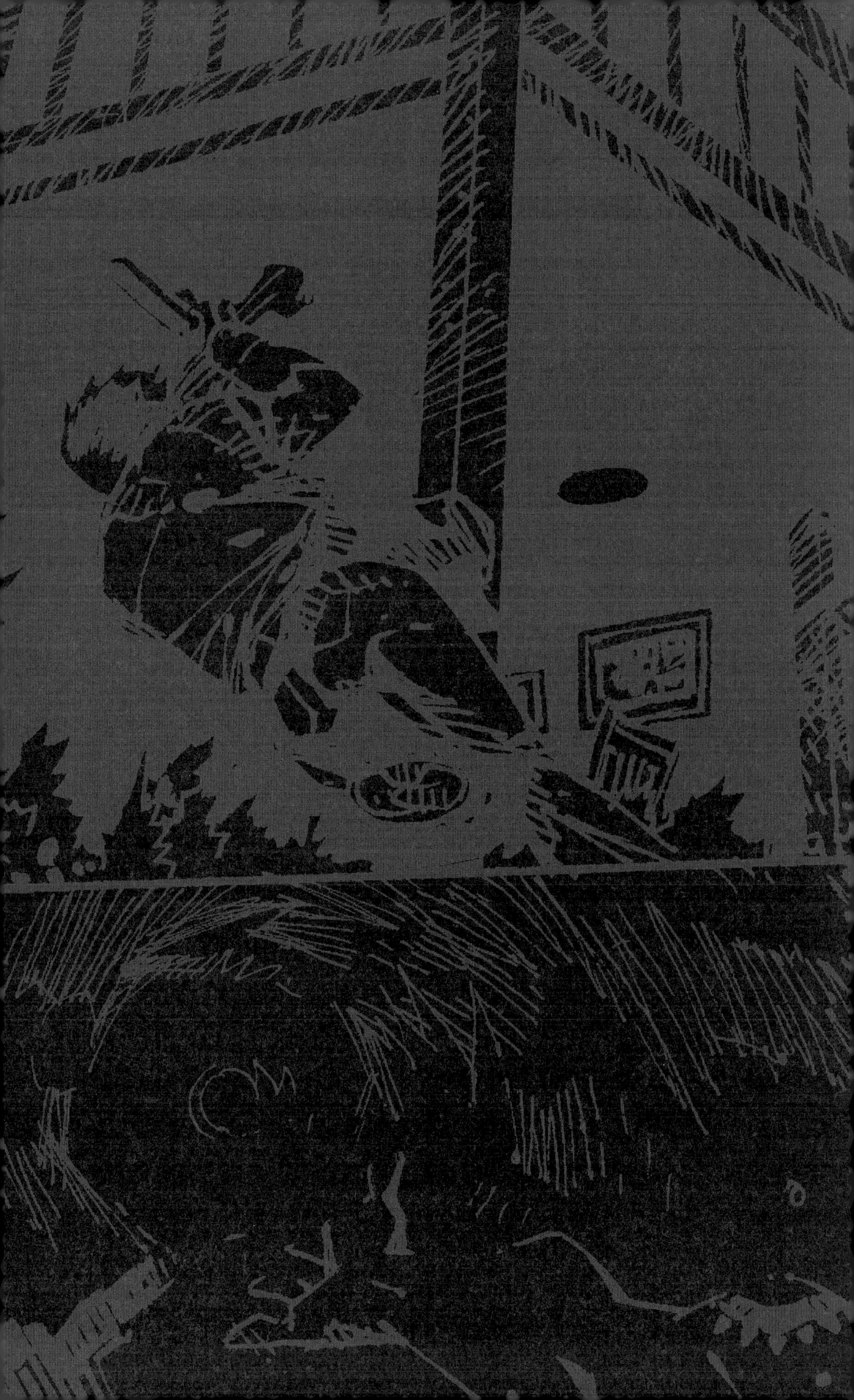

BURNING DESIRE
CHAPTER FOUR

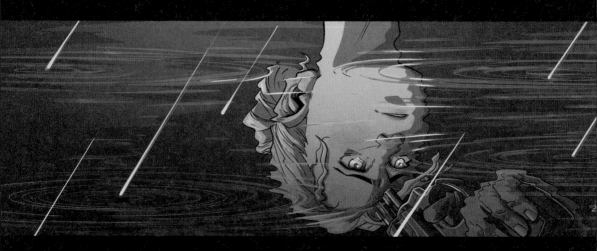

DOUG WAGNER
STORY

DANIEL HILLYARD
ART

CHARLIE KIRCHOFF

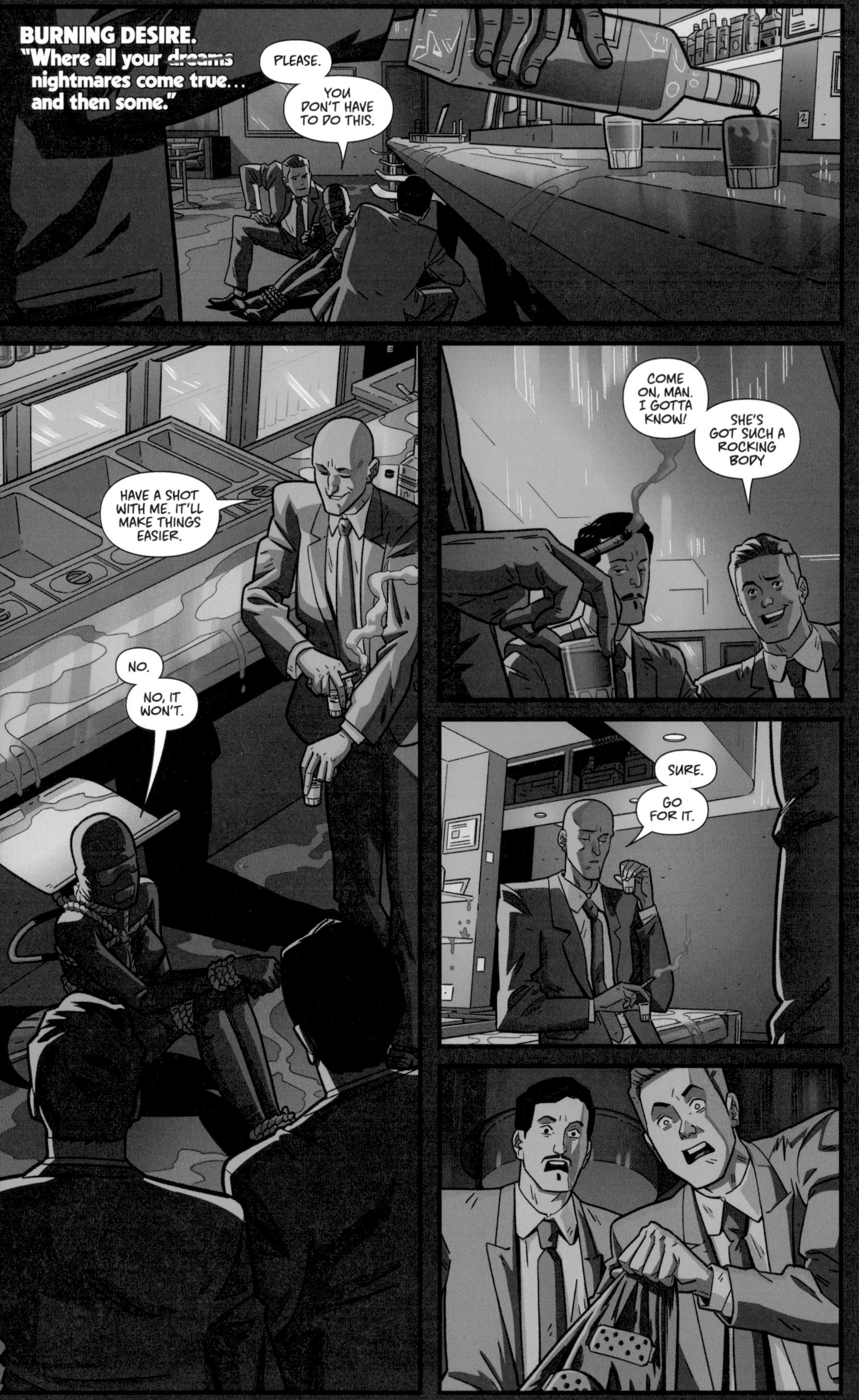
BURNING DESIRE.
"Where all your dreams nightmares come true... and then some."
PLEASE.
YOU DON'T HAVE TO DO THIS.
HAVE A SHOT WITH ME. IT'LL MAKE THINGS EASIER.
NO.
NO, IT WON'T.
COME ON, MAN. I GOTTA KNOW!
SHE'S GOT SUCH A ROCKING BODY
SURE.
GO FOR IT.

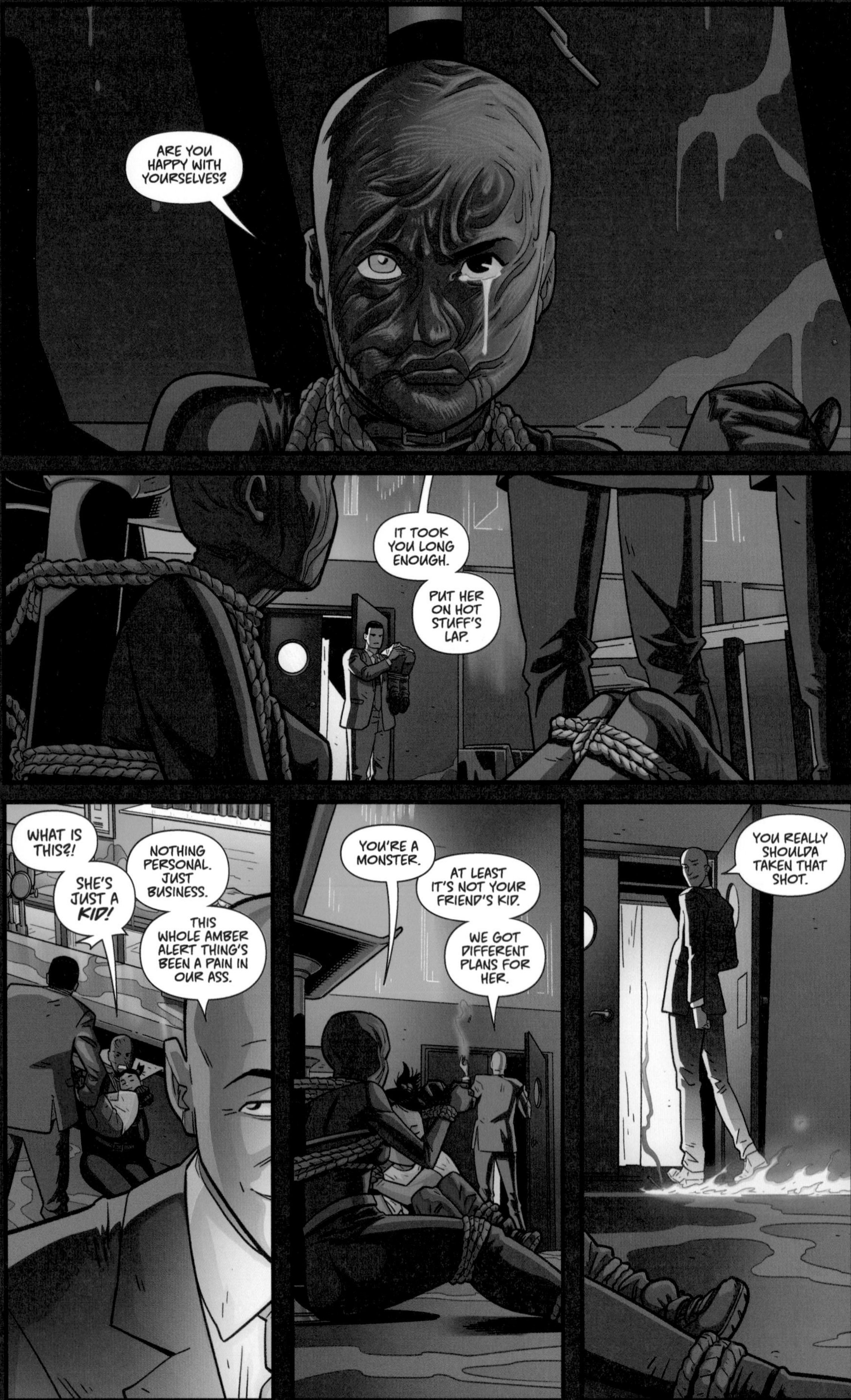
ARE YOU HAPPY WITH YOURSELVES?
IT TOOK YOU LONG ENOUGH.
PUT HER ON HOT STUFF'S LAP.
WHAT IS THIS?!
SHE'S JUST A KID!
NOTHING PERSONAL. JUST BUSINESS.
THIS WHOLE AMBER ALERT THING'S BEEN A PAIN IN OUR ASS.
YOU'RE A MONSTER.
AT LEAST IT'S NOT YOUR FRIEND'S KID.
WE GOT DIFFERENT PLANS FOR HER.
YOU REALLY SHOULDA TAKEN THAT SHOT.

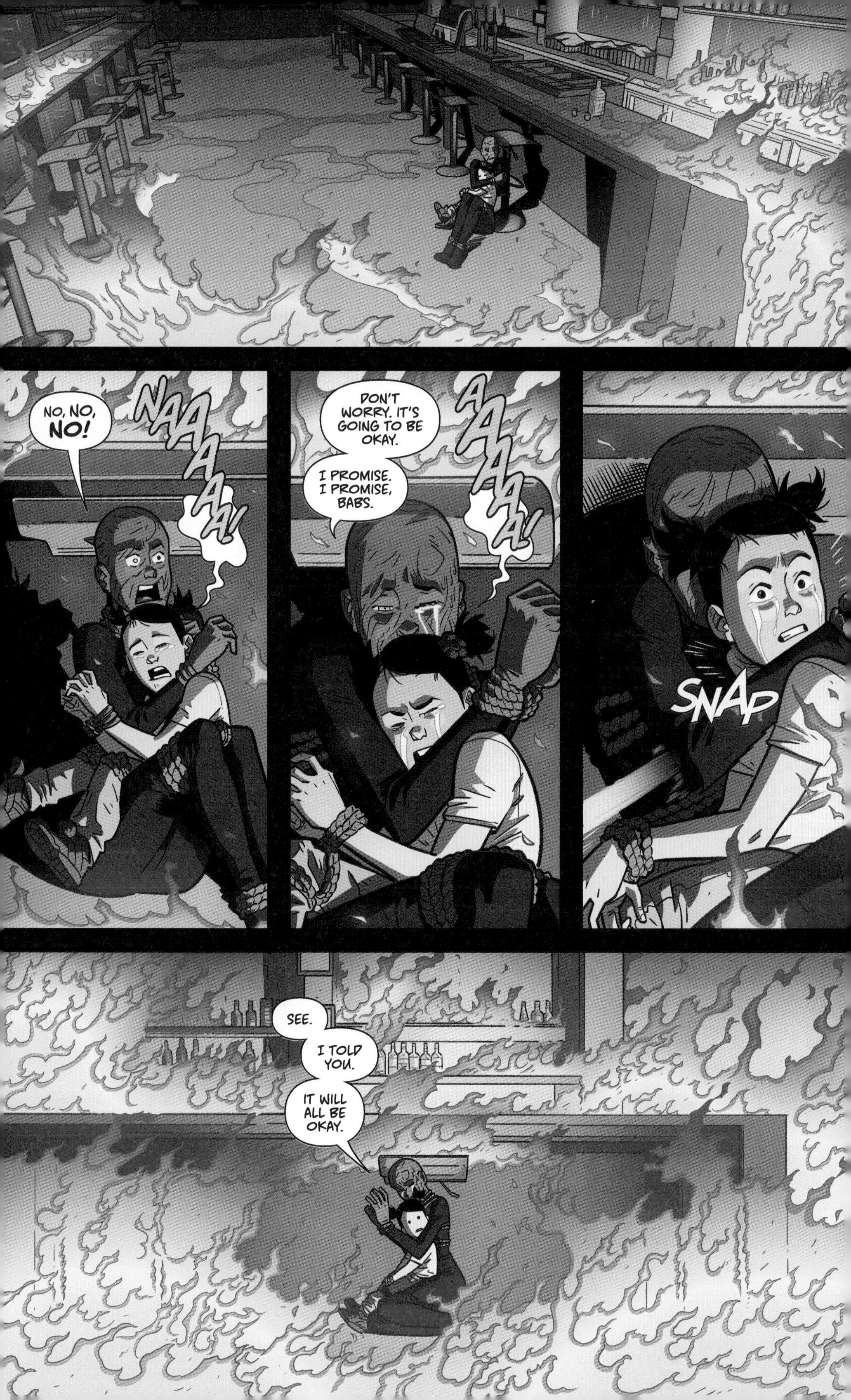
NO, NO, NO!
NAAAAAA!
DON'T WORRY. IT'S GOING TO BE OKAY.
I PROMISE. I PROMISE, BABS.
AAAAAA!
SNAP
SEE.
I TOLD YOU.
IT WILL ALL BE OKAY.

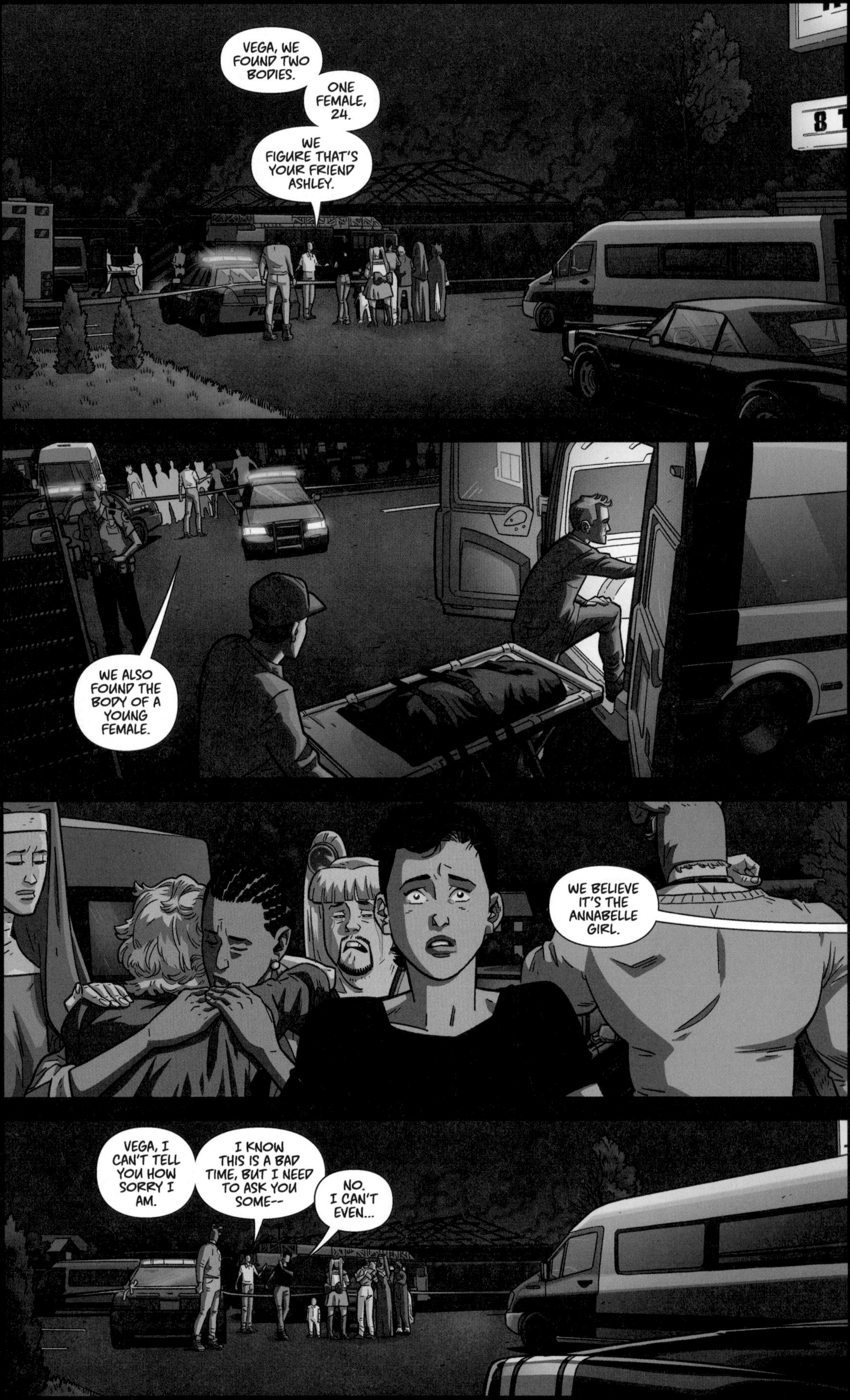
VEGA, WE FOUND TWO BODIES.
ONE FEMALE, 24.
WE FIGURE THAT'S YOUR FRIEND ASHLEY.
WE ALSO FOUND THE BODY OF A YOUNG FEMALE.
WE BELIEVE IT'S THE ANNABELLE GIRL.
VEGA, I CAN'T TELL YOU HOW SORRY I AM.
I KNOW THIS IS A BAD TIME, BUT I NEED TO ASK YOU SOME--
NO. I CAN'T EVEN...

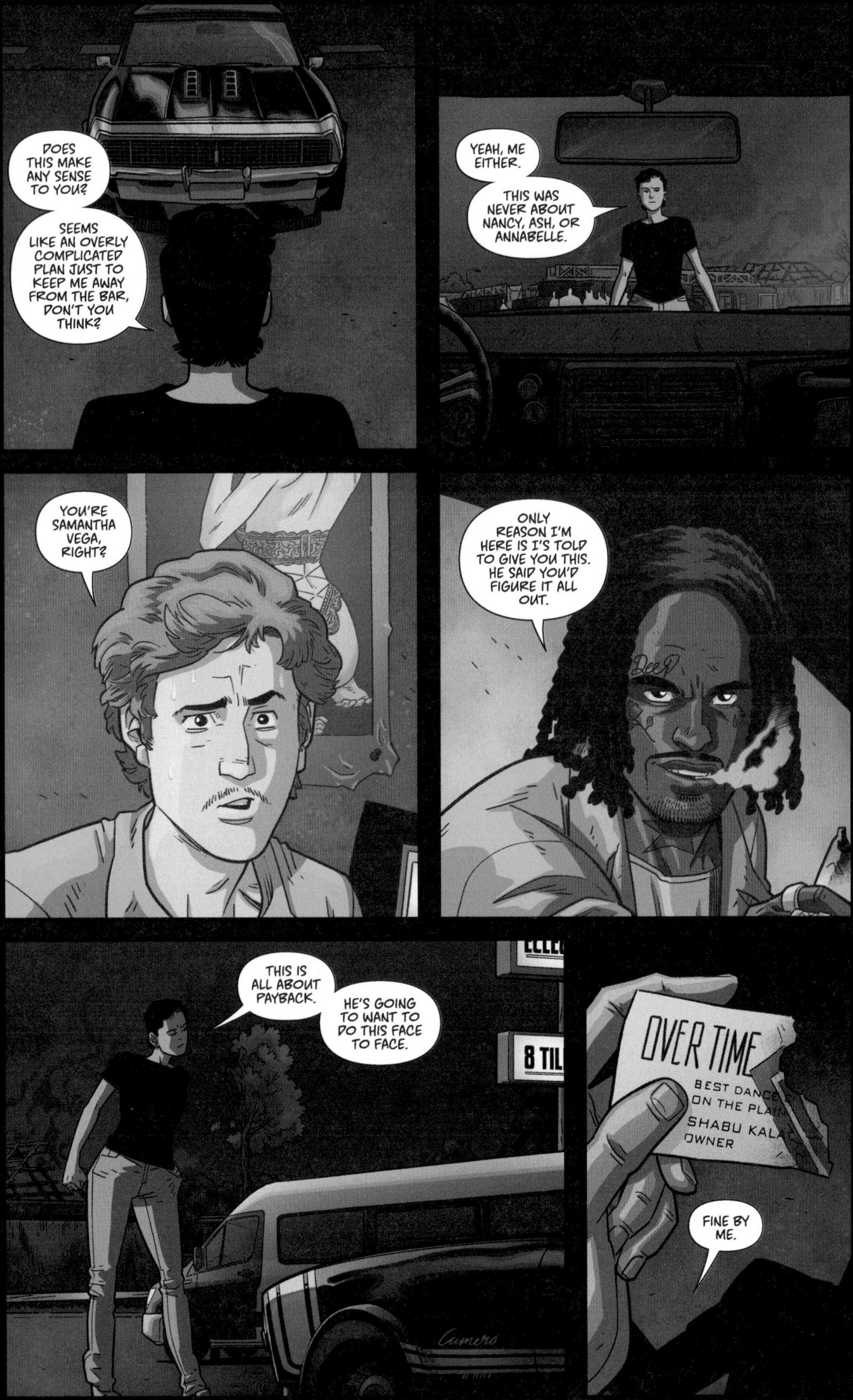
DOES THIS MAKE ANY SENSE TO YOU?
SEEMS LIKE AN OVERLY COMPLICATED PLAN JUST TO KEEP ME AWAY FROM THE BAR, DON'T YOU THINK?
YEAH, ME EITHER.
THIS WAS NEVER ABOUT NANCY, ASH, OR ANNABELLE.
YOU'RE SAMANTHA VEGA, RIGHT?
ONLY REASON I'M HERE IS I'S TOLD TO GIVE YOU THIS. HE SAID YOU'D FIGURE IT ALL OUT.
THIS IS ALL ABOUT PAYBACK.
HE'S GOING TO WANT TO DO THIS FACE TO FACE.
8 TIL
OVER TIME
BEST DANCE
ON THE PLAI
SHABU KALA
OWNER
FINE BY ME.
Camero

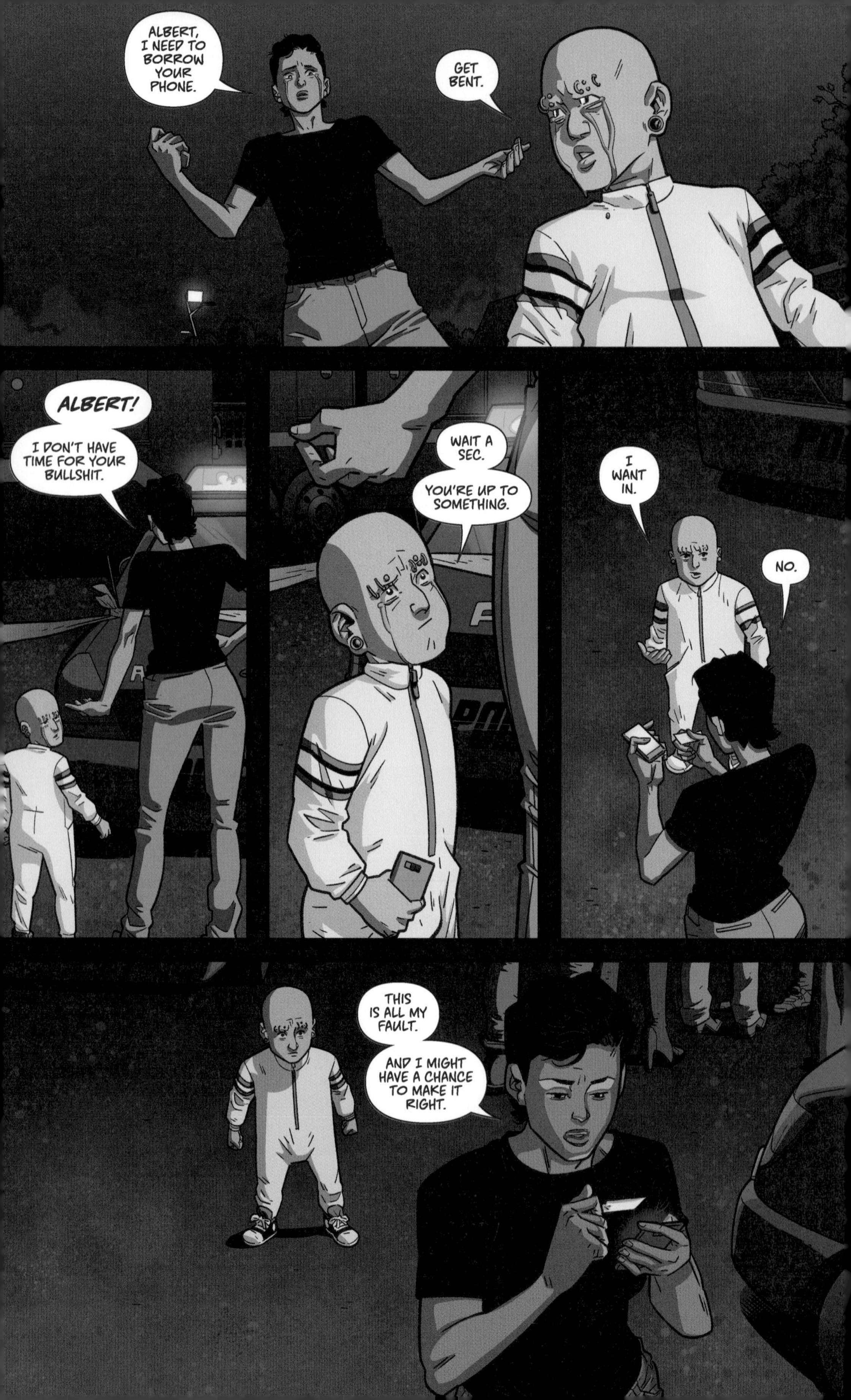
ALBERT, I NEED TO BORROW YOUR PHONE.
GET BENT.
ALBERT!
I DON'T HAVE TIME FOR YOUR BULLSHIT.
WAIT A SEC.
YOU'RE UP TO SOMETHING.
I WANT IN.
NO.
THIS IS ALL MY FAULT.
AND I MIGHT HAVE A CHANCE TO MAKE IT RIGHT.

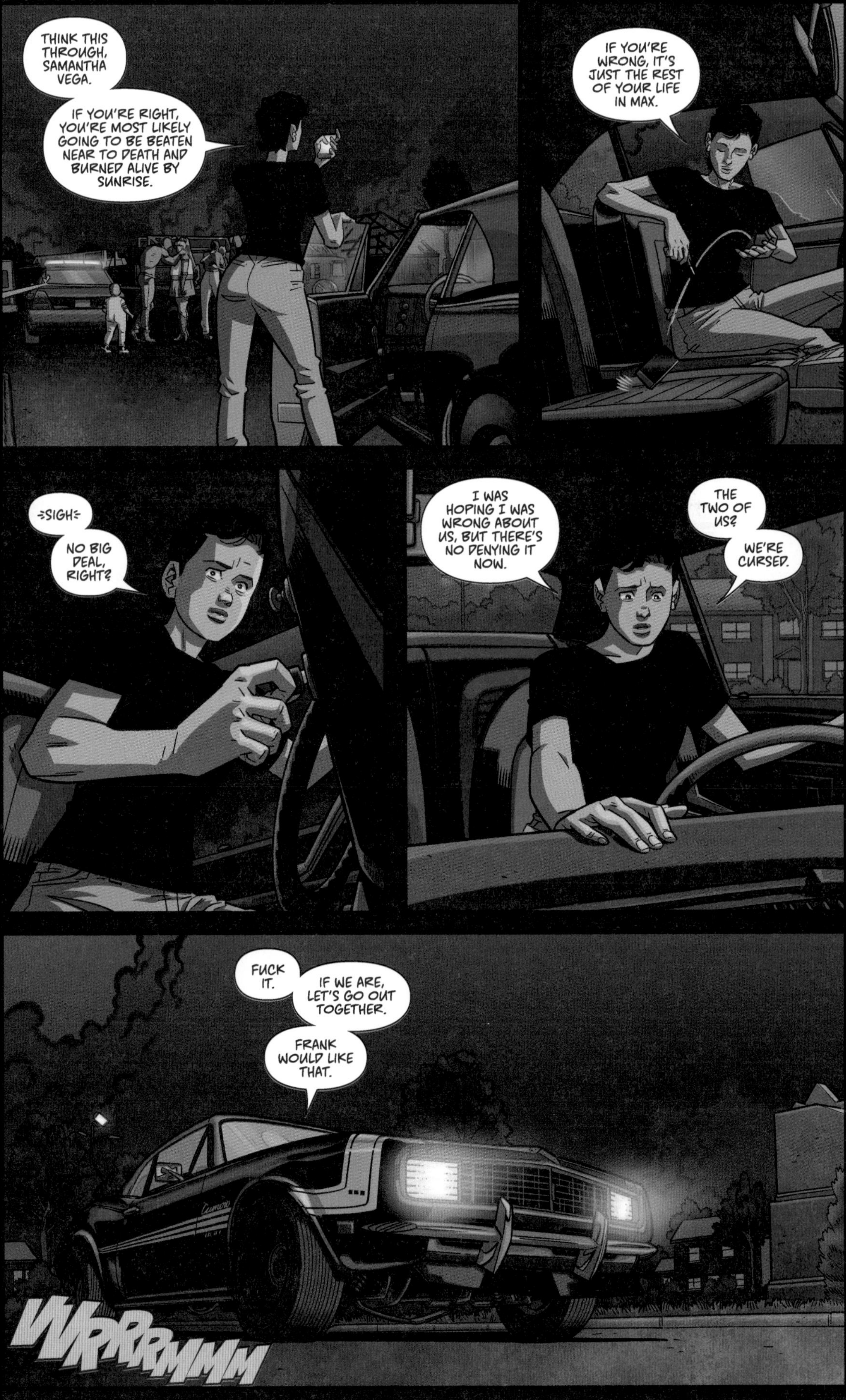
THINK THIS THROUGH, SAMANTHA VEGA.
IF YOU'RE RIGHT, YOU'RE MOST LIKELY GOING TO BE BEATEN NEAR TO DEATH AND BURNED ALIVE BY SUNRISE.
IF YOU'RE WRONG, IT'S JUST THE REST OF YOUR LIFE IN MAX.
=SIGH=
NO BIG DEAL, RIGHT?
I WAS HOPING I WAS WRONG ABOUT US, BUT THERE'S NO DENYING IT NOW.
THE TWO OF US?
WE'RE CURSED.
FUCK IT.
IF WE ARE, LET'S GO OUT TOGETHER.
FRANK WOULD LIKE THAT.
WRRRMMMM

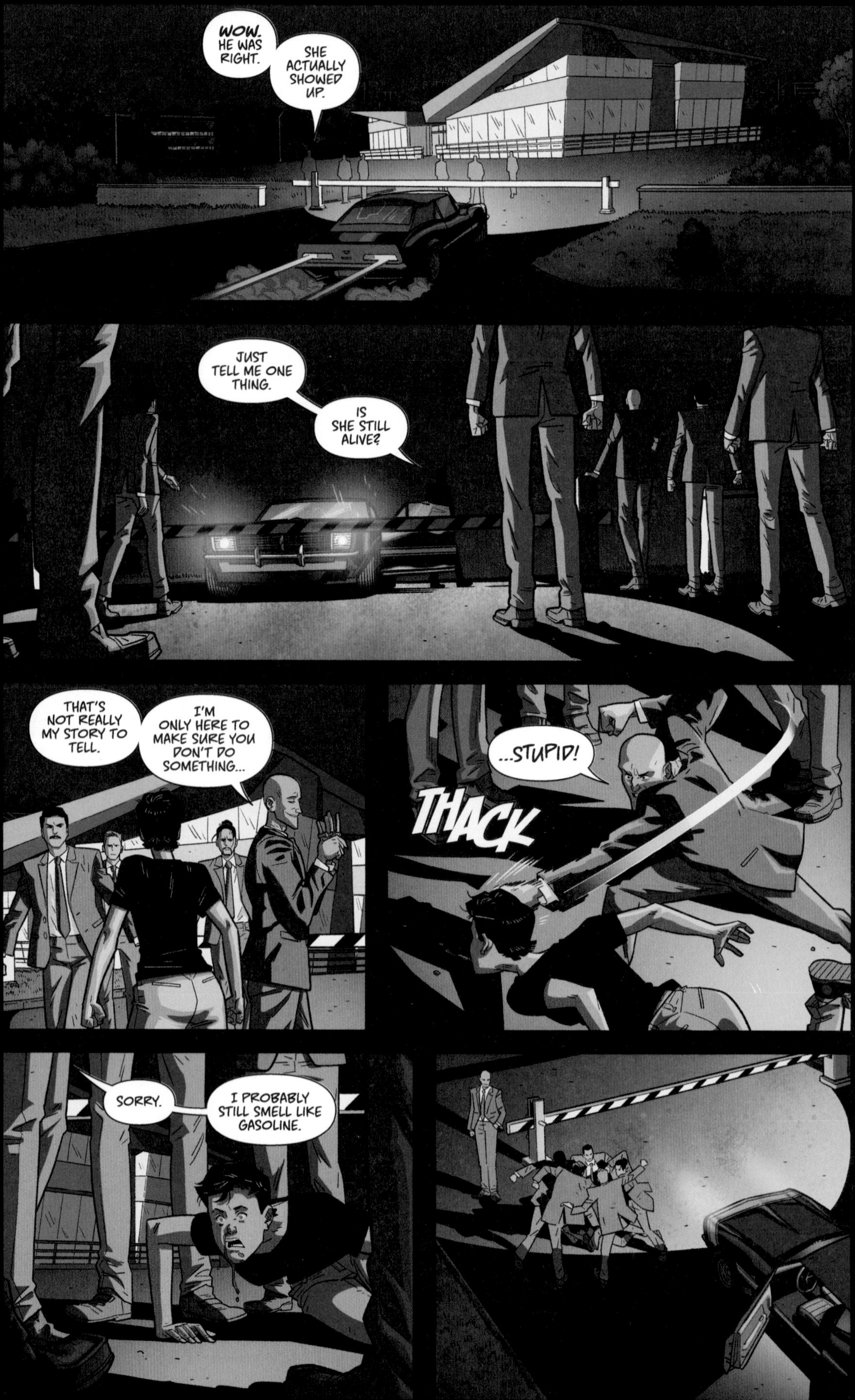
WOW. HE WAS RIGHT.
SHE ACTUALLY SHOWED UP.
JUST TELL ME ONE THING.
IS SHE STILL ALIVE?
THAT'S NOT REALLY MY STORY TO TELL.
I'M ONLY HERE TO MAKE SURE YOU DON'T DO SOMETHING...
...STUPID!
THACK
SORRY.
I PROBABLY STILL SMELL LIKE GASOLINE.

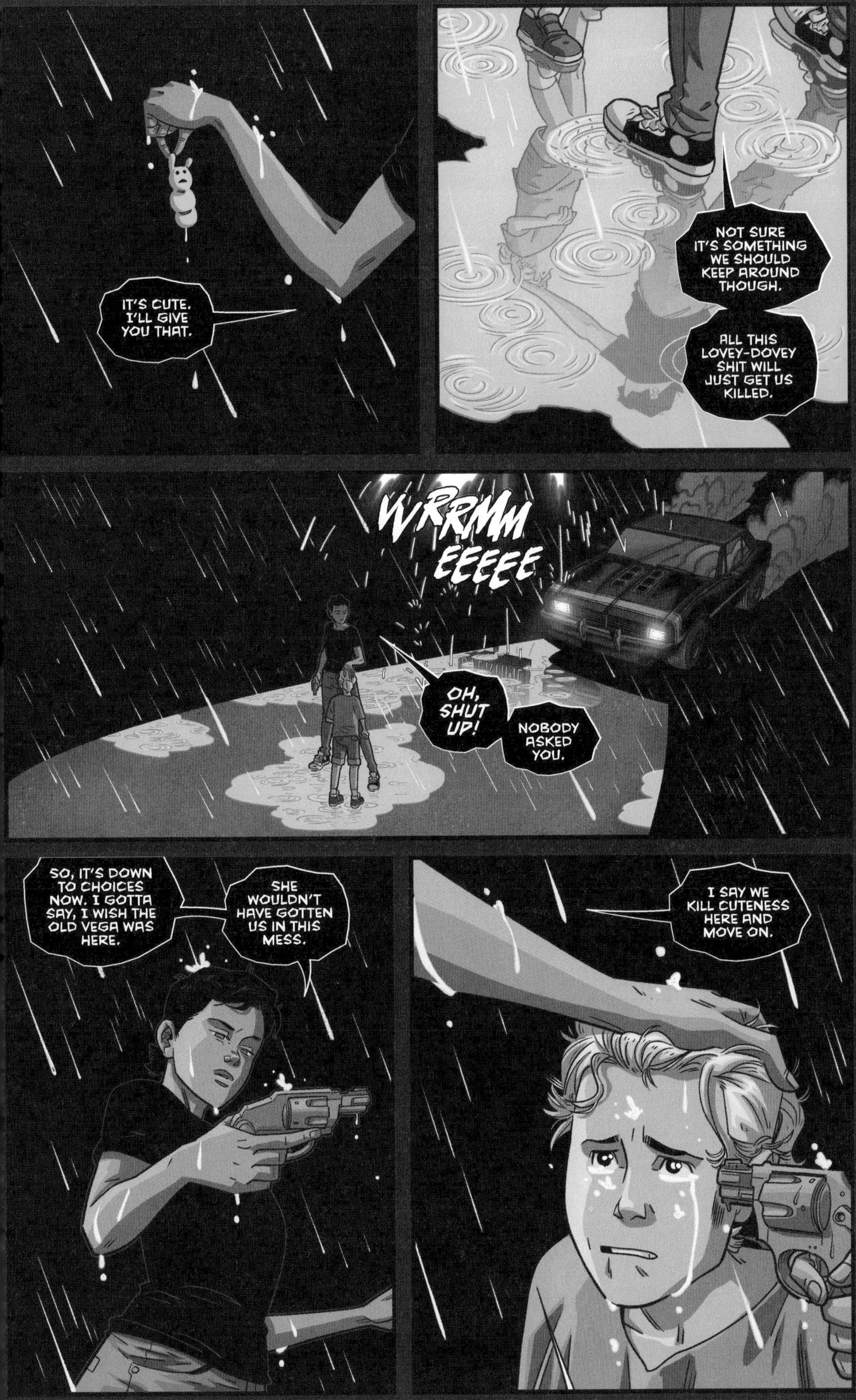
IT'S CUTE. I'LL GIVE YOU THAT.
NOT SURE IT'S SOMETHING WE SHOULD KEEP AROUND THOUGH.
ALL THIS LOVEY-DOVEY SHIT WILL JUST GET US KILLED.
WRRMM EEEEE
OH, SHUT UP!
NOBODY ASKED YOU.
SO, IT'S DOWN TO CHOICES NOW. I GOTTA SAY, I WISH THE OLD VEGA WAS HERE.
SHE WOULDN'T HAVE GOTTEN US IN THIS MESS.
I SAY WE KILL CUTENESS HERE AND MOVE ON.

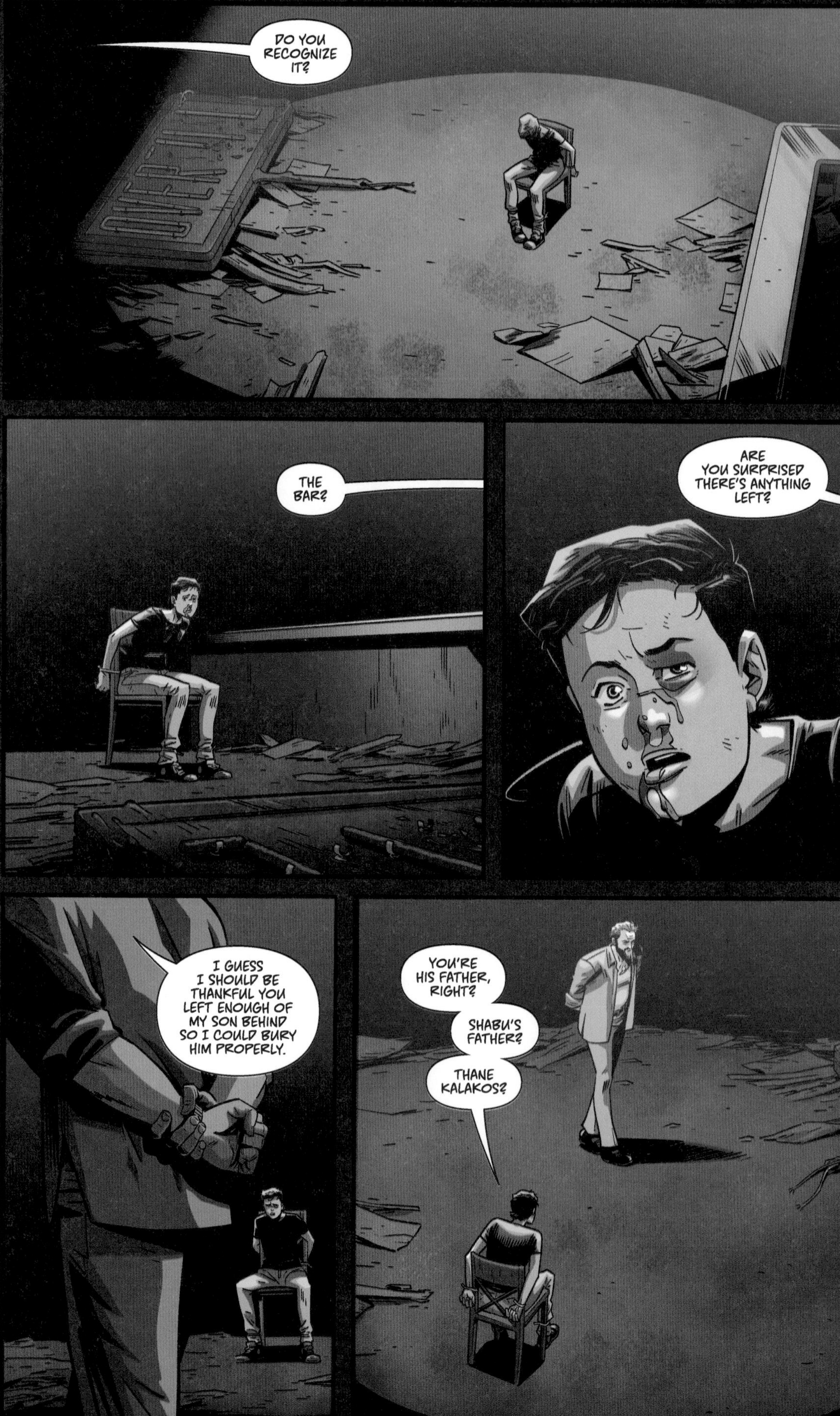
DO YOU RECOGNIZE IT?
THE BAR?
ARE YOU SURPRISED THERE'S ANYTHING LEFT?
I GUESS I SHOULD BE THANKFUL YOU LEFT ENOUGH OF MY SON BEHIND SO I COULD BURY HIM PROPERLY.
YOU'RE HIS FATHER, RIGHT?
SHABU'S FATHER?
THANE KALAKOS?

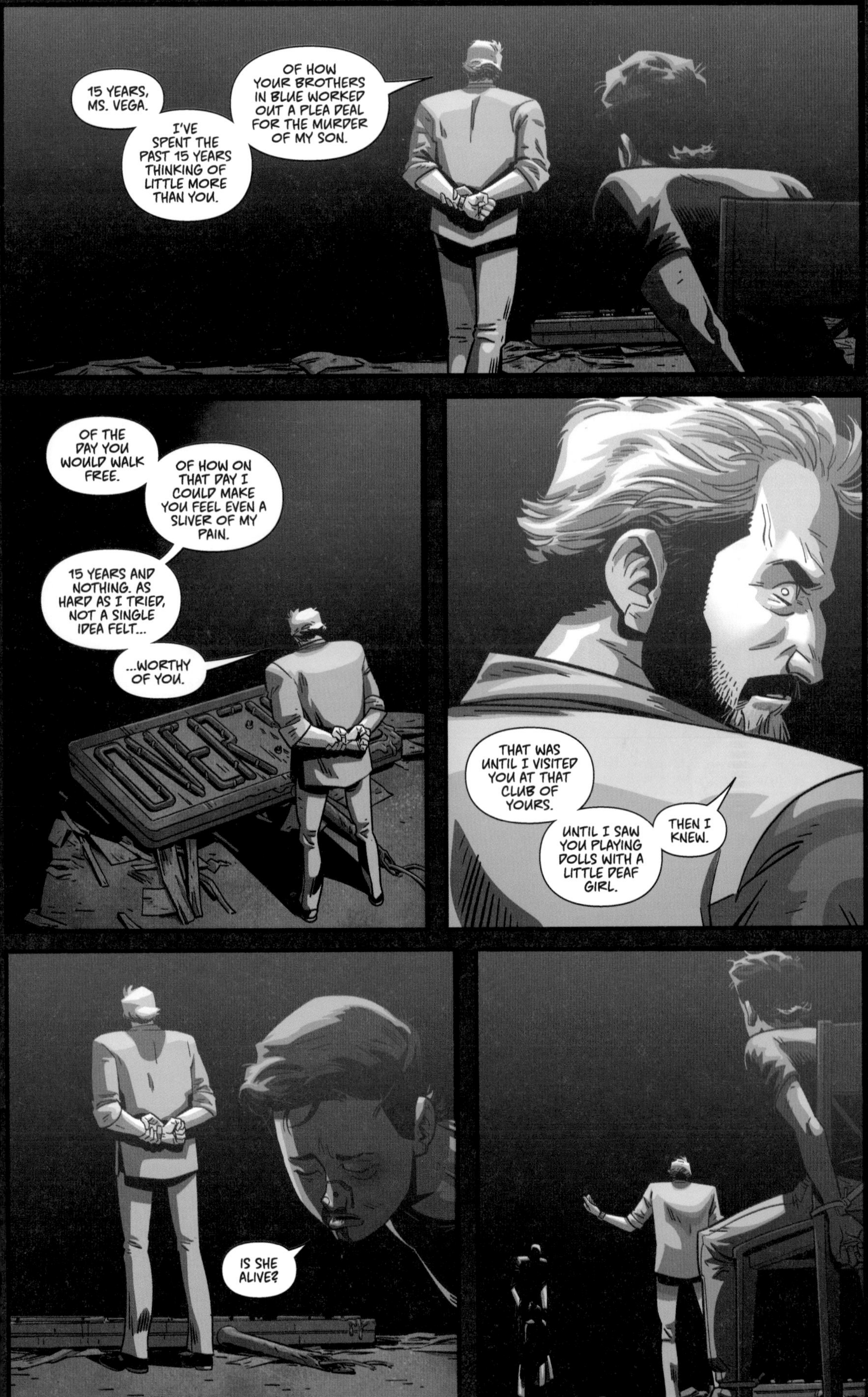
15 YEARS, MS. VEGA.
I'VE SPENT THE PAST 15 YEARS THINKING OF LITTLE MORE THAN YOU.
OF HOW YOUR BROTHERS IN BLUE WORKED OUT A PLEA DEAL FOR THE MURDER OF MY SON.
OF THE DAY YOU WOULD WALK FREE.
OF HOW ON THAT DAY I COULD MAKE YOU FEEL EVEN A SLIVER OF MY PAIN.
15 YEARS AND NOTHING. AS HARD AS I TRIED, NOT A SINGLE IDEA FELT...
...WORTHY OF YOU.
THAT WAS UNTIL I VISITED YOU AT THAT CLUB OF YOURS.
UNTIL I SAW YOU PLAYING DOLLS WITH A LITTLE DEAF GIRL.
THEN I KNEW.
IS SHE ALIVE?

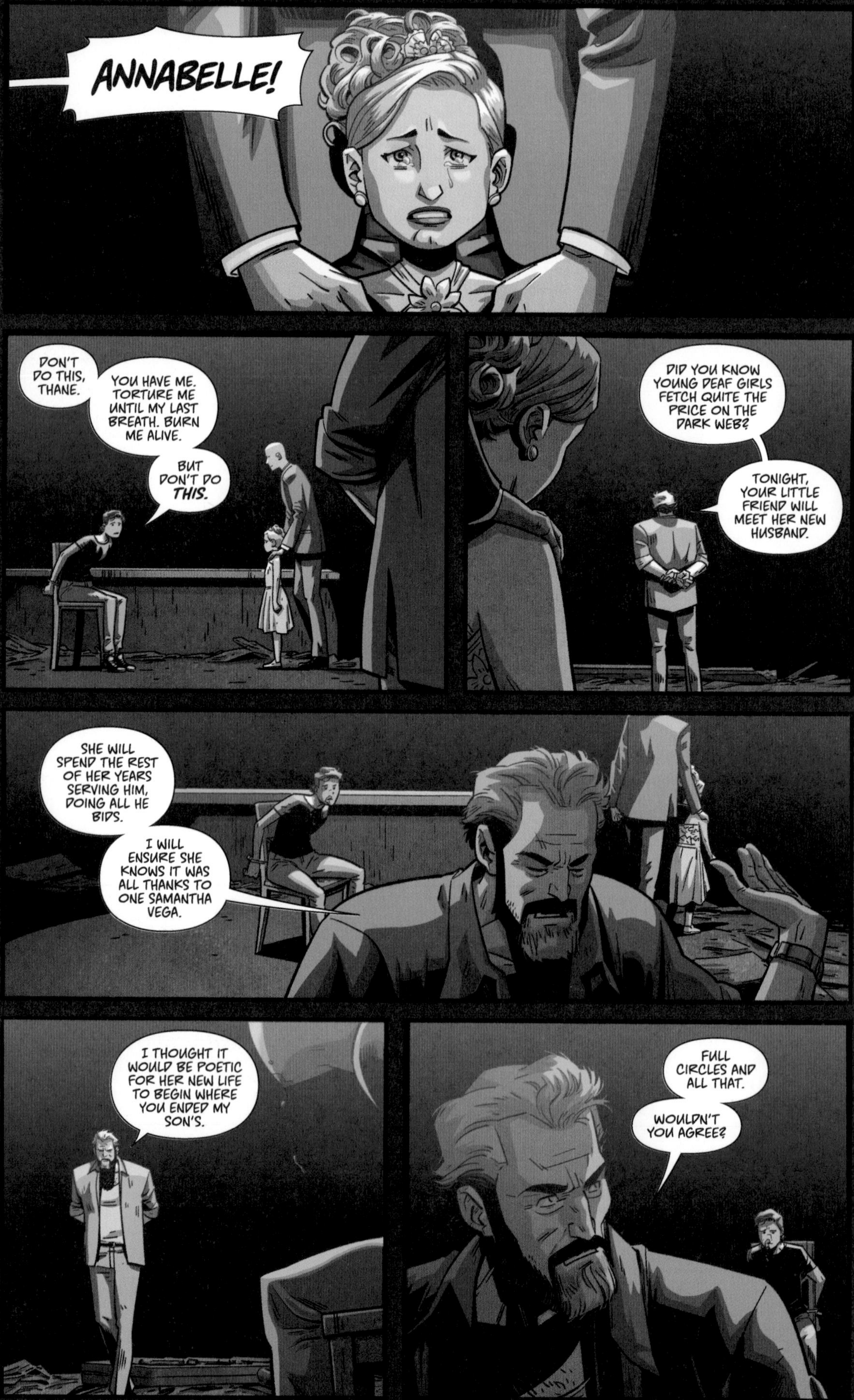
ANNABELLE!
DON'T DO THIS, THANE.
YOU HAVE ME. TORTURE ME UNTIL MY LAST BREATH. BURN ME ALIVE.
BUT DON'T DO THIS.
DID YOU KNOW YOUNG DEAF GIRLS FETCH QUITE THE PRICE ON THE DARK WEB?
TONIGHT, YOUR LITTLE FRIEND WILL MEET HER NEW HUSBAND.
SHE WILL SPEND THE REST OF HER YEARS SERVING HIM, DOING ALL HE BIDS.
I WILL ENSURE SHE KNOWS IT WAS ALL THANKS TO ONE SAMANTHA VEGA.
I THOUGHT IT WOULD BE POETIC FOR HER NEW LIFE TO BEGIN WHERE YOU ENDED MY SON'S.
FULL CIRCLES AND ALL THAT.
WOULDN'T YOU AGREE?

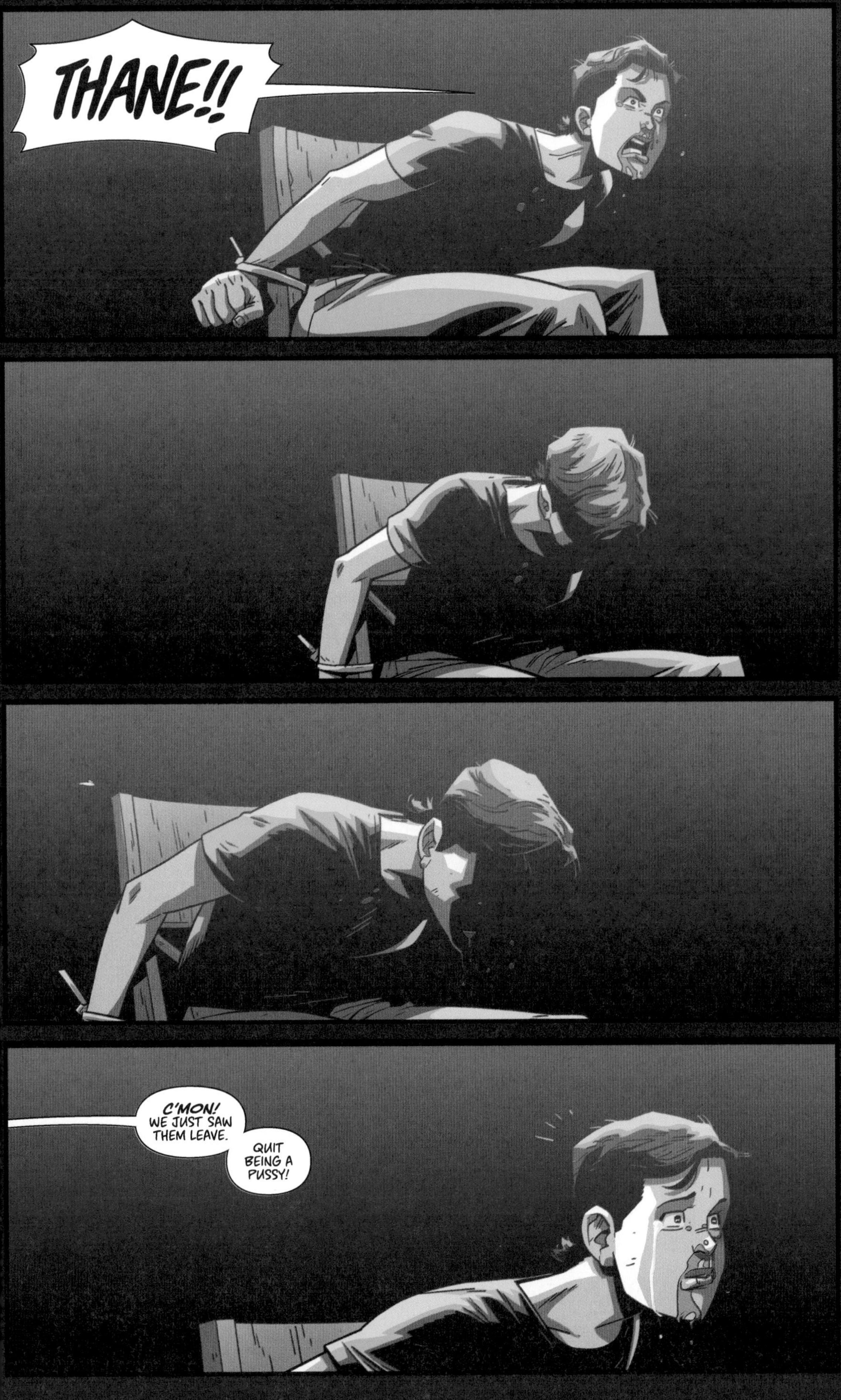
THANE!!
C'MON! WE JUST SAW THEM LEAVE.
QUIT BEING A PUSSY!

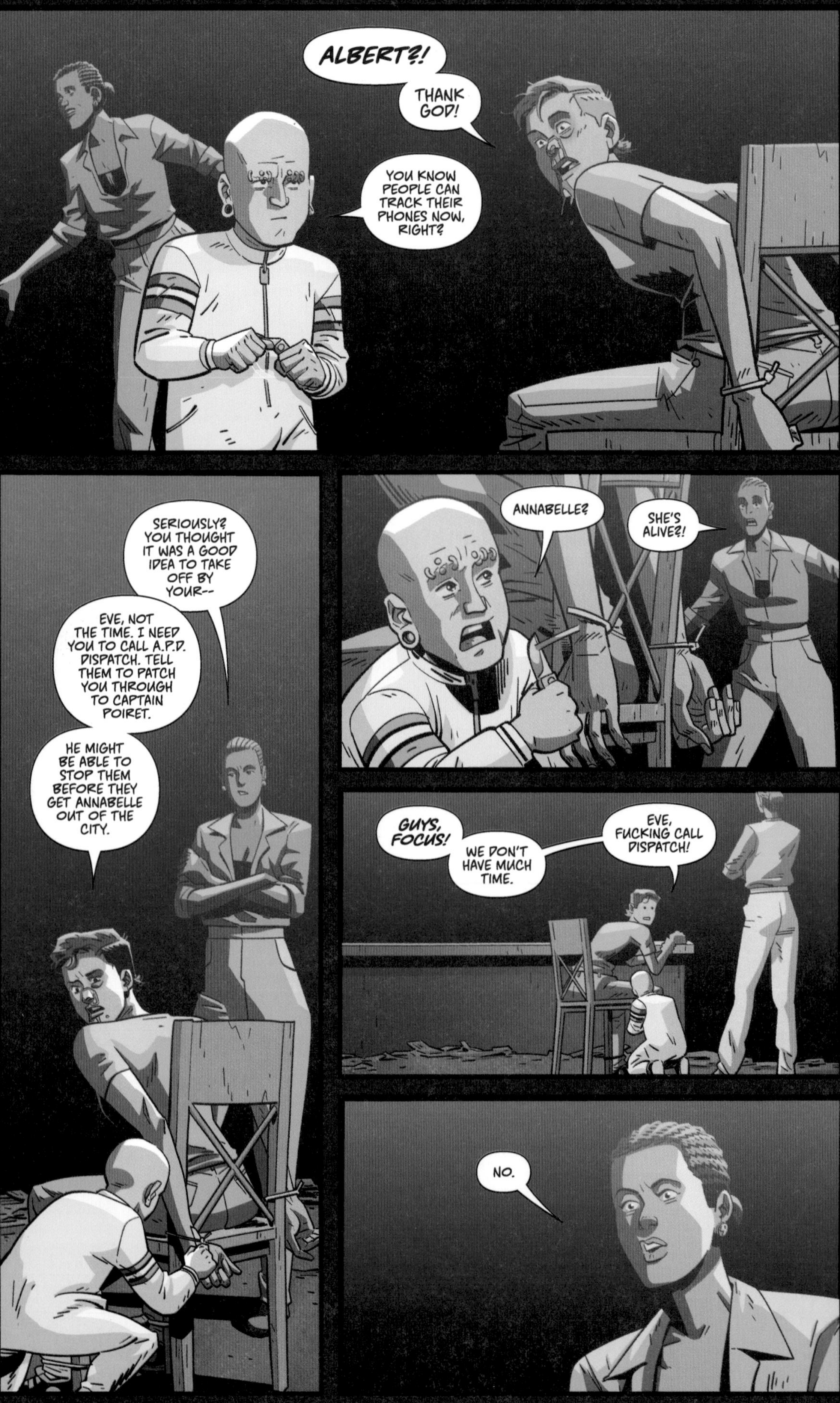
ALBERT?!
THANK GOD!
YOU KNOW PEOPLE CAN TRACK THEIR PHONES NOW, RIGHT?
SERIOUSLY? YOU THOUGHT IT WAS A GOOD IDEA TO TAKE OFF BY YOUR--
EVE, NOT THE TIME. I NEED YOU TO CALL A.P.D. DISPATCH. TELL THEM TO PATCH YOU THROUGH TO CAPTAIN POIRET.
HE MIGHT BE ABLE TO STOP THEM BEFORE THEY GET ANNABELLE OUT OF THE CITY.
ANNABELLE?
SHE'S ALIVE?!
GUYS, FOCUS!
WE DON'T HAVE MUCH TIME.
EVE, FUCKING CALL DISPATCH!
NO.

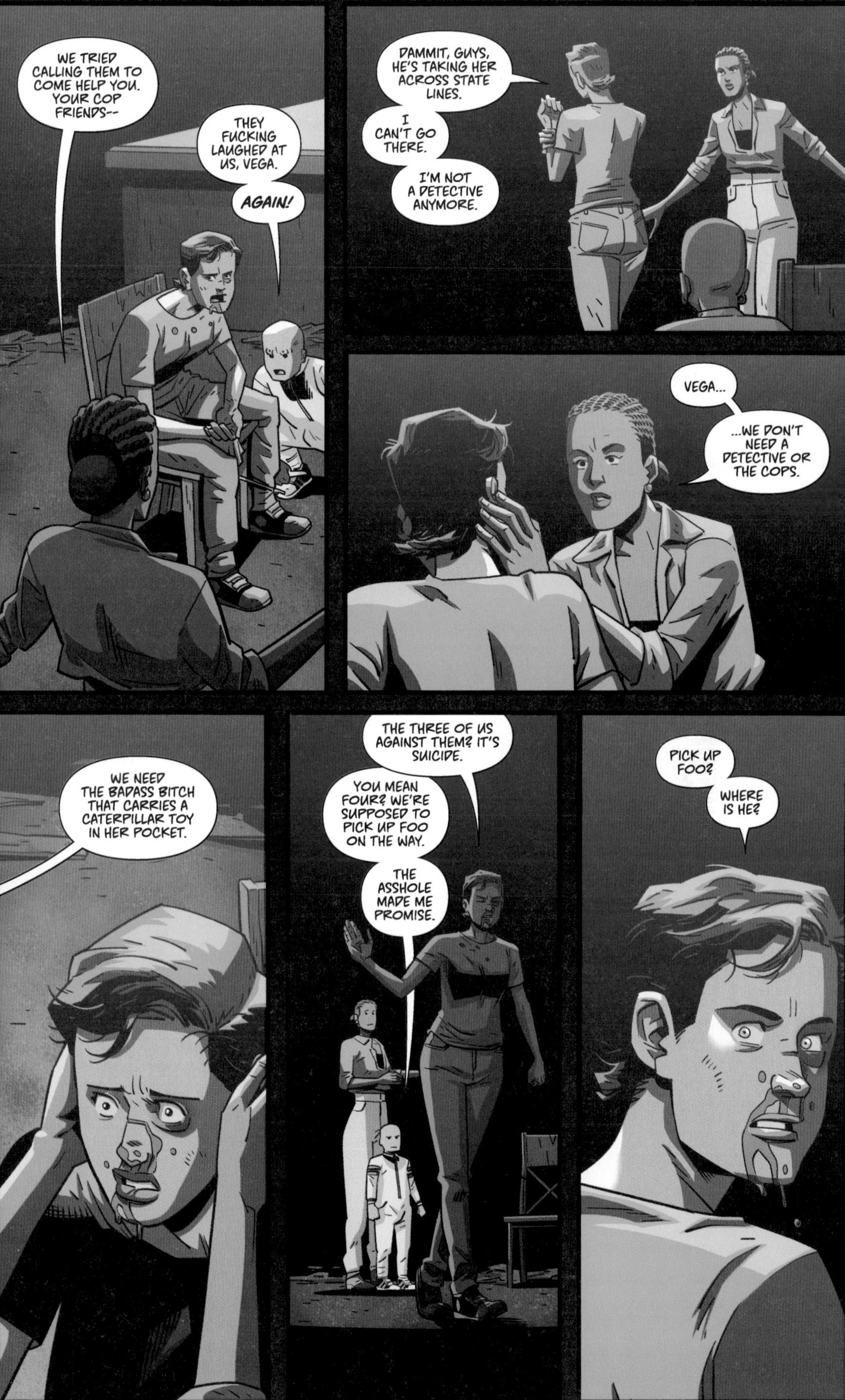
WE TRIED CALLING THEM TO COME HELP YOU. YOUR COP FRIENDS--
THEY FUCKING LAUGHED AT US, VEGA.
AGAIN!
DAMMIT, GUYS, HE'S TAKING HER ACROSS STATE LINES.
I CAN'T GO THERE.
I'M NOT A DETECTIVE ANYMORE.
VEGA...
...WE DON'T NEED A DETECTIVE OR THE COPS.
WE NEED THE BADASS BITCH THAT CARRIES A CATERPILLAR TOY IN HER POCKET.
THE THREE OF US AGAINST THEM? IT'S SUICIDE.
YOU MEAN FOUR? WE'RE SUPPOSED TO PICK UP FOO ON THE WAY.
THE ASSHOLE MADE ME PROMISE.
PICK UP FOO?
WHERE IS HE?

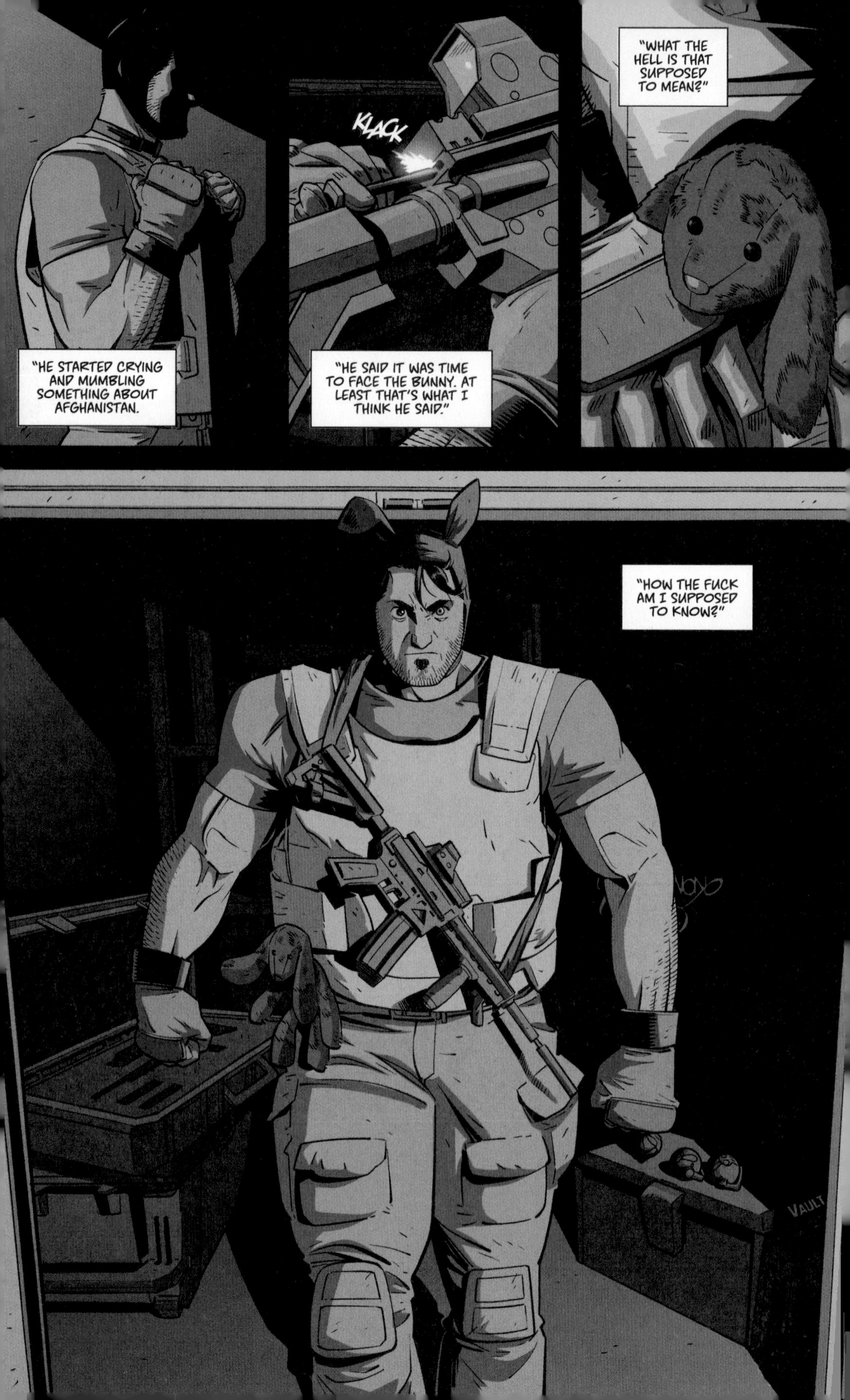
"HE STARTED CRYING AND MUMBLING SOMETHING ABOUT AFGHANISTAN.
KLACK
"HE SAID IT WAS TIME TO FACE THE BUNNY. AT LEAST THAT'S WHAT I THINK HE SAID."
"WHAT THE HELL IS THAT SUPPOSED TO MEAN?"
"HOW THE FUCK AM I SUPPOSED TO KNOW?"
VAULT

"Nun"

DOUG WAGNER

STORY

TOMM COKER

ART

ED DUKESHIRE

LETTERS

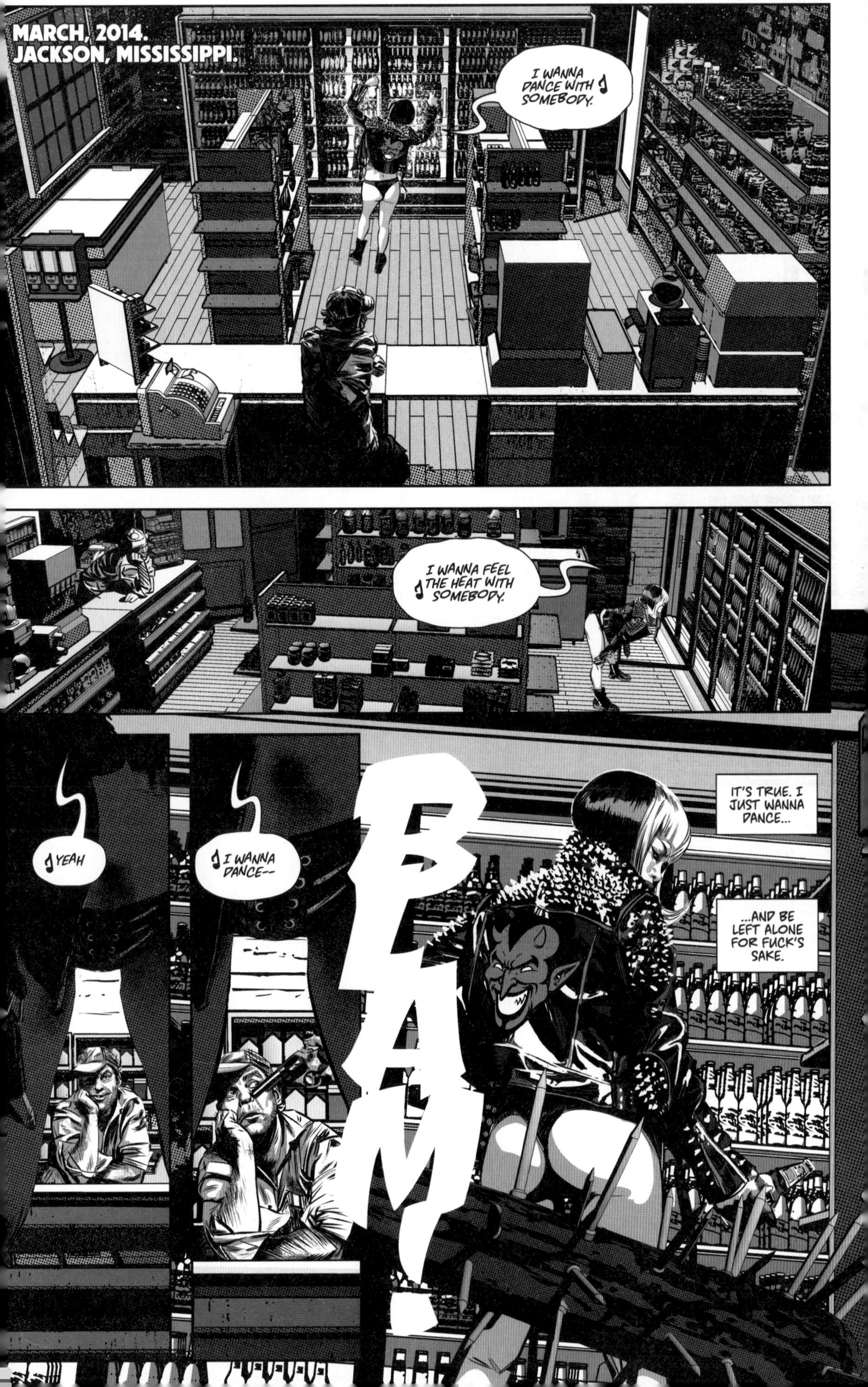
MARCH, 2014.
JACKSON, MISSISSIPPI.
I WANNA DANCE WITH ♪ SOMEBODY.
♪ I WANNA FEEL THE HEAT WITH SOMEBODY.
♪ YEAH
♪ I WANNA DANCE--
BLAM!
IT'S TRUE. I JUST WANNA DANCE...
...AND BE LEFT ALONE FOR FUCK'S SAKE.

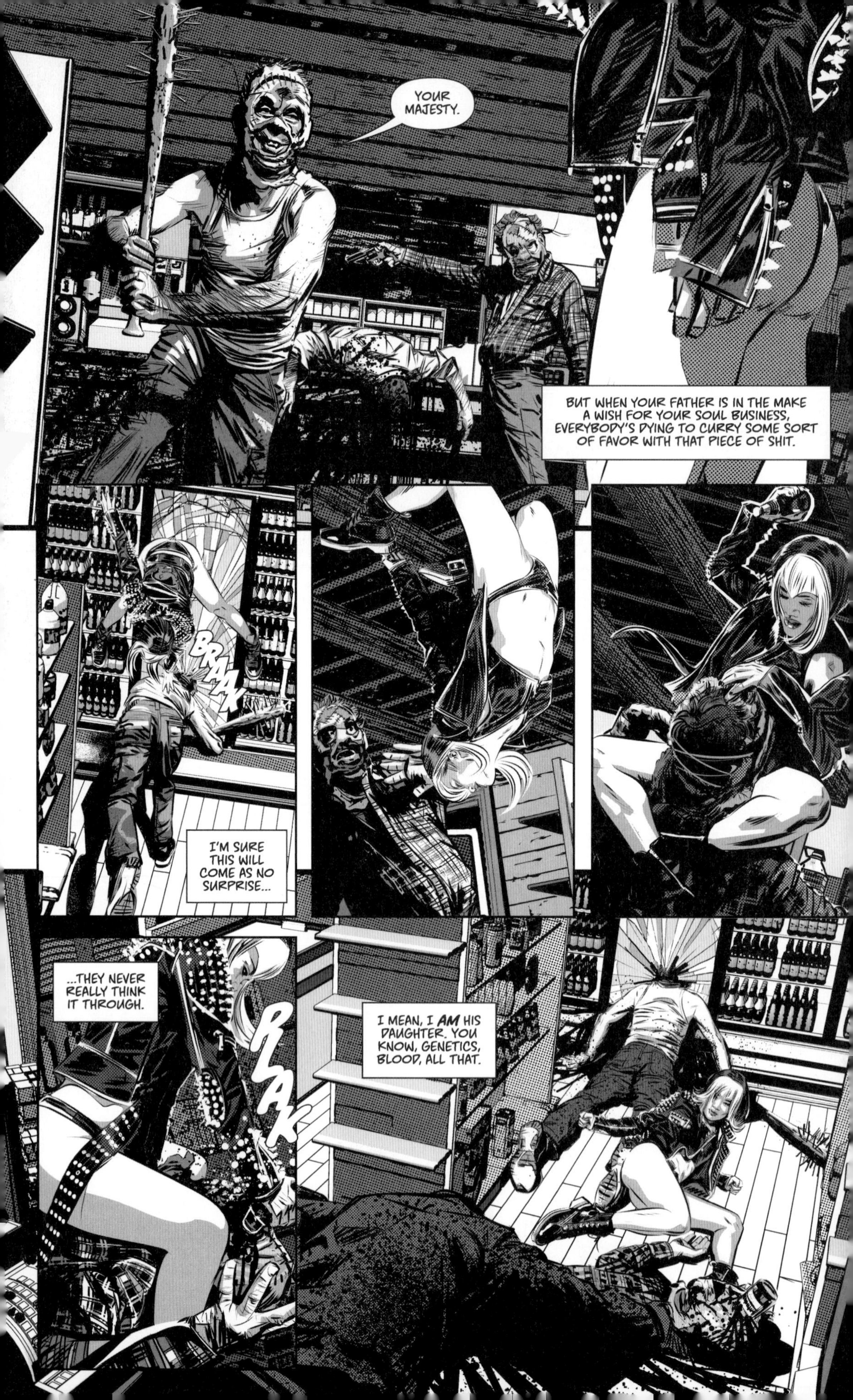
YOUR MAJESTY.
BUT WHEN YOUR FATHER IS IN THE MAKE A WISH FOR YOUR SOUL BUSINESS, EVERYBODY'S DYING TO CURRY SOME SORT OF FAVOR WITH THAT PIECE OF SHIT.
BRAAK
I'M SURE THIS WILL COME AS NO SURPRISE...
...THEY NEVER REALLY THINK IT THROUGH.
I MEAN, I **AM** HIS DAUGHTER. YOU KNOW, GENETICS, BLOOD, ALL THAT.

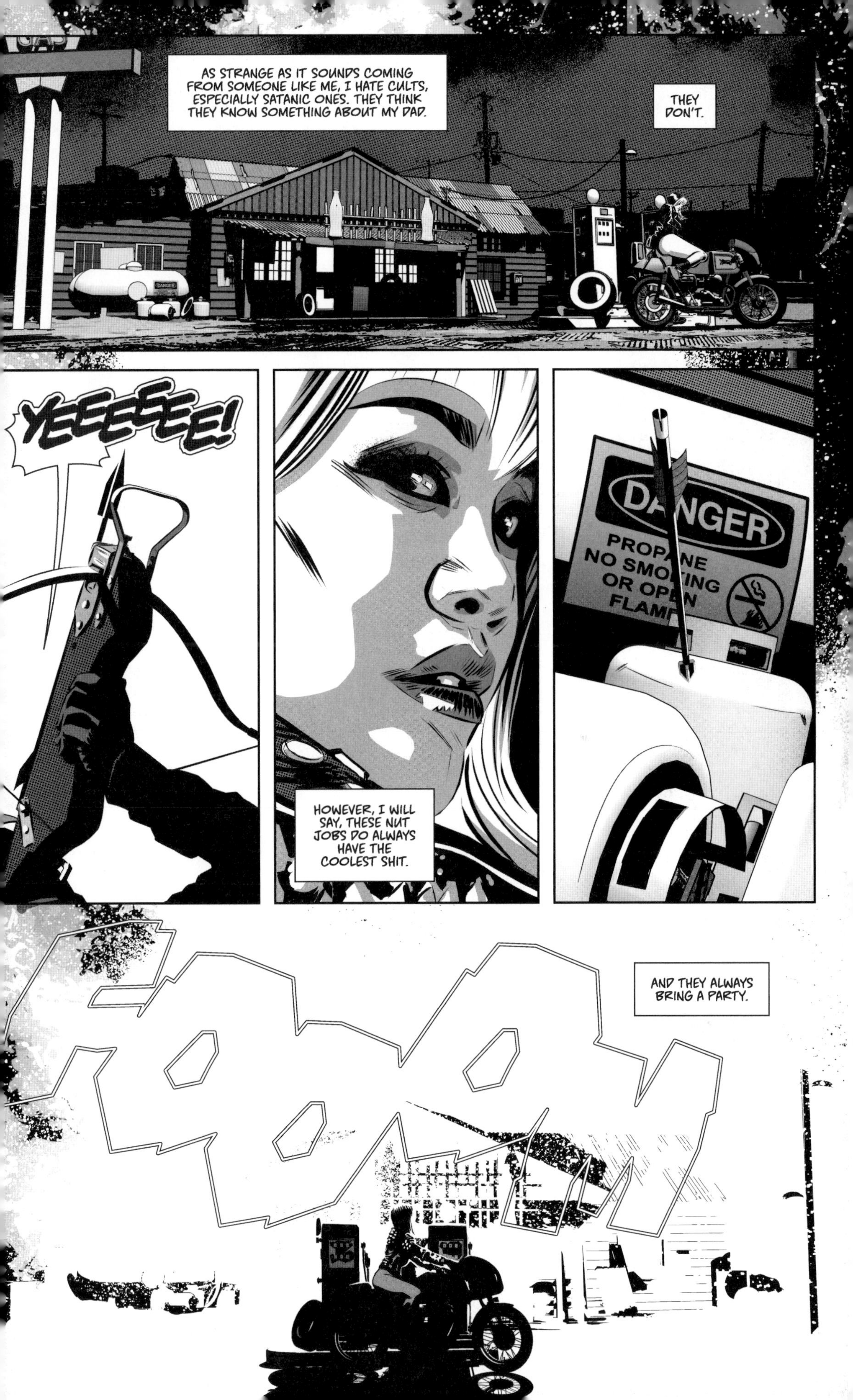
AS STRANGE AS IT SOUNDS COMING FROM SOMEONE LIKE ME, I HATE CULTS, ESPECIALLY SATANIC ONES. THEY THINK THEY KNOW SOMETHING ABOUT MY DAD.
THEY DON'T.
YEEEEEEE!
HOWEVER, I WILL SAY, THESE NUT JOBS DO ALWAYS HAVE THE COOLEST SHIT.
DANGER
PROPANE NO SMOKING OR OPEN FLAME
AND THEY ALWAYS BRING A PARTY.

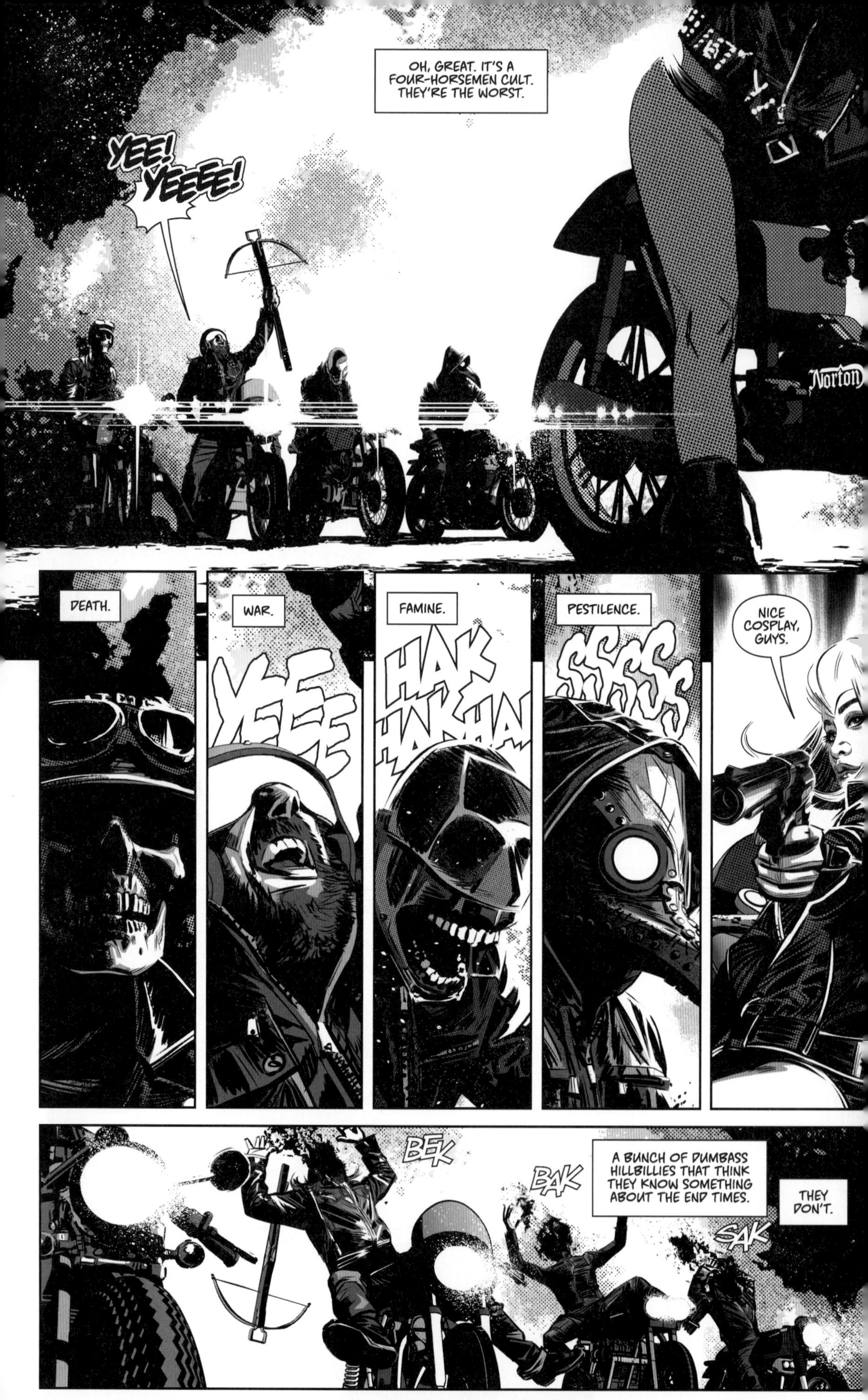
OH, GREAT. IT'S A FOUR-HORSEMEN CULT. THEY'RE THE WORST.
YEE! YEEEE!
Norton
DEATH.
WAR.
YEEE
FAMINE.
HAK HAKHA
PESTILENCE.
SSSSS
NICE COSPLAY, GUYS.
BEK
BAK
A BUNCH OF DUMBASS HILLBILLIES THAT THINK THEY KNOW SOMETHING ABOUT THE END TIMES.
THEY DON'T.
SAK

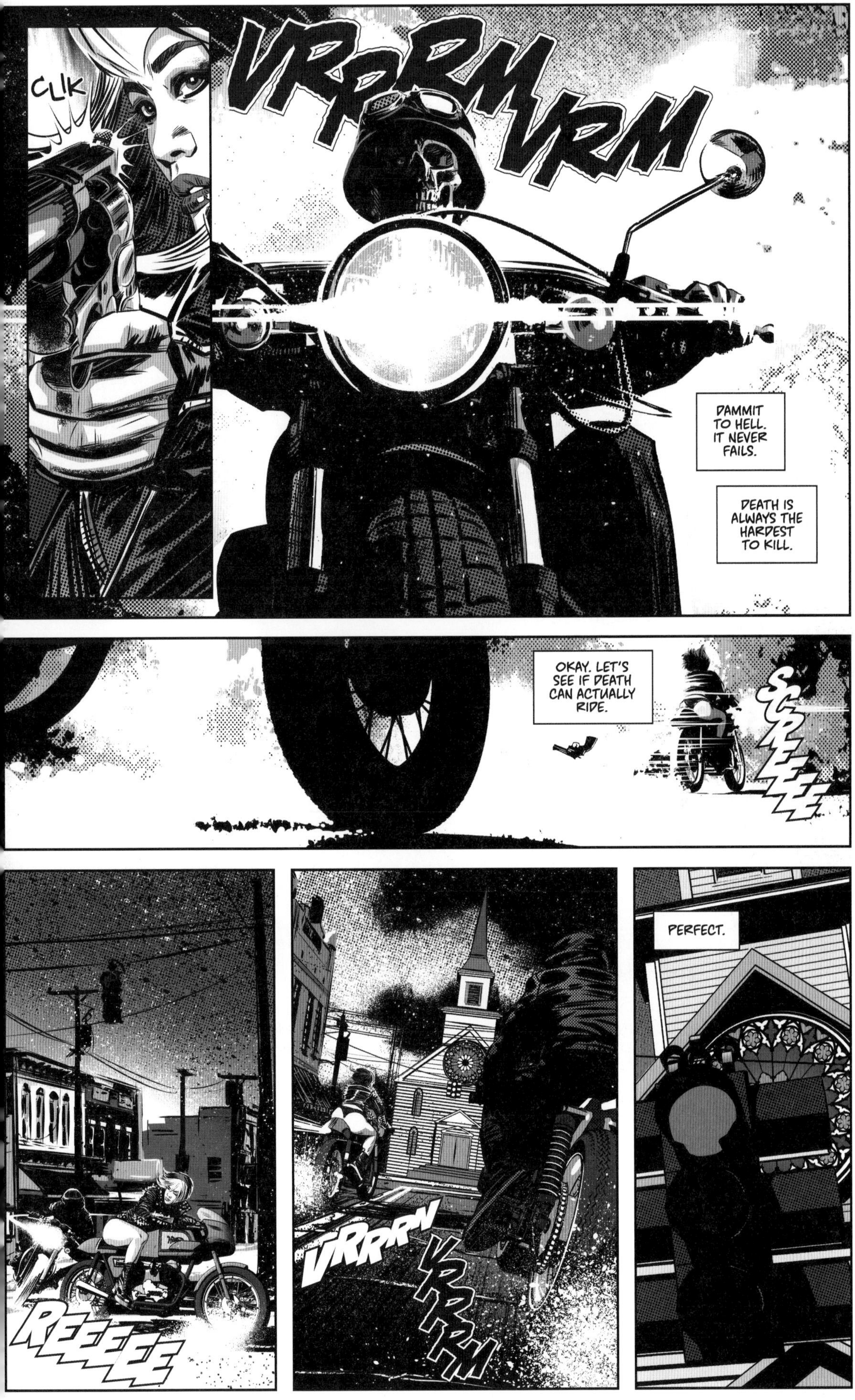
CLIK
VRRRM VRM
DAMMIT TO HELL. IT NEVER FAILS.
DEATH IS ALWAYS THE HARDEST TO KILL.
OKAY. LET'S SEE IF DEATH CAN ACTUALLY RIDE.
SCREEEE
REEEEEE
VRRRRN
VRRRM
PERFECT.

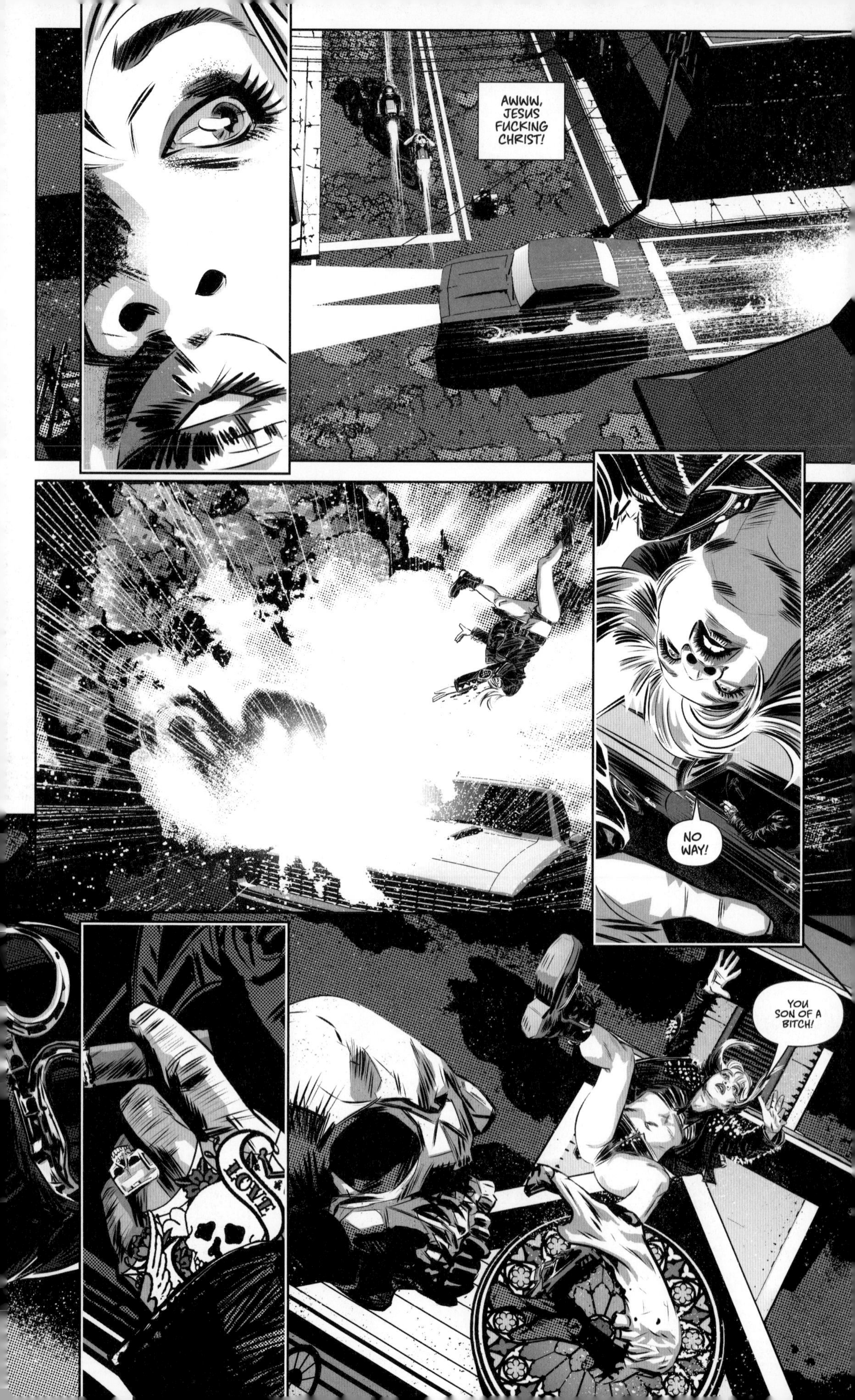
AWWW, JESUS FUCKING CHRIST!
NO WAY!
YOU SON OF A BITCH!

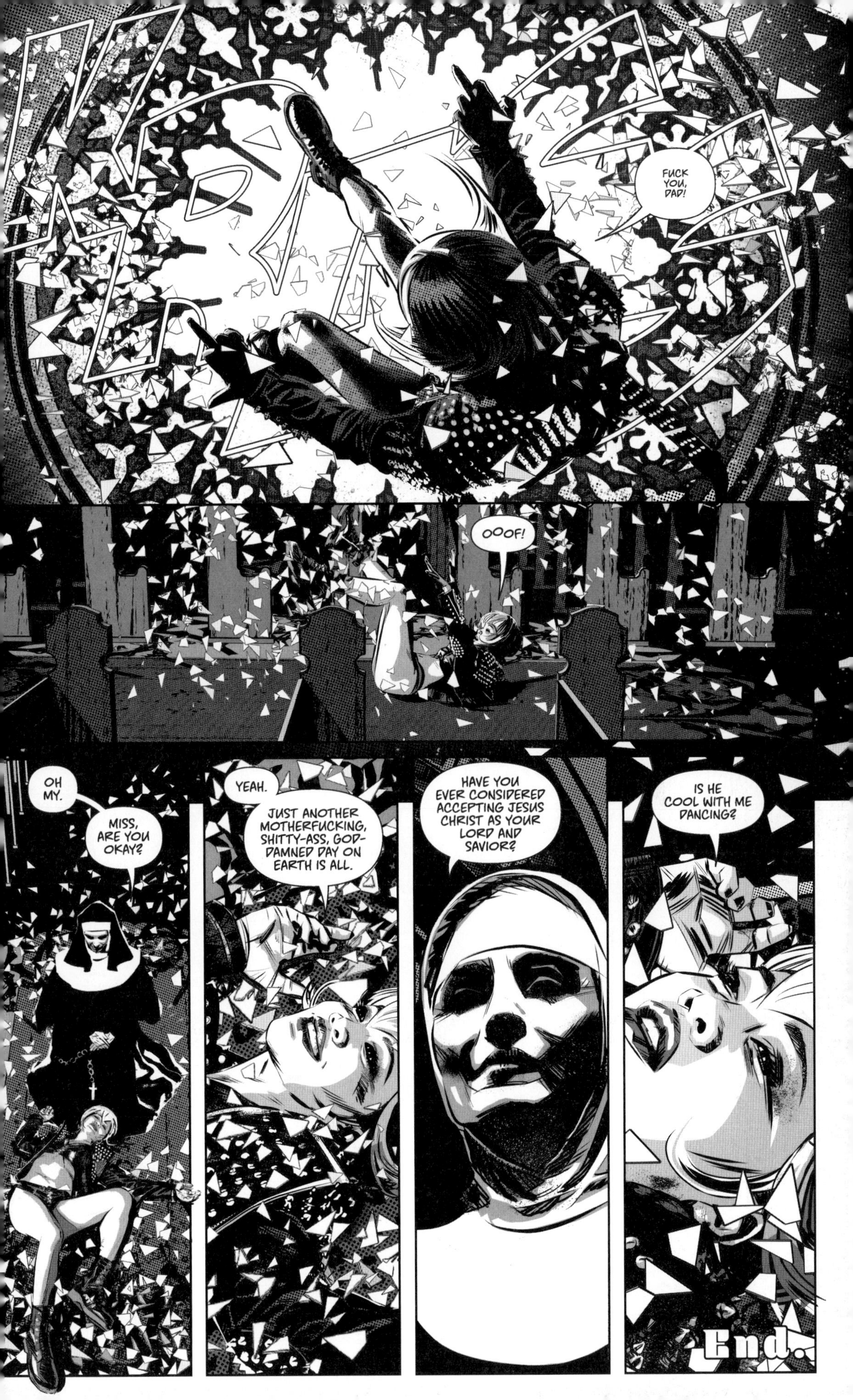
FUCK YOU, DAD!
OOOF!
OH MY.
MISS, ARE YOU OKAY?
YEAH.
JUST ANOTHER MOTHERFUCKING, SHITTY-ASS, GOD-DAMNED DAY ON EARTH IS ALL.
HAVE YOU EVER CONSIDERED ACCEPTING JESUS CHRIST AS YOUR LORD AND SAVIOR?
IS HE COOL WITH ME DANCING?
End.

BURNING DESIRE
CHAPTER FIVE

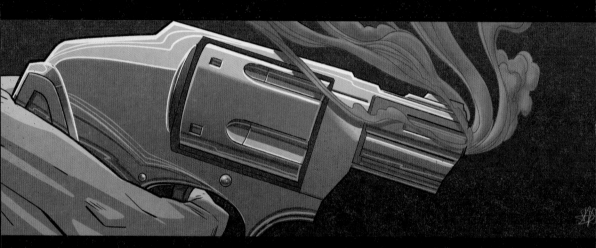

DOUG WAGNER

STORY

DANIEL HILLYARD

ART

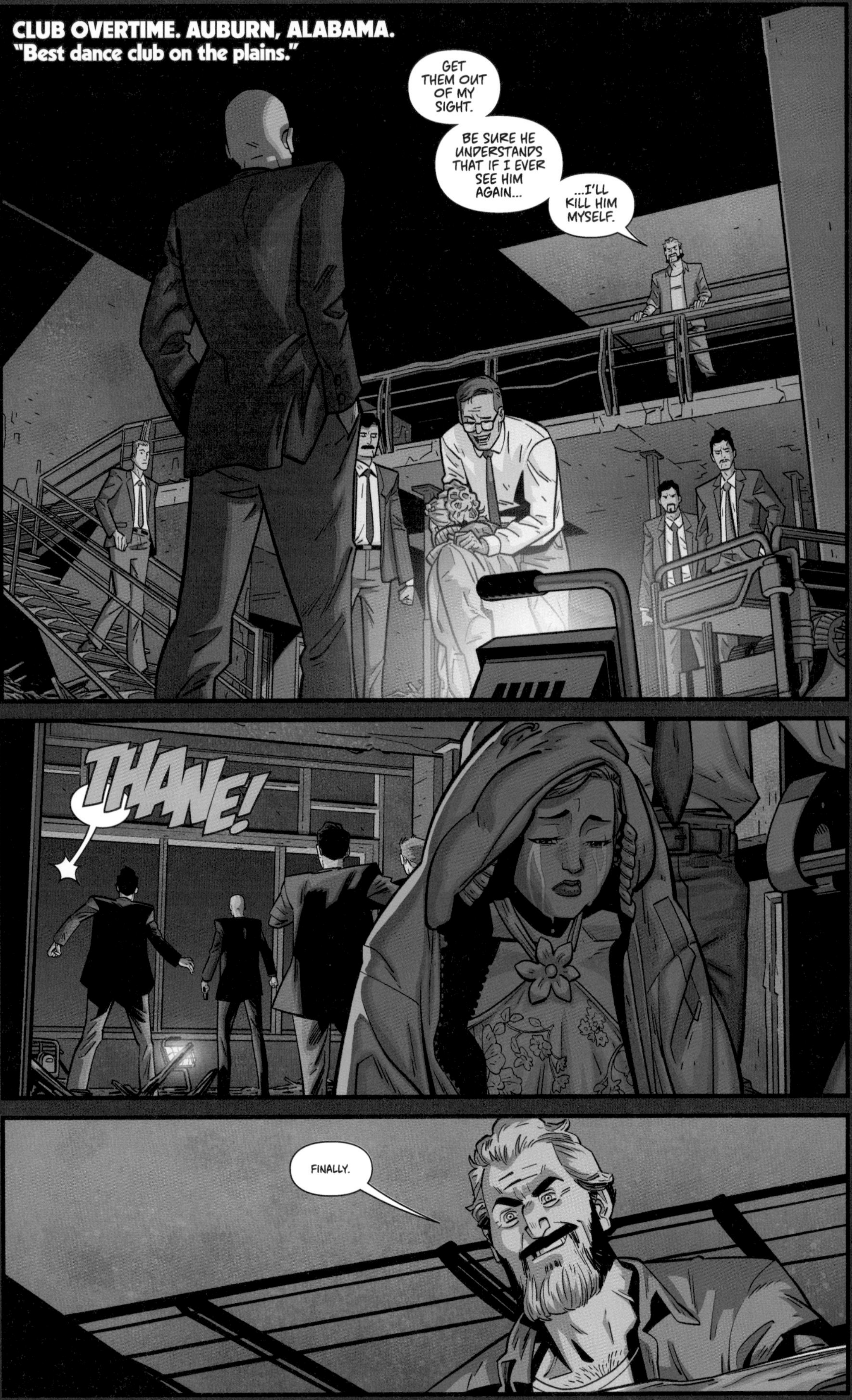
CLUB OVERTIME. AUBURN, ALABAMA.
"Best dance club on the plains."
GET THEM OUT OF MY SIGHT.
BE SURE HE UNDERSTANDS THAT IF I EVER SEE HIM AGAIN...
...I'LL KILL HIM MYSELF.
THANE!
FINALLY.

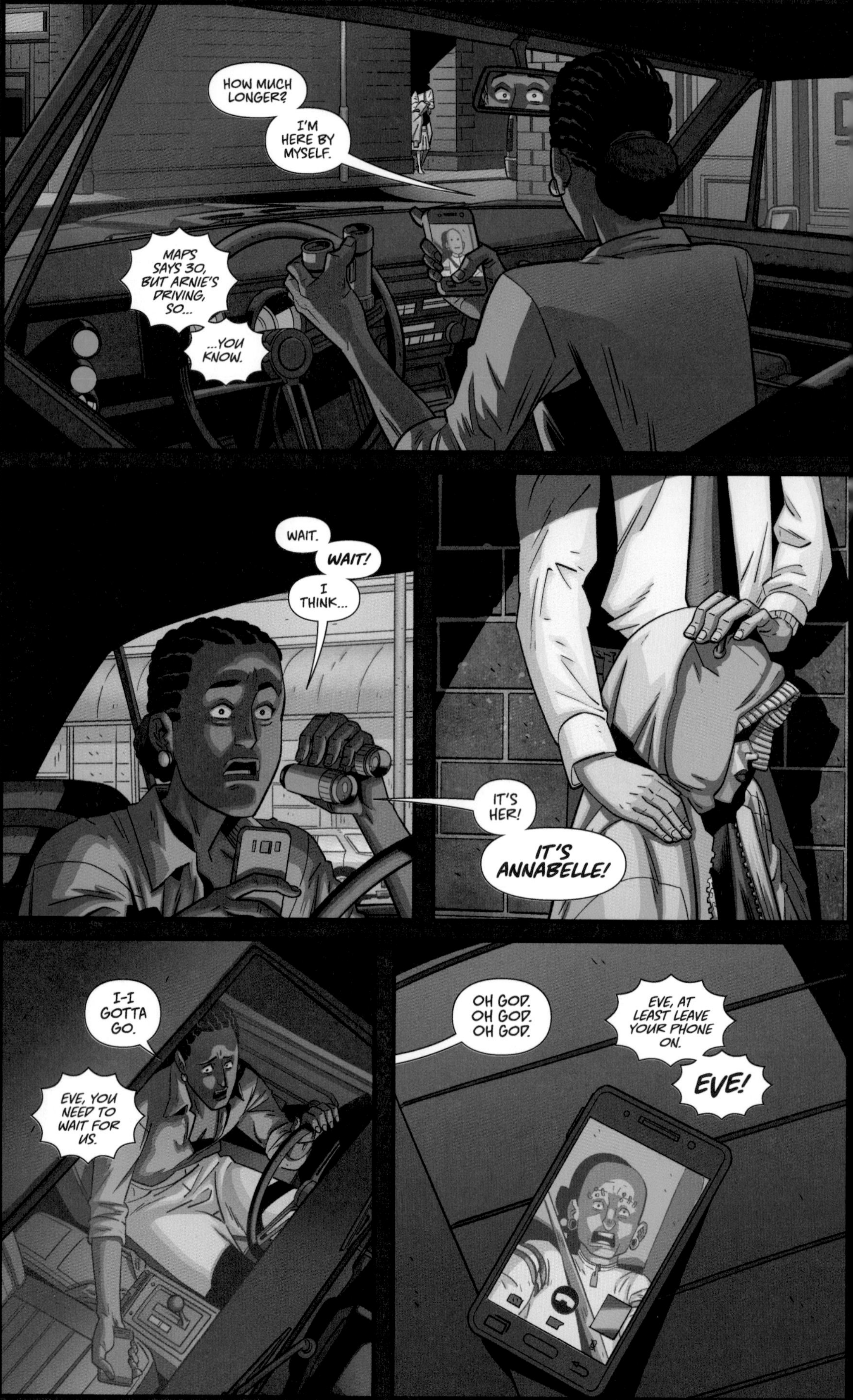
HOW MUCH LONGER?
I'M HERE BY MYSELF.
MAPS SAYS 30, BUT ARNIE'S DRIVING, SO...
...YOU KNOW.
WAIT.
WAIT!
I THINK...
IT'S HER!
IT'S ANNABELLE!
I-I GOTTA GO.
EVE, YOU NEED TO WAIT FOR US.
OH GOD. OH GOD. OH GOD.
EVE, AT LEAST LEAVE YOUR PHONE ON.
EVE!

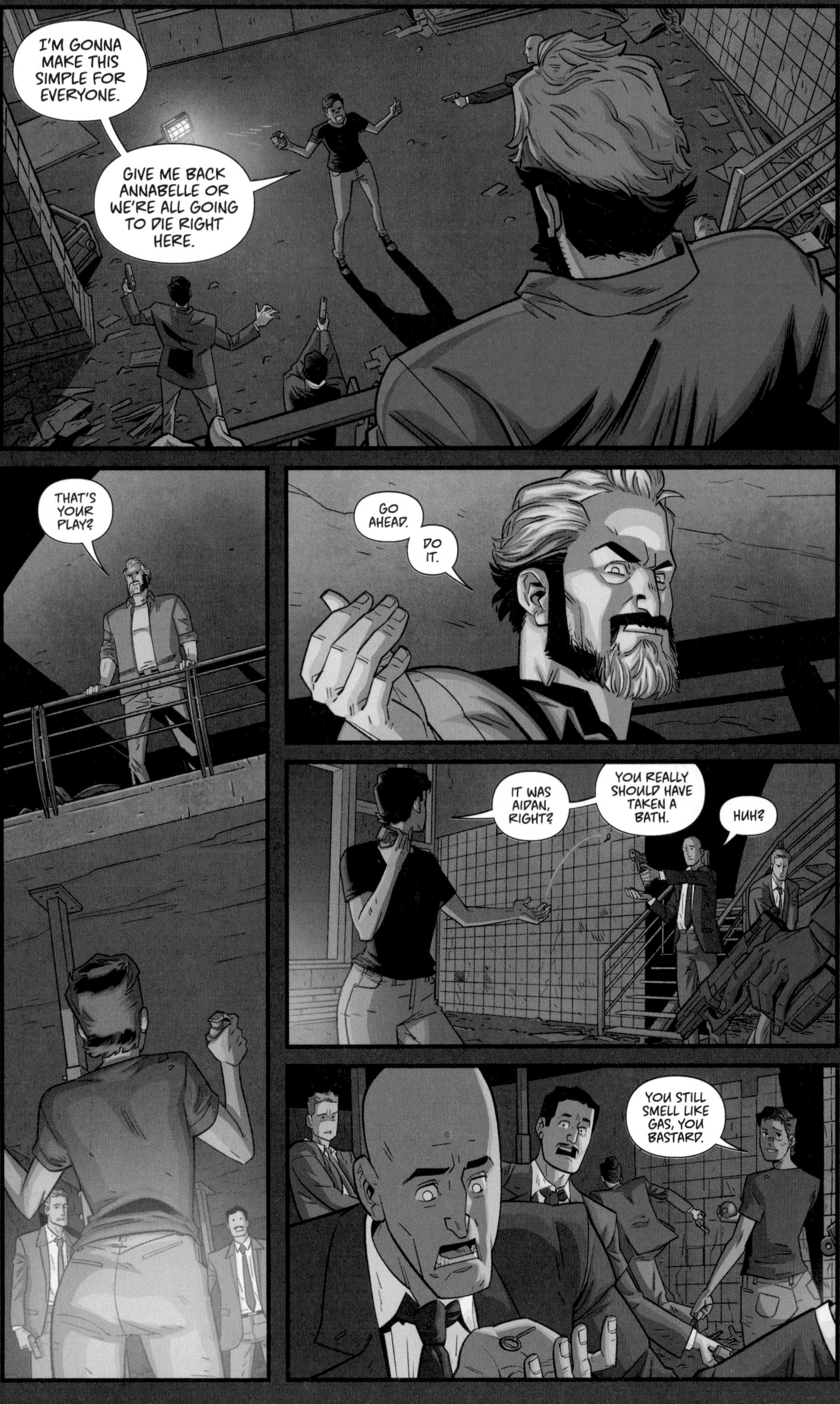
I'M GONNA MAKE THIS SIMPLE FOR EVERYONE.
GIVE ME BACK ANNABELLE OR WE'RE ALL GOING TO DIE RIGHT HERE.
THAT'S YOUR PLAY?
GO AHEAD.
DO IT.
IT WAS AIDAN, RIGHT?
YOU REALLY SHOULD HAVE TAKEN A BATH.
HUH?
YOU STILL SMELL LIKE GAS, YOU BASTARD.

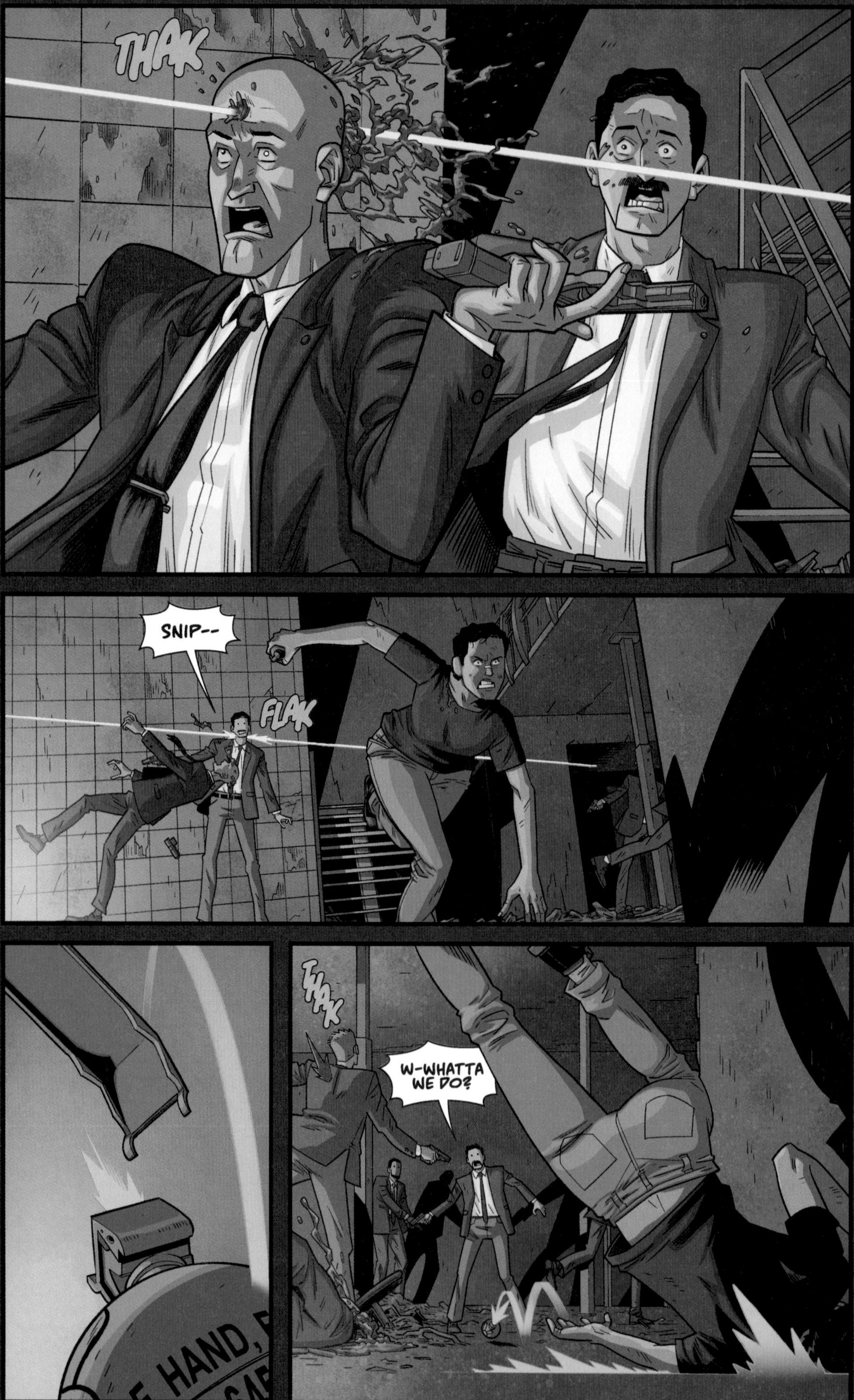
THAK
SNIP--
FLAK
THAK
W-WHATTA WE DO?
E HAND,

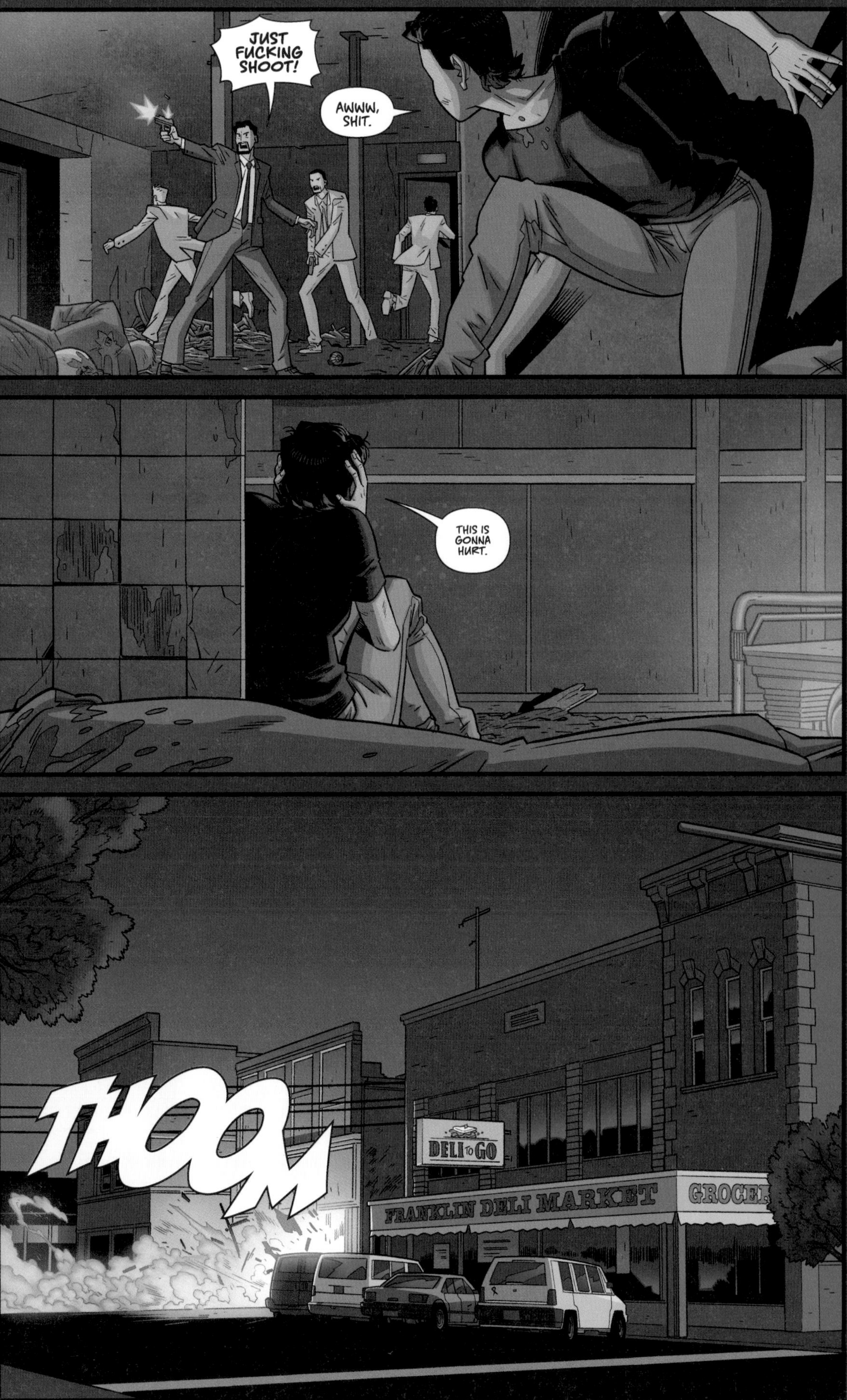
JUST FUCKING SHOOT!
AWWW, SHIT.
THIS IS GONNA HURT.
THOOM
DELI TO GO
FRANKLIN DELI MARKET
GROCE

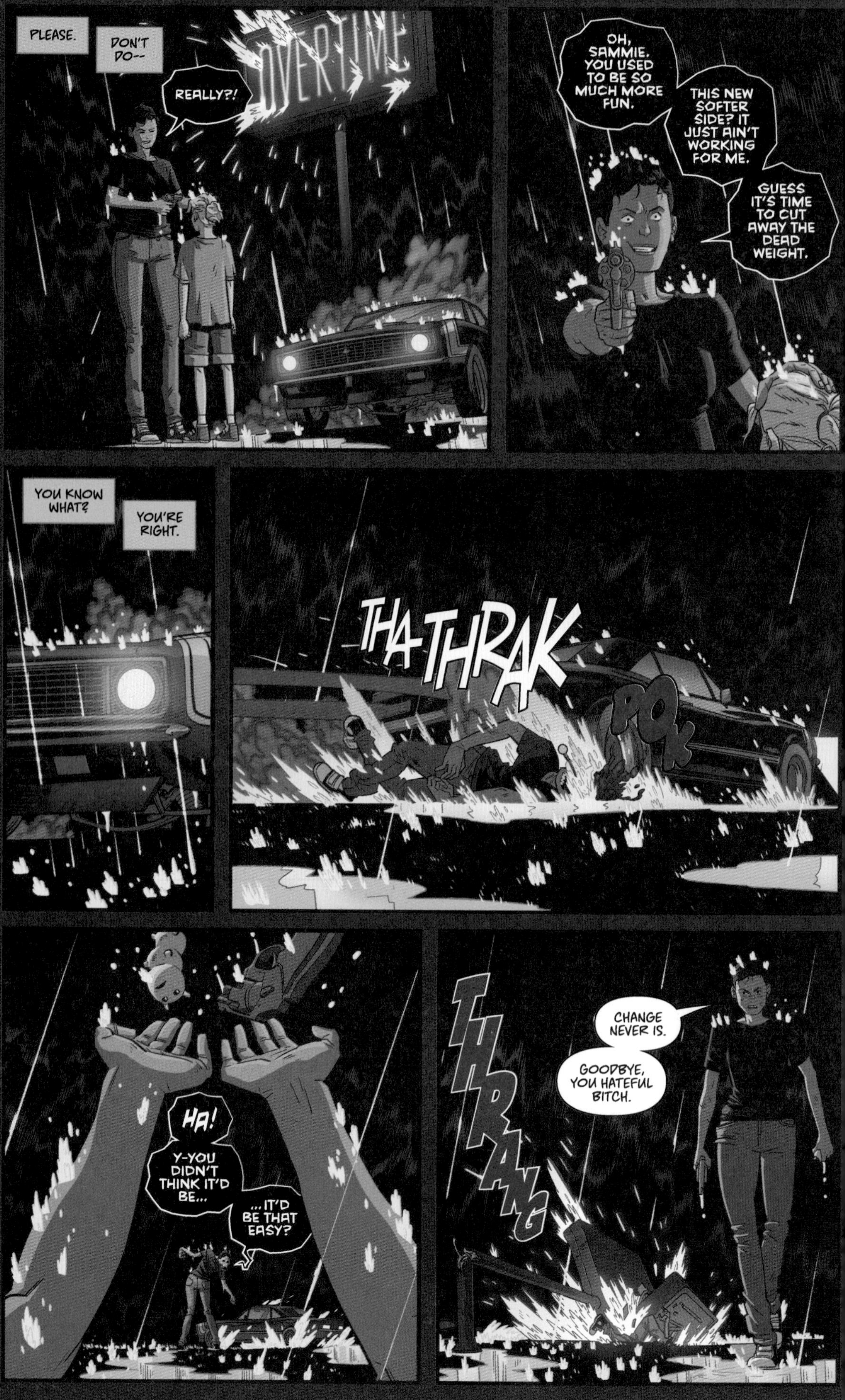
PLEASE.
DON'T DO--
REALLY?!
OVERTIME
OH, SAMMIE. YOU USED TO BE SO MUCH MORE FUN.
THIS NEW SOFTER SIDE? IT JUST AIN'T WORKING FOR ME.
GUESS IT'S TIME TO CUT AWAY THE DEAD WEIGHT.
YOU KNOW WHAT?
YOU'RE RIGHT.
THATHRAK
POK
HA!
Y-YOU DIDN'T THINK IT'D BE...
...IT'D BE THAT EASY?
THRANG
CHANGE NEVER IS.
GOODBYE, YOU HATEFUL BITCH.

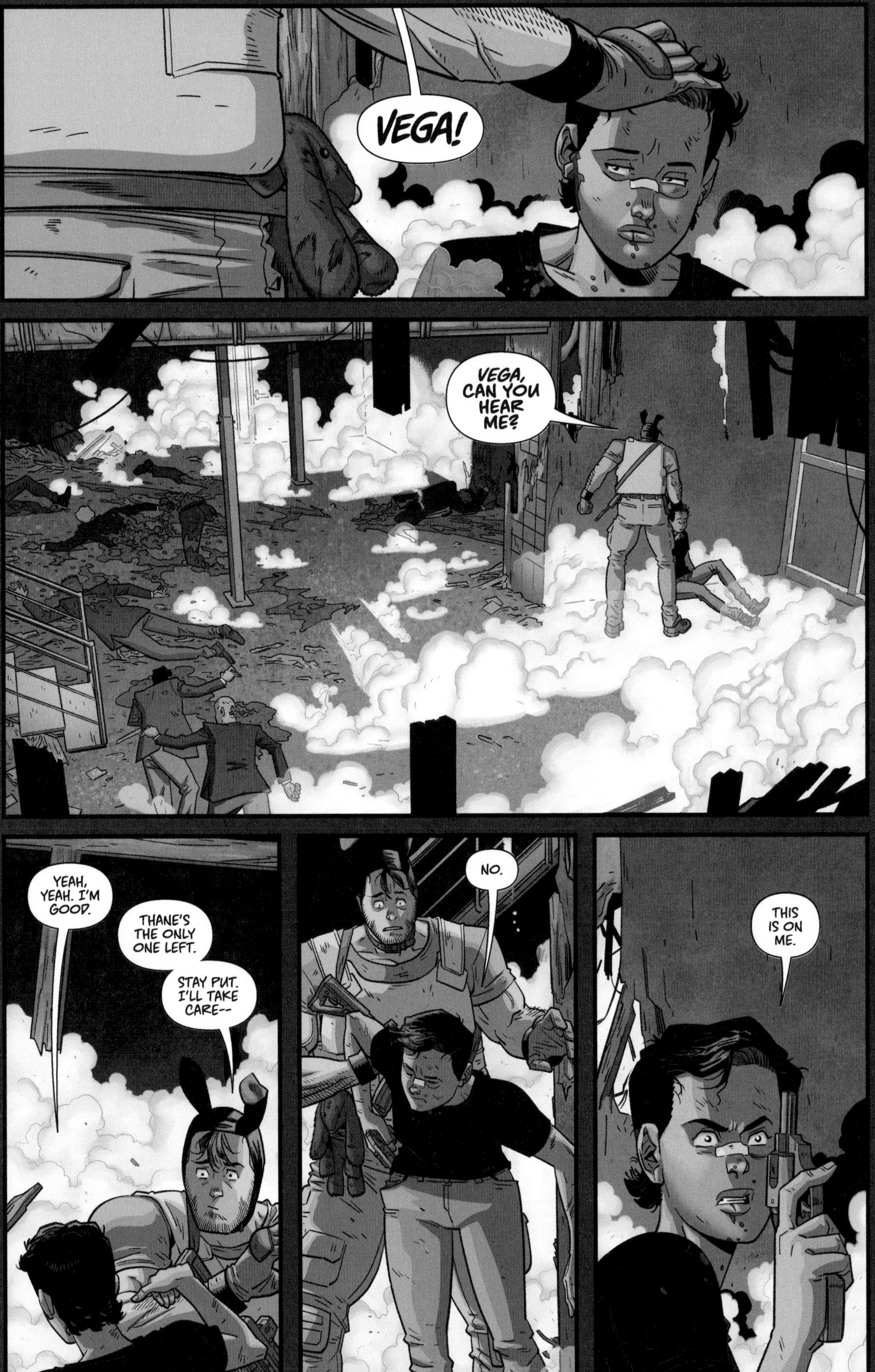
VEGA!
VEGA, CAN YOU HEAR ME?
YEAH, YEAH. I'M GOOD.
THANE'S THE ONLY ONE LEFT.
STAY PUT. I'LL TAKE CARE--
NO.
THIS IS ON ME.

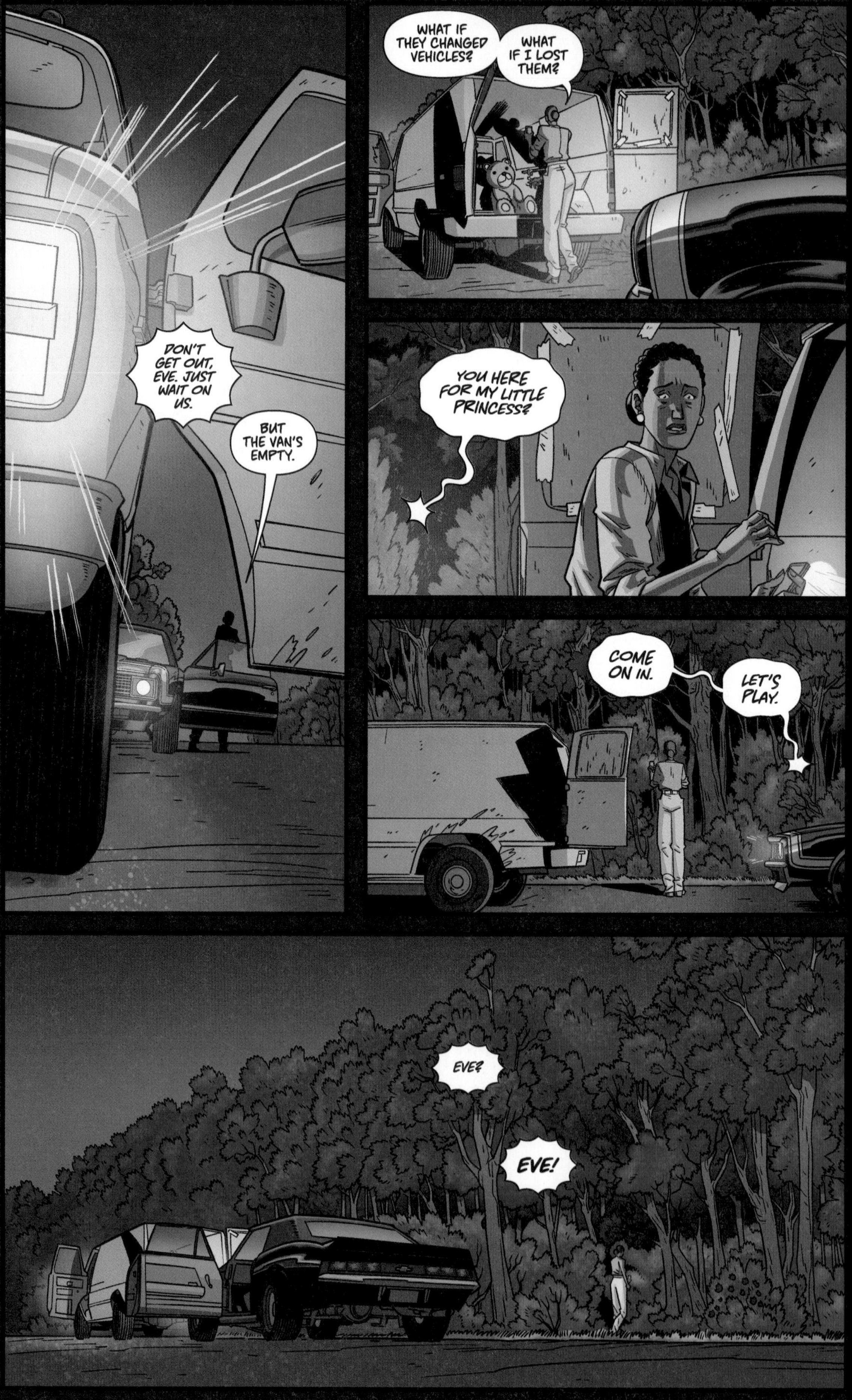
DON'T GET OUT, EVE. JUST WAIT ON US.
BUT THE VAN'S EMPTY.
WHAT IF THEY CHANGED VEHICLES?
WHAT IF I LOST THEM?
YOU HERE FOR MY LITTLE PRINCESS?
COME ON IN.
LET'S PLAY.
EVE?
EVE!

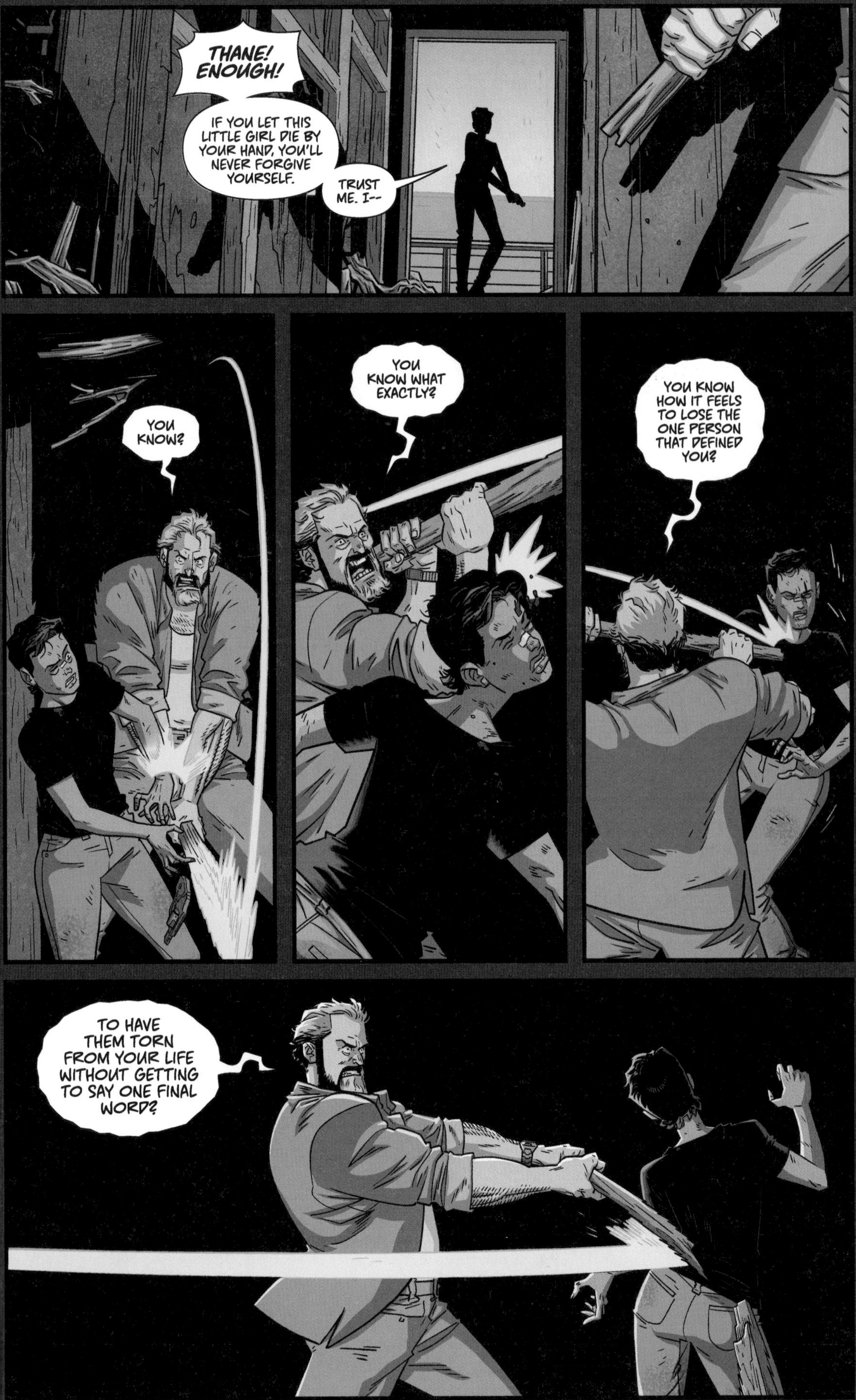
THANE! ENOUGH!
IF YOU LET THIS LITTLE GIRL DIE BY YOUR HAND, YOU'LL NEVER FORGIVE YOURSELF.
TRUST ME. I--
YOU KNOW?
YOU KNOW WHAT EXACTLY?
YOU KNOW HOW IT FEELS TO LOSE THE ONE PERSON THAT DEFINED YOU?
TO HAVE THEM TORN FROM YOUR LIFE WITHOUT GETTING TO SAY ONE FINAL WORD?

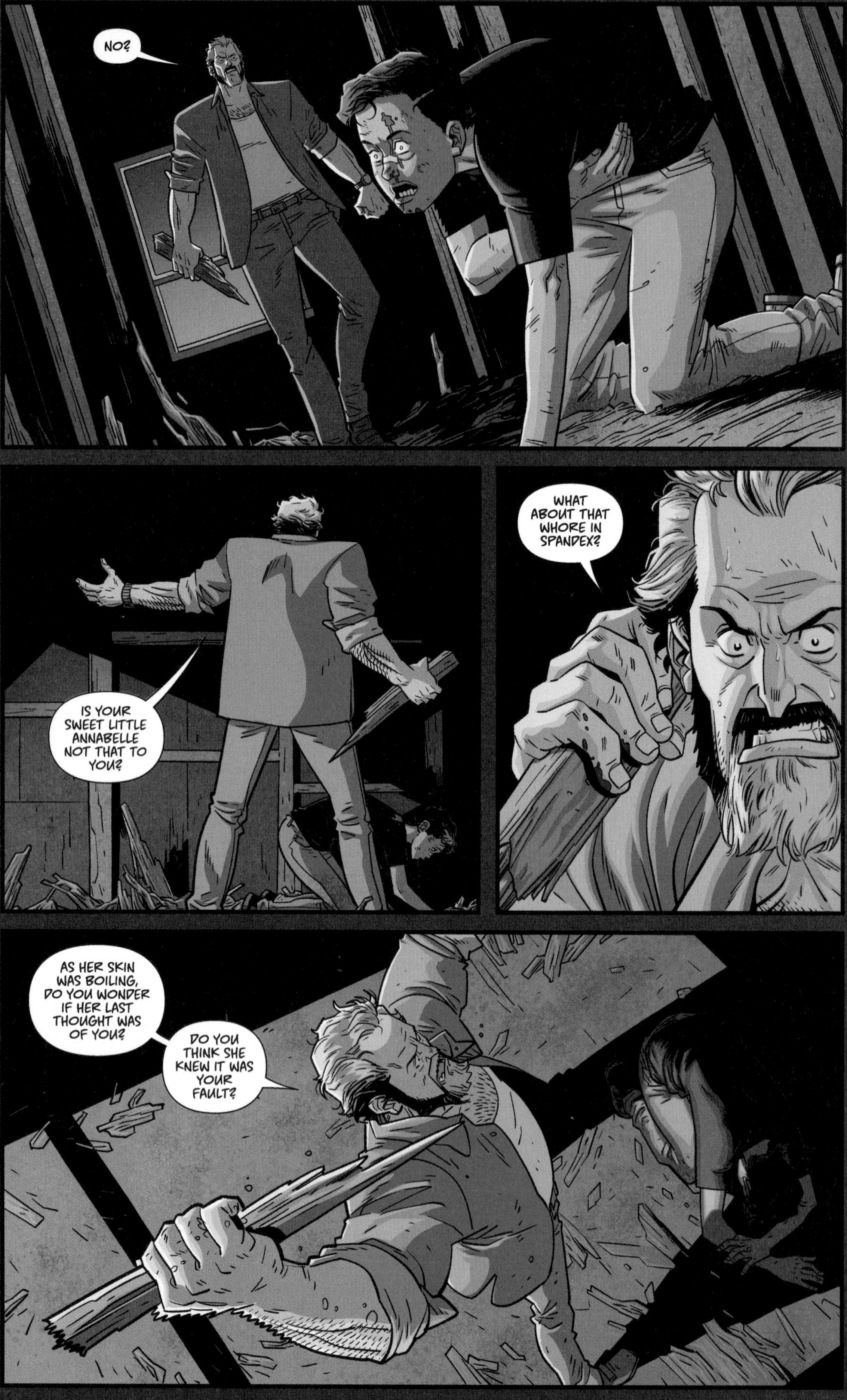
NO?
IS YOUR SWEET LITTLE ANNABELLE NOT THAT TO YOU?
WHAT ABOUT THAT WHORE IN SPANDEX?
AS HER SKIN WAS BOILING, DO YOU WONDER IF HER LAST THOUGHT WAS OF YOU?
DO YOU THINK SHE KNEW IT WAS YOUR FAULT?

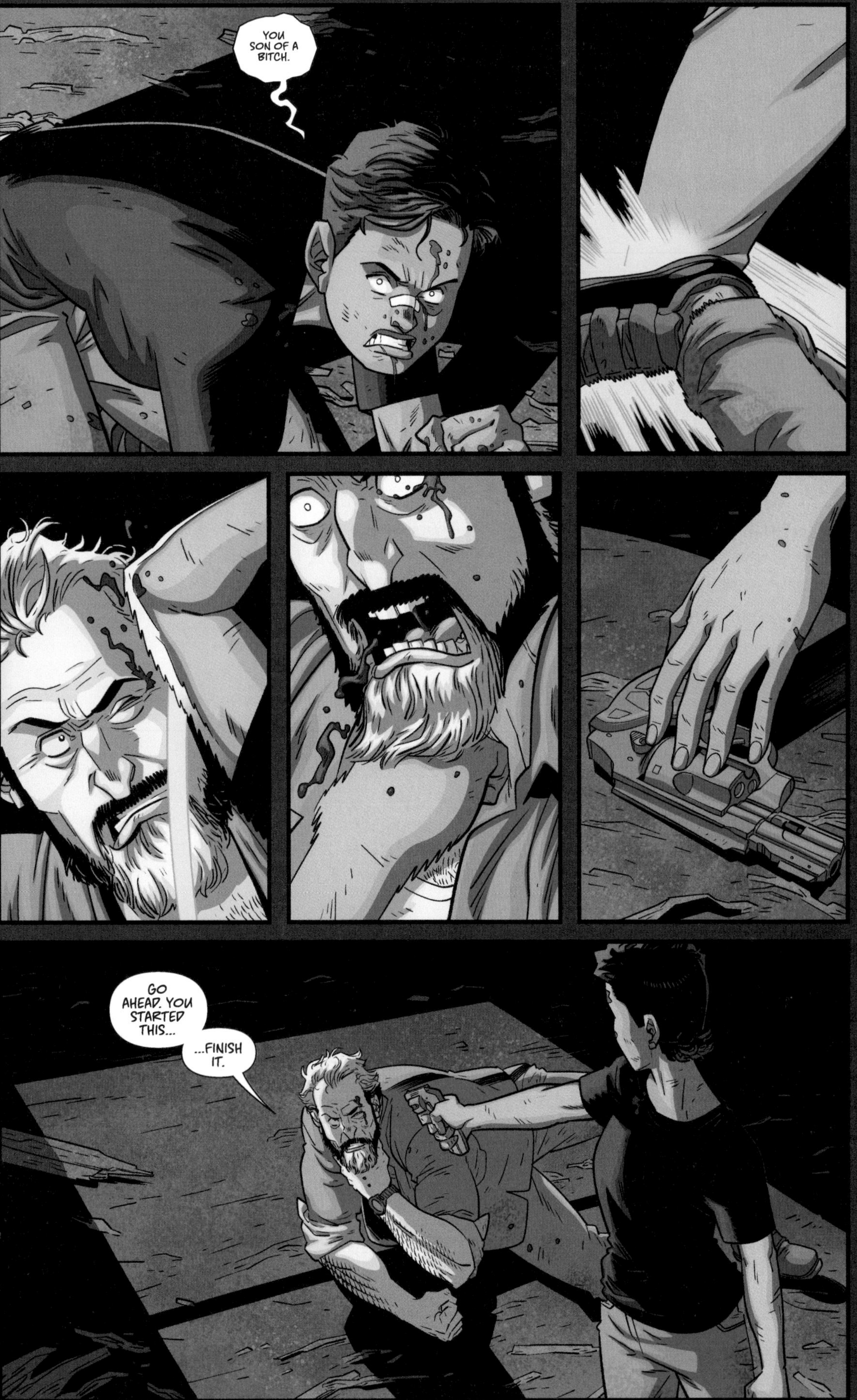
YOU SON OF A BITCH.
GO AHEAD. YOU STARTED THIS...
...FINISH IT.

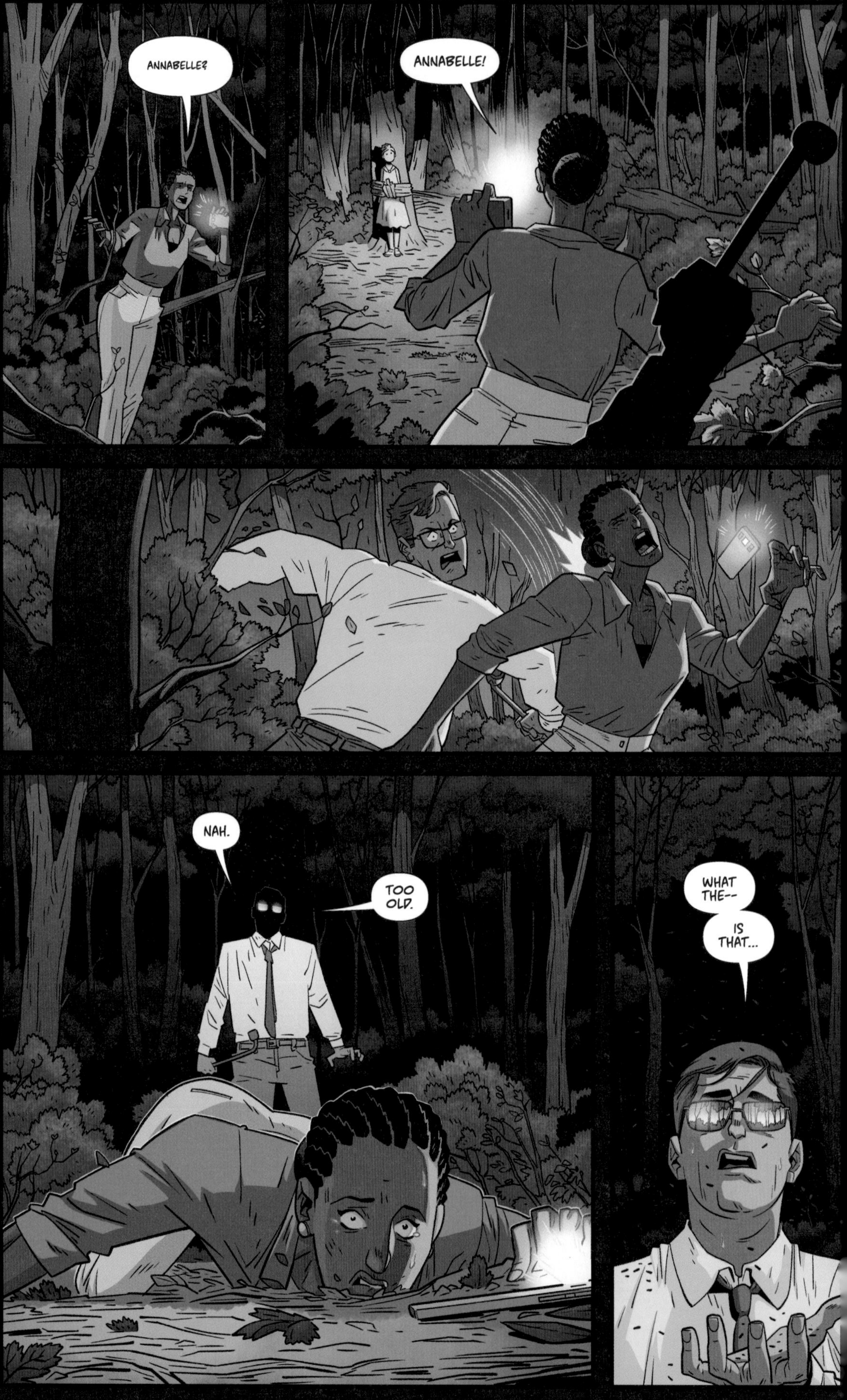
ANNABELLE?
ANNABELLE!
NAH.
TOO OLD.
WHAT THE--
IS THAT...

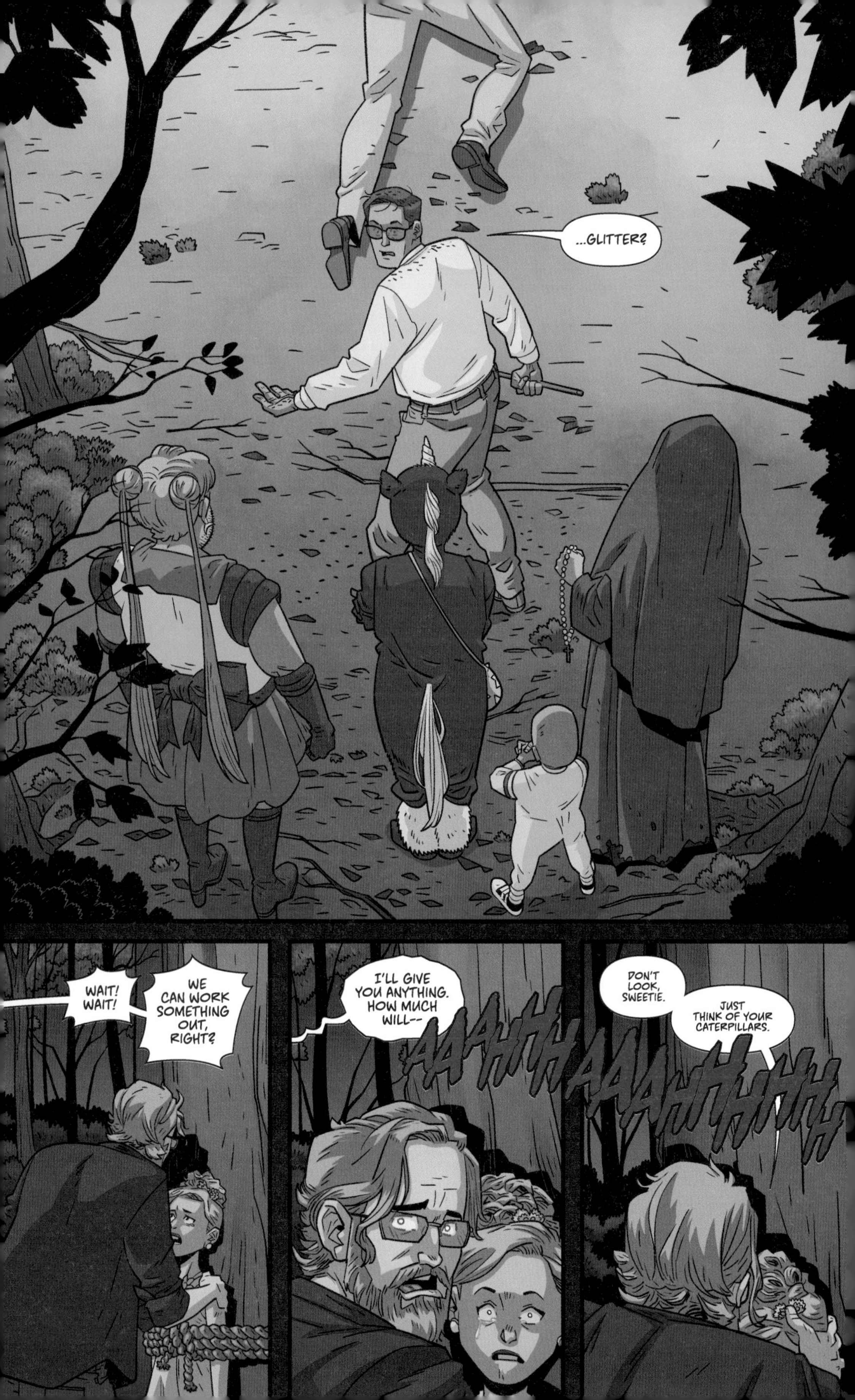
...GLITTER?
WAIT! WAIT!
WE CAN WORK SOMETHING OUT, RIGHT?
I'LL GIVE YOU ANYTHING. HOW MUCH WILL--
AAHHHAAAHHHHH
DON'T LOOK, SWEETIE.
JUST THINK OF YOUR CATERPILLARS.

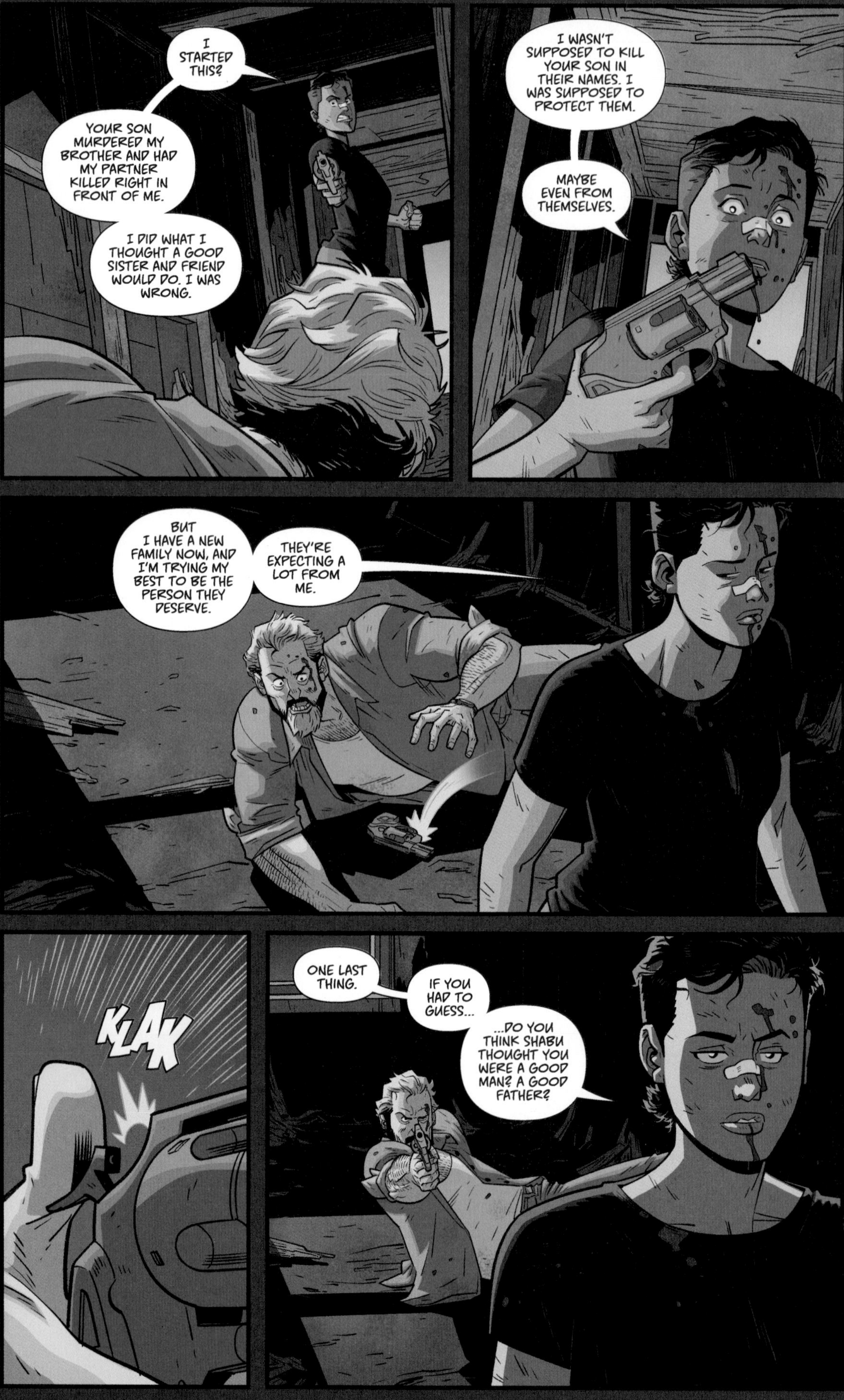
I STARTED THIS?
YOUR SON MURDERED MY BROTHER AND HAD MY PARTNER KILLED RIGHT IN FRONT OF ME.
I DID WHAT I THOUGHT A GOOD SISTER AND FRIEND WOULD DO. I WAS WRONG.
I WASN'T SUPPOSED TO KILL YOUR SON IN THEIR NAMES. I WAS SUPPOSED TO PROTECT THEM.
MAYBE EVEN FROM THEMSELVES.
BUT I HAVE A NEW FAMILY NOW, AND I'M TRYING MY BEST TO BE THE PERSON THEY DESERVE.
THEY'RE EXPECTING A LOT FROM ME.
KLAK
ONE LAST THING.
IF YOU HAD TO GUESS...
...DO YOU THINK SHABU THOUGHT YOU WERE A GOOD MAN? A GOOD FATHER?

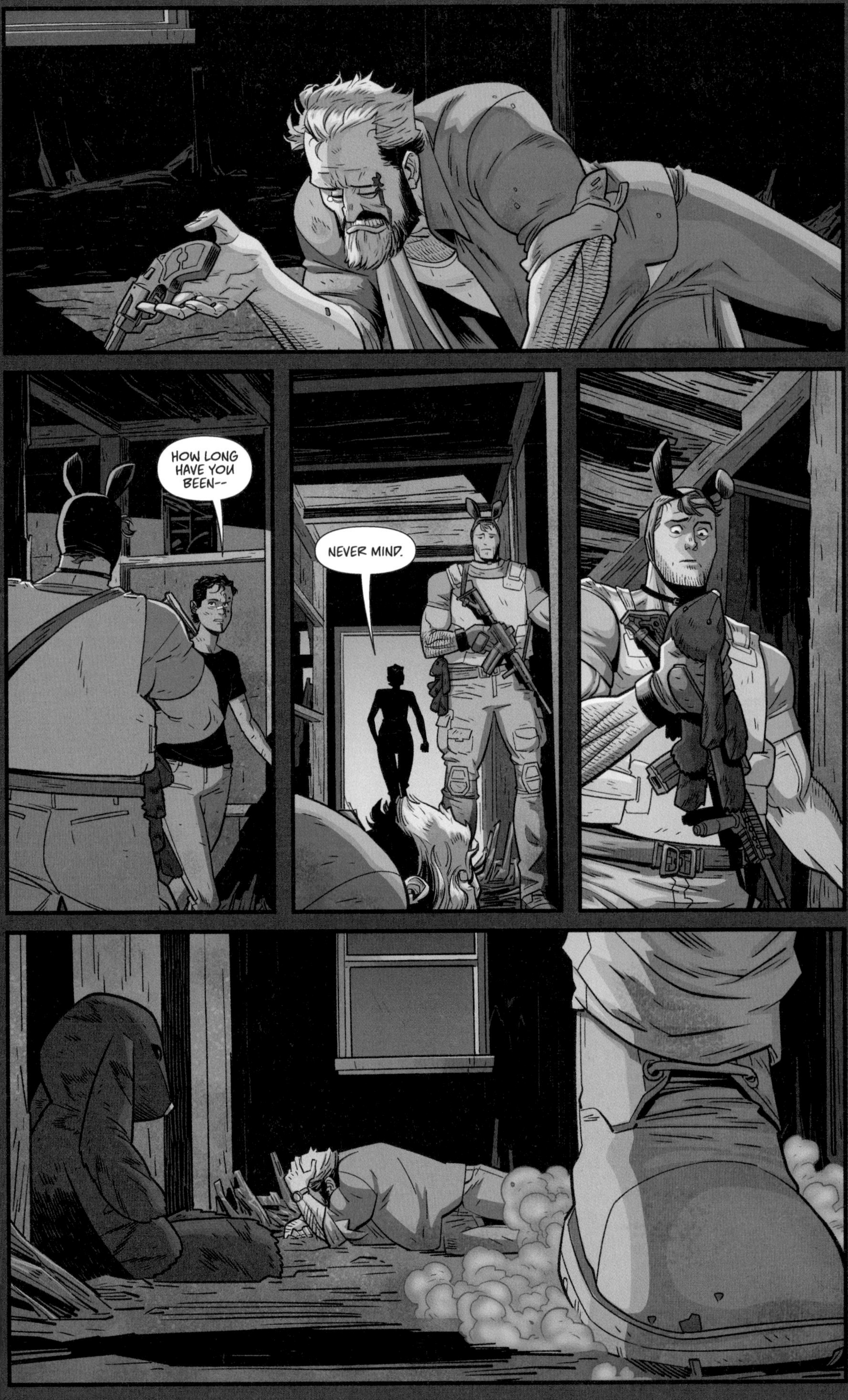
HOW LONG HAVE YOU BEEN--
NEVER MIND.

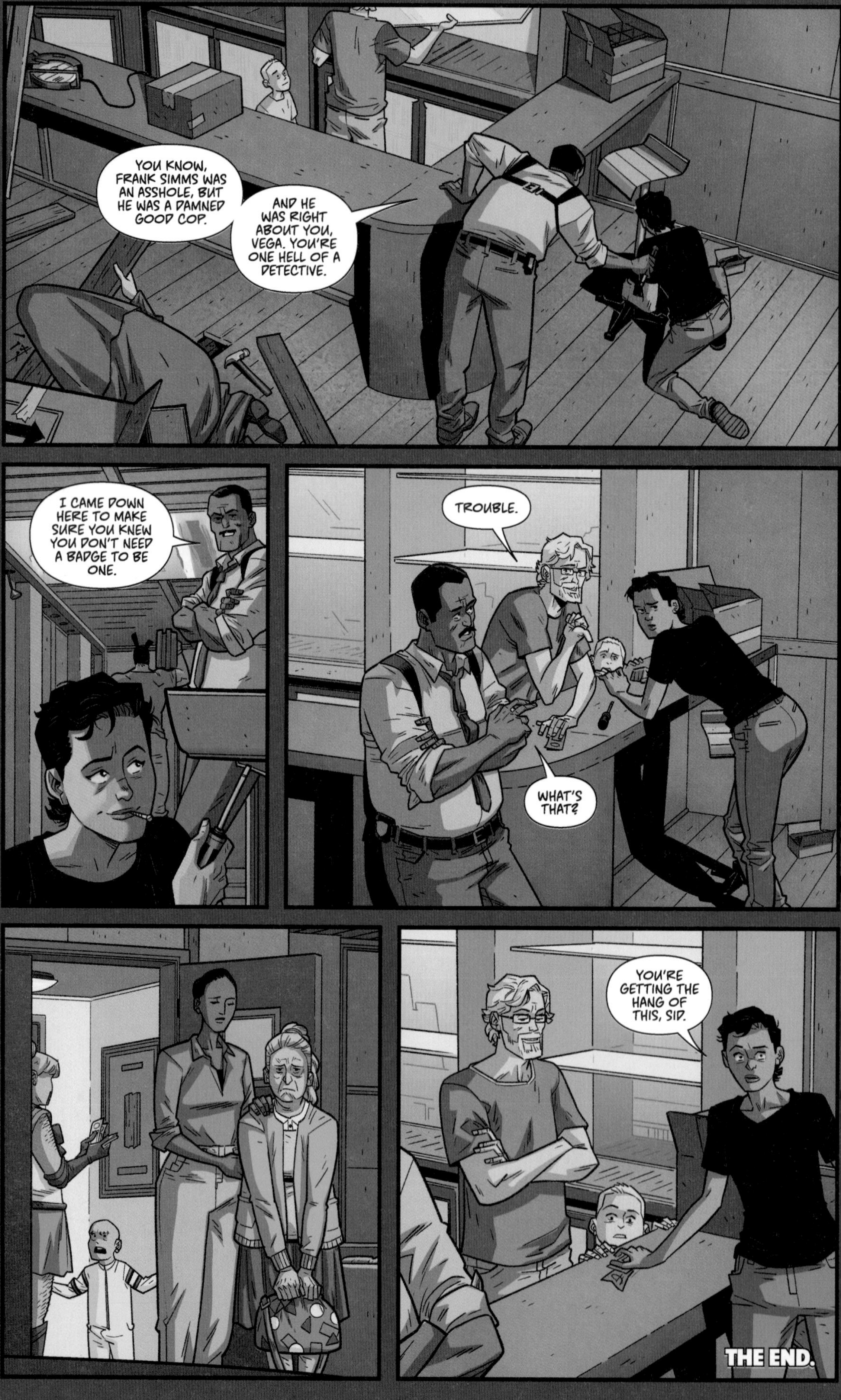
YOU KNOW, FRANK SIMMS WAS AN ASSHOLE, BUT HE WAS A DAMNED GOOD COP.
AND HE WAS RIGHT ABOUT YOU, VEGA. YOU'RE ONE HELL OF A DETECTIVE.
I CAME DOWN HERE TO MAKE SURE YOU KNEW YOU DON'T NEED A BADGE TO BE ONE.
TROUBLE.
WHAT'S THAT?
YOU'RE GETTING THE HANG OF THIS, SID.
THE END.

"Arnie & Albert"

DOUG WAGNER

STORY

DOUG DABBS

ART

ED DUKESHIRE

LETTERS

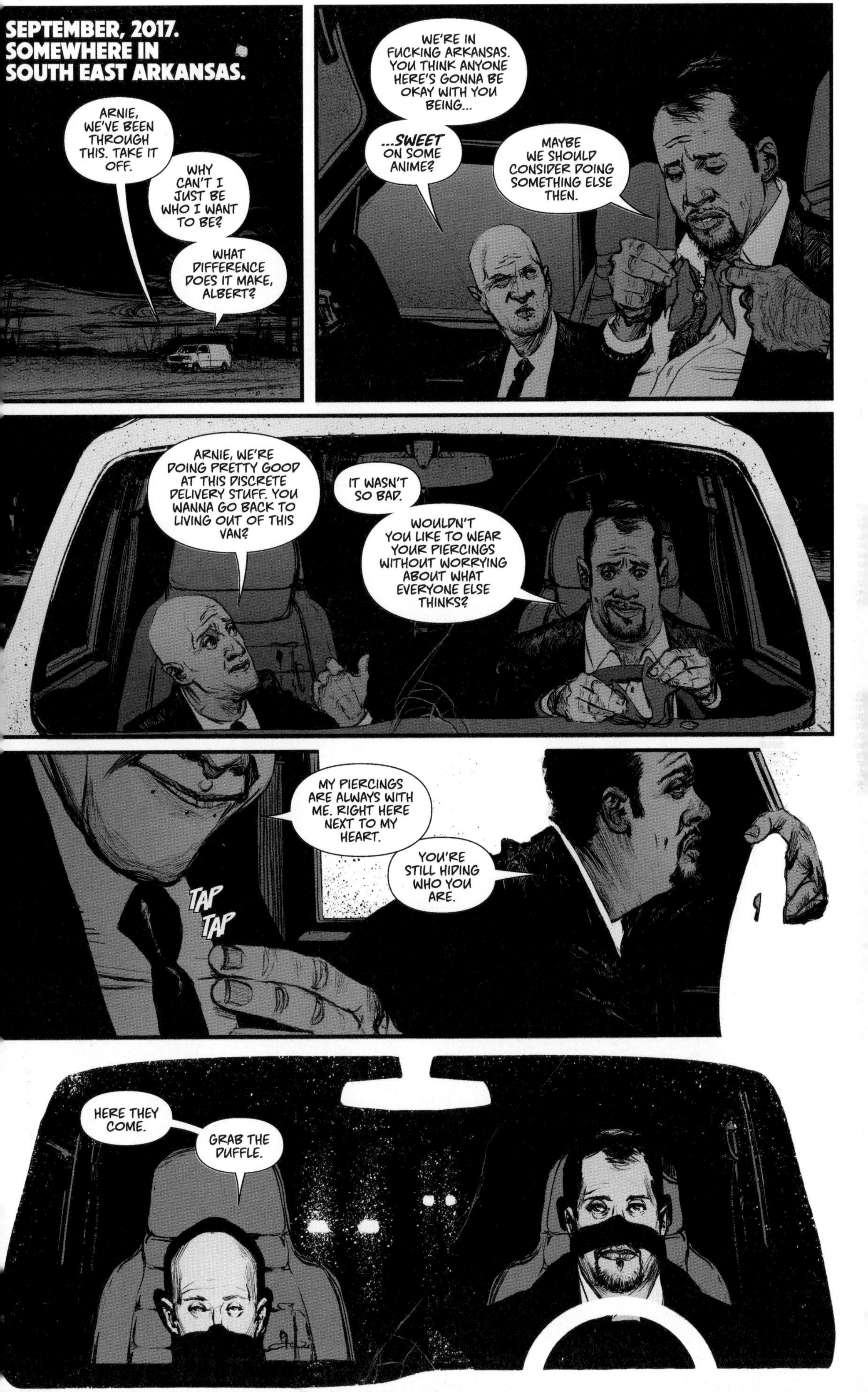
SEPTEMBER, 2017. SOMEWHERE IN SOUTH EAST ARKANSAS.
ARNIE, WE'VE BEEN THROUGH THIS. TAKE IT OFF.
WHY CAN'T I JUST BE WHO I WANT TO BE?
WHAT DIFFERENCE DOES IT MAKE, ALBERT?
WE'RE IN FUCKING ARKANSAS. YOU THINK ANYONE HERE'S GONNA BE OKAY WITH YOU BEING...
...SWEET ON SOME ANIME?
MAYBE WE SHOULD CONSIDER DOING SOMETHING ELSE THEN.
ARNIE, WE'RE DOING PRETTY GOOD AT THIS DISCRETE DELIVERY STUFF. YOU WANNA GO BACK TO LIVING OUT OF THIS VAN?
IT WASN'T SO BAD.
WOULDN'T YOU LIKE TO WEAR YOUR PIERCINGS WITHOUT WORRYING ABOUT WHAT EVERYONE ELSE THINKS?
MY PIERCINGS ARE ALWAYS WITH ME. RIGHT HERE NEXT TO MY HEART.
TAP TAP
YOU'RE STILL HIDING WHO YOU ARE.
HERE THEY COME.
GRAB THE DUFFLE.

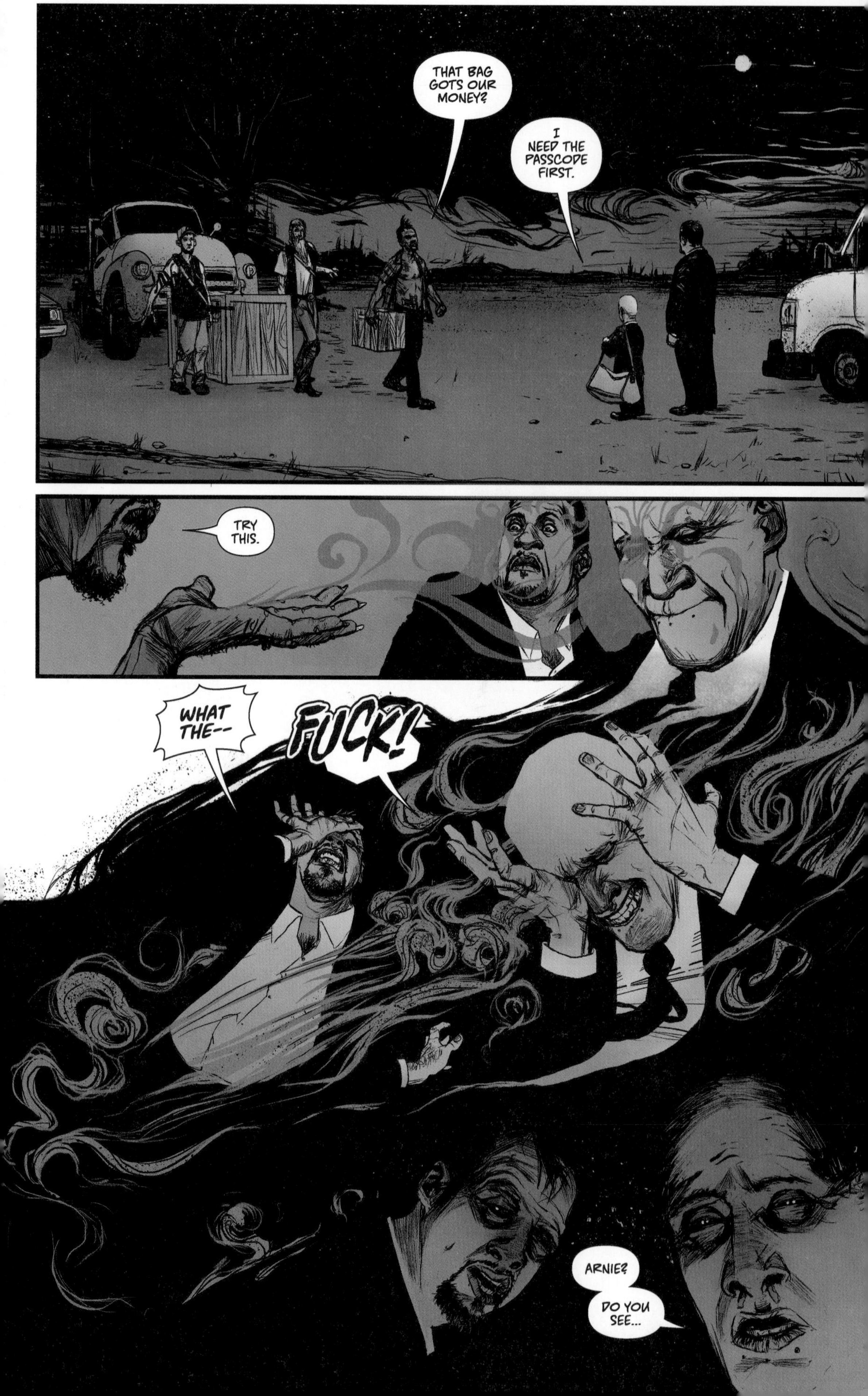
THAT BAG GOTS OUR MONEY?
I NEED THE PASSCODE FIRST.
TRY THIS.
WHAT THE--
FUCK!
ARNIE?
DO YOU SEE...

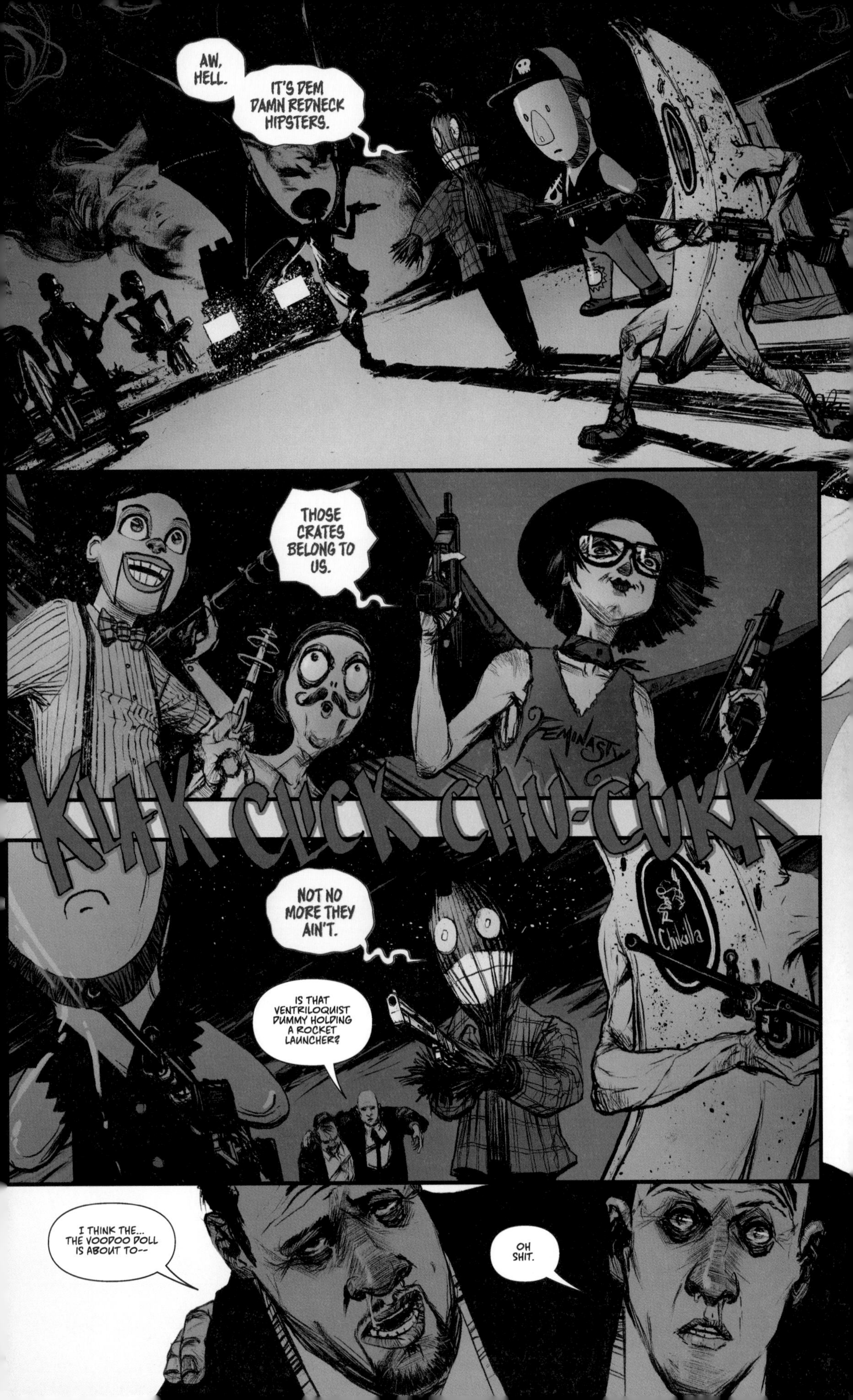

AW, HELL.
IT'S DEM DAMN REDNECK HIPSTERS.
THOSE CRATES BELONG TO US.
FEMINASTY
KLAK CLCK CHU-CUKK
NOT NO MORE THEY AIN'T.
Chikilla
IS THAT VENTRILOQUIST DUMMY HOLDING A ROCKET LAUNCHER?
I THINK THE... THE VOODOO DOLL IS ABOUT TO--
OH SHIT.

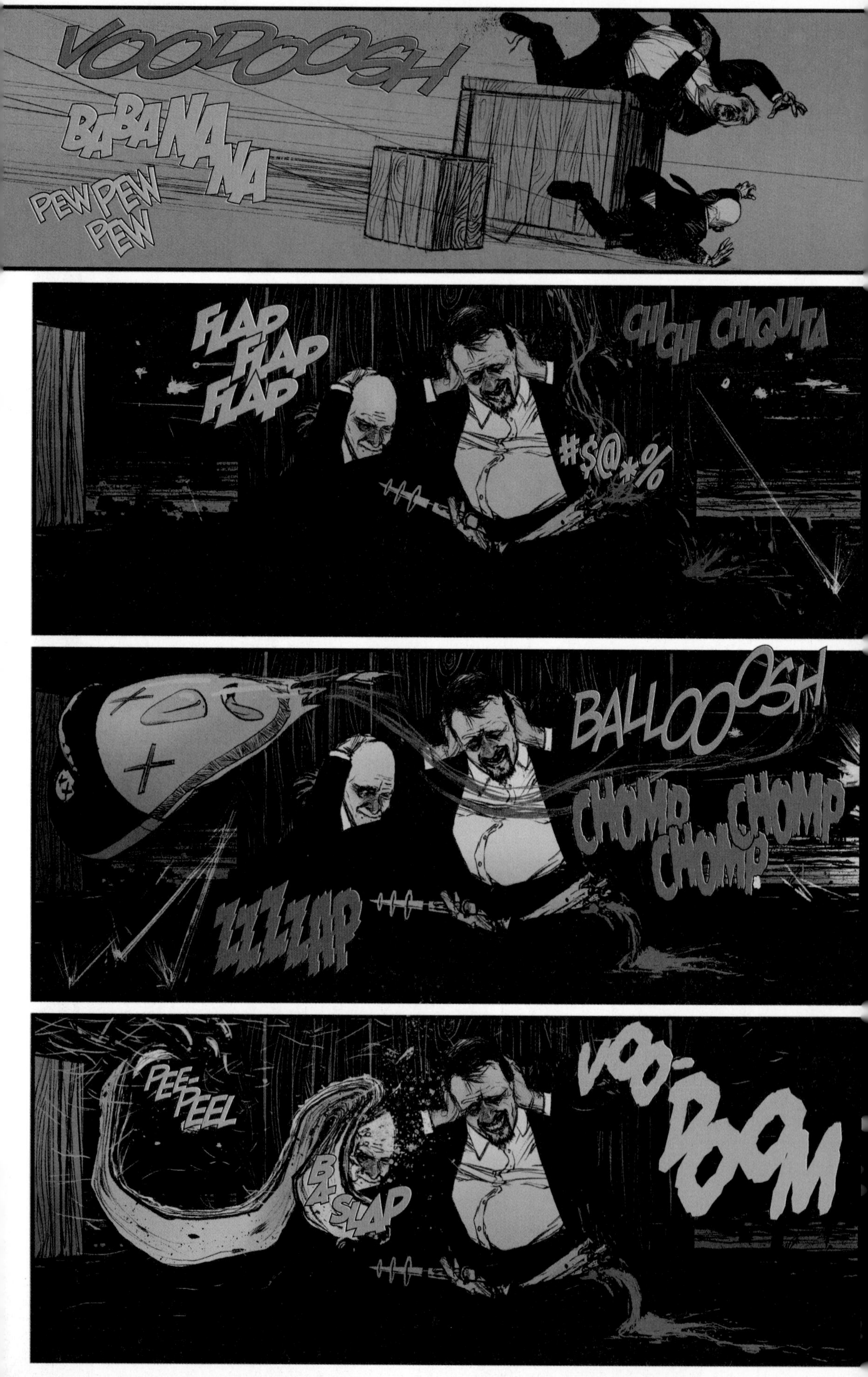
VOOPOOSH
BABANANA
PEW PEW PEW
FLAP FLAP FLAP
CHICHI CHIQUITA
#$@*%
BALLOOOSH
CHOMP CHOMP CHOMP
ZZZZAP
PEE-PEEL
BA-SLAP
VOO-DOOM

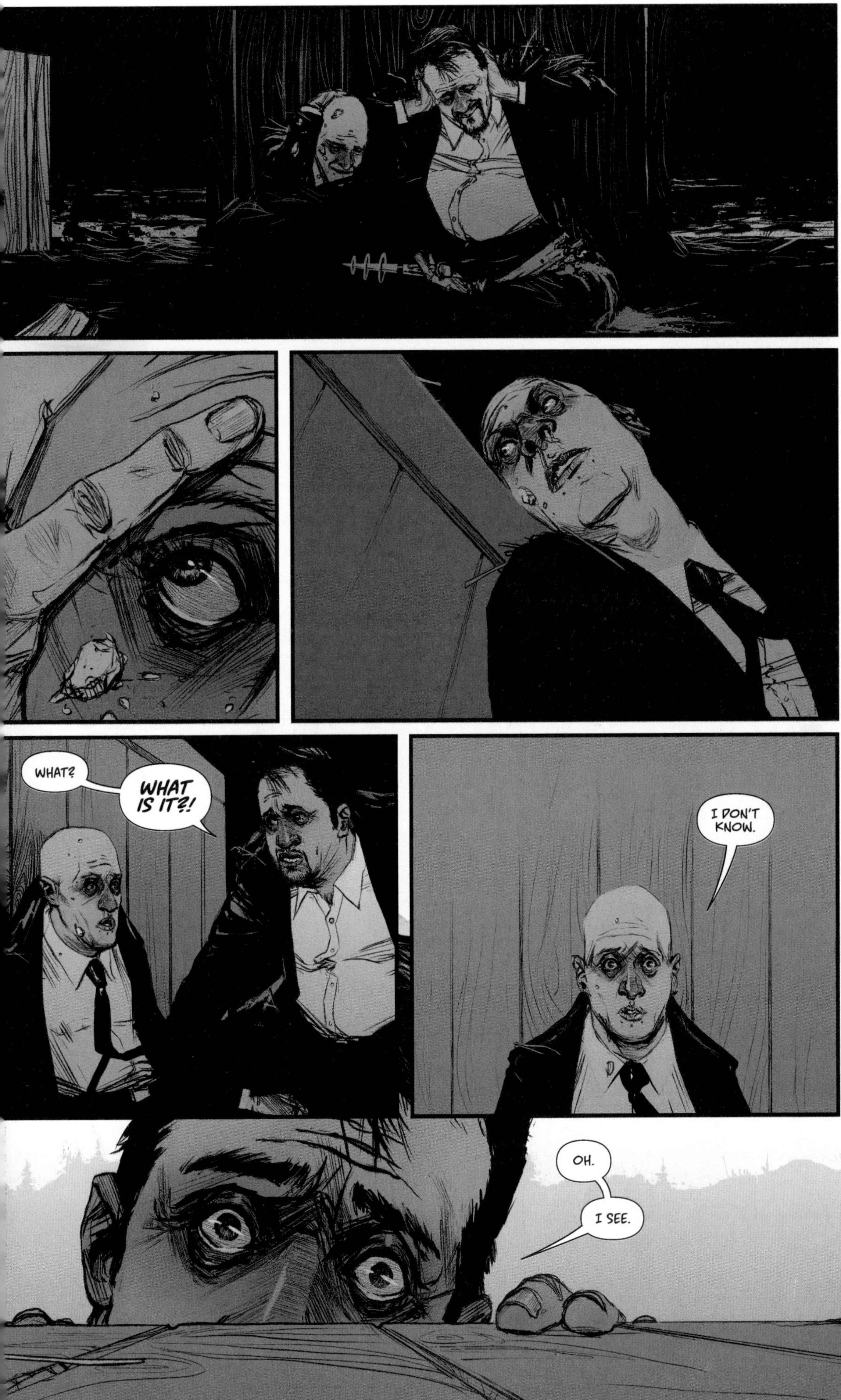
WHAT?
WHAT IS IT?!
I DON'T KNOW.
OH.
I SEE.

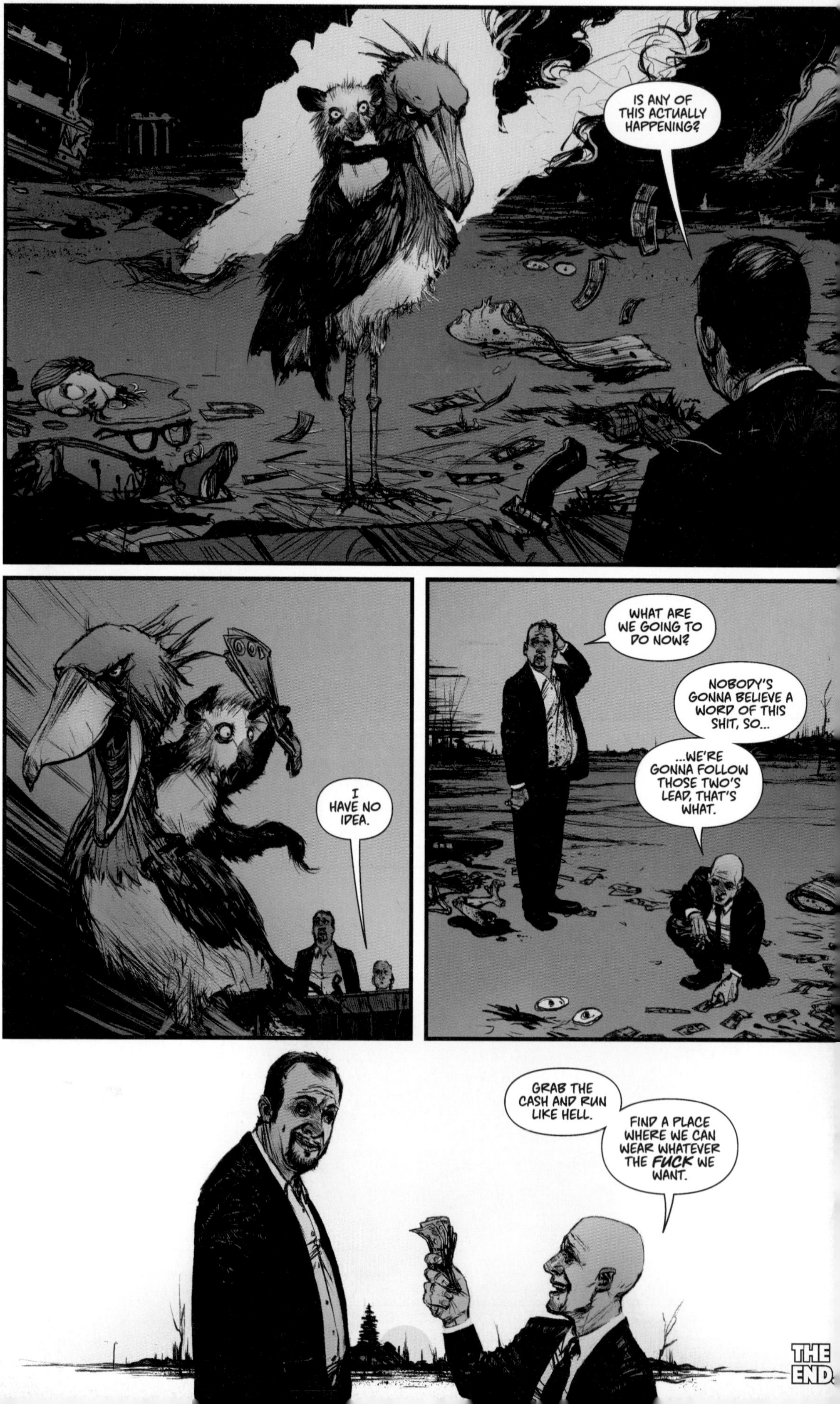
IS ANY OF THIS ACTUALLY HAPPENING?
I HAVE NO IDEA.
WHAT ARE WE GOING TO DO NOW?
NOBODY'S GONNA BELIEVE A WORD OF THIS SHIT, SO...
...WE'RE GONNA FOLLOW THOSE TWO'S LEAD, THAT'S WHAT.
GRAB THE CASH AND RUN LIKE HELL.
FIND A PLACE WHERE WE CAN WEAR WHATEVER THE FUCK WE WANT.
THE END

the Ride

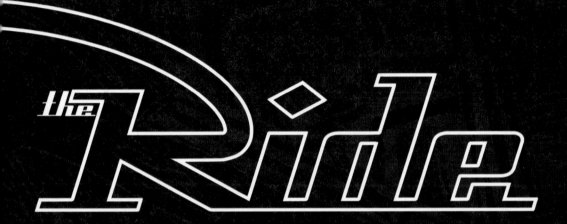

+ 15TH ANNIVERSARY INTERVIEW SERIES

+ COVER GALLERY

15TH ANNIVERSARY

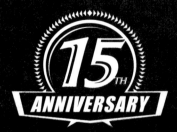

HOW IT ALL STARTED
A CONVERSATION WITH
DOUG WAGNER

The Ride: Wheels of Change #1
The Ride: Die Valkyrie #1 - #3
The Ride: Southern Gothic #2
The Ride: Burning Desire #1- #5

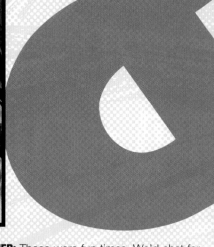

KEVEN GARDNER: Well, I guess you can blame this insanity on two guys — Doug Wagner and myself. Doug and I met back in the mid-nineties when we were both working in comic book stores. I had just met a few of the guys in Atlanta's famed Gaijin Studios (Adam Hughes, Brian Stelfreeze, Cully Hamner, Jason Pearson, Tony Harris, Joe Phillips, Karl Story, Dave Johnson) and as luck would have it, Doug and Cully were best buds from high school, so our friendship just sort of lined up at that moment in time. I eventually left retail to work at Valiant Comics, but a few years later, Doug and I ended up in the same town (Auburn, AL). I had caught the publishing bug while working at Valiant, and with Doug and I constantly talking about what comics we loved or ones we thought could be better, the seed for what would become *The Ride* was planted.

> ## "ONCE THE WORDS 'MUSCLE CAR' CAME OUT OF MY MOUTH, I KNEW WE HAD IT."

DOUG WAGNER: Those were fun times. We'd chat for hours about what we thought could help the industry, what wasn't working, and what we'd do if given the chance. You know, a lot of armchair quarterbacking. When you brought up the idea of us doing our own thing, I was immediately on board. All I'd ever wanted to do in my life was write comics. Man, we spent over a year trying to talk ourselves into it. Do you remember what finally made us pull the trigger?

KG: It was early-2003 when I finally said, "It's now or never," as my wife and I were expecting our first child, and I knew if I didn't take the plunge then I would probably never find the time.

DW: Yeah, that was a weird call. "Hey, I'm having a kid. Wanna put together a comic book?" We dove right in too, started plotting on how we could talk the Gaijin gang into this, or if we could dig up any blackmail material. I mean, we were talking about giants of the industry here. Guys that were offered work by EVERYONE. How could we possibly get them to work with us? We knew we were going to have

"HEY, I'M HAVING A KID. WANNA PUT TOGETHER A COMIC BOOK?"

to come up with a unique plan, present it well, and cross our fingers.

KG: From there it was about the format. How could we excite all of these talented guys creatively? We knew it had to be an anthology because none of them were going to be able to commit to multiple issues, but let's be honest, anthologies can be a tough sell. After a lot of debate on why anthologies often fail, we settled on needing an element that would tie these stories together. I'm not sure what all got thrown around, but once the words "muscle car" came out of my mouth, I knew we had it — these stories would focus on a particular 1968 Camaro and all the people who had owned it, stolen it, been run over by it, etc. The stories would mostly be crime and action, but with a splash of horror from time to time to mix things up. Most importantly, it was designed to allow creators to take a little joy ride away from the grind of doing editorially-driven comics for the big two.

KEVEN
GARDNER

And then all we had to do was convince some of the toughest creators in the business to buy in!
I think we called Pearson first, knowing that if we could at least get him to commit to the idea of it, that the other guys would have to listen. He grilled us for a while but eventually said he was in. From there it was a trip to Atlanta to sit down with Cully, Brian, Georges, Dexter, and Adam. We had our dream team picked, but still had to do a great sales job to get them all onboard.

DW: That was one of the most stressful days of my life. There I was sitting at a table with artists I revered. I picked up, and still pick up, every comic they do. I like to think we did a solid job pitching them the idea, but I'm still surprised they bought it. One of the smartest things I believe we did was that we had left a lot of the publishing details ambiguous. You thought we had a better chance of landing these guys if we had them

THE RIDE: BURNING DESIRE #1
cover by Daniel Hillyard

help mold the plan. Should we self-publish or go through a publisher? How many pages and issues should we do for our first run? Full color or black and white? That's where things got interesting. Clearly, the whole studio had been discussing their ideas on this for years. That late morning breakfast exploded in conversation and debate. Your plan was brilliant.

KG: I'd probably go with nuts, but whatever works! I just remember knowing this was going to happen when Brian, who had mostly been listening, took the floor and said, "If we're going to do this, each artist needs to be in for half of an issue. 11 pages each, and 44 total story pages. That's the format." It was like Moses came down from the mountain and gave us our instructions.

DW: You and I had been working out the foundation for the story, but I wanted to make sure the entire team enjoyed drawing each of their respective chapters. I managed to sit down and ask all of them, "What do you want to draw?" Brian wanted to blow stuff up and push the levels of good taste, Cully requested something moody and noir-ish, Georges asked for something action oriented but set in a unique location, and Jason demanded something brutal and harsh. It took some wrangling with the story, a few scenes moved here and there, but after it was done, everyone seemed happy with what I gave them. Of course, I worked closely with each one of them during the whole process to make sure they stayed happy. That was extremely important to me.

"I REALIZED I DIDN'T NEED ANYONE'S PERMISSION TO MAKE COMICS."

KG: A few months later we had pages coming in and it was time to figure out how to get the books into comic stores. One option was to go directly to Diamond, but we all knew getting it picked up by Image was the home run hit; Cully made some calls and came back to me with Eric Stephenson's name and phone number. At the time Jim Valentino was the publisher at Image and Eric was working under him, but someone had told Cully that Eric would really dig this title and we should talk to him first. I made the call and it went well, so Brian offered to put the official proposal together (it was an oversized comic of his finished pages and a synopsis of the concept and story, all under a black cover with *The Ride* logo on it — a logo he designed as a surprise to us) and we FedEx'd the package to Eric.

We quickly got the green light and man, that was the best feeling. We had an Image book on the way with all these amazing creators—it was a wonderful time.

DW: No doubt. It was a dream come true for me and changed my perspective on my comics career. For years I thought the only way to be successful and validated as a writer was to be hired by a major publisher. This two-issue story changed everything for me. I realized I didn't need anyone's permission to make comics. I just had to have the determination to do it.

KG: Then other creators started reaching out to us wanting to do their own stories, and I guess the rest is history. 15 years later, with this book that people now hold in their hands, it's all come full circle. You got to catch back up with Samantha Vega, which in a lot of ways had to be like seeing an old friend you lost touch with a very long time ago, but picking back up like you'd never been apart.

DW: You're absolutely correct. It was a joy to be cuddling up with Vega again; the young girl that saved me and changed my life. I just hope we aged well together.

CREATING HISTORY
A CONVERSATION WITH

CULLY HAMNER

The Ride: Wheels of Change #1
The Ride: 2 For The Road
The Ride: Burning Desire #3

KEVEN GARDNER: We couldn't do this interview series without sitting down with one of the guys who was in from day one, artist-extraordinaire, Cully Hamner.

Cully, since issue #1 of *The Ride* was first released back in 2004, you've been connected to this series in one form or another (both as an artist and a writer). Why do you keep coming back? Is it just because Doug Wagner and I pester the shit out of you, or something more?

CULLY HAMNER: That's most of it! You and Doug are very annoying. But really, it's also about maintaining a relationship with my own history. I look at everything that's come before as formative, and it's always fun to go back and touch on that again; like when you go back home to visit your parents and drive by your old high school, or the parking lot where you used to drink beer, or whatever… it's always fun when you get the opportunity to tour your old life and wonder how you might handle things now. Creatively, how would I approach material for *The Ride* now? Of course, the story in "Burning Desire" wasn't a Ride-proper story because the car

WHERE WOULD YOU BE IF I HADN'T GOT TO MY EXTRA IN TIME?

"YOU AND DOUG ARE VERY ANNOYING."

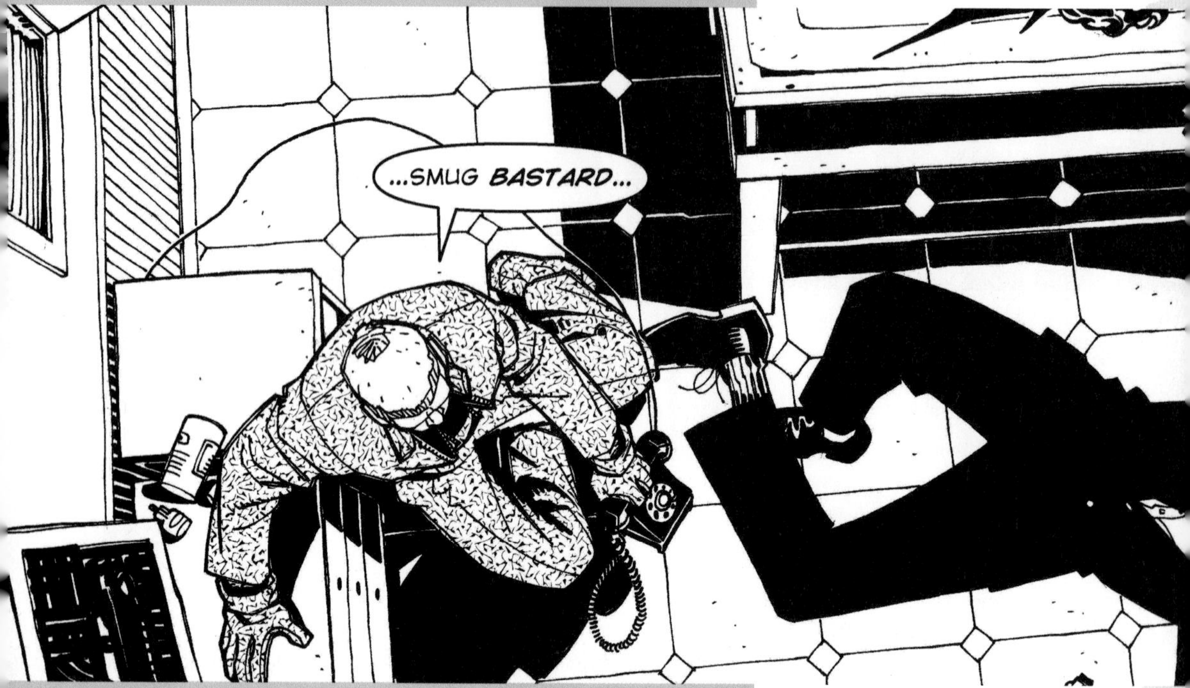
...SMUG BASTARD...

wasn't in it—not quite the same, but it certainly was familiar from the standpoint of working with Doug again. He and I go way, way back... I've known him for 35 years. When I was 15, we were talking about making comics together. And yet, it's worked out shockingly little at this point, which I don't quite understand other than it's just been horrible luck, but our only published stories together have been in *The Ride*. And that definitely makes it special.

KG: You'll always be the artist that drew the first chapter of the series. In the history of comics, *The Ride* is just a very small blip on the radar, but does something like that resonate with you when you look back at your storied career?

CH: Yeah, because it wasn't an existing thing before Brian Stelfreeze and I drew that first issue. Brian did his part after me, so I was kind of flying blind. And then I saw his pages, and I was like "I could have done this better, or could have drawn that..." But the reality is I had to set up the ball for Brian to hit it out of the park. What he did in his chapter was so sublime, where mine was more nuts and bolts, but hey... for better or worse, it was up to me to set the tone.

KG: And you got to co-create Frank Simms and Samantha Vega, and to this day, people still come up and want to talk about those characters.

CH: I honestly did not know that, and it's great to hear. I always felt that Laci was the breakout of that issue, but Frank and Vega hold a special place in my heart.

KG: Laci certainly stole the show because of that iconic page, but people always ask about Vega, and that's why we knew she had to star in this 15th Anniversary series. We actually set this one up a few years ago in Doug and Brian's "Die Valkyrie" mini-series, which got a little call back in issue #1 of "Burning Desire."

Switching gears, you both wrote and drew your "Big Plans" story in *The Ride* #3. Was it hard for you to tackle both duties?

CH: In the '80s, the writer/artist was king. So, I grew up admiring (and aspiring to be) Frank Miller, Walt Simonson, Howard Chaykin, John Byrne... right? It just felt like it was the next step that I was supposed to take. You've known me a long time; I'm a story-centric person and even if I'm not writing the script, I'm at least rewriting a part of the story by laying it out. So, this was a natural jump from that.

KG: With "Big Plans," were you itching to tell a story set in the '60s?

CH: Oh, yeah, it's a favorite period of mine. And with *The Ride*, there was only one rule, and it was that the car had to be on at least one page in the story. What I did was bend that rule as far is it would go without breaking it. I remember you being trepidatious about it, but I sold you on the idea that the car was there, or at least the idea of it was there.

KG: You definitely bent the rule pretty far, but still won me over. Plus, the main character had one hell of a cool outfit. I kind of think that's the reason you wrote the story— you just had to draw him!

CH: That's true, I really wanted to basically draw Lee Marvin in a turtle-neck. And you probably remember this, but no one else knows — his adversary in the story, in my head, was kind of a young Paul Moses from *Red*.

KG: Oh, I very much remember! It's been an Easter Egg that I've kept to myself since 2005.

CH: It isn't officially the same character, but in my head it's Moses— essentially the same version of the guy I wrote and drew in my *Red: Eyes Only* one-shot a few years later. Sort of like in the movie *The Rock*, where they never confirm Sean Connery is actually James Bond, but it's pretty strongly implied that it's supposed to be.

KG: Let's also touch on your story in "Burning Desire," which is quite different than your previous *The Ride* tales. When I first read Doug's script, I wasn't sure where it was going, but wow— what a tragic and emotional ending.

CH: Such a strong little story, right? The impression is that Foo was really good at what he did and he enjoyed it maybe a little too much, almost to the point that you don't think he understood the reality of it— it was like a game to him. So here he is having the best time in combat, smirking through

the story, until something he does kills a young girl. It smacks him right in the face, and he surrenders maybe for the first time in his life. Retreats from reality, actually. In some ways he was already operating in his own reality and just enjoying playing 'war.' He was already in retreat; he just wasn't aware of it himself when we first saw him in action.

KG: And it's not something that we often see in comics, which is the emotional scars of war, but here we see that up close and personal.

CH: You have to give it to Doug for pulling it off— so much meat in a 6-page story! Doug has become such an interesting writer, it's like some switch went off inside him and he's writing these searing, emotionally conflicted stories, usually with some sort of off-putting premise. It's like he's discovered how to purposely make you uncomfortable. And if you know Doug, he's the nicest guy in the world, and you read these stories and have to go, "What the fuck! Where is this coming from?!"

KG: I always believed in his writing, but the last few years he took it to another level, especially with *Plastic*, and now this series.

CH: I've said it before, but I was and remain jealous of Daniel Hillyard for getting to draw *Plastic*.

KG: I've got to wrap it up, but I want to thank you for all your contributions to this series since the beginning, when it was just a crazy idea. It wouldn't be the same without you.

CH: And I wouldn't be the same without *The Ride*, so back atcha'!

"..I REALLY WANTED TO BASICALLY DRAW LEE MARVIN IN A TURTLENECK."

STAYCATION

A CONVERSATION WITH TOMM COKER

The Ride: The Key To Survival
The Ride: Southern Gothic #2
The Ride: Burning Desire #4

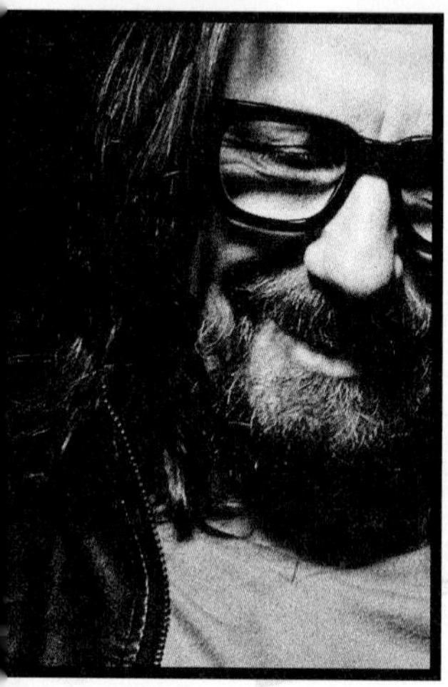

KEVEN GARDNER: Tomm Coker is one of the most gifted creators I've had the pleasure of working with; he can write and draw like a madman, and his three trips behind the wheel of our '68 Camaro have been stellar.

Tomm, we first met around 2006 when you were about to direct *Catacombs*, your feature film for Lionsgate. You were a fan of *The Ride* and didn't hesitate when I asked you to do a story. In fact, you seemed to be quite excited about doing a story in black and white.

TOMM COKER: At the time I'd been working for Wildstorm, Marvel, and Vertigo and the coloring on my books was fine, but I always felt that the colorists were trying to do too much. My stuff can be a little messy with splatters and razor blades, and that often led to the colorists adding more to the pages than necessary. So, I was excited to work without color. You asked me to do a horror story, and my favorite book ever was always *Creepy*, so I wanted to use this opportunity to figure out how to draw that *Creepy*-style like Al Williamson and Angelo Torres, while at the same time, revamping my style to make it colorist-proof going forward.

KG: I've always told artists that this was supposed to be a fun gig— just cut loose and do what the other editors won't let you do, but I had no idea how much you took advantage of that freedom.

TC: After editors saw my *Ride* story, I could tell them how my art should look by just adding values of color, and that was huge for me moving forward.

KG: Had you used the zipatone effects on your pages prior to drawing your first *Ride* story, "The Key to Survival"?

TC: I had used real zipatone on my pages, but that was the first time I figured out how to do it digitally; in fact, that was the last story that I drew on paper—although I was drawing panels on different pieces of paper and assembling them in Photoshop. And as I was playing around with them and adding effects, I figured out I could add zipatone digitally, and because of that, *The Ride* was a real transition point for me. It allowed me to do whatever I wanted—write my story and just run with the art.

KG: You may not know this, but you're one of two people to write and draw your own *Ride* story (along with Cully Hamner) but you are the only writer/artist to carry an entire issue on your own. I guess this is where you get a 'No- Prize' (Ha!).

TC: That story was a blast. *Ride* stories are really hard for a couple of reasons: first, you're competing with guys like Pearson, Stelfreeze, Hamner, Brunner— all these guys that I said I could never do what they do under any circumstances. Cully is so good at that clean, intense, action. Jason just draws so goddamn well. They all do! So, doing that story was intimidating, because of the level of quality that I had to live up to.

KG: Man, you are not giving yourself the credit you deserve. Now, let's talk about your second *Ride*

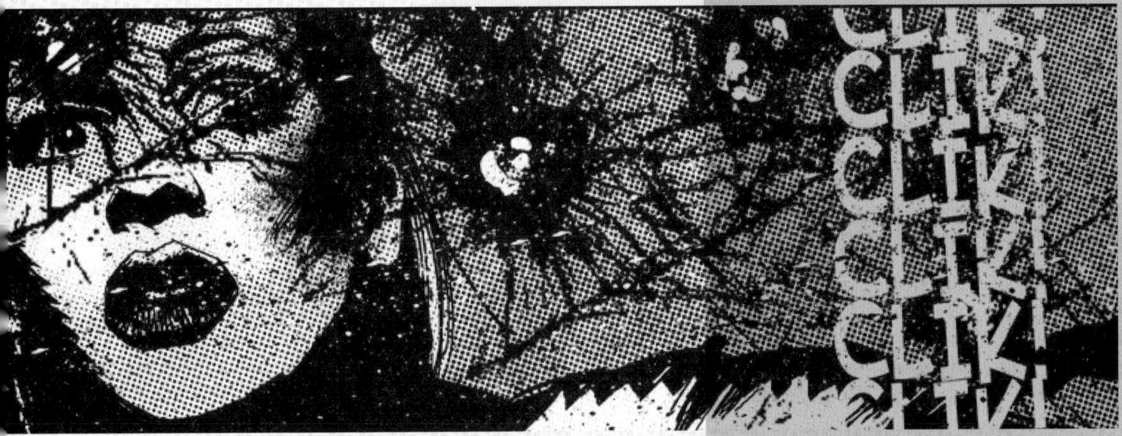
CLIK!
CLIK!
CLIK!
CLIK!
CLIK!

story, "The Devil Don't Sing No Blues," which was your version of the legendary Robert Johnson tale.

TC: I was in my studio listening to Robert Johnson recordings, while actually working on a different story idea. Then it hit me that if the devil had approached Johnson, he wouldn't have just walked up, he'd have been driving a nice car. As soon as I had that idea the rest was easy.

KG: And your "Burning Desire" short is a callback to "The Devil Don't Sing No Blues," because our nun is actually the devil's daughter.

TC: It's so much fun. And this is why I come back every time you ask. These stories are like 'staycations' for me. I get to go draw something fresh and different, and something I could never get to do under normal circumstances. Plus, these are challenging, but they are fun. I just laugh all day long when I'm drawing these stories, and I'm just so happy to be included. It's more than I ever expected (to be included with the caliber of guys that have worked on this series).

KG: For me, I love your pages and I love your stories, so I just cross my fingers and hope you say 'yes' every time we do a new series.

TC: I will always say yes to *The Ride*; don't you worry about that.

"...I JUST LAUGH ALL DAY LONG WHEN I'M DRAWING THESE STORIES..."

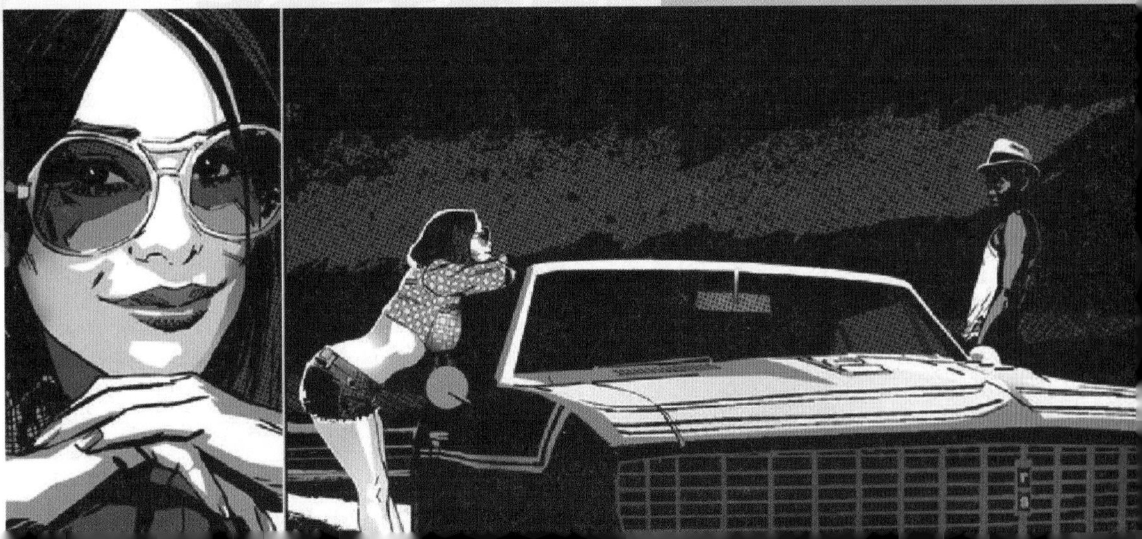

THIS IS WHAT FREEDOM FEELS LIKE
A CONVERSATION WITH
BRIAN STELFREEZE

The Ride: Wheels of Change #1
The Ride: Die Valkyrie #1 - #3
Gun Candy #1 & #2

KEVEN GARDNER: They say you should never meet your heroes because they'll only disappoint you. I'm here to say that's definitely not the case with Brian Stelfreeze. Like many others in this industry will tell you, Brian is not only one of the most talented creators around, he's also an amazing teacher and mentor to artists climbing the ranks, as well as a fantastic ambassador for the industry. And somehow, this guy has drawn more pages of *The Ride* than anyone else. How did that happen? Let's find out...

KG: Brian, when Doug Wagner and I first approached you about *The Ride*, what about the concept made you want to jump on board?

BRIAN STELFREEZE: It was a combination of things, but I think the main one was this anthology had one 'thing' that tied the stories together, and I'd never seen anything like that in comics. And the fact that the thing was a cool car, something that everyone can relate to— finally getting their first car or getting the car they've always desired— that's an inflection point in people's lives, and *The Ride* would explore that in every story.

KG: This was covered in the first part of this interview series, but Doug and I sat down with you and Cully for breakfast to do our pitch for the series, and you enthusiastically came on board and completely invested right then and there. Out of that, you and Doug created probably the most iconic character of the series— Laci, the

teen-assassin. How did she end up being so crazy?

BS: That was really just Doug and I trying to one-up each other. He described her, and I tried to push her look further than what he'd asked, and that led to Doug pushing her even more in the script. So, I kept ramping it up and wanted her to be crazier, which ended with me exploring Laci's hypersexual side.

KG: I remember the script to her 'big intro' splash page saying something along the lines of, "Laci stands on the car with a crashing bus exploding behind her, and you can really tell she gets off on killing."

And you took it literally.

BS: I started drawing that page in the studio, and I was drawing it hoping no one would pop in my office and see it. Cully was the first, and he just screamed, "Oh my God!" That caused my girlfriend, Stine, to walk back and see what was going on; she just stopped, said, "No," and walked out of my office. It was exactly the reaction I'd hoped for!

KG: And once you were done inking the page, you called me and said, "Kev, are you in front of a computer? Because I just sent you an email." I was, so I opened up the attachment and was immediately shocked, speechless, and then just started laughing. I'm pretty sure my initial thoughts were, "What the hell have I gotten myself into?"

BS: And we were friends, but I had no idea what was about to happen. I remember thinking you were going to say, "Dude, just don't." And you were quiet for like a full minute, and I was thinking, "Oh man, he's not liking this" but then you started chuckling and then full-blown laughing.

KG: One of the reasons I was so quiet, and I had forgotten this until now, but originally Vega and Laci were going to be partners on the force, but she was named 'Lucy' after my daughter who had just been born. Then Doug added Frank, and the 'Lucy' character changed to a nemesis, which was all fine with me until you drew that page… and she had to get a new name! After that, Laci was officially born.

BS: But for me, I had been working for Marvel and DC for so long, and now no one was telling me to stop. And knowing that I had no limits, I was having a blast. This is what freedom looked like!

KG: And with Laci being so popular, you and Doug immediately wanted to do more with her, and that's how her *Gun Candy* series came to be.

BS: When I was doing that first *Gun Candy* cover, I knew I had to come up with something as offensive as the bus scene from *The Ride*, and that's where the candy cane cover idea came from.

KG: That was another time you called me and said, "Are you in front of your computer…?"

BS: (laughter) But like I told you, if you saw something dirty or offensive, it was because your mind went there, and that's on you.

KG: And it was a great cover! After all that, the origin story was well-received, and that led to you and Doug teaming up once again for "Die Valkyrie" a few years later. That story starred Laci, but it wasn't a solo adventure.

BS: Doug called me with the idea of doing this Laci story, but also the story of a group of good girls who were trying to be bad, and a bad girl (Laci) trying to be good; but in the end they all realized what they truly were and that was their salvation. Man, did I love drawing that series. What a blast.

Something else that's really cool, for me, no matter what I do, and I've had this insane career, but *The Ride*, to me, and 12-Gauge in general, just feels like home. I will go off and do these wild adventures, but I'm always going to come home and I'm going to hang out with my brothers, and just have fun. It's awesome to have a home like that to come back to and have fun and stretch my wings.

KG: Having fun is the key. Comics should be fun. Yes, it's a lot of work and it's your job, but you should still have fun creating comic books.

BS: That's the edict— just have fun doing it. Working with you and working with Doug, and just coming up with these awesome, fun stories, and then having fun producing the art… there's nothing cooler than that as far as I'm concerned. And the next book I'm doing with you guys, that I'm working on right now, I'm home; I've got home field advantage on this one and I am having a great time. We are going to blow some people's minds when this new series is released.

KG: That's supposed to be a secret, so I'll cut you off before we get in trouble. Before we close, I want to tell you I will forever be in your debt for jumping on this train; maybe it was just a perfect storm— you were there looking for something to excite you, we pitched you *The Ride* and somehow it all came together. All I know for sure is that this thing would not exist without all your sacrifices along the way.

BS: *The Ride* wasn't a perfect storm to me, it was a Jupiter storm. A 5-million-year red spot as far as I'm concerned, and I've loved every minute of working with this team ever since.

"IF YOU SAW SOMETHING DIRTY OR OFFENSIVE, IT WAS BECAUSE YOUR MIND WENT THERE. AND THAT'S ON YOU."

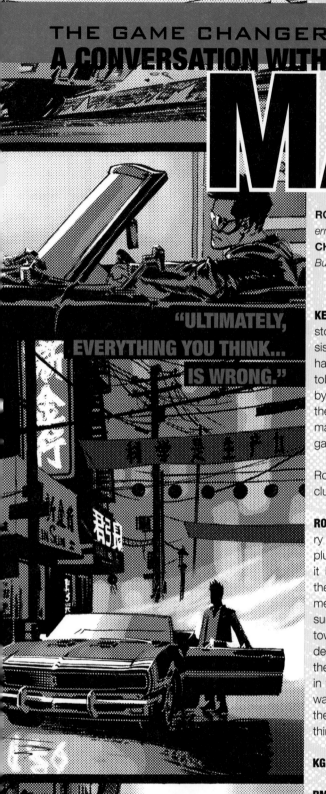

THE GAME CHANGER
A CONVERSATION WITH RON MARZ

"ULTIMATELY, EVERYTHING YOU THINK... IS WRONG."

F36

RON MARZ: *The Ride: Foreign Parts & The Ride: Southern Gothic #1 & #2*

CHRIS BRUNNER: *The Ride: Foreign Parts & The Ride: Burning Desire #2*

KEVEN GARDNER: With 15 years of great *The Ride* stories in the rear-view mirror, the one that has consistently been mentioned to me more than any other has to be "Language Barrier," which was brilliantly told by Ron Marz and Chris Brunner (with Zip FX by some kid named Rico Renzi). With that in mind, there's no better time than now to revisit that little masterpiece; one I've always referred to as "the game changer" of the series.

Ron, what inspired you to tell the story almost exclusively in Chinese?

RON MARZ: Honestly, I have no idea where the story came from. It was just... there, waiting to be plucked from the ether. Sometimes that's the way it happens, and when it does, those are usually the best stories. The only thing I can trace it to is meeting a friend a number of years ago at a dim sum breakfast in New York City. We were in Chinatown, and I was definitely the alien. I couldn't understand the language, I couldn't read the signs on the buildings. And I kind of loved it. I was immersed in this culture that was utterly different than what I was used to. I think "Language Barrier" kind of puts the reader in that place. Ultimately, everything you think... is wrong.

KG: Were you at all worried about how this might go?

RM: The only thing I worried about was whether the concept itself could be pulled off. I remember telling you, before I wrote it, that the story was either going to be great or a disaster, no middle ground.

KG: And that scared the hell out of me, but as we

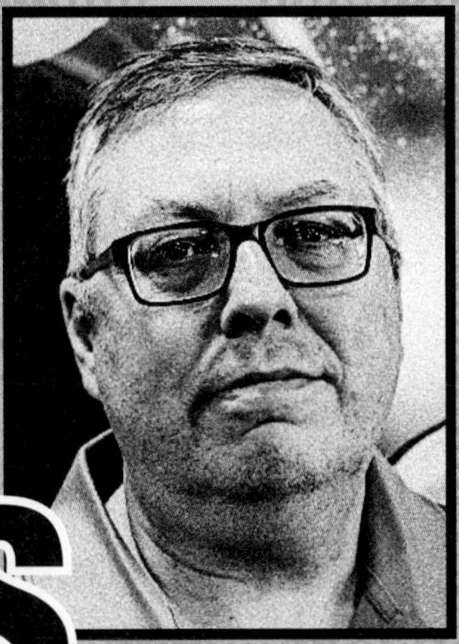

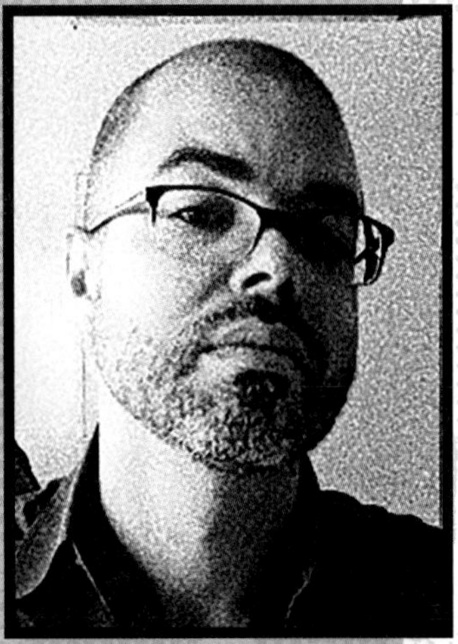

CHRIS BRUNNER

talked over how you envisioned the story, it really hit home that this was why I wanted to do the series to begin with— to give creators a chance to stretch their wings and take chances.

"I JUST DIDN'T REALIZE HOW RARE IT WAS TO GET A STORY LIKE THAT TO WORK ON."

Chris, what were your thoughts when you first read the script?

CHRIS BRUNNER: I'm glad I didn't appreciate how difficult it was going to be at the time—I just saw that the script worked and I trusted it; I could see it all in my head and that doesn't often happen. It opened up like a movie in my head and I just took notes on it. I followed that instinct so directly that I didn't think about what a hat trick it needed to be.

Ron, you said it was either going to be a success or a disaster; I think it succeeds because of the badge. Li flashes it on page two, right away. The badge is so visual and we all know what it means, so we can follow everything without it being confusing. In the absence of that visual device I don't know how the story would fly. It ended up being one of the most perfect hooks I've ever been given to work on. Had I appreciated that at the time I would have been a lot more nervous with a lot more stage fright. I just didn't realize how rare it was to get a story like that to work on.

KG: What kind of reaction did you guys get after it was released?

RM: The reaction was uniformly positive, from what I can remember, especially for Chris and Rico's work. I think it landed as we intended, with the audience having a real lightbulb moment when we reveal what's actually going on. That's the kind of thing you can do much better in a short story, more so than in a full issue.

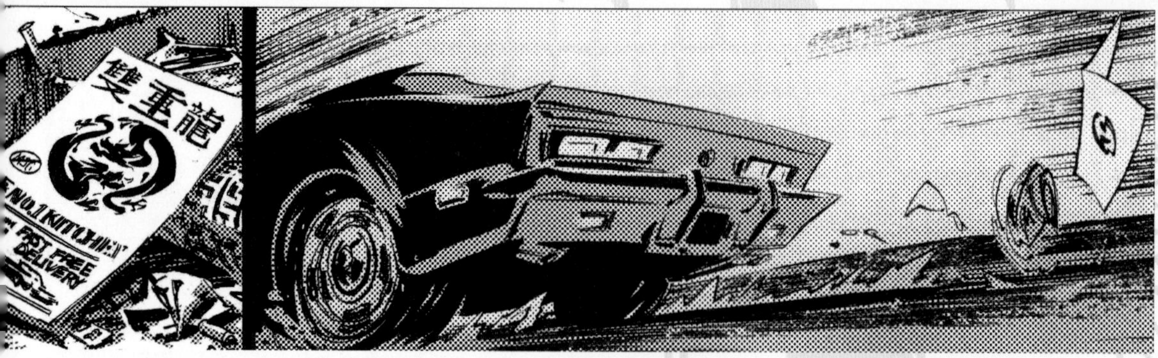
雙重龍
FAST FREE DELIVERY

CB: I'll never forget James O'Barr coming up to me at a con and introducing himself. He said that after he saw it he wanted to do his own *The Ride* story. James is, maybe more than anybody, responsible for the overwhelming force of "Language Barrier," because that's what he did in *The Crow*. That book was very influential to me. His comics were the kind of comics I wanted to make, where as an artist, I was saving nothing for the next page.

RM: As I recall, it also got a nice mention in *Entertainment Weekly*.

KG: Yes, it was reviewed in EW when the trade was released — "There is something undeniably captivating about balls-to-the-wall pulp storytelling. And that's just what *The Ride* is... Like any anthology, some of the stories misfire, but when they hit (like "Language Barrier," told almost entirely in Chinese...) they hit hard." A- —Marc Bernardin

I'm still not sure which story he considered a misfire, but that review, along with all the "Language Barrier" praise from the creative community, is why I always considered that particular issue the one that defined what the series was going to be moving forward; Chuck Dixon and Rob Haynes did the other story in that issue, "Iron Road," which was very unique and touching. Then you guys just blew the doors off and left people in awe. The bar was set pretty high and creators knew they had to do something special if they were going to participate. So, thanks guys… we might be on issue #100 by now if you hadn't backed me into a corner!

Chris, who made the call to use so much zipatone?

CB: The zipatone was Rico's idea, and what he really brought to the story. Guys in the industry at that time, we all grew up on and loved reading comics that used zipatone, so it really resonated with people. Rico and I had been trying to figure out how I could show off my realism chops without making it look corny, and the zipatone did that…it allowed my work not to look too slick and also gave it a visceral tone. It was also the timing, as we'd been looking for something to work on together. I had just done a Batman story, but DC wouldn't let Rico do the interior colors. You offered us this chance to work together and we were so excited, but shit, it was in black and white. How would we solve this problem? And he freaked me out with the way it looked. This was the first comic I'd made that I actually wanted to buy.

KG: Any last thoughts?

CB: Brian Stelfreeze told me it worked because the readers were so busy looking at everything that they were distracted from trying to figure out what was coming. If I'd drawn it simple and graphic, they may have tried to figure it out. I guess it just boils down to Ron wrote a perfect little script with a perfect hook; it set up the artist to show off, and it was all in service of a good story and a twist you'll always remember.

RM: This is comics. It's visual storytelling. The writing is pretty immaterial if the art doesn't work. If I write a genius script, and it's drawn by a hack artist, at the end of the day it's a lousy story. If I write a mediocre story and it's drawn by a genius artist, at the end of the day it's a great story. My success as a writer is dependent upon what you do as an artist. And obviously I'm pretty ecstatic about how this one turned out.

WE HOPE YOU ENJOYED *THE RIDE!*

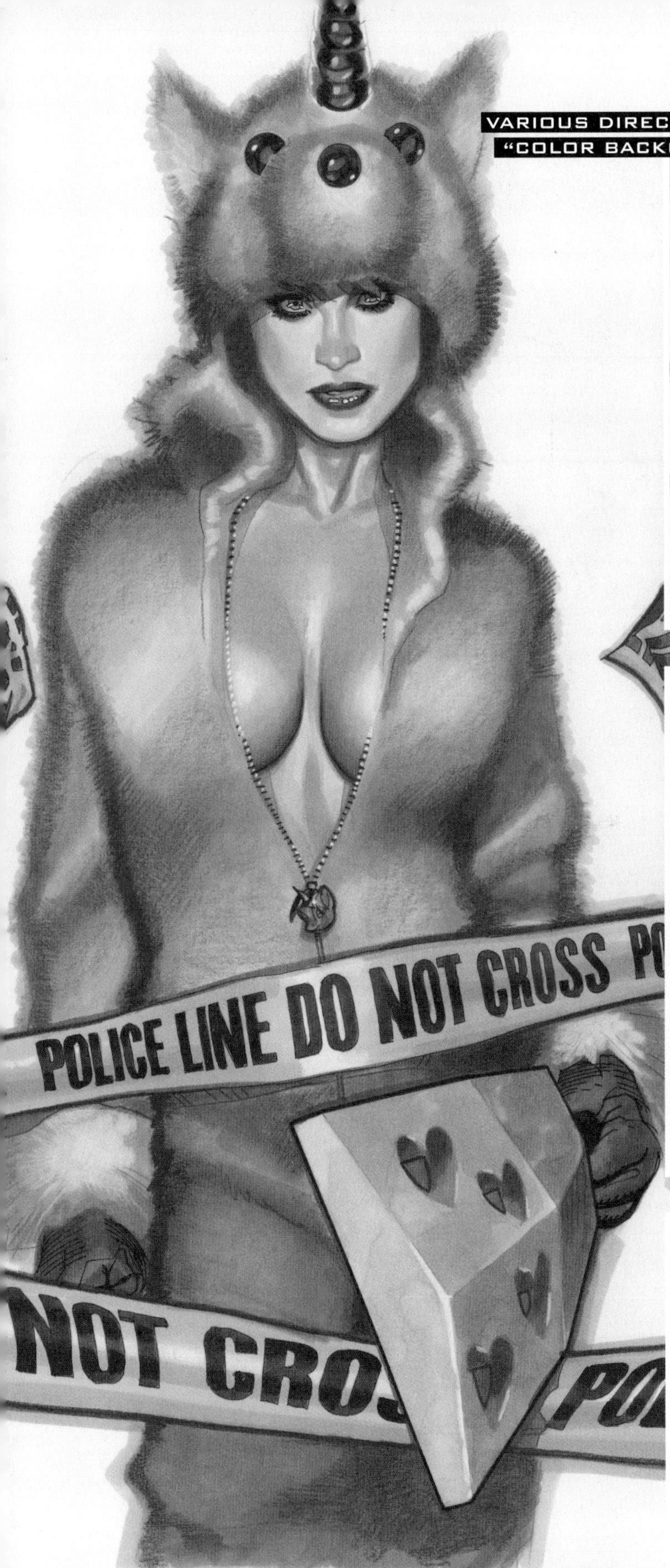
POLICE LINE DO NOT CROSS
NOT CROS

ADAM HUGHES
ISSUE #1 12-GAUGE
"MARKER COMP" CON VARIANT

ADAM HUGHES
ISSUE #1
VARIOUS DIRECT MARKET RETAILER
"COLOR BACKGROUND" VARIANTS

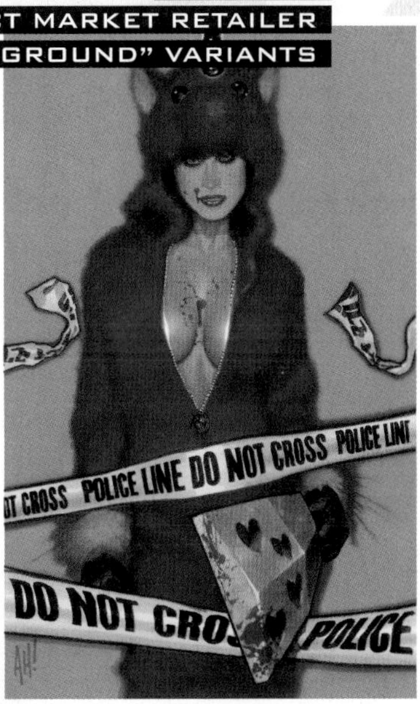
POLICE LINE DO NOT CROSS
DO NOT CRO
POLICE

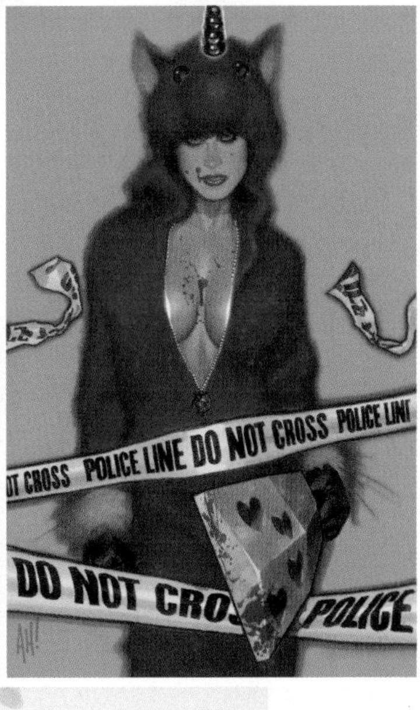
POLICE LINE DO NOT CROSS
DO NOT CRO
POLICE

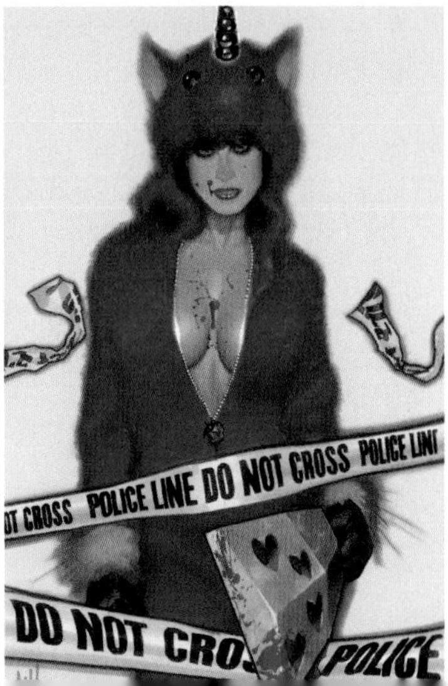
POLICE LINE DO NOT CROSS
DO NOT CRO
POLICE

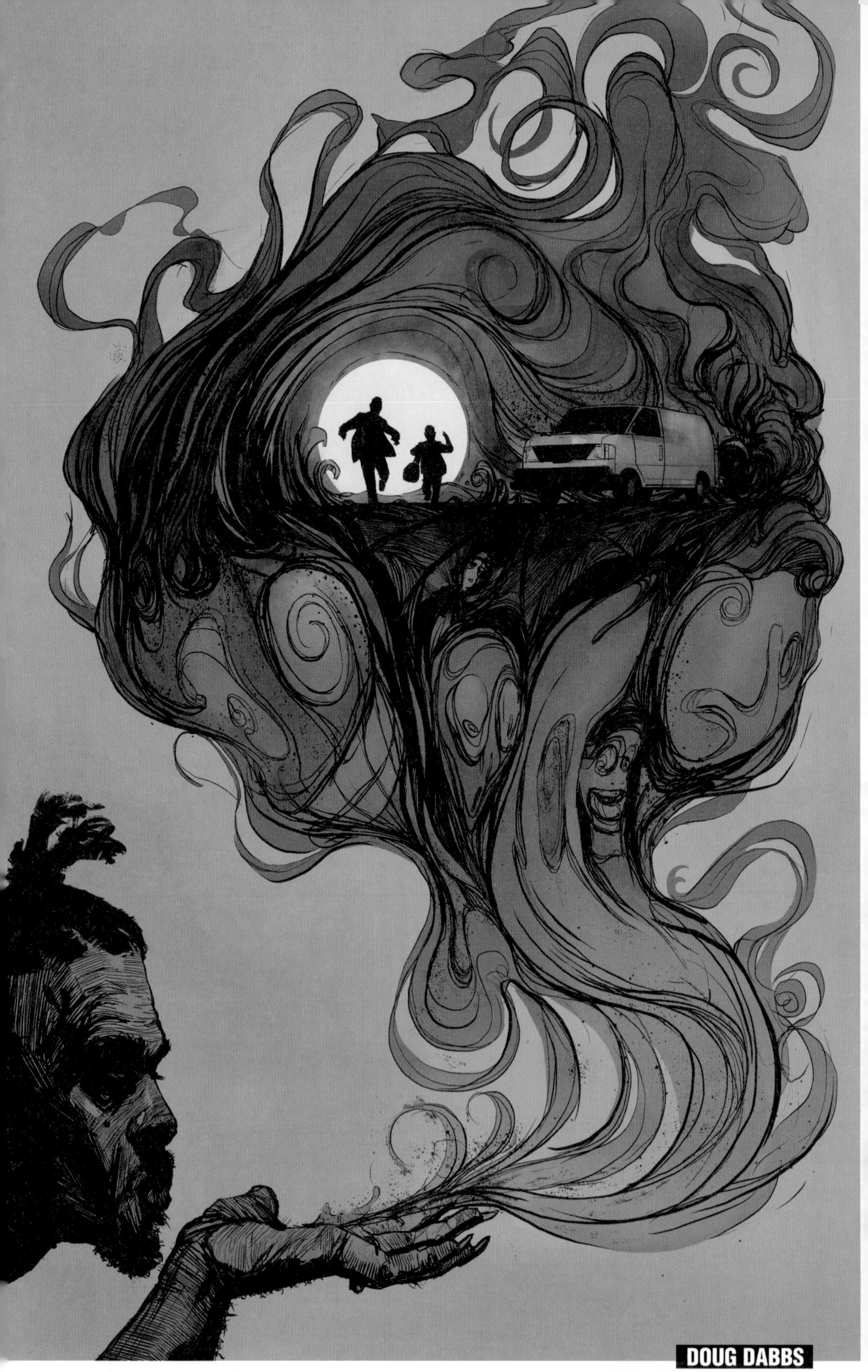

DOUG DABBS
ISSUE #5 COVER A

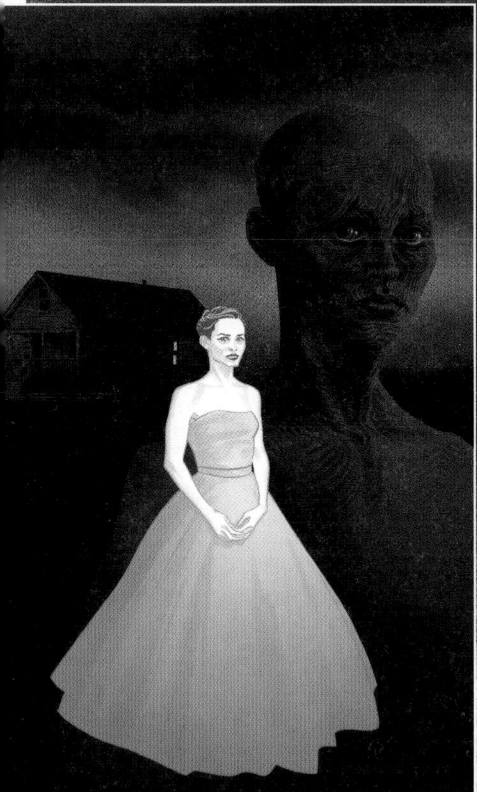

CHRIS BRUNNER

ISSUE #2 COVER A

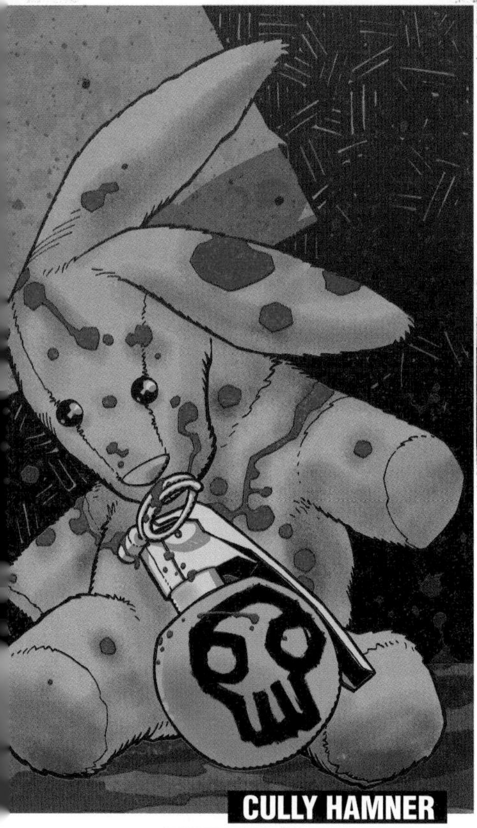

CULLY HAMNER

ISSUE #3 COVER A

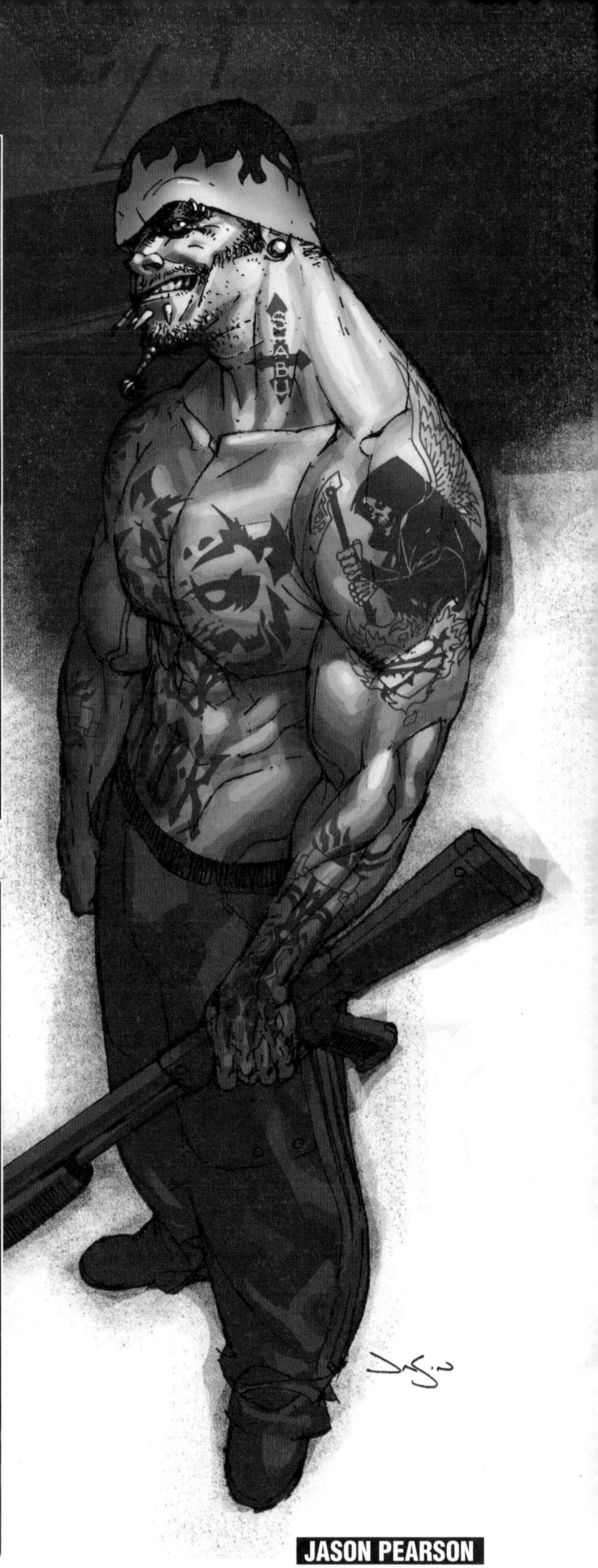
SABU

JASON PEARSON

ISSUE #5 BACK COVER

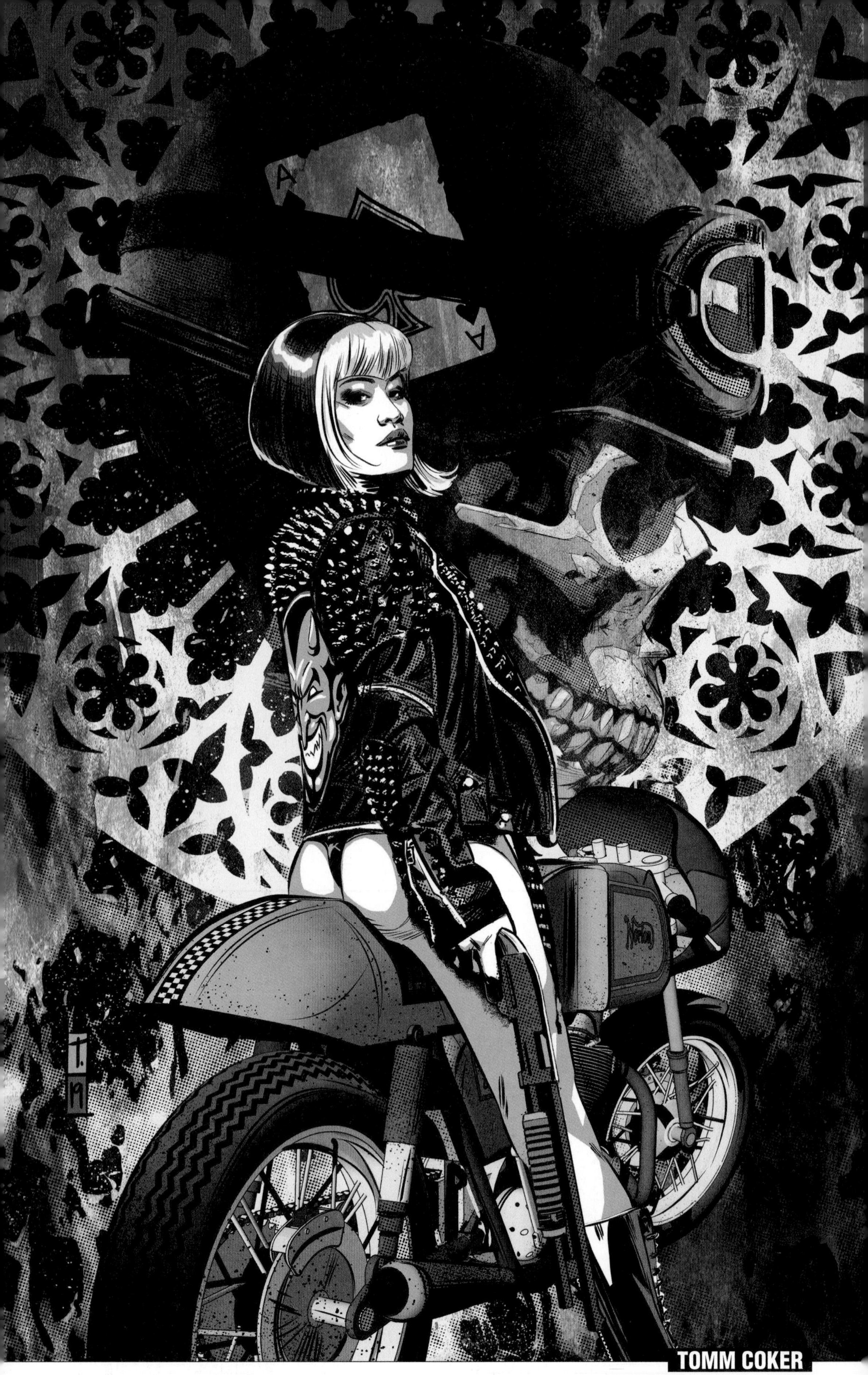
Norton

TOMM COKER

ISSUE #4 COVER A

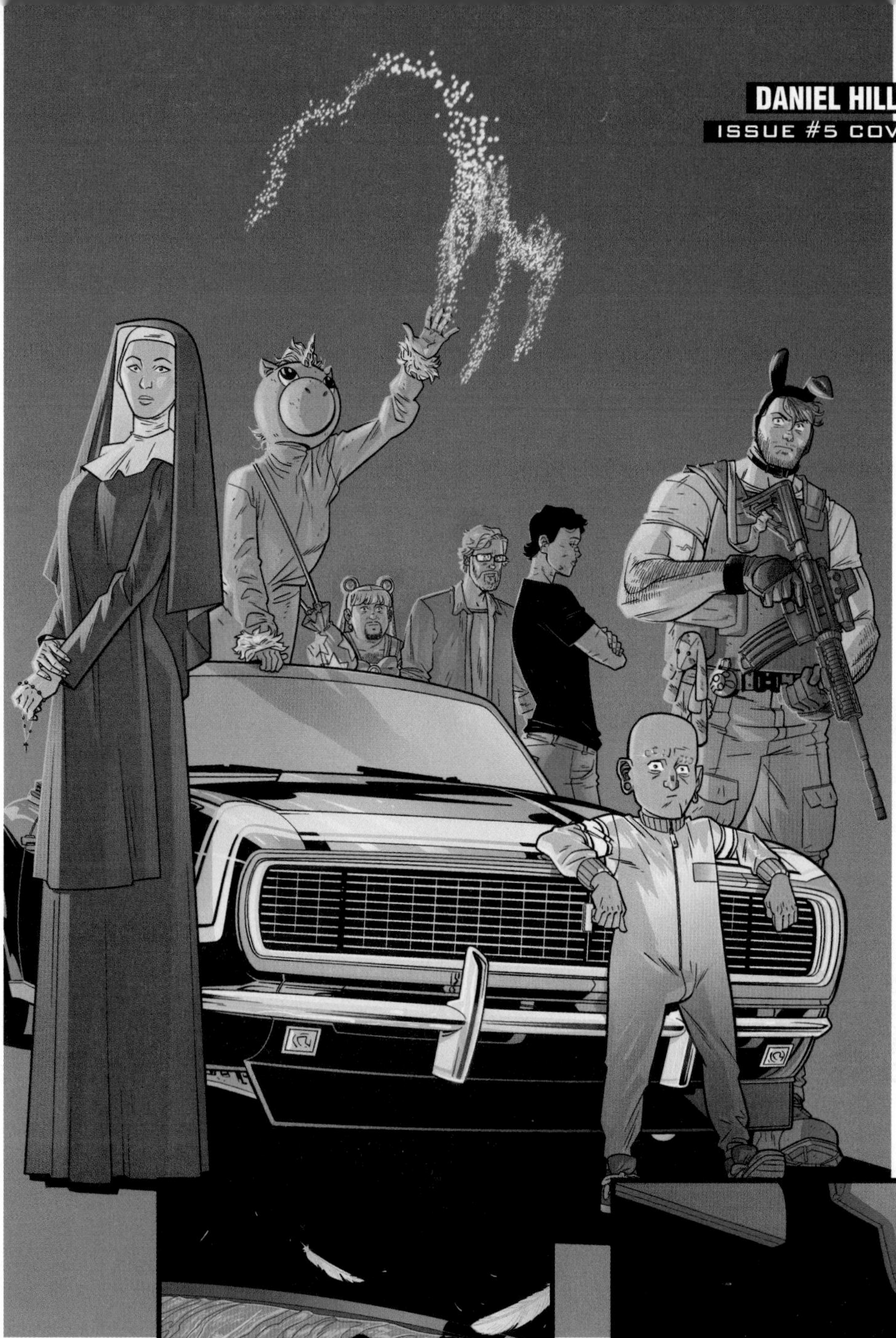

DANIEL HILLYARD

ISSUE #5 COVER B

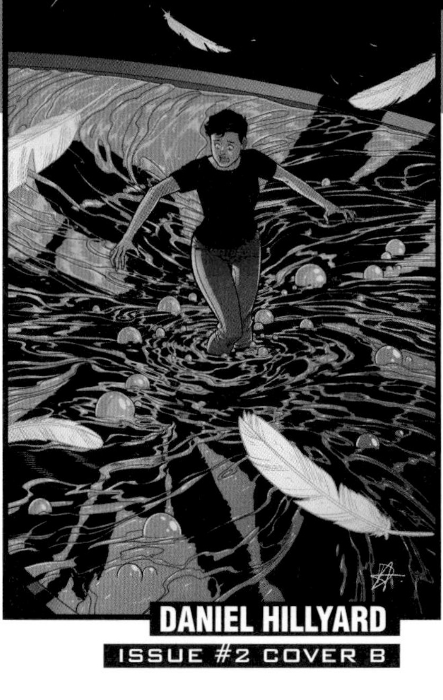

DANIEL HILLYARD

ISSUE #2 COVER B

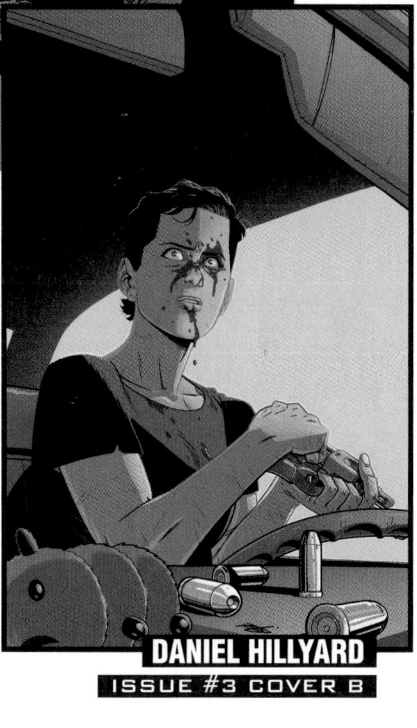

DANIEL HILLYARD

ISSUE #3 COVER B

DANIEL HILLYARD

ISSUE #4 COVER B

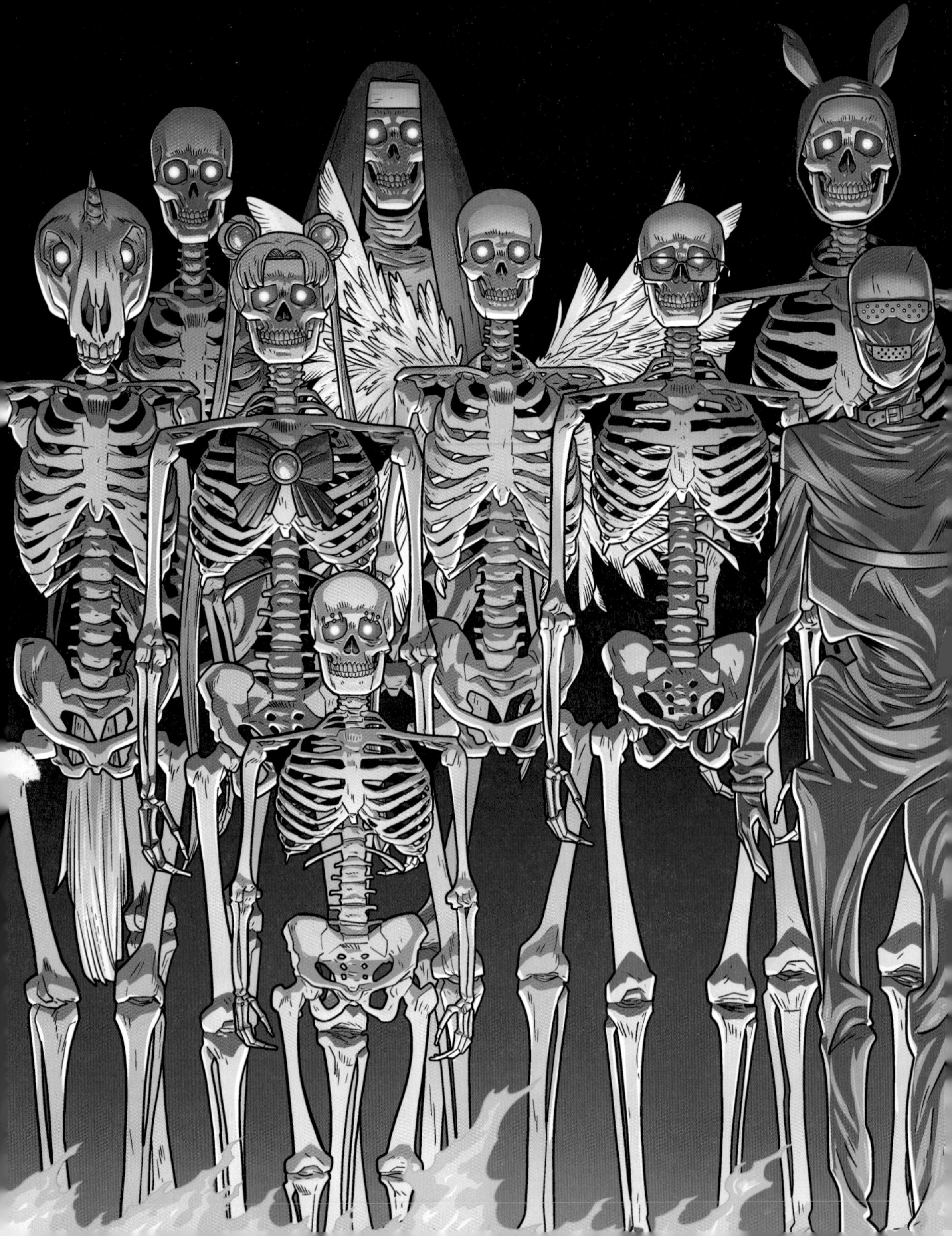